C000132426

Never Again

By Nicky Clifford

Copyright

Published by Nicola Clifford in 2016
Copyright © Nicky Clifford, 2016
All Rights Reserved

Publisher: Nicola Clifford
Email: cliffordnicky@gmail.com

Cover design by Daniela Owergoor

First Edition published by Nicola Clifford in October 2016

A CIP catalogue record for this book is available from the British Library

ISBN: 978-0-9956153-1-1

Dedication

Ailsa Boyle, my wonderful mum, for all she has done and does.

Ann Hope (my muse), without whom this book would never have been written.

Sam, Thomas and Mark, who make my life complete.

Chapter 1

Her mother would be turning in her grave. To have thrown away so much for so little.

Harriet was lost in her thoughts. She was oblivious to the majesty of the range of mountains stretching skyward around them. She didn't notice the excited voices rising and falling in the carriage as tourists pointed out the chalet-style houses dotted around the Lauterbrunnen valley far below, the houses that were growing ever smaller as the train climbed its effortful way up the funicular railway track.

No, having shooed away thoughts of her mother, all Harriet could hear ringing in her ears were Ed's last words to her: 'You're making a terrible, terrible mistake.'

'Can I see? Can I see?'

Beside Harriet, a tired-looking mum with lank, brown hair tied back in a ponytail, reached over and lifted a little boy onto her lap. His brown curls danced around his animated face as his eyes flitted in every direction, 'Mummy look! Look at *that*!'

Harriet felt raw emotion tugging at her, curling and twisting her stomach. She averted her eyes from the boy who reminded her so sharply of . . . She closed her eyes. No! She would not, could not think about him. That is why she had come here. To forget.

Harriet took a deep breath, then another. She wrapped her hands around the handles of her bag so no-one would notice them shaking.

She smoothed her hands over her taupe skirt. When she had left the house, what seemed like a lifetime ago, she had looked immaculate. Now her suit was creased and clung to her like a second skin. Why hadn't she realised how much hotter Switzerland would be at this time of year compared with England? Detail was supposed to be her "thing", or it had been.

After the last few months, she no longer knew what her "thing" was. She, Harriet, who always had a plan, who forged ahead in life

1

to get to where she wanted to be, was now floundering in self-doubt.

Harriet shook herself. She was not here to wallow. She had come here to clear her head, to move on from the grief that had dogged her for months. To work out a new life plan, one that did not involve . . .

'Scuse me, can I sit by the window for the last bit? Please.'

'Cameron, no!' his mum reprimanded him. 'Leave the lady alone.'

Harriet smiled, trying to swallow down the lump of emotion rising fast in her throat. He had the hugest blue eyes and the cutest brown curls. It would have been easier if he had been blond or ginger or if his hair had fallen as straight as a ruler, but no, it had to be brown and curly.

'It's okay. Really. I don't think my stop's much further.' Harriet stood up and allowed the little boy and his mum to slide along the seat next to the window.

Before Harriet could settle back into her thoughts, a loud voice with a distinct American twang cut across the general chatter:

'It's exquisite, don't you think? Freddie got down on one knee in the ice caves on Jungfrau. Yesterday! It was so cool!'

Engaged? Ouch! That hurt. Would reminders of her past never stop?

With the ring of congratulations circling the carriage, curiosity overcame her. Harriet turned her eyes slightly to the left. She watched as a young woman swished her hand from side to side, drawing admiring gasps from the other passengers, who were fast becoming an enthralled audience. A large diamond sparkled on her left hand.

Harriet reckoned she was in her mid-twenties. Her glossy auburn hair cascaded in perfect waves, as if she had just walked out of the pages of a shampoo advertisement. In fact, she was perfectly formed in every way. If she had looked like that, Harriet was certain that Greg would never have walked away.

As she struggled to bring her emotions under control, the train slowed before pulling into Wengen station. Harriet pushed all thoughts of Greg aside.

Finally, she was here, in Switzerland. It was hard to believe. Her life had been such a whirlwind over the last few months, with so many decisions taken in such a short period of time.

Harriet took a deep breath and stepped onto the platform, the wheels of her modest suitcase clicking behind her. The warmth lapped at her skin. She was grateful for the bob she had insisted upon two days ago – her new shorter style allowed the breeze to cool her neck and shoulders.

Ali had needed a lot of persuading to cut off her long, blond hair.

'You'll regret it!' he warned, shaking his head. 'Such a pity – your beautiful hair.'

'It has to come off,' Harriet insisted. It was time for a change.

All she felt with every snip of the scissors and every strand falling to the floor was a sense of freedom. If only the rest of her ties could be released that easily.

Before she had time to walk across the platform, the recently engaged brunette tapped her on the shoulder.

'Geez! Move along, can't you? Move along! I have to get my cases off the train.'

Stepping aside, Harriet scowled. '"Please" would've been nice,' she muttered under her breath.

Harriet's docility was astounding. A few short months ago Harriet would have confronted such rudeness head-on. When you were directly in charge of ten staff and had a building full of employees to oversee, you could not afford to be undermined. Anyway, her staff would never have spoken to her like that. It was all about mutual respect.

A sharp retort hovered on Harriet's tongue, but she bit it back. The battering that life had given her recently had knocked her confidence and dimmed the spark inside that had driven her.

Instead, Harriet watched as three men jostled with each other to help the brunette with her three bulging suitcases. Harriet shook her head and turned away.

3

Unsure what to do next, Harriet dived into her handbag. What was it the letter had said? She pulled out a piece of paper and unfolded it. Ah yes, there it was in black and white: one of the porters would meet her at the station.

Harriet looked up. She saw several smart mini-vans assembled in the road next to the station. Each of them had a different hotel logo emblazoned across the paintwork. It didn't take her long to spot one with 'Hotel Neueranfang' written in gold writing on a dark blue background. She sighed with relief.

A dour-looking man with grey hair and a droopy moustache snatched her case from her and shoved it into the back of the van. Harriet hesitated. Should she get in the front or side door? The porter glared at Harriet. He jabbed towards the side door with his index finger. Harriet shuddered as she climbed in under the watchful scowl of the porter. She sincerely hoped that this was not the kind of welcome waiting for her at the hotel.

A shrill voice rang out behind Harriet.

'Hey! You there! I need some help here!'

Harriet turned around to see the brunette tottering on what had to be three inch heels, trying and failing to drag one of her cases behind her.

A long groan escaped from the porter's lips as he spotted her making her way towards him.

'Over here!' The brunette beckoned over and over again with her free hand. 'MY CASES IN THERE.' Her words were clipped and concise. She motioned towards her suitcases and then back to the porter and again to her suitcases.

The porter shrugged and made his way towards her, muttering under his breath.

A few minutes later, with the brunette's cases thrown into the back of the van to the high-pitched cries of: 'Careful! Can't you be careful!' the brunette settled herself next to Harriet. The porter huffed and puffed as the little van whirred its electric way through the streets of Wengen.

4

'I'll sue!' The brunette glared at the back of the porter's head as he navigated the narrow roads. 'If anything in my cases has been ruined, I swear I'll—'

'Are you staying at Hotel Neueranfang?' Harriet asked. The brunette's whining was getting on her nerves.

'Well, not exactly. Oh, by the way, I'm Becky. Becky Randalph-Goodheim.'

Harriet raised an eyebrow. She should not have been surprised: a diva's surname to match a diva personality.

'I'm Harriet.' Despite her reluctance to encourage any sort of friendship with this American, she could not ignore Becky's outstretched hand. She gave it the briefest of shakes before folding her hands back into her lap.

She could not help noticing Becky's beautifully manicured finger nails. She curled her own into her palm. Biting her nails was one habit from her childhood she had never been able to kick. For years she had disguised the nibbled nails with a trip to her manicurist, but the sort of work she would be doing for the next few months would not make great bed-partners with false nails.

As they drew up outside the hotel, an elegant woman in her mid-fifties appeared at the entrance. Her suit was beautifully tailored, and no doubt came from an expensive Swiss boutique. She shot a few rapid words to the porter, who nodded his head and began lifting their cases out of the van with the greatest care.

Becky tossed her hair over her shoulder and tutted loudly. She had a good mind to tell his boss exactly how he had treated her cases minutes before.

'Welcome to you both. I am Frau Tanner.' The woman smiled at the two of them. She had shoulder-length blond hair, which swung around her face in a long bob. Her hazel eyes sparkled with a sense of fun and yet, there was something steely about them, which warned you not to cross her. What surprised Harriet, however, was her accent – it had a definite Irish twang to it.

Becky introduced herself. 'What a journey! I'm dead beat. I hope your showers are powerful. I'm gonna have to stand under a shower for hours to wash off all the grime that's accumulated on this exhausting journey.'

Harriet wanted to laugh. Given Becky had been at the Jungfrau yesterday, which could be reached by staying on the same train they had recently alighted from, Becky could not have travelled very far.

'I am sure you will find everything sufficient.' Frau Tanner's tone was as cool as the air in the ice caves that Becky had been boasting about earlier. Turning her back on Becky, Frau Tanner smiled at Harriet.

'I'm Harriet.' She took hold of Frau Tanner's hand and shook it. 'Lovely to meet you.'

A tiny grin formed in the corners of Harriet's mouth. Ever since she had replied to the advertisement in The Lady magazine a couple of months ago, doubts had been nagging at her. The 'what ifs?' had been stalking her, eating away at the courage it had taken her to apply. She had to keep reminding herself that this was something she had dreamed of doing for years.

In her late teens, she was stuck in a deep rut of responsibility and accountability, helping her mum to make ends meet. Her best friend at the time, Mel, begged her to come to Spain to waitress in a seaside hotel for the summer holidays. Harriet refused. How could she leave her mum on her own with their heavy burden of debt, the one and only thing they had inherited from her father?

So, Mel flew to Spain on her own. She bombarded Harriet with postcards and photos and long enthusiastic rants about the "ball" she was having. This only served to fan the flames of Harriet's jealousy into a roaring fire. Harriet swore to herself that one day she would do the same thing. She would escape abroad, work in a hotel and shed the burden of being a grown-up.

Several months ago, when her life crashed around her, memories of Mel's summer in Spain provided her with a perfect solution: she could escape somewhere hot to lick her wounds, at the same time as fulfilling her childhood dream.

As the day of departure drew nearer, the enormity of leaving her well-paid job and her home settled over her like a dense fog. And

6

yet, she knew she couldn't stay where she was. It was too painful. She needed to get away to clear her head, to grieve and to work out where her life was heading.

Standing there, in front of Hotel Neueranfang, Harriet started to believe that travelling to Wengen had been exactly the right decision. This was her chance to put the last few months behind her. To move on.

'I am very pleased to see you both. You really could not have come at a better time. Guests start arriving the day after tomorrow so we have not got long to show you the ropes.'

Harriet stared at Becky. Surely she was a guest? Even with the largest stretch of her imagination, she could not picture Becky pulling up her shirt sleeves and getting stuck in. As for being at others' beck, or in her case 'Becky' and call . . .

Becky grimaced.

It was clear to Harriet that Becky was not an enthusiastic participant, quite the opposite in fact.

Frau Tanner led Becky and Harriet over to a traditional Swiss chalet to the right of the main hotel. Window boxes overflowing with pink and white flowers lined the windows on all three levels. Several small balconies with intricately carved designs allowed guests to admire the views.

'How quaint!' The sarcasm dripping from Becky's voice did not go unnoticed by Frau Tanner. Harriet watched annoyance flicker across her face.

To Harriet's satisfaction, Frau Tanner ignored Becky's comment and showed both women to their rooms on the first floor of the chalet.

'Once you have had a chance to freshen up, come down to reception and I will sort out some refreshments before we organise your uniform.'

Harriet thanked Frau Tanner. With a sigh of relief, she closed the door and flopped onto her bed. Thank goodness it was a single room. The thought of having to share with Miss High and Mighty could well have driven her straight back to England.

Harriet closed her eyes. The pull of sleep tugged at her. No, she could not stay where she was. It would not look good to oversleep on her first day.

Harriet forced herself to stand up. Her eyes scanned the room. It wasn't big, but it was cosy. Wooden panels lined the walls, ceiling and floor. Several woven rugs boasting multiple colours like a shaken up rainbow were scattered on the floor making the room feel homely. An imposing wardrobe stood next to an ornate chest of drawers with an aged mirror balanced on top. Plenty of room for her clothes, though she doubted Becky would be able to cram even half of her stuff into the same space, that is, if their rooms were a similar size.

As Harriet's eyes scanned the room, she noticed a second door at the end of the bed. Curious, she turned the handle. Immediately her eyes lit up. An en-suite! That was an unexpected surprise. Space was always at a premium in hotels and she had imagined that 'en-suite' would be solely for paying guests.

Her suitcase sat in the middle of the room mocking her. She knew it would be sensible to unpack now. If she left it until later that evening, she knew she would ignore her suitcase and collapse straight into bed.

Given the long hours she had worked at Hardacres her current lack of energy was bewildering. It wasn't as if she had travelled across the world. She had only flown from Heathrow that morning. And she had packed so conservatively, unpacking would be quick. She grinned as she tried to work out how long Becky would take to unpack her gigantic cases.

When Harriet unzipped her suitcase and opened the lid, the pungent smell of coconut assaulted her nose. Dark stains had soaked into her two favourite bikinis. That stupid shampoo! She had definitely checked the lid was screwed on tightly before packing it. If only she had taken the time to zip it into her washbag. She knew that if her mum was here she would be citing "poetic justice" and telling her that it served her right for poking fun at someone else. Hmmm.

A loud crash outside followed by some rapid shouting drew Harriet over to the large window at the head of her bed. The window was hinged on both sides, with traditional wooden shutters behind the glass. Harriet unhooked the catches and pushed the window and shutters open, flooding the small room with light.

Harriet looked out. She could see two men facing each other. She was pretty certain the older man was the porter who had collected them from the station. Scattered on the ground at their feet was an explosion of fruit: apples, oranges, bananas, kiwis and others she couldn't identify.

Their raised voices were getting louder and louder. Harriet's full attention was focused on the two men and the fruit at their feet. She did not notice the man sitting at a table on the hotel terrace opposite her window. As the terrace was raised a few feet up from the road where the men were still arguing, it meant that anyone sitting along the outer rim of the terrace could look straight into her room.

Harriet watched as a tall, silver-haired man strode with complete authority towards the commotion. With his jaw set at a determined angle and his shoulders pulled right back, Harriet did not envy the two men locked in a heated argument, who were as yet unaware of his presence.

That was when she saw him. He was sitting alone at one of the tables on the terrace. His eyes were locked on hers. Unwavering. Breath caught in Harriet's chest. Every cell in her body screamed at her to turn away, but she was caught up in his gaze as if he had cast a spell over her.

Then, as suddenly as a guillotine dropping, the connection broke. He looked away. His eyes focused down onto the pile of paperwork in front of him as if they had never left it.

Harriet threw herself back from the window, her heart galloping as if she had just completed a hundred metre sprint in record time. She closed her eyes tight to rid herself of the image that seemed indelibly imprinted in her mind: his sun-streaked hair, which flopped over his forehead and around his neck; his tan, which only served to highlight his piercing eyes; and the dark-blond shadow that traced his jaw.

'Stop it! Just stop it!' Harriet shook her head. It was ridiculous. Completely ridiculous. She was behaving like a love-struck teenager rather than the woman she was. A woman in her late twenties, and a successful business woman at that.

She grabbed a towel from the end of her bed and headed into her bathroom. Forget unpacking. Forget sleeping. What she needed before she faced Frau Tanner and Becky Randalph-Goodheim, in particular, was an extremely cold shower.

Chapter 2

The morning had flown by. Even though there were no guests in the hotel, there was no shortage of jobs to be done. Glasses and cutlery had to be polished, salt and pepper pots topped up and napkins folded. And that was without starting on the bar.

Harriet concentrated on polishing a particularly tarnished fork. Her mind drifted back to Hardacres Ltd. This was so different from her previous job. If Ed could see her now, he would be shaking his head in despair. But she had come here for a purpose. She was not going to be side-tracked by dwelling on the very past that she was trying to escape from.

Looking up from the pile of silver cutlery in front of her, Harriet wondered what type of guests the hotel attracted. Fairly wealthy ones by the look of the room prices listed in the reception area.

She could see why they charged so much. The restaurant itself was spacious, but cosy. It was divided into sections, presumably to give diners an element of privacy. With starched white squares over sea-green tablecloths, the now gleaming cutlery, sparkling glasses and a candle on every table, the effect was dramatic.

With the candles flickering in the evening, it would provide a perfect atmosphere for a romantic dinner for two. Shaking her head, she brushed that thought away. Would everything here keep reminding her of England?

'She's a bit of a slave-driver. She needs to chill out!' Becky glanced over to where Frau Tanner was giving instructions to another waitress.

'Depends what you're used to,' Harriet replied. Compared with her twelve hour days at Hardacres, this was a holiday.

'I'm used to daddy's expense account and lots of vacations,' Becky explained, without any embarrassment, shoving her cloth down on the table.

'Well, this is quite a change for you, isn't it? Did daddy's credit card dry up?' Harriet knew she was being catty, but honestly, her mother had worked three jobs to keep them afloat when she was Becky's age and here was Becky in what must be her first job.

'Something like that.' Becky examined her fingers. 'Geez! Now look what that dumb cutlery has done to one of my nails.'

Harriet eyed the broken nail and tried hard not to smile. She had made the right decision getting rid of her false talons before starting here.

'Right, follow me! Time to initiate you into the delights of our rather temperamental drinks machine.' Frau Tanner led the way through to the bar.

'Where would I rather be?' a sing-songy voice behind her asked.

Harriet looked over her shoulder. A willowy redhead grinned back. Her long hair was struggling to stay contained within the confines of its band.

'On a beach in the Caribbean?' Harriet suggested.

'I wish! Although the pool in Wengen isn't too bad. I'm Jo by the way.'

'I'm Harriet. So how come you've already found the pool?'

'Ah, you see, this is my second season. I'm a sucker for punishment. What's your excuse?' Jo's eyes sparkled.

'No excuse I'm afraid. I just needed a change.'

'Don't we all?' Jo nodded her agreement.

'Right, listen up!'

Frau Tanner explained the various buttons and levers and the process to make drinks ranging from tea to coffee to hot chocolate.

After several practices and a couple of scorched fingers, a cafetiere of coffee sat neatly on a doily-lined tray along with a bowl of sugar, a jug of milk and a couple of homemade cookies.

'I thought guests didn't arrive until tomorrow.' Becky leaned down to rub her foot. Her shoes were killing her. She was not used to being on her feet all day.

'This is an exception.' Frau Tanner began to search through the cupboard next to the coffee machine. 'Herr Smith arrived a week ago.'

'He's our resident writer, isn't he?' Jo asked.

'Herr Smith is staying with us for the season. What he does is none of our business.'

Jo pulled a face at Harriet over the top of Frau Tanner's head. Harriet suppressed a giggle.

'This is Herr Smith's personal mug. Do not forget! And please, please do not give it to any other guests.' Frau Tanner placed the mug on the tray with such care, you would be forgiven for thinking it was a priceless antique.

Personal mug? Who did he think he was? Why couldn't he drink from the hotel mugs like everyone else? Harriet looked over at Jo who raised her eyes to the sky.

Harriet's eyes widened as she studied the mug. "Forever Yours" was written in curly writing around the mug. She moved closer to Jo, speaking quietly into her ear, 'Oh dear! Talk about sentimental.'

Jo made a face.

For whatever reason, Harriet's mother, once again, leapt into her mind. Her mother had always seen the best in everyone. If she did not stop being so judgemental, she would end up a bitter old lady, just like one of their neighbours who died lonely and angry at the age of 99. No-one attended the funeral except for Harriet and her mother. 'You never know what goes on behind closed doors Harriet, so you have no right to judge.' That was what her mother used to say to her. She would be wise to start following that advice.

And anyway, the writer was probably a wrinkled old man, who had been scribbling away on his novels for years. Perhaps his wife had presented the mug to him weeks before she died. Or maybe his only daughter had flown off to Australia and this was her parting gift to him.

'Harriet, you can take Herr Smith his drink. He is out on the terrace.'

Harriet was grateful there was only one pot of coffee. She had seen waiters in hotels carrying trays laden with multiple pots of tea, together with cups and saucers for a table of eight. The thought filled her with trepidation.

Fortunately, she had swapped her business heels for a pair of comfortable black loafers, so at least she had less chance of tripping over. The same could not be said for Becky. Harriet glanced over to where Becky was still massaging her feet, her three inch heels discarded next to the chair she had collapsed into.

The sunlight was dazzling as she moved from inside the bar to the outside terrace. Squinting, Harriet scanned the tables. Herr Smith was the only guest so he was easy to spot hunched over his laptop at the far edge of the terrace.

Typical. If he had any consideration at all for other people, he could at least have sat a bit nearer the bar.

'Coffee, Herr Smith?' Harriet forced a smile.

'Leave it there!' Herr Smith's command was reinforced by a dismissive wave of his hand motioning towards the table. He did not look up.

Harriet seethed. How dare he talk to her like she was some kind of skivvy?

Harriet dropped the tray onto the table with a clatter. The milk jug rattled as it lurched against the coffee pot, half of it spilling onto the tray.

The speed of Herr Smith's reactions took Harriet by surprise. His hand shot out and steadied the jug before the remainder of its contents tipped onto the table.

Herr Smith's head snapped up. Every fibre in Harriet's body started doing uncontrollable back-flips. She found herself staring into the most disturbing grey eyes she had ever seen. The same eyes that had locked with hers yesterday afternoon. The very eyes that she had been unable to shake from her mind, however hard she tried.

'Don't *ever* do that again!' He spat out his words with such venom that Harriet was silenced.

It didn't take her long to recover. 'It was an accident.' Harriet said the words through clenched teeth, her eyes challenging his.

Herr Smith closed his laptop and moved it across to an adjacent table, away from the coffee. 'If that milk had spilled onto my laptop, it would have been a disaster.'

Harriet tried not to notice his muscles flexing on his tanned arms. She tried to avert her eyes from his face. She tried to imagine him as an elderly author bent over his notepad. She tried. She failed.

He was rude and arrogant and she was determined not to let herself be distracted by his looks. He was making a drama out of nothing.

'But it didn't. *Spill.*'

'Your name?'

Harriet held her head high. 'Harriet.'

'Well, *Harriet*, I do not pay an extortionate room rate to take that risk.' Herr Smith stood up. Harriet hadn't realised how tall he was. He must be at least 6', and despite her respectable 5'8", he still towered over her.

Gathering up her courage, which was starting to flag, Harriet glared at him. 'Well, I don't get paid a pittance to be spoken to like a child!'

With that, Harriet turned on her heel and strode back across the terrace towards the bar. If steam could stream from ears, then at that moment hers would have been billowing with the stuff.

Quite clearly her former assertiveness was still simmering just below the surface. But why the hell did it have to be a guest who stirred up the embers of her temper? She would have to watch herself or she would be out before she had properly started.

Oh boy! Herr Smith watched as Harriet strode away from him. He could feel the blood pumping fast around his body.

Unbelievable! That woman had to be the clumsiest and most infuriating person he had ever had the displeasure to meet. And there had been no shortage of irritating people in his previous line of work.

Still, he could not tear his eyes away from her as she stalked towards the bar: her head held high; her blond hair swinging from side to side; and there was an alluring sway to her hips, which filled her black skirt in a way that was far too distracting. The aroma of her perfume still lingered. It took him straight back to summer picnics in his parents' garden when the flowers in full bloom infused the air with lavender, rose and wisteria.

He shook his head at his foolishness, and yet, he only looked away when she was completely out of sight. He leaned over and retrieved his laptop from where he had placed it on a neighbouring table away from *her*. An accident waiting to happen, that's what she was.

He tried to concentrate on the words in front of him, the words that had been flowing freely before the interruption. Before that English girl had rampaged like a bulldozer into his train of thought and derailed his creativity.

All he could picture now as he stared at the jumble of words on the document in front of him was her bewitching green eyes. They had done enough to rattle him yesterday from afar, but close up . . . Slamming down the lid of his laptop, Herr Smith pushed back his chair.

Women! They were all the same - enchanted you, and then let you down. Well he was not about to fall for that again. Anyway, he had his hands full with Sophie. The last thing he needed was another woman in his life to complicate things.

Wengen had seemed the ideal place to escape. He could simply leave everything behind. The remoteness of a village surrounded by mountains had appealed to him. It was only accessible via the funicular railway or by donning a sturdy pair of walking boots. What he had found here, up until she arrived to rattle his equilibrium, was the peace and quiet he craved.

He had to get away from the publicity, from the expectations being hurled at him from every direction. He had even taken the unprecedented step of leaving his mobile at home. Unheard of. No-one apart from his agent knew how to contact him.

And they had been warned that if they wanted book number two to be written within the deadline, they would have to leave him in peace to write it. Fortunately, his first novel had been a best seller, so they weren't about to upset him by ignoring his wishes. He hoped not anyway.

Thousands of words were hidden in the depths of his mind just waiting to be released in some kind of order to form a coherent first draft. Philippe looked at his laptop, but his eyes were drawn past it to the path that led out of the hotel grounds and on up the mountain.

Yesterday he discovered a café, which served the most delicious hot chocolate. Okay, so it could be seen as an odd choice considering it was late spring, but hot chocolate had always been one of his favourites. And it was Sophie's favourite too, or it had been until she discovered alcohol.

From the café's terrace he could see for miles. It helped to keep his thoughts in the present moment where they belonged, and put a stop to any reminiscing.

As he was deliberating whether to stay and try to write through the disoriented state that Harriet had hurled him into minutes before, a loud American voice shivered up his spine. He could not believe it. *That* accent? Here? Very slowly he turned around.

'Hey there, Harriet mentioned you might need some more milk.' Becky wiggled her way towards Philippe, making the most of her high heels.

Philippe closed his open mouth. It was the exact same accent, but instead of Lauren, a tall brunette stood in front of him. Philippe inhaled sharply. She was a carbon-copy of Lauren, minus the blond hair.

As Becky held out the milk jug, the clouds parted and the sun beamed down onto the terrace. Philippe turned his face up to the sky, drinking in the warmth, wondering if he would ever be able to erase Lauren from his mind now that this American had put her firmly back into his thoughts.

'Milk?' Becky repeated, fluttering her eyelashes. She was not used to being ignored.

Philippe looked right into her eyes, but instead of the brown eyes staring back at him, all he could see were Harriet's cat-green eyes. Blinking hard to dispel the image, Philippe scooped up his laptop.

'No, I don't think so.' He turned his back on Becky and walked down the steps to the road.

17

Becky stood with her hands on her hips staring after him.

What was it with this place? He had expected strapping village women carrying countless jars of beer around the bar, not a procession of attractive waitresses. Harriet, yet again, sprang into his mind. He rolled her name around his head briefly, before sighing with frustration. This had got to stop, and it had to stop now!

He decided that a brisk walk up the mountain would clear his head and get his endorphins rolling. His exercise intake had reduced by at least 90 per cent since his accident, and it wasn't suiting him. If he rounded off this expedition with a drink and the perspective that seeing the valleys and mountains stretched out before him could bring, he was pretty confident that Harriet would recede into the background, exactly where she belonged.

Chapter 3

Philippe threw his pen onto the desk. It was no good. Whether he used the laptop or tried to scribble directly onto his pad, his writing was not flowing. In fact, ever since Harriet had gate-crashed into his life, his creativity had shrivelled to almost nothing.

Every time he sat down to a blank screen or a blank page, all he could see were her green eyes staring back at him: how they flashed with anger when she argued with him; and the way her blond hair flicked across her forehead.

So he had kept himself holed up in his room. The last thing he wanted was to bump into *her* again. Fat lot of good that had done. In some ways it had intensified his memories of her, with nothing more real or recent to base them on.

It was impossible to fathom why he was so entranced by her. She had not exactly endeared herself to him, quite the opposite; she had been extremely rude. Although - a lick of shame washed over him - if he was honest with himself, he had not exactly been polite either.

Maybe it was because of her rudeness. He was used to women fawning over him, using all their wiles to attract his attention and keep it. When you rose to the top of your career, you attracted countless groupies, all wanting a piece of you, of your fame. At the beginning, it had been exciting. His ego had been stroked and he had lapped up the attention.

But pretty quickly he realised it was all part of their game-plan. These women were playing him. He was simply one of their chess pieces. That was, until he met Lauren. She played her hand much closer to her chest. He truly believed she was different from other women, and if it hadn't been for the accident, she would have landed him, hook, line and sinker. Although looking back now, he was incredulous that he hadn't seen straight through her.

The sun streamed through the open doors that led out onto his balcony. From there he could see right down into Lauterbrunnen. With the white tip of the Jungfrau to his left and the waterfall to his right, it should have formed the perfect backdrop to write his crime novel.

Philippe sighed. This was fruitless. He had been sitting at his desk hour after hour with nothing more to show for it than multiple erased lines. Enough was enough! He rummaged in his drawer and managed to locate a pair of swimming trunks.

Becky had raved about the pool, which was, according to her, only a short walk from the hotel. He tried to ignore most of the never-ending conversation that flowed from Becky's mouth when she delivered his meals. But today, dipping into a pool's liquid depths seemed a tempting alternative to his current reclusive existence. It did not take him long to throw his things into a rucksack. He set off up the steep path leading to the pool with a shiver of anticipation.

Philippe spotted Harriet the moment he stepped in through the gate. She was lying flat out on a towel in the tiniest and brightest of bikinis. His eyes drank in every last detail of her body. He knew he should drag his eyes away from her, but found himself transfixed.

Harriet was starting to relax. Her eyes were closed. She stretched out her body, luxuriating in the heat of the sun. By all accounts, it was raining in England. She smiled. She knew that fact should not give her so much satisfaction, but she could not help feeling a little bit smug.

If someone had told her a year ago that she would be here, lying next to a swimming pool surrounded by skyscraper-mountains without even a whisper of breeze, she would have thought they were joking. But that was before a bomb, or rather two simultaneous bombs, exploded into her life.

'Shouldn't you be working?'

Harriet's skin prickled at the sound of the deep voice a breath away from her.

Surely not? She hadn't seen a glimpse of him since the milk incident on the terrace. At first, she thought he had left, packed up his things and gone in search of a hotel where the waitresses were efficient and polite rather than clumsy and impertinent.

Instead, according to Becky, he had hidden himself away in suite number 208 and ordered room service. Unsurprisingly, Becky had been quick to volunteer herself as his *personal* waitress.

Harriet's eyes shot open. She immediately regretted it as the sun dazzled her, forcing her to shut her eyes again.

'Don't creep up on people like that!'

'Here, that should be better.'

Very slowly, Harriet squinted towards the voice. All she could see looming above her was a dark shadow, which was blocking out the light.

Groping around, Harriet managed to locate her sunglasses. Once she had settled them on the bridge of her nose, she looked up and up until she caught the full impact of his eyes.

Somehow, she managed to tear her gaze away from his face and yet, from behind the safety of her sunglasses, she could not help herself zooming in on the outline of his chest through his white T-shirt.

She was at a considerable disadvantage here; Herr Smith was fully clothed and she was barely covered in one of her friend's bikinis. Beth, her next door neighbour, had insisted that Harriet would need at least three bikinis. She had thrown her fluorescent pink two-piece into Harriet's case as a spare. As fate would have it, her more modest bikinis were the ones that got soaked in shampoo. Typical!

Feeling her cheeks flaming, Harriet sat up and pulled on her shirt.

'Don't leave on my behalf.' A smile hovered at the corners of his mouth. 'It's me taking the risk.'

Harriet pulled the shirt tighter around her. She scowled up at him. 'I don't know what you mean?'

Herr Smith scrutinised her intently. In an effort to avoid his eyes, Harriet tried to focus on the pool. It was impossible, however, to avoid him. He was much closer to her than she would have liked, and yet in another way, not nearly close enough.

Her eyes were drawn to his unfairly tanned legs. In comparison, hers were almost luminous. She wondered how he could boast such a golden tan when the weather in Britain had been less than sunny during the winter they had just had.

She fiddled with her sunglasses and racked her brains to find anything intelligent, or in fact anything at all, to say to him. It was as if the power of speech had been plucked from her. At last, in desperation, with the silence stretching between them, she blurted out the first thing that came into her mind.

'You're a fan of sunbeds, Herr Smith?'

Herr Smith threw his towel onto the grass next to Harriet's. 'Call me Philippe,' he told her. 'Herr Smith makes me sound so old.'

'Philippe.' Harriet paused. He was impossible to tie down, this Philippe Smith. She took a deep breath. 'Do you always avoid answering questions?'

'Okay, you've got me there. Yes, I do avoid answering questions. But for you, I'll make an exception. My risk? Remember the milk?' Philippe smiled. 'And no, I don't like sunbeds; I prefer to spend my time in hot countries, and recently I've had more than enough spare time to lounge in the sun. How's that? Have I fully satisfied your curiosity? Or do you have anything else you'd like to ask me?'

Despite trying to look severe, Harriet felt her lips twitching.

'Is there a chance I've melted the ice-queen?' Philippe leaned up on one elbow and faced Harriet.

A giggle escaped out of her mouth. 'Maybe not melted, exactly, but perhaps you've coaxed a little bit of water to dribble down her side.' Harriet groaned inwardly. Oh hell! What a terrible image. "Dribble down her side?" What was she thinking? Had she lost control of her mouth as well as her senses?

Philippe cocked an eyebrow. A blush spread across Harriet's cheeks. She had to find something to say to move on from her disastrous analogy.

'So why are you spending the whole summer in a hotel?' Harriet managed to peel off her shirt without, she hoped, attracting too much attention. Today was such a scorcher; it was far too hot to lie in the sun's gaze with a stitch of extra clothing on than was

absolutely necessary. Beth's bikini would just
Tomorrow she would post it back to England, out

'You're not a reporter are you?' Philippe asked.

Harriet looked at him quizzically. 'What, an underc
sent here to discover Herr Philippe Smith's hidden secrets

'Something like that.' Philippe looked away.

A loud splash, followed by bellows of laughter, crashed int
former silence. Hans and Fred, two of the hotel's chefs, stood in t
middle of the pool play-fighting. Harriet smiled as she watched
them messing around. They were always joking those two, much to
the frustration of the rather terrifying head chef.

She could not work Philippe out. He did not seem the reclusive
type, but then who could definitively describe a writer? In her very
limited experience of them, they were their own breed.

'Are you going to tell me where you get the inspiration for your
books?'

'Tell me which one you've read, and I'll let you know where I got
my inspiration.'

'Well . . .' Harriet's voice tailed off. He wrote crime, Jo had told
her, and she knew she hadn't read any of them. She was more of a
romance or period drama type of girl. Best to be vague. 'Not many.'

Philippe laughed. His whole face transformed. His lips curled,
his grey eyes sparkled and his blond hair flicked off his forehead as
he threw back his head. She looked away. She must not let down
her guard. Men were unreliable. All of them. She was not about to
be taken in by a great body and a cheeky smile, or the most
enchanting grey eyes.

'I've only written one,' Philippe admitted.

'So why all the fuss? Frau Tanner treats you like royalty . . .'
Harriet stopped as she saw Philippe's face harden.

'Maybe because I'm staying all season,' Philippe's grey eyes
glittered. 'I wouldn't want you to think I was anyone special.'

Harriet hung her head. 'Sorry, I didn't mean . . .'

Honestly, he must be the touchiest man she had ever come
across. Greg sprang into her mind. He had been loving and caring,
well right at the beginning he had, she was certain. He had always

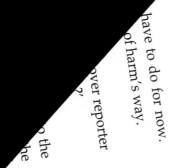

d her like a precious jewel, although
anted something. And then he had
warning. Just a curt text. She could
at again.

ʒ real, she supposed. He wasn't
manipulate her. Like Greg.

le knew he was being a jerk. He
 , years at the top of his game, before the accident.
.. was hard to come crashing down, physically and professionally. Any inference that he was not quite as important as he seemed sent his hackles rising. He knew that this was his new reality, but he did not like being reminded.

It was hardly Harriet's fault. She only knew him as Philippe Smith, author of one crime novel, which she hadn't even read. There was a whole other life that she was ignorant of. And he wanted it to stay that way.

But it was his intense reaction to her that bewildered him. She was completely different to most women he had dated and the polar opposite to Lauren. Lauren was 100 percent styled. She had been a model since her early teens. The clothes she wore, the make-up she applied, how she walked and what she said were of utmost importance. All of it was carefully choreographed to maximum effect.

Harriet, in comparison, was so natural. The barely-there make-up, her hair styled, yet at the same time casual, her impulsiveness. She intrigued him. He suspected that where Lauren had been as shallow as a mountain stream, Harriet's character ran as deep as a river cutting through a mighty canyon.

He wanted to know what she was doing waitressing in a hotel in the middle of nowhere. There must be a story behind it. Although any kind of attachment was the last thing he needed right now. He had to get his first draft finished and more importantly, he had to sort out his life. And then, of course, there was Sophie.

Harriet lay back down on her towel.

'You're burning.'

Harriet wriggled onto her side so she was facing Philippe. 'Am I? Where?'

'Just. There.' Philippe pointed. 'Oh, and there.' He wanted to run his finger down her neck, along her collar bone and on down . . .

'I don't feel sore!'

There were her claws again. It didn't seem to take much for Harriet to jump to the offensive. 'Well of course, if you're happy to risk burning, then . . .'

Harriet looked sheepish. 'Okay, so last time I burnt, I didn't feel sore until I got home and then, well, it was torture.'

Philippe sat up on his haunches, holding out his hand. 'Where's your sun cream?'

It didn't take long for Harriet to locate a bottle of Factor 50. As she placed it into his hand, their fingers touched. Harriet whipped her hand back double quick, averting her eyes from Philippe.

Had she felt that too? The jolt as their fingers met had kicked his heart into an altogether faster rhythm. The electric current descended into his stomach where it churned madly like a dog chasing its tail, before spiralling upwards, making him feel light-headed. If there was *that* much heat between them when the tips of their fingers touched, what would happen when he rubbed sun cream on her back?

'Don't bother!' Becky appeared out of nowhere. She snatched the bottle of suntan lotion out of Philippe's hand. 'Frau Tanner wants to see you, Harriet. Says it's urgent.'

Harriet sat up. 'What, now?'

'Yeah now. Immediately!'

'Did she say what it was about?' Harriet asked. 'I'm not due in until five.'

Becky shook her head. 'Something about a phone call.'

Harriet pulled on her shirt, her mind whirring. How strange. A phone call? Who could it be? Nobody knew she was here. Well, nobody apart from Beth. And she had been instructed to only call

25

her in an emergency. She knew Beth wouldn't disturb her for anything less.

But what if it was something serious? Reason teetered on the edge of the abyss of full blown panic. Not wanting Philippe, or Becky for that matter, to witness her melt-down, Harriet threw all her things into her bag as fast as she could. She grabbed her towel. She shoved her feet into her waiting flip flops. As she set off towards the gate, Philippe spoke.

'Is everything okay?' A frown creased his forehead.

'Yes! No! I don't know.' She must calm down. There was probably a rational explanation. Maybe if she pictured herself in her old office, sitting behind her old desk; if she imagined herself dealing efficiently with every challenge, she would morph back into that person, that person who was totally in control.

'D'you want me to come with you?' Philippe got to his feet.

'No. It's okay.' Harriet watched Philippe's face fall. 'But. Thanks.' Harriet turned away and walked towards the exit, but not before hearing Becky's next words.

'Philippe, you couldn't be a darling and do my back?'

Harriet made the mistake of glancing back. Becky had shed her clothes in record time and was stretching her long, toned body on a towel placed very close to Philippe's.

A slither of irritation interrupted Harriet's panic. Becky was unbelievable! She had no morals. Engaged to be married and yet throwing herself at any available man, well at Philippe anyway. Not that she cared. A man was the last thing she needed in her life right now. Particularly a man like Philippe.

When Harriet reached the hotel reception, Frau Tanner was nowhere to be seen. Karina, the German receptionist, was poring over some receipts. Harriet could not help but smile. With her two thick, dark plaits wound around her head, her no-nonsense clothes and clumpy, practical shoes, she looked like the stereotypical German waitress.

'Can I help you?' Karina's words were clipped. 'I am very busy.'

'Sorry, yes. I'd like to speak to Frau Tanner.'

Without looking up, Karina turned over a letter and scrutinised a column of figures. 'She is out.'

'D'you know when she'll be back?' Harriet's mind had dreamed up all manner of scenarios based on this one call. She would not be able to settle until she knew what it was about. And to top it all, her back was beginning to sting.

'She has been out all morning. I am not her PA.'

'Out all morning? Are you sure?'

Karina gave Harriet a look that would have had Harriet scurrying for safety, had this not been so important. Very important. Gearing up her courage, she persevered.

'Has there been a phone call for me?'

'Why would there be?' Karina turned her back on Harriet. 'I am very busy. Can you not see that?'

Harriet slammed her bedroom door and threw her bag into the corner of the room. How dare Becky Randalph-Goodheim lie to her like that? Who did she think she was? She had a good mind to go and tell Becky exactly what she thought of her. Although, on second thoughts, that would mean a show down in front of Philippe, and he had already seen her kicking off once before.

Instead, she lay on her bed and played in her mind all the things she wanted to say to Miss Becky Randalph-Goodheim. She tried not to imagine Philippe smoothing sun cream across Becky's back, of Becky reciprocating, her hands running across his stomach.

For the first time since she had landed in Zürich, Harriet regretted ditching her mobile. It had been an impulsive decision. The moment her feet stepped onto Swiss soil, or tarmac to be more accurate, she dropped it into the nearest bin. She told herself that she could not have a clean break with constant reminders of her old life interrupting her.

Yet, at this moment in time, she could have done with some music to distract her. She thought of all the tracks she had painstakingly downloaded onto her phone. Damn! Instead, she would have to make do with a couple of English magazines, which one of the guests had left in reception. So much for her quiet getaway. This trip was turning out very differently indeed.

Chapter 4

Jo sat at the table with her feet propped up on the chair opposite.

'Ah, lush.' Jo took a long drink of iced lemonade, which had been left out for the staff after lunch service. 'I love this weather, but sometimes it's far too hot outside. Especially when you're working in it.'

The staff room was basic with none of the home comforts that were spread liberally throughout the guest areas of the hotel. Not that this deterred the staff from taking full advantage of the space. It was a sanctuary where they could relax, let off steam, share a joke, and for a brief period of time not be accountable to anyone but themselves.

'Would you rather be back in Wales?' Harriet asked. 'They had gale force winds there yesterday.'

Jo picked up a biscuit and began to nibble the chocolate from around the outside. 'You've got a point. I promise never to moan about being too hot ever again.'

Harriet crossed one leg over the other and started to massage her left foot. 'They're killing me.'

Even though she had chosen the most comfortable loafers she could find, she was not used to being on her feet for so many hours at a time. Yes, she used to walk around the office and speak to different departments, but most of her day had been spent sitting behind a desk.

'You can't take the pace,' Jo teased. 'We need to toughen you up.'

'What do you suggest? A few years toiling on a farm in the middle of the Welsh countryside? Would that do it?'

Jo jutted out her chin. 'Are we all just walking clichés to you? Farmers from Wales, brash Americans from - America.'

Becky, huddled in the corner, scowled at her.

Harriet giggled. 'What, and a pale English rose from England?'

In the few weeks they had known each other, Jo frequently talked about her family. She was the youngest and had three elder brothers. Her dad worked the farm, as had his father and his grandfather before him. Her mother was the heart of the family. Harriet wondered what it would have been like to have been brought up in such a large family. Her experience had been so different.

'Yes, and that pale English rose needs to spend a few months sweating it out on our farm. That would be a good start. A bit of waitressing would be a breeze after that. It certainly didn't do me any harm.' Jo raised her arm and flexed her non-existent muscles.

'Well,' Harriet cocked her head on one side, 'I wouldn't bet on you in an arm wrestle.'

'You're not going on about the bracing air in Wales again, are you?' A tall, slim man with a riot of red hair sticking up inches above his scalp pulled up a chair beside Jo.

Jo blushed. 'You're just jealous! You wish you had mountains in Germany as impressive as Snowdon and Cader Idris.'

'You'll have to come to the Black Forest with me, young lady, then I'll show you what a *real* mountain looks like.' Hans turned to Fred who had just walked in. 'Isn't that right, Fred?'

Fred was as broad as Hans was slim. His previously bushy brown beard was neatly trimmed. Herr König, the head chef, had insisted on it; strict hygiene was practised in his kitchen at all times.

'I reckon you're hogging all the women.' Fred squeezed onto the end of the bench.

'And why not?' Hans stretched out his arms, trying to loop Jo and Harriet within them.

Harriet dodged away from him. 'I wouldn't get too cosy. Jo's big brothers will be here next week.'

Hans quickly withdrew his arms, looking sheepish.

'So what's with this Herr Smith?' Jo sipped her drink, looking from Hans to Fred to Harriet.

Harriet could feel the heat rising into her face. Since the day she had left the swimming pool to find Frau Tanner, she hadn't spoken to Philippe. She had caught sight of him briefly across the restaurant or out on the terrace. She didn't know whether to be relieved or disappointed that his table was not in her section of the restaurant.

The effect he had on her was infuriating. Even when she spotted him out of the corner of her eye, she could not concentrate on anything else; her eyes zoomed in on him as if they were the lens of an expensive SLR camera.

The other evening, Philippe walked past to get to his table. He gave her a brief nod in acknowledgement. She was so flustered, she served the only vegetarian in her section with Steak Tartar and offered Mrs Evetts, who had a nut allergy, some peanut sauce.

Occasionally, she sensed him watching her. It took all her willpower not to lock eyes with him. The rest of the time wasn't much better. Despite trying to keep him out of her thoughts, vivid memories of him on the terrace and at the swimming pool haunted her waking hours and infiltrated her dreams.

'Ask Becky!' Fred nodded to where Becky was sitting on her own at the other end of the table. 'Isn't she his *personal* waitress?'

Becky ignored him.

Hans sniggered. 'A lot more than that if you ask me.'

Harriet felt the blood draining from her face. Ever since the swimming pool incident, she had stayed out of Becky's way, as far as was possible given they had to work together. There had been a few times when a cutting retort had quivered on the edge of her tongue: something about the fabricated phone call, but it would only look like she was being petty.

Laughter burst out of Hans. He raised his eyebrows at Jo. 'Will you be my *personal* waitress?'

Jo whacked him across the legs with a napkin. 'You wish!'

'I guess that is a "no".' Hans grinned from ear to ear as he tried to protect himself from Jo's highly ineffective weapon.

Harriet pushed back her chair. 'Right, I'm on bar duty in five minutes. I'll see you lot later.'

The midday shift was normally quiet. Only one waitress was needed. Most of the guests were out walking in the mountains or visiting the lakes at Interlaken or on some other trip. She dreaded this time of day. Her mind invariably bombarded her with memories: of her mother; of her office; of Greg; and of Toby.

Sighing, she stepped out onto the terrace. It was surprisingly busy. Six of the tables were occupied.

Harriet made her way around the tables, smiling and chatting as she took orders for coffee and cold drinks. She recognised most of the guests as they tended to stay at least one to two weeks at a time, if not longer. Although what had really surprised her at the beginning was how many of the guests were English.

'How are you today, dear?' Elspeth Beecham smiled up at Harriet. A mischievous twinkle shone out of her blue eyes as she spoke. It was difficult to work out her age. Despite having snow white hair cropped close to her scalp, she was wiry. She looked as if she could out-walk a person half her age.

'I'm okay, Elspeth.' Harriet flipped over the page of her notebook ready to take Elspeth's order. Elspeth had insisted on first-name terms at their first meeting: "Call me Elspeth. Please. Mrs Beecham makes me sound like I'm a matron."

Elspeth studied Harriet's face. Her smile didn't quite reach her eyes. There was a sadness that seemed to follow her about like a shadow.

'You know, my dear,' Elspeth reached out her hand and touched Harriet's shoulder, 'I may not have children of my own, but I have ten godchildren, a gaggle of adopted nephews and nieces, and very broad shoulders. If you ever want to talk about anything, I'm in room 310. You'd be very welcome. Anytime.'

Harriet blinked back the tears, which were rising fast to the surface. It made her ache for her mother. It was still hard to believe that she was dead. Part of her wanted to be folded up in Elspeth's arms, to shed the tears that she hadn't been able to let loose at the funeral. But not only was she working, she was also terrified that once she opened the floodgates, she would never stop crying.

'Thank you.' Harriet squeezed the old lady's hands. 'That's lovely of you.'

'Right, I'm keeping you waiting.' Elspeth turned to the menu. 'From the look on that man's face, I am extremely unpopular.'

31

Harriet looked over to where Elspeth had gestured. She saw Philippe, arms crossed, his eyes fixed in her direction. Her heart jumped in her chest.

Her mind shot back in time, first to her dad and then to Greg. They had both been users of the worst kind. They had charmed her, and then grabbed what they could before scarpering. She knew it had made her cynical. It was hard not to be when the two most important men in your life, the ones who had meant everything, betrayed you.

Anyway, she had come to the conclusion weeks ago that if you loved someone, it led to heartache. You loved them, you invested yourself in them and then they left you.

It took concerted effort for Harriet to look away from Philippe, as if his coordinates had been pre-programmed into her brain. Somehow, however, she did manage to drag her eyes away before turning back to Elspeth. 'Not out walking today?' Harriet asked, hoping that a change of subject would distract her.

'No dear. I'm having a rest day. Never a bad thing. Now, what I would love is a glass of apple juice and some of that heavenly chocolate ice cream.'

Harriet nodded. 'I'll bring it over in a minute.'

'I think that man is trying to attract your attention.' Elspeth looked over to where Philippe was beckoning. Elspeth nudged Harriet with her elbow. 'He's a bit of a dish. There was a time when I would have jumped at the chance.'

"Jumped at the chance?" Harriet stared at Elspeth as if seeing her for the first time.

'Off you go – better see what he wants,' Elspeth encouraged, giving her a little shove in Philippe's direction.

Harriet made her way across the terrace. She tried to keep herself calm. It was difficult. The arms of his sleeves were rolled up exposing his tanned biceps. It was outrageous, that's what it was. He should, by rights, be pasty and puny. What she wanted to know was how a writer sitting at his desk day in, day out had managed to build up a body like that? She shook herself and tried to focus away from his bare skin.

'What can I get you?' Harriet stared at the table to avoid catching his eyes, or any part of him, for that matter.

'A smile would be nice?' A cheeky grin spread across Philippe's face.

Harriet's sharp intake of breath broadened his grin to a full-wattage smile.

Tilting her chin, Harriet kept full control of her face. Who did he think he was asking her to perform on demand? He might be able to twist Becky around his little finger, but she was not about to be taken in by his banter.

'Shame that's not on the menu,' Harriet retorted. 'Now if there's nothing I can get you, I need to serve guests who actually want to place an order.'

A muscle pulsed in Philippe's cheek. His former humour vanished. 'Get me a coffee. Without milk. I still remember what happened last time.'

'Fine!' Harriet snatched the menu out of Philippe's outstretched hand and marched off towards the bar.

Philippe shook his head. He seemed to spend far too much time watching Harriet's retreating back, and an angry one at that. Women! They were impossible to work out. One moment they were chatty and friendly, the next moment they morphed into a convincing impersonation of Cruella de Vil.

He should have learned his lesson with Lauren. When he dropped down on one knee and she said yes, he had meant forever. Was it so wrong to have believed that she felt the same? And yet, it turned out that he had been a fool to think she would stick with him after the accident.

His career had lain in tatters and then, the icing on the cake: Lauren dumped him, moved onto a new, improved model; one that hadn't been injured; one who was still a rising star; one who was going somewhere.

He had to stop this, this hankering back to the past. He had to focus. Finish the book he had promised his publishers. He came here to get away from the reporters still sniffing around for any gossip they could spread across the media. He did not come here to dwell on the past or to complicate his future.

Philippe remembered the promise he made himself the day he opened the paper to find his fiancé in the arms of another man. At that moment, he had drawn a line under women. He had sworn to himself that he would be a confirmed bachelor. Forever.

He would do well to keep that fact lodged firmly in the forefront of his mind. Especially around Harriet. There was something frustratingly compelling about her.

His manuscript, as thin as it was, sat in front of him. He stared at the chapter he was working on. Instead of making the occasional edit, he picked up his pen and crossed out paragraph after paragraph. If he carried on like this, he would work his way backwards to chapter one and having nothing to show for the hours he had already invested in this book.

As it was, he had only got to chapter five of the first draft, and even that was looking sketchy. This frustrated him, particularly as his first book had poured out of him as effortlessly as a raging downhill river during snowmelt. What he was experiencing now was far more like an obstinate drip, drip, drip: one that kept drying up. And he had Harriet to blame for that. She was the exact opposite of a muse.

Sitting back in his chair, Philippe gazed at the peaks rising in every direction. It really was paradise here: mountains, valleys, the snow-capped Jungfrau. He needed to open his eyes to the beauty around him, stop mourning the loss of his career and Lauren, and move on. Otherwise he would end up like Scrooge, and *that* wasn't going to help anyone, least of all himself.

Philippe's thoughts were interrupted as a coffee pot was banged down onto the table beside him, followed by his mug and the milk jug, which, to give Harriet her due, was put down rather more gently than the rest. He was about to mention that he had specifically ordered coffee *without* milk, when he caught sight of Harriet's stony face staring down at him.

The question: "Is that any way to treat a guest?" hovered on the tip of his tongue. Fortunately, his mother's parting words, about hoping that a few months away would knock the arrogance out of him, curbed this impulse.

Maybe he should try and be a bit nicer. 'Bad day?'

'I'm surprised you noticed.' Harriet glared at him. Her next words came out in a rush, tumbling over each other to be aired. 'Actually, I thought you'd be at the pool tracking down more women to rub sun cream on.'

Harriet clapped her hand over her mouth, a look of mortification mingling with an ever-deepening red blush.

A smug grin stretched across Philippe's face. He tried to halt his ever growing smile, but his mouth refused to cooperate.

With her head held high, Harriet swung around. She was about to escape when Philippe's hand shot out and grabbed her wrist. She tried to yank her hand away, but his grip was too firm.

'Will you let go!' Harriet pulled at her arm.

Harriet reminded him of a fierce tiger, in which case he was the ineffective lion-tamer. Eventually, Harriet stood still. Anger bristled out of her. Philippe dared to look deep into her eyes, as if he was reaching right into her soul.

'Not until you hear what I have to say. I want to make one thing very clear. I did not go anywhere near Becky with the sun cream, nor any other woman for that matter. And to make up for that slur on my character, you and I are taking a little walk this afternoon.'

'I'm working.' The warmth of Philippe's fingers was scorching her skin.

'You're off at five,' Philippe replied. 'I checked.'

Harriet stared at him in disbelief.

Philippe dropped Harriet's hand. 'Look, it's your choice. I'm not going to force you.'

The atmosphere hung heavily between them. Harriet watched as Philippe turned away from her, back to his papers.

The words slipped out of Harriet's mouth as if they too had a mind of their own. 'Okay.'

Philippe smiled up at her. 'I'll see you by the gate at five-thirty. I want to show you something.'

Harriet nodded, turning away from the table as if in a dream.

As Harriet walked back across the terrace, she glanced over at Elspeth who winked at her. The enormity of what she had just agreed to started to sink in. Oh dear, oh dear. What had she let herself in for?

Chapter 5

The sun's heat had mellowed from fiercely hot to pleasantly warm. As Philippe and Harriet made their way up the mountain path, Harriet wished she was fitter. Philippe had led the way from the hotel. She could tell he was shortening his stride to allow her to keep up.

Harriet hadn't had much time to get ready. Despite that, for the first time in months, she had chosen her clothes carefully, and even made time to re-apply her make-up. She always tried to look smart and neat for work, but ever since her mum had died, six months ago, spending time on preening seemed superficial. It also demanded a level of concentration and motivation, which seemed to have deserted her.

As they reached the top of a particularly steep section, Harriet paused to catch her breath. This allowed her to watch Philippe as he strode on ahead. The one advantage of walking behind was that she could study him unobserved. A grey T-shirt was pulled tight across his broad back. The muscles on his tanned legs flexed as he walked. She wondered what it would feel like to be wrapped in his arms, to be pulled close to his chest. Her pulse quickened. This was no good for her at all. What she had to do was to focus on something else. She was already out of breath from walking up the mountain, she did not need anything else to take her breath away.

Try as she might, however, she could not tear her eyes away. The meadow scattered with hundreds of colourful wild flowers on one side and the valley flanked by craggy rocks clinging to the edge of the mountains on the other did not draw her gaze as Philippe did.

As she stared, she noticed his gait swung more to the right as though his left leg was slowing him down. Her brows pulled together. Was he limping? As she watched, she noticed vivid red scars zigzagging down the length of his left leg from where his shorts ended to the top of his socks. How come she had never noticed these before? Well, how could she? Most of the time he was sitting at a table on the terrace or in the restaurant, and that one time at the pool, she had had other things on her mind.

'We're nearly there.' Philippe paused, allowing Harriet to catch up with him. The scree covering the path was making progress slippery. 'Would you like a hand?'

Harriet looked at Philippe's outstretched hand, then to his face and back again. Reaching up, she felt his fingers curl around hers. A shiver ran through her. What was it with her body? Yet again, it had taken on a life of its own.

At the touch of Harriet's fingers on his, Philippe's breath caught in his throat. He immediately regretted offering his help. In fact, he regretted asking her out at all this afternoon.

Being in strict control one hundred per cent of the time had been crucial as he had flown up the ranks in his career. Trying to outrun his emotions by charging up the hill ahead of Harriet had failed miserably. All it had done was to aggravate his leg. It was taking monumental effort to keep from limping.

'Could we have a breather?' Harriet's breath was coming out in short gasps.

Philippe lowered himself onto a patch of grass straightening his left leg out in front of him.

'What happened to your leg?' Harriet found it impossible not to stare at the deeply entrenched scars zigzagging his leg.

Clenching his lips together, Philippe took a deep breath. He hated it when anyone commented on his leg. It represented all that he had lost.

'It's nothing.' Philippe kept his eyes focused on two birds gliding effortlessly above them. If he had half as much freedom and movement as them, he would still be flying high himself, being held up as the champion he used to be, with Lauren by his side.

'Heaven's above! That's terrifying. Why would anyone do that? It's insanity!' Harriet shouted, covering her eyes with her hands, although Philippe could see her peeking through the gaps in her fingers. She was like a rubbernecker on the motorway, who slowed down to drink in the carnage of an accident, when all the while her conscience was imploring her to look away.

Philippe looked over to where Harriet had been pointing. A man was paragliding down into the valley, soaring like an eagle.

They both watched, Philippe entranced, Harriet petrified, as the red and orange parachute rippled in the breeze.

Philippe turned to Harriet. 'It must feel like flying!'

'Only if I had a gun to my head,' Even the thought of it made Harriet feel dizzy. A shiver ran through her.

'I guess you'd never give it a try?' Philippe's eyes challenged hers.

Harriet stared at Philippe. So many images flew through Harriet's mind: her mum's funeral, Greg's text, Ed's face when she told him she was leaving, and finally, Toby.

Each blow had knocked her confidence until she was curled up so tight like a prickly hedgehog with all its spikes out. She wasn't sure she was ready to uncurl and embrace life again. It all felt too risky.

'Unless you're too chicken?' Philippe's voice had a teasing note in it.

The words took Harriet straight back to primary school. Up until that day she had been shy. If anyone spoke to her, she would blush bright red. To survive school, she kept quiet and stayed in the background.

On this particular day, a group of boys found a huge worm in the field, which they pulled out of the ground. It was unfortunate that Harriet was sitting on the tarmac beside the field, her head buried in a book. The boys approached her. They told her that she could join their gang if she picked up the worm and put it down Maisie's back. Maisie was the school swot, complete with big round glasses, which made her eyes pop out, and an immaculate uniform.

Harriet stood up, ready to run. She hated slimy things, but she hated being picked on more. The words "gang" and "join" were almost enough to tempt her to pick up the disgusting creature and do the dirty deed. And Maisie was always lording it over her, smiling smugly each time Harriet got a bad mark. Well, she had had enough!

'Unless you're too chicken?' Tom taunted, holding the wriggling worm out towards her.

'I'm not a chicken!' she shouted back.

The three boys stared in astonishment as quiet, meek Harriet Anderson grabbed the worm in her hand, stomped over to Maisie Wright, yanked back her T-shirt and shoved the worm down her back.

Maisie screamed loudly. She jumped up, shaking her shirt, desperately trying to dislodge the slimy creature, which was wiggling its way down her back. 'HELP ME! HELP ME! HELP MEEEEE!'

One of the teachers grabbed hold of Maisie and demanded she stay still. She was wriggling around as frantically as the worm lodged in her shirt, which made it impossible to grab hold of the slimy creature. At last, with the help of another teacher, the worm was removed. Maisie then had complete hysterics. Harriet, in contrast, felt completely calm. In fact, she felt on top of the world.

That was her turning point. That one incident gained her three ardent male admirers, an open invitation to join groups of girls in the playground and a severe reprimand from both the headmaster and her mother. But it had been worth it.

'I'm not a chicken!' Harriet retorted, her flashing eyes meeting his.

But this time, her words were pure bravado. Even the sight of someone gliding hundreds of metres above the ground made her feel decidedly queasy. The thought of actually dangling from a harness suspended in mid-air paralysed her with fear.

She was terrified of heights; heights where she didn't have her feet firmly placed on solid ground. She could put it down to the time she fell out of a friend's tree house; or when the roller coaster a friend dared her to ride on got stuck at the top of a loop with the carriage and each of its occupants hanging upside down for 60 seconds, which at the time felt like 60 hours; or when they were on a rare holiday by the sea, her dad hung her upside down by her ankles over the balcony, four flights up, when she was five years old, just before he left them. Her mum, who had been at the local shop at the end of the street buying cigarettes for her dad, said she could hear Harriet's screams as she was paying.

In any case, Harriet didn't much care why she was scared. All she knew was that she and heights did not mix. Ever.

To be able to get on the plane to Switzerland, she had to have weeks of hypnosis. Before she could even step into the airport, let alone get on the plane, she had to swallow a couple of prescribed Valium.

The steep train ride up the mountainside, although not her favourite mode of transport, was bearable; the train was connected to the rails and these in turn were connected to the ground. But hand gliding? No way!

So why then did she find herself agreeing? As soon as the word "okay" was out in the open air, she clapped her hands over her mouth. It was her stupid, stupid pride, which refused to let that word - that simple, compact word "No" release itself from her mouth.

'That's a date then,' Philippe smiled.

A "date"? Despite her terror, Harriet's heart soared - pity it wasn't *that* easy to go hand-gliding.

'I'll ask Herr Tanner where to go. We don't want any cowboys.'

The word "cowboys" flew around Harriet's mind. 'No, you're right. No cowboys!'

Although it hardly mattered. If she had anything to do with it, there was no way that her feet would be leaving the ground harnessed by several strings to a flimsy bit of silk, cowboys or not. Absolutely no way!

Anyway, surely Herr and Frau Tanner would object to her dating one of the guests, and participating in dangerous sports at the same time. Maybe that would save her. But then, it wasn't even a real date. It was just a dare. Wasn't it?

Twenty minutes later Harriet and Philippe were sitting side by side on a wooden table on a small terrace. Two steaming hot

41

chocolates, with cream swirled up high above the mugs' rims, sprinkled with grated chocolate, sat in front of them.

Philippe was in turmoil. His conscience prodded him. He hated lying, particularly to Harriet. He hated the fact that he had to pretend to be something he wasn't. But he was fed up with people wanting him for his name and his past. How could he move on and try and re-build a new future when everyone was so intent on dragging him back to his former life? How could he know whether people were being friendly because of who he used to be rather than who he wanted to become? He used to think he was a good judge of character, but look what had happened with Lauren. No, this was the only way he could start making sense of himself and his new life, by being Philippe Smith, not Philippe Myers. His mum had suggested he drop the 'pe' and go back to his original spelling, but there were still elements of his stardom that he wasn't willing to let go. In any case, he'd got used to "Philippe" over the years and couldn't see himself ever going back to plain old "Philip". And in his defence, his publishers preferred the new version; they said it was more "artistic".

'Hot chocolate on a hot day? Are you sure about this?' Harriet asked, eyeing the hot chocolate with suspicion.

'It is the best hot chocolate ever. You have to try it.' Philippe forced himself to concentrate on Harriet, pushing his worries to the back of his mind. And it wasn't hard to keep his attention on her, she was beautiful.

Philippe had insisted they sit on the same side of the table, even though it was slightly cramped for both of them on the small bench, but that way they both got to admire the view. He could feel the heat of her leg pushed up close to his, the brush of her arm as she raised her drink to her lips. The impulse to run his hand down her arm and to sweep the lock of blond hair behind her ear, was becoming stronger by the minute.

Focus on something else, he kept telling himself. Anything else.

42

'So what do you do for fun?' Philippe found himself asking – anything that would distract himself from her proximity.

'Fun? If only I could remember what that was.' Harriet took a sip of her hot chocolate, wincing as the scalding liquid burnt her tongue.

'Well, I'll have to see what I can do to remedy that.' Philippe smiled at Harriet, imagining them holding hands ice-skating or rowing a boat across a lake armed with a picnic or ambling around a zoo or lounging on a beach.

'Ah, so you've taken on the role as my 'Fun-Planner' have you? I'm afraid you'll have to get to know me a lot better if you're going to tick all my boxes.'

'It would be my pleasure.' Philippe's eyes held hers. Within seconds, she looked away, breaking the connection between them.

A question had been hovering in Philippe's mind during their walk up the mountain. Okay, so he was pretty sure of the answer, but he had to be certain. There was no way he would risk putting himself in a vulnerable situation so soon after Lauren. Not that he wanted anything serious with Harriet, but getting involved with someone who was committed or married, well, for him, it would be like jumping head first into a pit of vipers. That was definitely a no-go area. A sharp tug of disappointment ran through him at the thought of Harriet sharing her life with another man.

He took a deep breath. It was now or never. 'So have you left a boyfriend or husband pining for you back in England?'

A shadow clouded Harriet's face before she spoke. 'No, there's no boyfriend or husband. Just me.'

As Philippe watched Harriet, a tear rolled down her cheek, then another. He moved closer. He gathered her into his arms and pulled her to him. He expected her to push him away, but she sank into him. His hand automatically reached up and stroked her hair. It made him think of Sophie. The hundreds of times he had comforted her. What he did know, without any doubt, was that having Harriet here in his arms was exactly where she was meant to be.

43

After a few minutes, Harriet pulled away from him. Her cheeks were pink and streaked with traces of mascara, which had run down them along with the tears.

'Here.' Philippe took the tissue out of Harriet's hand. He gently wiped away the brown stains with the edge of the tissue before returning it to Harriet.

'Are you okay?'

Harriet's eyes were focused on her lap. 'My m-mother died. S-six months ago. She got cancer. I looked after her. I thought she'd be okay. They said she had a chance. A small one. But she died.'

Philippe put his hand over Harriet's and squeezed it. 'I'm so sorry.' The intensity of emotion rampaging through him was confusing: her pale face streaked with tears; her small hand tucked in his, shaking slightly; the need to protect and comfort her. He had never felt anything like that for Lauren. The only person who had come close to triggering such intense reaction was Sophie. But that was different. Completely different.

Harriet struggled to compose herself. She had only cried once since her mother had died. Why her body had decided to choose this precise moment, sitting next to Philippe, to let go, was beyond her. It was the last place she would have chosen to allow tears to fall. Somewhere quiet and private would have been preferable. Although when his arms wrapped around her, so close that she could feel his heart beating against hers, when he wiped the tears from her face with such tenderness, she found it was the one place she wanted to be, to stay.

It didn't make any sense. She hadn't known Philippe that long. Greg had been attentive and caring right at the beginning of their relationship, until he hooked her good and proper. Then the evasive answers and excuses started, and the late nights working. Yet, she had still hoped that he would change back into the loving man she had fallen in love with. Until she read the text he sent her during the night. Despicable coward that he was.

Reluctantly, Harriet disentangled her hand from Philippe's. She was left feeling slightly bereft. It would have been so easy to reach out and take his hand in hers again to feel the gentle pressure, the reassurance. But she must stay strong. It was easier in the long run.

'Thank you.' Harriet looked at the mountains wondering who lived in the chalets perched on the slopes leading down to the valley below. They became smaller and smaller the further down the mountain she looked. She had to try something to regain her composure. She knew it would take only the slightest thing to set off her tears again, and she was feeling foolish enough as it was.

'What about you?' Harriet hoped a change of subject would distract her from the grief over her mum and stop her feeling so conscious of Philippe's close proximity. 'Where do you live when you're not hiding out in a hotel?'

'London.'

'Mum and I used to go shopping in London. We'd tour the museums and treat ourselves to a posh tea at The Ritz.' Harriet smiled at the memory.

'I bet they didn't serve hot chocolates as delicious as these.' Philippe raised an eyebrow as he licked the last of the cream off his teaspoon, glancing over at her.

Harriet grinned. 'I couldn't tell you. We only ever had tea and cucumber sandwiches.'

'With bone china handles and your little finger out at an angle?' Philippe smiled.

'Of course. I'm not an amateur tea drinker, you know. I can crook my little finger with the best of them.'

Philippe turned to face her. 'Well we'll just have to test that out, won't we? In fact, when we get back to England, you'll have to prove it to me.'

Resisting the impulse to look into his eyes, which she knew were trained on hers, she pushed aside her empty mug and swung her legs over the bench.

'Right! Let's head back.' Harriet waited for Philippe to extract his long legs from under the low bench.

45

'So that's a yes?' Philippe picked up his wallet and tucked it back into his pocket.

'Okay, yes, or I'll never hear the end of it.'

A burst of giggling caught Harriet's attention. She watched as two young women walked onto the terrace. One of them pointed at Philippe and gasped loudly. 'Oh my God, it's Philippe Myers!' The blond woman grabbed her friend's arm and squealed.

The dark-haired woman's eyes widened. 'I can't believe it. Philippe Myers, here!'

Harriet's eyes shot up taking in Philippe's expression of horror. He stood frozen to the spot, like a naughty child who had been spotted with his hand in the cookie jar.

Before either of them could move, the two women crowded around Philippe shoving a piece of paper and a pen at him, begging for his autograph.

Autograph? Philippe Myers? Then it clicked. She could not believe she hadn't realised before now. Okay, so he had shaved off his iconic beard and cut his hair, but it was glaringly obvious. Philippe Smith was none other than Philippe Myers, the former tennis champion. If she had been at all interested in tennis, she would probably have recognised him, but her career and then Greg had consumed 100 percent of her time for so many years. It had never occurred to her that the English writer by the name of Herr Smith was anything but that: a writer.

He had lied to her! All this stuff about taking her to tea at The Ritz and going paragliding as if they were suddenly the best of friends, and yet he hadn't even had the decency to be honest with her. So who was he? A writer? A tennis champion? The only thing she did know without question was that he was a liar, and she had had enough of them to last her a lifetime.

Grabbing her cardigan, Harriet took off down the path towards the hotel, muttering to herself. Men! How could she have been taken in again? Would she never learn?

She did not notice the quizzical looks from other walkers as she stormed past. She didn't even see the scenery, which had captivated her on the way up. Her anger, and watching her footing as she strode crossly down the mountain, consumed her whole being.

So she didn't hear the footsteps behind her until someone grabbed her arm. Whipping around, she found herself face to face with Philippe, concern etched across his face.

'I'm sorry Harriet. I should have told you.'

'Don't bother!' Harriet tried to yank her arm away.

Placing his hands on her shoulders, Philippe leaned over. He kissed Harriet full on the mouth. Her whole body melted against him, giving herself up to his lips, his arms, his kiss.

Greg's smug face blurred, unasked, into her vision: his countless apologies; his lies; the time after time she had taken him back. She was such a pushover! One kiss and all was forgiven. Well. Not this time.

Gasping with the effort it took to tear herself away, Harriet put both hands against his chest and pushed.

Taken by surprise, Philippe struggled to retain his balance, his left leg throbbing with the speed he had run down the mountain to catch up with Harriet.

Harriet used this opportunity to extricate herself. She headed off down the path towards the hotel, towards the sanctuary of her room. She could hear Philippe calling her name, but she ran on, her breath catching in her chest as she pushed herself onward.

The chalet was quiet. At least that was something to be grateful for. No-one to witness her flushed face and dishevelled appearance. Harriet let herself into her room, panting hard. She sank down onto the bed, holding her head in her hands. Never again, she told herself, her breath gradually slowing. Never, ever again! And yet, the one image, which kept flashing into her mind, that she could not eradicate, was Philippe's kiss. She pressed the back of her hand against her lips. It was as if she could still feel his lips pressed hard against hers.

Frustration bubbled up and overwhelmed her. She picked up her pillow and threw it against the door. This man was *not* getting under her skin, no matter what. She would rather leave the hotel than allow that to happen.

What she needed was a stiff drink. Pity she didn't have any alcohol in her room. Occasions like this called for something stronger than coffee. As it was, coffee was all that was on offer, that or peppermint tea. She flicked on the kettle. One thing she was certain of - it sure as hell would not be a hot chocolate this time. Harriet spooned heaps of coffee into a mug. Her half-read novel lying on the bedside table caught her attention. She opened it. If *Birdsong* couldn't distract her, then she wasn't sure what would.

Harriet curled up at the end of her bed. The novel, though normally gripping, was failing to hold her attention. She sat up, leaning against the wall, sipping her coffee. This getaway of hers was turning out to be nothing at all like she had imagined. Instead, she had walked into a nightmare. It may be a different country, but it looked as if history was repeating itself.

Chapter 6

Harriet was surprised she had managed to sleep so soundly. It was probably, in part, due to her impetuous sprint down the mountain the day before. It certainly could not be attributed to Philippe's kiss, which had at the time and for a good few hours afterwards, awakened every nerve-ending in her body.

The alarm had woken Harriet abruptly from a dream, a dream surprisingly not about Philippe. A dream where Harriet lost Toby. She hunted everywhere: behind trees in the woods; under rocks by the sea; in boxes at the shops. With each step her search became more frantic. She despaired of ever finding him. Yet every time she looked up, she saw the back of his head disappearing around a corner or behind a car, and once again set off at a run to try and catch up with him. It was like the cat and mouse in Tom and Jerry except in this version the mouse was far too clever to ever get caught.

Her eyes catapulted open. It took a while to orientate herself and for her breathing to calm to a measured pace. She swung her legs out of bed and padded over to her wardrobe. She lifted up a pile of jumpers and slid out an envelope. Her fingers trembled slightly as she extracted a torn photograph, holding it up in front of her.

'Oh Toby,' she sighed. 'I do miss you.'

A boy of about six years old smiled back at her, his curly brown hair framing his cherub-like face. Images of Toby flooded into her mind: of her running beside him, holding fast to the saddle of his bike; of his face covered in a bright green cake mixture, which she allowed him to scrape from the bowl; of tears streaming from his eyes as she patched up his scraped knee, which was oozing bright red blood.

Wiping away her own tears, Harriet pushed the photograph back into the envelope. She could not think about him anymore. He was in her past and she had to forget him. The trouble was, she didn't know how she ever could.

Towelling her hair after a particularly cool shower, Harriet's mind continued to play games with her. First Toby took pride of place, his cute smile tugging at her heart strings. Then he faded away and Philippe's grey eyes swam into her field of vision. They stared at her, as if they could reach into every hidden corner of her mind. Once again, she pushed her hand up against her mouth as if she could still feel the imprint of his lips.

In a fit of impatience, she threw on her waitress outfit and slammed the door on her way out. Thank goodness she was working this morning. It would take her mind off everything. At least that's what she hoped.

The terrace was bustling with guests when Harriet arrived. It was a scorcher of a day and all the walkers who might otherwise have trudged past the hotel and continued on their journey were lured in by the smell of coffee and the clinking of ice cubes as cold drinks were served.

Young children slurped at ice creams, adults loosened walking boots and ran their eyes over the headlines of complimentary papers. Jo had been asked to help Harriet out. She would have been run off her feet on her own.

It was just past 11am when Jo grabbed Harriet by the arm and pulled her to one side. 'Harriet! What IS wrong with you? You have just served Elspeth's ice cream to that little girl over there. And her parents do not look happy.'

Harriet clapped her hand over her mouth. Stupid! Stupid! What had she been thinking? Her mind had been so full of Toby, and though she hated to admit it, of Philippe, that she knew she hadn't been concentrating. How could she when her mind was performing Groundhog Day on that kiss? That one stupid kiss. One of the thousands of kisses and goodness knows what else he had no doubt bestowed on his millions of hysterical fans.

Well, there was no way she was going to join the queue of girls that was likely to start forming once word got around that the reclusive writer, Herr Smith, was in fact the famous tennis player,

Philippe Myers, minus the trademark beard, of course. Not that that would put any of them off.

'Harriet.' Jo stood bodily in front of Harriet and made her look into her eyes. 'The dad's coming over. NOW!'

Piercing screams echoed across the terrace followed by a pink ball of fury, who pummelled her chubby arms into her dad's legs as he made his way across the terrace with her precious bowl of ice cream.

'Mein! Papa! Mein! Ich liebe es! Mein!' the girl screeched, grabbing at her father's trouser legs.

Watching the drama unfold in front of her, Harriet racked her brain. How could she calm this down before Frau or Herr Tanner came out to investigate the rising noise levels? She knew they would not be pleased, especially when they realised it was all down to her stupid mistake.

Other guests, most of them elderly, turned in their seats and frowned, their peaceful morning coffee shattered.

Before Harriet could open her mouth to try to form some coherent excuse, Elspeth appeared beside the puce-faced father and his hysterical young daughter.

'I am so very sorry.' Elspeth placed her hand on the father's arm. 'My fault completely. Your daughter, you see, looks exactly like my granddaughter. I miss her, you know.' She sniffed, holding up a tissue and dabbing the corner of both of her eyes.

'And the one thing that my granddaughter loves more than anything else in the world is ice cream. So when I saw your daughter sitting with you, as good as gold, I ordered her some ice cream. That's the trouble with me. I'm too impulsive. My daughter always says so.'

Harriet was puzzled. Elspeth didn't have any children, did she?

Elspeth raised her eyes to the father. She patted them with the tissue once again, staring round-eyed into his. 'I am so extremely sorry. I should have asked you first, of course.'

The transformation in the girl's dad was like magic. The father's anger melted away faster than the ice cream that had caused all the fuss. Bending down to his daughter, he scooped her up in his arms.

'For once, you can have something sweet, even though you know it is not good for your teeth.' He turned to Elspeth. 'I am a dentist, you see.' He smiled back at his daughter. 'Thank this nice lady for your ice cream.'

The demon of two minutes before beamed up at Elspeth: 'Danke. Ich mag Eis sehr.'

Harriet's shoulders sagged with relief. 'Thank you,' she mouthed to Elspeth, before heading back into the bar to get the drinks that had been ordered by Tables four and seven.

As soon as Harriet had taken out the drinks, she presented Elspeth with a coffee and an extra-large bowl of strawberry ice cream as a thank you. 'You're a miracle-worker.'

Elspeth smiled. 'It's a pleasure my dear, always happy to help out.'

'And your granddaughter, Elspeth?' Harriet grinned at her.

'What granddaughter?' Elspeth replied, winking.

Harriet shook her head in disbelief. 'Remind me never to get on the wrong side of you.'

Once Elspeth had stirred three heaped spoonfuls of sugar into her coffee, she fixed Harriet with her beady eyes. 'So, how was your walk with that dishy young man?'

'Well, you know in the fairy tale the princess kisses the frog and he turns into a prince?'

Elspeth raised her eyes just beyond Harriet and started to say something, but Harriet didn't notice. She was on a roll. 'This was the opposite. I thought he was a prince, but it turns out that he was a frog all along!'

Before Elspeth had a chance to say anything, Harriet saw a shadow looming behind her.

'A frog?'

Harriet spun around in the direction of the voice and came face to face with Herr Smith, no Myers. Oh, who cared anyway! An infuriating smile curved his lips and his eyes sparkled mischievously. Well he might think it was funny, but she certainly didn't.

Gritting her teeth, Harriet turned back to Elspeth. 'Can I get you anything else?'

'I think the *frog* wants your attention,' Elspeth whispered. She moved her eyes over to where Philippe was standing, less than a foot away from Harriet.

'Well the frog needs to find himself a slimy pond to wallow in because he certainly doesn't have any playmates here.'

From the look on Elspeth's face, Harriet knew she had gone too far. But what did she care? There was no way she was going to let Philippe get under her skin. She knew she couldn't cope with another rejection.

Harriet squared her shoulders, lifted her chin as far in the air as she dared and strode back across the terrace to the bar area without so much as a backward glance.

It was good to get out of her work clothes and into the fresh air. The sky was cobalt blue. Not a trace of cloud blurred the vivid sky. No hint of a breeze ruffled the leaves in the surrounding trees. The sun's heat created a haze, which forced walkers to don sunglasses, strip down to the bare essentials and take mouthfuls of refreshing water every few paces.

When Harriet first arrived in Wengen, she found the heat exhausting and relentless. But now, several weeks on, she revelled in the warmth, took regular gulps of the fresh, clean air, and was still enthralled by the scenery, which surrounded her.

Jo had gone on ahead, running up to the train as it pulled into the station. Harriet hung back.

Even from a distance, Jo's squeal of excitement made Harriet jump. Launching herself into the air, Jo threw herself shamelessly at a large, fiery-haired man who had hardly stepped out of the train. Three men, in turn, were pounced on as if Jo was their puppy and they were the owners returning from an extremely long holiday.

Harriet stood back and watched the four of them embracing. One big happy family. It made Harriet miss her mother more than ever. She had never wished for brothers or sisters before. She and her mum had forged such a strong bond that they hadn't needed anyone else. But now, watching the love between Jo and her brothers, made her heart ache with sadness.

Their closeness made her feel like a spare part. If only she had stayed in the chalet. She could have met up with them later, after they had greeted each other. But Jo had been very insistent about her coming to the station.

'Harriet. Come and meet my brothers. This is Tom, he's the eldest, and then Andy and Gareth - they're twins.'

A blur of stretched-out hands and grins ranging from cheeky to shy bombarded Harriet. Tom and Andy looked muscly and rugged, just as she imagined Welsh farmers should look. In fact, if she'd had to guess, she would have said these two were the twins.

Gareth, in contrast, was surprisingly willowy, given he worked full-time with his brothers on the farm. He looked as if he would have been more at home in front of an easel and a palette of paints, but then that was stereotyping before she had even said two words to him.

Their skin was burnished by the sun, which for them meant a thicket of freckles across their faces. Tom and Andy's backs were broad and their arms sculpted from lugging hay bales around and wrestling sheep to the ground to relieve them of their winter fleeces. However, there was no doubting their genes, all of them had inherited the same orange/red hair.

'Frau Tanner has given them a special rate for the chalet,' Jo told Harriet, linking arms with two of her brothers and leading the way out of the station and down the lane towards the hotel.

'So how come you can be spared in the middle of the summer?' Harriet asked.

Jo grinned. 'Yes, well, dad wasn't thrilled about it, but our neighbour owed us a lot of favours. He's pulled in some of his nephews to help out. It's only for two weeks and they haven't had a holiday for the last couple of years—'

Tom's low whistle brought them all to an abrupt halt. At first Harriet thought it was the sight of the snow-capped Jungfrau. It frequently stopped people in their tracks and initiated 'wows' and gasps and other outpourings of appreciation.

But no, on this occasion, no such luck. Sashaying towards them in another of her miniscule skirts, displaying her long and now tanned legs, was Becky.

'Uh oh, man-eater alert,' Jo whispered to Harriet. She raised her eyebrows. My brothers are suckers for a pretty face.'

'And a short skirt,' Harriet added.

'Well, looky here.' Becky batted her overly made-up eyes at every one of Jo's brothers in turn, although her gaze settled for a moment longer on Tom before she looked away. 'It looks like Wengen has just got three times more interesting!'

'You can say that again!' Tom nodded, running his eyes appreciatively down the full length of Becky.

Allowing her shirt to hang open just enough to display a large amount of cleavage encased in a small amount of electric blue bikini, Becky pushed her shades back onto her nose. 'Off for a dip in the local pool. Such a shame I can't reach my back with the sun cream . . .'

'Can't you call your fiancé?' Jo asked. 'I'm sure he'd oblige.'

Becky's scowl was quickly hidden with a wide smile. 'Shame he's in the States. I'll just have to ask someone more local to help me out. Yet again, as if her eyes had taken on a mind of their own, they sought out Tom without quite meeting his gaze.'

Jo turned towards Harriet. 'She's completely brazen. And just look at them.' She nodded towards her brothers all of whom, without exception, had their tongues practically hanging out of their mouths. 'It's pathetic!'

There was something about the way the three of them watched, totally hypnotised by Becky, as she swung her hips and wiggled her way up the road towards the village. They were like mindless puppets and Becky was, with very little effort, holding each of their strings as they danced to her tune.

Harriet tried to smother her giggle but it exploded out of her, releasing the tension that had lain heavy within her since the day before. Catching Harriet's eye, Jo hiccupped with the effort of keeping herself under control. Tom's raised eyebrow finished her off. Laughter howled out of her and before long both of them were bent double, their whole bodies shaking, their eyes streaming with tears.

'Women!' Tom shook his head. 'Come on guys, let's leave these two here. I've got sun cream to administer.'

The three men shouldered their rucksacks, and with cheeky grins all round, they continued on down the road towards the hotel, leaving Jo and Harriet hanging onto each other in the middle of the road, still helpless with hysterics.

Chapter 7

A 'frog'? The cheeky mare had called *him* a 'frog'! It wasn't so long ago that girls used to clamour for a touch, for his sweaty T-shirt, for any acknowledgement. What they would have given for just one kiss. And yet Harriet, she had not only pushed him away, but had now insulted him.

Yes, at first he had found it amusing to be called a frog. But the more he thought about it, the more indignant he became.

He tried not to think about the kiss. The kiss where she melted into him. Where the heat of her lips trembled through his body as he pulled her closer and closer. The kiss that he had wanted to go on and on and never stop. The kiss that was unlike anything he and Lauren had ever shared. And then she had abruptly shoved him away. If she had thrown a full bucket of icy water over him, it wouldn't have felt as traumatic.

Anyway, what had possessed him to kiss her? She was hardly his type. She was too natural, too spiky. For goodness sake, she didn't even bother with her nails. Did she have no pride? He was used to women who looked immaculate 24/7. It's not as if she had a proper excuse by being stuck in a tiny village way up in the mountains. Half the hotels had beauty parlours attached to them to pander to the wealthy ladies who visited Wengen for its reviving Alpine air and first class service.

Okay, so he admitted that waitressing was not conducive to immaculate false nails, but that other waitress, the American one, she seemed to manage. A tiny part of him buried deep knew he was being unreasonable, but he couldn't help himself. The 'frog' comment had got under his skin and was niggling away at him. No-one, but no-one had ever insulted him like that before. Flashes of newspaper articles with critics panning his arrogance sprang to mind. He shoved it aside. It was hardly comparable. Reporters were paid to write that nonsense.

Philippe pictured Harriet, tears glistening in her eyes as she told him about her mother. It had unlocked the same protective instinct in him that he felt with Sophie. He saw the hurt in her face when the groupies had approached, thrusting pen and paper at him. What terrible timing. All these weeks in Wengen and he had managed to stay anonymous. But just as Harriet and he had started to get close, his cover had been blown.

It was Harriet's flaring green eyes as she pushed him away from her that caught in his memory. The fury that swirled within them had taken his breath away. Hurt, anger, betrayal, all of these emotions had flown out of her eyes as if they were poisoned darts, aimed at him, primed to inflict wound after wound.

Shaking his head, he tried to dismiss these vivid images, which were stubbornly hijacking his mind.

'Damn her!' Philippe pushed his chair away from his desk where he had been hoping to finish the chapter he had been working on for far too long.

Philippe wandered over to the balcony. He watched the waterfall opposite. If only the power with which the water crashed down into the Lauterbrunnen valley could be harnessed and converted into creative energy. He marvelled at the mini prisms of multi-coloured light that bounced off the water as the sun's rays stroked its surface. To the left the snowy peaks of the Jungfrau swirled with mist. Who would have thought that thousands of visitors each year shivered their way through its ice caves when here in Wengen the sun was scorching hot?

If only the beauty surrounding him was enough to inspire him to write. A meagre eight chapters nestled in the folder on his laptop, but they were rough, not nearly written to the same standard he had produced the first time around. Perhaps the cauldron of emotions he had been experiencing when he wrote his first novel had been the motivating factor.

But God knows he couldn't go through anything like that again - he would not survive it. And it wasn't as if he was devoid of feeling this time around. Every time he saw Harriet she inspired in him huge emotional swings from anger to compassion to frustration to . . . well, that infernal woman had called him a 'frog'! Hardly the ideal recipe for a relationship. Not that he was in the least bit interested in one of those.

Having paced up and down his room countless times, Philippe could not settle at his desk, no matter how hard he tried. Instead, he strode into the bedroom, pulled on his swimming trunks, threw on some clothes and shoved his towel and latest crime novel into his bag. He kept hoping that by reading a gripping plot with the necessary twists and turns, he might gain some much-needed inspiration.

Anyway, the weather was too hot to be cooped up like a battery-hen, even if he had the luxury of an air-conditioned room. Maybe he would get some ideas by the pool. As an afterthought, he picked up his pad and a couple of pens and slipped them into his bag.

The first thing he heard when he made his way up the hill to the pool was wild splashing and shrieks of laughter. He had hoped that the pool would be quiet today. No such luck.

Philippe rounded the corner and paid his fee to the man sitting in the kiosk. He was surprised to find that apart from a large group of boisterous adults at one end, the rest of the pool was quiet. That, at least, was a relief. If he kept down the opposite end from the hijinks, he might even enjoy a bit of peace.

He was about to spread out his towel when he noticed a woman approaching him. Oh no! That was all he needed. It was the 'Lauren lookalike' who had taken on the role as his personal waitress and wasted no time in offering more services to him than was strictly professional or within the remit of "waitress". So far he had managed to keep her at arm's length, but she was persistent and not a woman who was used to being refused.

By the time he had racked his brain for excuses or avoidance tactics, Becky was invading his personal space. If she moved any closer, they would be touching.

'Either I can join you . . .' Becky was practically purring, her eyes never leaving his face, 'or you can come and join us. I know which I'd prefer.'

Philippe was on the verge of telling Becky precisely what she could do with her offer when he heard a peal of laughter ring out above the others. He would know that laugh anywhere. Harriet was here with that group? It made sense, he supposed. They did work in the same hotel, although he couldn't recall having seen either of them socialising together before now.

The group had spread themselves across the grass at the far end of the pool. Philippe spotted Harriet holding court, surrounded by at least three men. It was as if a freezing hand had clenched his stomach, sending icicles shooting through his veins. This was a feeling he recognised. It was how he had felt when he'd read about Lauren's engagement to an up and coming tennis star four short weeks after his accident.

At the time, it had only just become clear to him that he would have to retire from professional tennis. Not only was he no longer a number one tennis star, but there was very little hope of that ever changing. Lauren, it seemed, had cottoned on a lot faster. He was now superfluous to her requirements; discarded like an unwanted toy whose batteries had corroded rendering its mechanism unusable. As far as Lauren was concerned, he had been tossed on the "has been" scrap heap, along with goodness knows how many others, which she had rejected before him.

A few months on, with the clarity that hiding away in the Swiss mountains, and if he was honest having met Harriet, had given him, he could see how fortunate it was that they had never actually got married. Their long engagement had saved him from a messy and high profile divorce. Not that the papers needed any excuse. His near fatal motorbike accident, followed by Lauren's whirlwind engagement to another tennis player, was splattered across National papers for weeks.

'Well?' Becky stood with her arms crossed, tapping her foot.

'Thank you for your kind offer, but it wouldn't feel right keeping you all to myself.'

Philippe walked next to Becky, trying to keep his eyes from seeking out Harriet. What on earth had possessed him to acquiesce to Becky's pleading? Watching Harriet flirting with other men and knowing she thought of him as an abhorrent slimy frog wouldn't exactly do a lot for his ego, even with Becky drooling next to him. It did not make any sense. His decisions no longer made any sense.

'Hi Philippe.' Jo jumped up and smiled at him.

She was a sweet girl. Always friendly and good fun. Why couldn't he fall for someone uncomplicated like her? The words "fall for" stunned him into silence. That, well that was plain ludicrous. Okay, he had to admit that Harriet had somehow got under his skin. She was like a grain of sand, which had got lodged inside him so he carried around a constant reminder of her, despite his best efforts to erase her from his mind. But love? No way!

Each of the men introduced themselves. With extreme effort, Philippe managed to avoid looking at Harriet, so he missed the shock that continued to dance across her face at his unexpected appearance.

'Sorry, who did you say you were?' Harriet asked, confronting him. 'Philippe Smith or Philippe—'

Philippe's eyes narrowed. She was playing games with him. Well he would not allow it. He was done with game-playing. He had had enough of that with Lauren and the media fiasco, which had followed him around like a dark shadow. He was not going to let her hang this over him like some weapon.

'Philippe Myers, former tennis player. Philippe Smith, author of one rather inadequate crime novel. Now if you'll excuse me, I'm going for a swim.'

And with that, Philippe flung off his clothes, walked to the pool and dived in, immersing himself in its cool depths.

The group fell silent as they watched in astonishment as Philippe dived into the pool. All at once questions rang around the group. Becky's grin became even wider at the news. Not only was he a looker and wealthy and British and an author, but he was also Philippe Myers. Wow! She thought of her engagement ring tucked safely in its box in the hotel safe and was extremely glad she hadn't kept it on. There was all the more to play for now.

Jo hushed her brothers, whose over-excitement at the unexpected arrival of a former star in their midst was becoming louder and more heated. The few other sunbathers around the pool were looking over at them.

What have I done? Harriet looked over to where Philippe was swimming length after length as though his life depended on it. Yes, she was mad at him for not telling her, but it was hardly fair of her to blow his cover so publicly. It wasn't as if they had spent lots of time together and could call themselves friends. He didn't owe her anything. All the poor chap wanted was to hide himself away and forget the nightmare that his life had become.

She had been entirely selfish. It had been all about her. She had taken it so personally when she had found out that he was Philippe Myers. All she could think about at the time was that he had deceived her. Just like Greg. But she realised now, too late, that his motives for withholding who he was from her was not personal. It was self-protection. She had to apologise.

Untying her sarong, she hot-footed it over to the pool and jumped in. She hoped that the others would stay where they were. The last thing she needed was three red-haired men crowding her apology.

Harriet started swimming, trying to keep up with Philippe, but he was slicing through the water like a dolphin. His head was down in the water. He was focused only on his breathing and the movement of his limbs as he ate up metre after metre.

Desperate times called for desperate measures. Harriet waited until he swam back past her, and then she launched herself directly into his path, in full flow. Philippe collided with Harriet, knocking her under the water.

'What the hell?' Philippe righted himself, water spraying off his hair.

Reaching over he grasped Harriet's arm and yanked her up out of the water until she found her feet. Gasping and spluttering, Harriet tried to draw breath. He had winded her good and proper. But what did she expect by throwing herself in front of such a determined swimmer?

'Are you insane?' Philippe glared at her. 'Of all the crazy things to do!'

Harriet was shaking now. It reminded her of the time Toby nearly drowned. She had only been distracted for one minute, but that had been enough time for him to lose his footing and fall into the lake. Somehow she had managed to drag him out. He was right as rain after a hot drink and being forced into dry clothes, but it had scared the life out of her.

'Well?' Philippe demanded.

To her utter shame, tears started to stream down Harriet's face. Her whole body was trembling.

'I'm s-s-so sorry,' Harriet sobbed, 'f-f-for everything.'

Philippe watched as Harriet dissolved into tears, her whole body shaking with shock. All he wanted to do was take her in his arms and soothe her. After everything she had done, he couldn't stay angry with her. His protective instinct kicked in as it would if he had been presented with an abandoned puppy. Although he had to admit that the feelings weren't quite the same. He knew that once his arms were around her and she was pressed up close to him, his feelings would be anything but protective.

Before he could pull her to him, loud splashes rocked the water as several ginger heads appeared beside them.

'Are you okay, Harriet?' Andy asked.

'You look like you need a hot drink inside you,' Gareth said.

Andy took the initiative and slipped his hand into Harriet's. 'Come on! Let's get you out of the pool.'

'I'll help you dry off.' Andy winked at Tom who had reluctantly dragged himself away from Becky.

As if in a trance, Harriet dragged her eyes from Philippe's, obediently grasped Andy's hand and allowed herself to be led away.

Gareth turned towards Philippe. 'You alright, mate?'

Philippe nodded, trying to quell the emotions attacking him from every angle. As he watched Harriet climbing up the ladder, being helped up every step by a very attentive Andy, a wave of jealousy roared through him.

At the same time, sentences bombarded him so fast he felt winded. Paragraph after paragraph crowded into his mind. He had to get back to his room. He had to write it all down before the words dissipated into thin air. If nothing else, today's fiasco had reignited his creativity and that was worth something.

Heaving himself out of the pool, he quickly towelled himself dry. He tried to ignore Becky's doe eyes, which never left his body, but it was impossible not to notice.

Although it dented his pride to do so, he leaned over to where Harriet was sipping some water, under the protective shadow of Andy. He checked that she was okay. Harriet nodded, her eyes sliding quickly away from his.

Did she really think so badly of him that she couldn't even look at him?

Another few sentences flew through his mind. This was insane. Every second he was here he was losing paragraph after paragraph.

'Want some company?' Becky batted her eyelashes at him.

Tom, who had just sat down very close to Becky, scowled.

Philippe shook his head dismissively and strode off towards the pool's exit before Becky could think of coming after him. His sole focus at that moment was his laptop and the churning of ideas exploding in his brain. Finally, he was going to make headway on his novel, and not before time.

'Geez! What a loser!' Becky shook her head. 'He sure is a cold fish.'

Tom grinned at Becky. 'Lucky you've got a warm-blooded Welshman here. I'll look after you.'

'Shame you don't sound "Welsh".' Becky shot back, not that she knew what "Welsh" was supposed to sound like, but Tom was getting far too close to her.

Tom wasn't easily irritated, but Becky was starting to get under his skin. 'What, d'you want us to say: "boyo" and "valleys" in every second sentence? Anyway, how would you know what a Welshman sounds like?'

'I know a lot of things,' Becky stuck her nose in the air and tried not to look at him.

'So you sound American, do you?' Tom challenged.

'Of course not. Finishing school took as much of the American out of me as it could.'

Becky glanced at Tom. Despite his anger, she could not miss the full impact of the adoration shining out of his eyes. A tingle skittered down her spine. There was something surprisingly compelling about him. She couldn't understand it. He was nothing like the cultured men she socialised with in LA. He wouldn't know a label if it wrapped itself around him. He clearly had no money to speak of. He was also a redhead, and worst of all, he lived on a farm.

And yet, she found herself drawn to him. Somehow, on his first night in Wengen, he had persuaded her to join him for dinner. Since then, they had spent a few evenings together. He teased her. He made her laugh. He listened to her as if she might have something valuable to say. With Tom, she found herself dropping her guard and a large amount of the pretension, which she automatically pulled on with her clothes each morning.

But how could she relinquish the hopes she had pinned on Philippe? He was everything she had ever hoped for. The only problem was, he seemed to only have eyes for that creep, Harriet. Becky looked over to where Andy was fussing around Harriet like a mother hen. Andy was understandable, he was an ignorant farmer, but Philippe? She shook her head at the idea that Philippe was stupid enough to prefer a dim-wit like Harriet over *her*. Maybe all Philippe needed was a bit more persuading.

Becky thought of Freddie. What an epic fail he had turned out to be. How could he have agreed to her daddy's insane plan? Her daddy's parting words to her were: 'that she needed to be brought down a peg or two and learn what it was like to work for a living'. Could you credit it?

And as for Freddie, the bastard hadn't contacted her since he dropped her off in Switzerland. Not once. And that left him vulnerable to no end of tacky gold-diggers who would try to snare him for themselves. That thought incensed her. And it was one of the many reasons why she had identified Philippe as her reserve, just in case.

Okay, so she had insisted that Daddy let her work in Europe rather than the States. God forbid anyone in the States getting wind of her working, let alone getting her hands dirty in such a crappy hotel. She wouldn't grace the covers of top magazines again if it came out. Instead, she would be gracing the covers of the rags for all the wrong reasons, and she did not fancy that one little bit.

When Freddie first agreed to Daddy's plan, she had assumed, naively, that he would book a suite for the duration, stay with her and of course spoil her when she wasn't working. Maybe swap in a "double" from time to time so she could bunk off. As it turned out, she couldn't have been more wrong. All she got from Freddie was a quick peck on the cheek in Lauterbrunnen before he hopped onto the first plane back to the States. Double bastard that he was!

And all of this fuss just because she borrowed Daddy's credit card again. It was hardly a crime. I mean she was his daughter, after all. It wasn't like she'd maxed it out or splashed out on a Ferrari or anything extravagant. All she'd bought was a few pieces from Tiffany's.

'Anyone free to sun cream my back?' Becky glanced at each of the brothers in turn, apart from Tom. He had wriggled too far under her guard as it was, there was no way she was letting him get any closer. She had to stay focused on her future, which meant a rich and successful husband at the very least. Unfortunately, a poor farmer from Wales did not fall into that category.

Tom, oblivious of Becky's alternative agenda, leapt forward anyway, ready to oblige.

'No, not you.' The chill in her voice stopped Tom in his tracks.

Becky handed the sun cream to Gareth. He didn't often get the opportunity to outshine his brothers, so he made a great show of rubbing every inch of her back in slow, deliberate movements. From behind her sunglasses, Becky watched Tom as he gathered up his things and made his way to the exit. He didn't look back. Not once.

Becky felt something bitter in her mouth. With a jolt, she recognised it as regret.

'Where are you off to?' Andy yelled. 'Got another woman hidden away?'

Tom ignored them all. He kept on walking.

Becky rolled over. Another woman? Of course he couldn't have another woman. Could he? She snatched the sun cream out of Gareth's hand. He was starting to irritate her. 'Enough!'

Gareth narrowed his eyes at her.

As for Andy, he was so enthralled by Harriet, he barely gave Becky another glance. This wasn't good. Two things she hated with a passion were rejection and being ignored by the male of the species. If she carried on like this she, The Pied Piper of Wengen, would lose her loyal rats, which in turn would be a disaster if her master plan of capturing Philippe was to be a success. Without loyal rats trailing her, how else could she make Philippe jealous?

'Anyone for a dip?' Becky stuck out her chest and wiggled her hips as she walked over to the pool.

Gareth jumped up, his former grin reinstated.

Andy stayed seated, his eyes were trained solely on Harriet.

Becky almost spat in disgust. Oh well, despite the earlier putdown, Gareth was still chomping at the bit. As for Tom, she would have a lot of ground to cover if she was going to bring him back on board. Not that she intended to go anywhere near him again. Why would she?

Jo watched Gareth drooling over Becky. She raised her eyebrows heavenwards.

Harriet saw her and grinned. She extracted herself from Andy's very touching, if a bit suffocating, mother hen act and laid her towel next to Jo's.

'Why are men so predictable? Long legs, false breasts and fluttering eyelashes, and they are lost.' Jo lay on her back allowing the sun's warmth to stroke her face.

'It must go back to their caveman days where they dragged their prized possession around by the hair.'

Jo giggled, imagining Becky being pulled around by her hair by each of her brothers in turn.

'Although they do have an excuse. We live in a tiny valley. Most women are married off or are as broad as they are tall or well, they've been around the block a few times.'

'What, dragged by their hair?'

'More the other way around. They can be scary!' Jo shot a sly grin at Harriet, 'so on the subject of my brothers, you and Andy seem to be getting on well if I might say. Very well, in fact.'

'Now, now! Don't go all Cupid on me. I've already told you, I've had it with men.'

'I know you said that, but I can't help thinking what a perfect sister-in-law you would make.'

Harriet picked up her sarong and threw it at Jo. 'Don't get any ideas. From now on, I'm a confirmed spinster.'

'Shame! Although if you do change your mind, I'd make an ideal bridesmaid.'

The picture of a church and a flowing white dress conjured itself up in her mind. Her groom was standing at the altar, facing away from the congregation, away from her. As she walked closer, he turned around. It wasn't Andy standing in the morning suit waiting for her. It was Philippe.

Chapter 8

The morning light shone brightly through the thin gingham curtains. Harriet squinted at the illuminated panel on her clock. Only six 'o' clock? She groaned and pulled the covers high over her head. Why was it that on her day off, and a much needed one at that, she woke up this early? And yet, when it was a work day, her alarm had to battle its way through layers of sleep to rouse her.

As much as she squeezed her eyes shut and willed herself to go back to sleep, her brain had already begun whirring. Try as she might, sleep would not throw its dusty cloak back over her. With a loud groan, she swung her legs out of bed and stretched high in the air, yawning.

What a contrary body she lived in. It point-blank refused to return to the sleep it so desperately needed, despite being drop-dead tired from the physical exertion of waitressing. Added to that was the emotional exhaustion of her grief, and whilst she couldn't admit it out loud, there was a constant niggle at the back of her mind that refused to dislodge itself: Philippe. And yet, here she was, up and about at such an unearthly time on her day off.

Harriet flicked on the kettle, split open a pouch of coffee and breathed in the rich aroma. Switzerland did sell the most delicious coffee: strong, yet aromatic. Anyone who started their day in any other way was uncivilised, she decided. Smiling, she realised how arrogant she sounded. Not that she cared one jot. She was fed up with bending over backwards to conform.

At Hardacres, one or two of the staff called her the "Ice Queen". Behind her back, of course. She preferred to see herself as being "super-efficient" and "decisive". If you let emotion get in the way, you were walked over. She had seen it time and time again. Her determination not to screw up her life like her dad was her driving force. He gambled away their house and their money, deserted them when she was five years old, and then a year later, he dropped dead.

With Greg's sudden departure, the loss of Toby and then losing her mother to cancer, it tipped Harriet well and truly over the edge.

Her life and her self-confidence shattered into tiny shards. At the time she did not think she would ever recover. Everything, except her job, had been snatched from her. And even that had become too much. It was all too much for her.

So she ditched the job, much to Ed's horror. He had been her mentor and had promoted her quickly up the ranks to the position of HR Director at the age of 28. He tried everything to persuade her to stay, but she had made up her mind.

Feeling nostalgia threatening to overwhelm her, Harriet banged her hand down hard on the chest of drawers. The past had to stay in the past. She could not keep dwelling on it. Harriet poured the steaming water into her coffee, her hand shaking slightly.

Well, she was not going to sit around and mope. Today she would tackle Männlichen and Kleine Scheidegg. Even at the thought of what lay ahead of her, her heart thundered in her chest. She took a few deep breaths. She must not allow fear to overwhelm her like this. The only way she was going to conquer her fear of heights was to face it head on, and today was the day.

Harriet's eyes wandered to her walking boots, which she had bought specifically for Switzerland. They had only been aired once. And that had not ended well. Harriet found her mind drifting back to Philippe's kiss. Pushing it, along with him and her fear out of her mind, Harriet switched on the radio, which Jo had lent her, and climbed into the shower. Today would be an adventure and she was not going to allow anything to spoil it for her.

One floor above, Philippe paced up and down his lounge, running his eyes over the pages and pages of manuscript laid out before him. Since the swimming pool incident over a week ago, he had been like a writing machine. From the moment he awoke at the crack of dawn until the sun went down and the night time chill descended, he had churned out page after page of his novel.

He walked over to the mirror. His reflection was not what he had expected. His stubble had grown quickly. If he let it grow much longer, he would look too much like Philippe Myers. Whilst half the hotel seemed to know who he was, he wanted to stay as incognito as possible. Red-rimmed eyes stared back at him. Had a talent scout walked past looking for extras for a vampire movie, his eyes alone would have recommended him.

The sheaf of paper lying next to his computer brought a beaming smile to his face. Fifteen chapters, half of the book, with very few corrections, lay within its pages. If he continued at this rate, he wouldn't need to be here for more than a month. This thought depressed him. He pushed Harriet out of his mind. She was irrelevant. It was not about her. The stark reality was that he no longer had a life to go back to.

He had spotted Harriet a couple of times when he had forced himself out of his suite to stretch his legs. She had been serving in the restaurant or chatting to customers on the terrace on the rare occasions he ventured out. His breath had caught at the sight of her. It infuriated him how aware he was of her and how much her presence distracted him.

Now, however, was not the time to get distracted. He stared at the pile of paper. His novel had reached an impasse. One section had been closed off and he hadn't yet figured out how to begin the next. There were a number of different options, and each of them affected the ending. Two main characters jostled for position in his thoughts, each wanting to be the star of the show. He had grown fond of them both and could not see a way forward where both retained supremacy. One of them would have to take a back seat, and neither was happy about it.

What he needed was some space to think through each scenario. Staying here, shut away in his room, was becoming counterproductive. It pained him to acknowledge this as his laptop was calling strongly, but there was no point staring blankly at the keys, not until he had solved the dilemma of the plot's next steps.

His rucksack lay in the corner in a crumpled heap. He picked it up, threw in a map, half a dozen snacks, a couple of drinks, his cap, and at the last minute, his camera. Once he had laced up his hiking boots, he left the room, locking the door behind him. Today was going to be his day off. Even writers needed one of those.

It was quiet as he walked through Wengen, although it was still early. Many of the walkers staying in Wengen were elderly and didn't rise until after 8am, followed by a leisurely breakfast and an even more leisurely stroll around the countryside.

The sound of a tennis ball being batted backwards and forwards by a young couple made him look up. He felt a pang of loss. Since his motorbike accident he had not picked up a racket or stepped onto a court. What would be the point? All it would show him was how far he had fallen.

'Vorsicht!' The milkman's shouted warning made Philippe jump to one side as the electric milk wagon whirred past. A handful of tourists, puzzling over maps, indulged in strong coffee and cool water, sitting outside the cafés to make the most of the warm morning air.

His left leg was throbbing by the time he reached the cable car. It still frustrated him that he was no longer a highly toned athlete.

To his relief, there was no queue at the cable car, which would take him from Wengen up to the top of Männlichen. He had walked this route a dozen or so times since his arrival in Wengen, mostly stomping each step in frustration as his writer's block continued to produce page after page of scribbled out paragraphs.

'Quiet today,' Philippe said to the elderly man, 'Henry' according to his badge, cooped up inside the ticket booth.

Henry jerked his head towards the cable car currently climbing its way slowly up the sheer mountainside. 'It was not earlier. Those school children. They were noisy.'

Philippe paid for his ticket and smiled. 'Good timing then.'

Henry nodded, handing Philippe his ticket.

A total of four elderly hikers emerged from the cable car once it had ground to a halt. Philippe stepped inside, liking the idea that there wouldn't be many people in the capsule. This would allow him to move around freely without anyone getting in his way. He could then take photographs of the best views to put up in his room. Maybe they would provide him with additional inspiration to keep his writing flowing.

'Oh!'

Philippe had been too engrossed with his camera to hear the footsteps. He turned towards the voice. His eyes nearly burst through their sockets. She was the last person he expected to see.

'Harriet?'

'D'you want me to leave?' Harriet surveyed him through her lashes.

She was wearing black shorts. If they had been an inch or two longer, they would have been far better for his peace of mind. The hiking boots she was wearing with thick walking socks peeking out of the top did little to disguise the shapeliness of her long legs.

Before Philippe could answer the doors slid closed.

'Yes please,' Philippe answered, a smile curling his lips.

Harriet grinned. 'I guess you're stuck with me now!'

They were both silent as the cable car clunked its way out of the terminal. Harriet gripped the bar next to her as hard as she could. She stared at her feet. Sweat had formed a light sheen across her forehead.

Even though his camera was trained on the scenery, every fibre in Philippe's body was conscious of Harriet standing a few feet away from him. The silence hovered between them.

'Harriet, I . . .' He turned towards her. The colour had drained clean out of her face and she was visibly shaking.

In two strides, Philippe had closed the gap between them. He put his arms around her and held her tight.

'It's going to be okay. I've got you, Harriet. You're going to be fine. We're going to be fine.'

Initially, Harriet was ramrod straight within his arms, as if she had a metal poker stuck up her T-shirt. But as the warmth of his embrace reached into her rigid limbs, she relaxed against him.

'I-I-I am so stupid. I-I-I don't know why I thought I could do this.' Harriet's words trembled in tune with her body.

Philippe increased the pressure of his arms, holding her closer to him.

Harriet opened her eyes just a crack. She slammed them shut again.

'Are you feeling okay?' Philippe asked.

'I-I feel dizzy.'

Philippe released one of his arms from around her so he could stroke her hair.

'Don't let go!' Harriet pleaded, panic gripping her.

'I'm here. I'm not going anywhere.'

After five minutes, the cable car creaked. It swung alarmingly as it juddered into the terminal. Harriet's body shook. Philippe held her tighter as he felt tension course through her body. He kept his arm around her until they had made their way out of the terminal. There was an empty bench right in front of them. Philippe manoeuvred her over to it and helped her sit down.

'Right Harriet, breathe in and out deeply and don't move. I'm going to get you some water.'

Harriet did what she was told. She sat on the bench breathing in and out. She sipped the water that Philippe handed to her. Gradually, everything inside her settled back to normal, apart from her heartbeat, which was still hammering away inside her chest.

'Sorry,' Harriet whispered. 'I wanted to conquer it. I wanted to show my fear who was boss.'

Philippe reached out a hand and tucked a tendril of hair back behind her ear. 'You did. Show it. Look how far you've come, literally!'

Harriet lifted her head up and took a good look around her. In every direction valley upon valley was flanked by mountain after mountain.

'How are you feeling this high up?'

'I know it's strange, but I'm okay now we're here. As long as my feet are on firm ground, I feel safe. Even the train is okay because the rails are fixed into the ground.'

'And the plane? You did fly to Switzerland?'

Harriet blushed. 'I had to be sedated.'

Philippe squeezed her hand. 'Guess we'd better give the paragliding a miss!'

Harriet grinned at him.

What she didn't realise was how her smile lit up her face. Her eyes sparkled and she looked radiant. Completely different from when Lauren smiled. Lauren smiled for the press, for photos or when she wanted something. She smiled with satisfaction when she got what she wanted and she smiled when someone else didn't. All of her smiles were calculated. None of them were spontaneous, like Harriet's.

So why did she run out on you after the kiss? Why did she try to blow your cover at the pool in front of Becky and Jo and goodness knows who else? These questions had not stopped niggling Philippe since the day they had hiked to the café and that day at the swimming pool. He knew she was upset he hadn't confided in her about his past, but surely there must be more to it than that?

Harriet stood up. 'Which way are you heading?'

'Over to Kleine Scheidegg, for lunch, I thought. And you?' The question seemed so casual, but in fact it was fully loaded. Whatever her answer, he would make sure he headed in the same direction as her. He was not walking alone today, not knowing she was on the same mountain, and especially not if she was prone to fainting.

'Same. Shall we . . .?'

Philippe grinned. 'Would be silly not to. Anyway, I have to stick with you in case you have another funny turn!'

Harriet shoved him playfully. 'Right then macho man, which way are we heading?'

Reaching into his rucksack, he pulled out his map. Shaking it out, he turned it over a few times before pointing to a path to their left. 'You ready Scott?'

'Aye Aye, Captain!' Harriet giggled.

'Ah, so this is a nautical adventure now is it?'

'No, sorry,' Harriet admitted, 'I just couldn't think of another name of an adventurer.'

'Edmund Hilary?'

An impish smile crossed Harriet's face. 'Smart Alec, maybe?'

Harriet ducked as Philippe reached forward to ruffle her hair. Experience had taught him that girls were not fond of that.

'Follow me.' Philippe set off along the mountain path, closely followed by Harriet.

It didn't take many strides for Harriet to draw level with him. They walked side by side, pointing out the chalets dotted around the valley, commenting on rock formations or admiring how nimble the goats were as they jumped from rock to rock. But mostly, they walked in silence, both of them lost in their own thoughts and their own awareness of each other.

Chapter 9

'Can we stop for a break?' Harriet asked. She noticed Philippe's limp was getting more pronounced, and anyway they had been walking for over an hour. She could do with resting her legs.

They had paused briefly on several occasions to soak up the scenery or for Philippe to take photos. He had even asked a couple to take one of them both. Harriet was reluctant at first - that was what real couples did. However, she felt backed into a corner.

A flattish outcrop of rock provided an ideal seat. Philippe reached into his rucksack and pulled out two cartons of juice and a couple of packets of biscuits, clearly provided by the hotel.

'You're like a magician. You keep pulling things out of your rucksack. I keep wondering what's going to appear next.'

'Well if you're hoping for a white rabbit, I'm afraid you're going to be sorely disappointed.'

Harriet grinned. Sticking the straw into the apple juice, she drank thirstily. With the sun beating down and no cloud cover, the day was turning out to be scorching hot. She had put on a healthy dose of sun cream but wished she'd brought her hat with her. There was very little shade so high up.

'I don't suppose you have a spare cap with you?'

Philippe rooted around in his rucksack. 'Ta Da!'

To Harriet's surprise, Philippe held out two caps; he handed the bright blue one to her and placed the black cap onto his own head.

'Expecting company were you?' Harriet knew her voice sounded spiky, but she couldn't stop herself. The thought of him walking this same route with another woman, hand in hand, made her furious. She knew she had no right to feel jealous. It wasn't as if they were going out together or anything like that.

Philippe nodded to a zealous walker as he strode past, who in turn raised his hand to acknowledge them.

Philippe flicked his eyes over to Harriet's face. She was still frowning at him. Well, two could play at this game. Donning his very best scowl, he glared at Harriet. 'Not that it's any of your business, but I didn't realise I already had a cap in my rucksack when I packed my black one. Does that satisfy you?'

Looking down at her feet, which were starting to ache, Harriet nodded. What was wrong with her? The poor chap did not know whether he was coming or going. She was blowing hotter and colder than a roaring fire on a winter's day.

'Because if it bothers you *that* much, you can hand it back. I'm perfectly willing to lend it to the next bare-headed person I come across. I'm sure they'd be very grateful for it.'

A small smile quivered at the corner of Harriet's mouth. She coughed to conceal it. The harder she tried to stop, the wider her grin became. Before long she was bent double, helpless with laughter. The more baffled Philippe looked by her outburst, the harder she laughed until her stomach ached.

When she finally managed to bring herself under control, Philippe shook his head, a grin spreading across his face. 'I didn't realise I was that funny.'

'You're not!' Harriet grinned at him. 'It was the thought of you rushing up to anyone without a hat on and asking them if they'd like to borrow your cap. It conjured up some hilarious images.'

'Glad I've managed to amuse you.' Philippe smiled at her.

Harriet took a deep breath. She may as well ask him now. It would stand like a barrier between them unless she did. 'So would you have told me who you were if those fans hadn't approached you first?'

'I don't know, Harriet. I wasn't purposely withholding it from you to trick you. I wanted you to get to know me, not Philippe Myers, the tennis star.'

'And you think that would have influenced me?' Harriet looked hurt.

'Can you honestly tell me that you wouldn't have had any preconceptions about me? None at all?'

Harriet stared into the distance. Of course she would. It was naïve of her to think she would be immune.

'The whole point of me coming here was to leave Philippe Myers behind. My birth name was Philip Smith. It was too boring, so my

78

manager added the 'pe' and I took on my mother's maiden name, hence Philip Smith was buried in my past and Philippe Myers was born.'

'But you called yourself "Philippe" when I met you.'

'I know. Force of habit. I'd been known as Philippe for so many years, it slips off my tongue without thinking. And,' Philippe looked sheepish, 'I must admit, I prefer it to Philip and so do my publishers.'

Harriet twirled a lock of hair around and around her finger, glancing at Philippe and then towards the intimidating face of the Eiger where it reared up, casting a shadow over the majority of the valley below. So many men had died trying to reach its summit. It was a sobering thought.

'You heard about the accident?' Philippe asked.

'Was it on a motorbike?'

'Yes. I was reckless. When you keep winning at something and get to the top, you start to feel you're invincible. That's what happened to me. So when a friend asked me if I wanted to take a spin on his new bike, I didn't think twice. He made me put on his helmet, thank God, but I refused his leathers. The open road was calling.'

A loud yapping startled Harriet. Out of nowhere a small terrier shot past, diving down the rocky path with the agility of a mountain goat. Philippe was just about to continue his story when two large elderly women puffed around the corner, yelling loudly. 'Hübschen! Hübschen! Komm! Hübschen!'

They stopped in front of Philippe and Harriet. 'Haben Sie schon unser Hund gesehen?'

'Sorry, we are English,' Harriet said, in a loud and clear voice.

'Our dog! Have you seen our dog?' Both of the women were panting hard, their rotund faces puce with exertion.

Philippe nodded and pointed in the direction the terrier had raced seconds before.

'Danke! Danke Sehr!'

Harriet and Philippe watched as they disappeared around a bend, their panicked voices still echoing long after they were out of sight.

'I wonder if we'll see them reunited at Kleine Scheidegg.' Harriet asked.

Philippe stood up. 'Not if we don't get a move on.'

'But you haven't finished telling me about the crash—'

'It's not something I like talking about. It brings it all back.'

Harriet nodded, but at the same time, her face fell.

'Look it's simple, okay. In a nutshell: I crashed the bike. I smashed up my leg. I lost my career. My fiancée married someone else. I was publicly humiliated. Is that enough detail for you?' Philippe's words were shot out as harshly as if they had been peppered from a BB gun.

Harriet swung around and faced Philippe. 'You've had a horrible time. And I'm sorry. But you don't have to take it out on me!'

'Oh, so you're sorry, are you? As if you'd know anything about losing your whole life . . .' The moment Philippe had said the words, he clapped his hands over his mouth. 'Harriet, I—'

It was too late. Harriet's face had flushed red. Her green eyes flashed. With her hands lodged firmly on her hips she leaned in close to Philippe's face. 'How DARE you! You don't know anything about me. After mum died of cancer, my so called fiancé dumped me. And . . .' Harriet fought to regain control. 'I couldn't function anymore. So I left my bloody good job because I couldn't cope and I came here. So don't you ever talk to me about not understanding!'

And with that, Harriet spun around. She marched off along the mountain path, head held high, tears streaming unchecked down her cheeks.

Philippe stood frozen to the spot. He stared out at the valley stretching below him. What had he become? As he rose up the ranks to the heights of a famous tennis player, his ego had grown with him. If you are treated like a king and worshipped for long enough, you start to believe you are a king. You become arrogant and believe you have rights: a lot of them.

When all of that is ripped away, you become a "nobody". In fact, you are worse than a "nobody", because you are then a "has been". You lose yourself and you become rudderless.

He had behaved like a complete idiot. Goodness knows if Harriet would ever forgive him. And at that moment in time, her forgiveness was more important to him than anything else.

Slinging his rucksack over his shoulder, he set off after Harriet. He had already wasted precious minutes letting his thoughts whirl around his mind. Whether he could catch up with her with his stupid leg, he had no idea. One thing he was certain of: he was going to give it his best shot. His leg could ache all it liked. He did not intend to leave this mountain until he had made his peace with Harriet.

Not much further along the path, Harriet sat on a bench, curled up in a ball, her arms wrapped tightly around her knees. Tears slipped down her cheeks, wetting her legs.

Bit by bit, her tears receded. A light breeze blew around her, a welcome release from the scorching sun, which shone down, unchallenged by a single cloud. Laughter rang out from one of the many paths built into the mountain.

She jerked her head up at the sound of feet pounding towards her. Philippe came into view, his forehead glistening with sweat. He spotted her and stopped abruptly.

'I'm so very sorry, Harriet. It was inexcusable of me. I—'

Harriet patted the seat beside her, shaking her head. 'No. No, Philippe, it was my fault. I shouldn't have overreacted like that. You've been through so much.'

Emotions crackled between them. Reaching across, Philippe took one of Harriet's hands, enveloping her dainty fingers in his.

'Shall we call a truce?'

They both watched as two Red Kites soared through the air in front of them, being lifted and dropped with the ebb and flow of the breeze. Harriet sighed.

'Well?'

'Yes, a truce.' Harriet nodded, a slight smile lighting up her face.

By the time they reached Kleine Scheidegg, they were both tired and hungry, but in good spirits. They had managed to enjoy each other's company for the rest of their trek across the mountain to their destination.

Once they were seated at the largest restaurant, which boasted panoramic views, Philippe bent down to rub his left leg.

'Is it sore?' Harriet asked.

Swallowing his pride, Philippe answered. 'A little stiff. Nothing a hearty meal won't fix.'

'That's an interesting remedy for sore legs,' Harriet grinned. 'Suddenly mine are both feeling achy.'

It was the truth. Walking around the hotel serving food and drink to customers used very different muscles from scaling mountainous terrain, both up and down hill. With Philippe's injury, it was hardly surprising that his leg was painful.

The sound of animated chattering filled the restaurant. Large picture-windows allowed diners to see down into Grindlewald on one side and towards Wengen on the other. Photos of the local mountains covered in snow and dotted with skiers clad in a rainbow of different coloured ski suits filled every free space of wall. Harriet smoothed the red and green checked table cloth with her hands before reaching for a menu.

A blond-haired, blue-eyed waitress, her hair hanging in neat pigtails either side of her face, bounded up to the table. Without even glancing at Harriet, the waitress focused her full attention on Philippe.

'Do you see anything you like?' she asked in perfect English. She leaned towards him, the buttons on her blouse gaping under the strain.

Clearly not impressed with this, Philippe ignored her. Instead, he turned to Harriet. 'What would you like?'

Once they had both ordered soup and bread, followed by Black Forest Gateau with cream, the waitress flounced off. She was a former child model and did not appreciate rebuffs of any kind.

Harriet unwrapped a breadstick and nibbled the end of it. In spite of the snacks that Philippe had handed out en route, she was starving. She raised her eyes to Philippe's. 'How's your novel coming along?'

'I hardly dare say this, but it's been flowing.' Philippe smiled. 'The publishers would have a breakdown if they knew how little I'd written, particularly up until a week ago.'

The waitress slammed two hot chocolates onto the table, dropped their cutlery and napkins in front of them and then stalked off to another table.

Philippe raised his eyebrows. Harriet grinned back.

'Nothing quite as scary as a woman scorned!'

'Don't I know it!' Philippe picked up his hot chocolate. Peaks of cream balanced on the top. Sipping the rich chocolate through the cool cream tasted like heaven.

Harriet raised the steaming mug to her lips. 'That's delicious.'

'Almost as good as the hot chocolate at my café?'

Harriet's head jerked up. She did not want to think about that afternoon. Changing the subject, she brought the conversation back to his novel. 'So when's your deadline?'

'What, my deadline to determine the best mug of hot chocolate in Switzerland?'

Loving the banter that was toing and froing easily between them, Harriet giggled. 'No silly! Your novel.'

'My first draft is due in a matter of weeks and I've only written half of it . . . so, you might wonder why I'm not slaving away on it now?'

Harriet snapped another breadstick in half. She looked over at Philippe. 'Everyone needs a break. Even writers.'

The delicious smell of French onion soup wafted in their direction, followed by two bowls being dumped in front of them. Large croutons covered with melted cheese bobbed up and down on top as the soup struggled to recover its equilibrium.

'Can I get you anything else?' The waitress scowled at Philippe and then Harriet in turn.

'No thank you,' Philippe replied, looking pointedly at Harriet. 'I have everything I need right here.'

Harriet gave Philippe a shy smile.

A loud snort of disgust emanated from the waitress.

Both Harriet and Philippe struggled to control their laughter.

Neither spoke much as they devoured the soup, every scrap of bread and two slices of gateau. Harriet placed both her hands onto her stomach and groaned. 'I don't think I'll ever eat again.'

'Lightweight!' Philippe teased.

'I'll give you lightweight! You've left that last spoonful of gateau.'

The outraged expression on Harriet's face was too much for Philippe. Laughter burst out of him. Harriet couldn't help but join in. Before long, both of them were bent double with laughter.

Sometime later, stirring creamy milk into his strong coffee, Philippe glanced at Harriet, who was spooning more sugar than was good for her into her mug. Reaching over, he took one of her hands in his. 'How are you, Harriet?'

Harriet bowed her head. The real sympathy shining out of his eyes was too much for her. If she said anything, she knew she would start crying again. It baffled her. She had never been a crier, not before she arrived in Switzerland. It appeared that her body was making up for lost time. All the unshed tears over each year of her life had stored themselves up in a great well and had chosen her arrival in this country to release the deluge.

'I know the last year's been really tough for you.' Philippe paused. 'What I'm trying to say is if you ever want to talk or cry or anything, you know where I am.'

Images of her mum in the years before cancer crippled her and visions of Toby laughing as she pushed him faster and faster on the roundabout, crowded into her mind. Greg's strikingly handsome face hovered in the background. She could feel more tears gathering behind her lids. Although she couldn't speak, she squeezed

84

Philippe's hand and hoped her eyes conveyed how much she appreciated his concern.

Philippe squeezed back. 'Right, are you ready to tackle the downward climb or shall we cheat and get the train?'

'How could you suggest such a thing?' Harriet gasped, her eyes shining, and not just from the tears. 'Turns out you're the lightweight!'

Philippe tossed a few notes on top of the till receipt served on a little metal platter. 'I'll give you "lightweight"! Come on! Race you to the door?' Philippe challenged.

Pushing back her chair, Harriet raced through the restaurant, swerving adeptly in and out of the tables, hotly pursued by Philippe. Several customers stared after them in amusement. A couple of old ladies sitting with their half-drunk beers clicked their tongues with disapproval. The blond, pig-tailed waitress muttered 'Good riddance!' under her breath.

Both Harriet and Philippe were unaware of the attention they had attracted. Neither cared. They reached the beginning of the downward slope and stood gasping for breath and laughing like adolescents. Harriet looked across at Philippe and he smiled back. All she wished, with all her heart, was that this moment could last forever.

Chapter 10

The clock in the staffroom ticked loudly, counting down the minutes until their breakfast break was over and the hard work began. It was already warm outside and there was a dozen or so people crowded around the terrace tables. The ancient air conditioning unit in the staffroom was struggling to keep the rising heat at bay.

Aromas of baking bread wafted from the kitchen combining with the smell of over-brewed coffee and hot bodies.

Hans stretched his arms above his head and yawned. He watched Fred as he sloped in through the door. Tapping his watch, he raised his eyebrows. 'Good of you to join us, Fred.'

'Late night,' Fred answered, looking sheepish. His eyes were puffy slits and his face as pasty as the pastry he would be rolling out that morning.

'Not the blonde from the Taverne again?'

Fred shrugged his shoulders, reaching for the coffee. His normal mischievousness was hidden deep below his raging hangover.

Hans shook his head and turned to the others. 'It's that aftershave I lent him – it's irresistible!'

Jo looked up from her croissant, which was crumbling all over the table. She fixed her eyes on Hans. 'Maybe you should try wearing some. It might improve your chances!'

Snatching a piece of paper off the noticeboard behind him, Hans crumpled it into a ball and threw it at Jo. Unfortunately, he was a bad shot and the ball bounced off Becky's chest.

'Geez Hans! Cut that out. I'm trying to do my nails here.'

Hans failed miserably at hiding his smirk and even Fred in his delicate state was not able to suppress a chuckle.

Both were rewarded with a furious scowl, which was almost harsh enough to turn them to stone had she possessed powers anything like that of Medusa.

'Mine next.' Jo pushed her fingers towards Becky and wiggled them hopefully.

Becky glared back at her. 'You gotta be kidding!'

Curled up in the corner, cocooned in her own thoughts, Harriet was re-living every step of their trek across the mountains. When they made it back to the hotel, Philippe stroked her cheek and told her how much he had enjoyed her company. She somehow resisted the impulse to throw her arms around him, to kiss him, to tell him how special and how amazing and how incredible he made her feel.

They stood there, so close they were almost touching, his hand on her cheek. Neither moved. She held her breath, waiting for him to lean over, to push his lips against hers.

Instead, he turned away. He disappeared into the chalet without another word, without looking back. It happened so suddenly, it left her feeling bereft.

No matter how many times she re-ran the scenario in her head, she could not make sense of it. She had spent hours wondering what she had done wrong, trying to work out whether she had offended him, thinking she must have got his signals all wrong. Could he just want her as a friend?

She swung from relief she hadn't thrown herself at him to confusion about his behaviour to fury that he had behaved so coldly. For him to have brushed her off as if she was no-one hurt her more than even she wanted to admit. However, she had to acknowledge that by shoving Philippe away last time he kissed her, it would hardly encourage him to initiate a repeat performance. Honestly, her head was pounding. She was more confused than ever.

Two days had passed since their trek across the mountains. She had spotted Philippe across the restaurant once, but apart from that, she hadn't seen him at all. If it wasn't for Becky's constant updates, she could be forgiven for thinking, not for the first time, that he had packed up and left.

'Penny for them!' Jo squeezed in beside her on the bench.

There had been many occasions when she had almost confided in Jo. For various reasons, she had resisted. If she started talking about Philippe, it would make her feelings for him too real. And she couldn't bring herself to voice how Philippe had walked away and left her standing there. On her own. Feeling bereft.

'Sorry. Day dreaming.' Harriet turned to her friend. 'So what are your brothers up to today?'

'I strongly suspect they're lazing in their beds until we meet them at the café for lunch. Lazy so and so's!'

'Don't tell me, they were out partying hard last night?'

'Tell me about it. I can't believe how much beer they managed to sink between them. Although Tom disappeared off early. I don't know what's got into him.'

'A secret fancy woman?' Harriet suggested.

'Nothing would surprise me.' Jo's eyes wandered over to Hans, who was deep in conversation with Fred.

Harriet studied Jo's face, watching a blush creep between her freckles. 'So, how's it going with you two?'

'We might have been out for drinks a couple of times.' Jo looked coy. 'But nothing serious. Just drinks. As friends. You know.'

At that moment, Hans looked up and caught Jo's eye. He winked at her. Jo gave him a cheeky grin before turning back to Harriet.

'Hmmm, just friends, heh?'

Jo giggled.

Harriet pushed her plate away from her and took a sip of milky coffee. Before she had a chance to quiz Jo further about Hans, Jo pounced on her abandoned croissant.

'Aren't you eating that?' Jo asked.

'It's all yours.'

Whilst Jo munched on Harriet's croissant, Harriet concentrated on keeping her mind off Philippe. Yesterday she had, yet again, been so distracted she managed to serve three guests with the wrong meals and spill two drinks, fortunately not over any of the guests, or guests' laptops or guests' electronic devices, but still, Herr Tanner was not happy with her. She would have to buck up or she would be out, and then what would she do?

'You're still coming to lunch with us?' Jo asked.

'Now that my blisters have gone down, I should be able to make it to the café.'

Everyone looked up as Becky rapped hard on the table. 'I've got some gossip that I might share with you all, but only if you treat me nice.'

'Fat chance,' Jo said, under her breath.

'Come on Becky, spit it out!' Hans shouted, glad for the opportunity to use some recently learned English slang.

Becky looked down her nose at him. 'That's the best you can do? Your parents should've sent you to finishing school. It would have improved your manners no end.'

'Pity it didn't do you any good,' Hans retorted, his cheeks flushing.

Before the two became locked in combat, Jo clapped her hands like a school teacher. 'Come on you two, stop bickering. Becky, dish the dirt!'

With her hands on her hips and a pout on her lips, Becky looked as if she was going to stall. She glared at the faces staring at her expectantly. Never one, however, to be able to resist being centre of attention, she caved in. 'OK. Guess who I saw sneaking out of Philippe's room this morning at the crack of dawn?'

A hush fell over the room. Harriet's heart started pounding in her chest.

'Who? Who?' Jo hoped it was someone famous. All of them knew that Herr Smith was also the renowned tennis player, Herr Myers.

'This stunning blond girl,' Becky's eyes flitted around her audience, lapping up the attention, and yet, there was more than a flash of anger flickering through her tone. 'Although she looked like a right tart, if you ask me. Can't think what Philippe is doing with *her*. Not when there are other far superior women around here.' Becky's eyes scanned her "audience". She waited, as if she was expecting one of them to single her out for this prestigious title. As the silence lapped around them, Becky huffed, and then continued with her gossip. 'And her nighty was very, very short.'

Hans looked Becky up and down. 'A bit like your dresses!'

'Is that all?' Even Fred, in his hungover state, was expecting greater things than the vague description Becky had given them. 'Can't you even give us a name?'

Becky shoved back her chair. Her head whipped around. 'You losers need to lighten up!'

'That's ruined your chances!' Fred glared at Becky as if she was a nasty smell.

'If you think a blond bit of nothing like that will stop me, then you are as ignorant as you look!' And with that, Becky gathered up her nail varnish, her nail file and her nail varnish remover. She shot them all a withering glare before stalking out of the room.

Harriet sat motionless like a statue. This was like a bad dream: a girl, in a nighty, and a right "tart" by all accounts, in Philippe's room. No! No! No!

Harriet didn't know how she got through the next few hours. It was as if she was sleep-walking. She was taking part in life, but completely disconnected from it. By the time Jo dragged her halfway up the mountain to the café, and Philippe's café at that, she was fit to drop.

The restaurant was dark inside; all the outside tables having been taken. And it smelt of boiled cabbage. Harriet pushed a pork chop around and around her plate, hardly seeing what was in front of her. Jo's brothers were packed around their small table and in high spirits after a long sleep and several pints of black coffee. The chatter circled around her. Loud howls of raucous laughter were making her head ache.

She had tried her hardest to wriggle out of today, protesting exhaustion, but Jo was not having any of it. 'The fresh air will do you the world of good,' Jo had insisted. So here she was, squeezed in between Andy and Tom, wishing she was anywhere else, but preferably under her duvet in the sanctuary of her bedroom.

'What's with the long face?' Tom asked.

Harriet's eyes narrowed.

Andy didn't need much encouragement to join in. 'Yeah, where's the "fun" Harriet disappeared to?'

All three brothers looked at Harriet, who in turn shrank from them like a cornered rabbit.

'Poor girl!' Jo reached over and grabbed Harriet's hand. 'It's hardly surprising she looks so pale with you three ugly mugs gawping at her.'

'Could a large slice of cake come to the rescue?' Gareth suggested, his mouth watering at the thought of the Black Forest Gateau he had spotted at the counter.

Andy pulled his hat down over his eyes and made strange mumbling noises. 'What am I?' he asked, hoping to bring a smile to her face.

'An idiot?' Gareth suggested.

'By gum, the boy speaks,' Tom taunted, throwing his hat at his brother.

'Now! Now! Children! That's enough bickering.' Jo glared at each of them in turn.

Seeing the exuberant expressions on the men's faces start to fall, Harriet decided that enough was enough. They had been trying to cheer her up, and she was being a total misery. No, this could not carry on. She would not sit here moping a minute longer. It was pathetic. And over a man. Again. If Philippe was that fickle, that blond bimbo was welcome to him.

Somehow, Harriet managed to force a smile. 'Did anyone mention gateau?'

'Now you're talking!' Andy patted her on the back. 'Tom, call the waitress. You're always so good at attracting the girls!'

The boys jostled amongst themselves. Jo ordered Tom out of his seat and slipped in next to Harriet. 'Are you okay? You haven't been yourself today.'

'I can't talk about it. Not yet.' Harriet said.

Jo picked up a sugar sachet and tore off the end ready to pour it into her coffee. 'What about a problem shared is a problem halved?'

'Let me come to terms with it myself first. Please Jo.'

Jo was about to reply when several shouts rang through the café. Everyone turned their heads towards the door in time to see a tall, slim girl, with a head full of blond curls, shove her hands on her hips. 'You were the one who promised me hot chocolate. I told you I'd have settled for whisky. So now you've dragged me up this stupid mountain, I am not leaving until we've had that damn hot chocolate. And it'd better be good!'

'If you'll just be quiet for one moment and stop making such a fuss, I'll get you a hot chocolate.' Philippe's words came out in an anguished hiss.

Horrified, as if she had been dropped slap bang in the middle of a really bad movie, Harriet watched Philippe lead the girl into the café. Becky was right. She was stunning. Why did she have to be stunning?

Gareth, uncharacteristically, let out a long, low whistle. The girl turned towards the table and winked at him before Philippe grabbed her arm and guided her to a table at the far end of the café.

He hadn't looked in her direction once. And no wonder. If he had any conscience at all he should be ashamed of himself. How could he play relay with women in this way, without even giving them time to hand on the baton?

'Can we go now?' Harriet whispered. 'I'm feeling a bit sick.'

Gareth couldn't take his eyes off the girl who was now seated at the table, making eyes at him and no doubt any other male within a thirty-mile radius.

Philippe really had no taste at all. Becky was right, again. She was a complete strumpet.

'Things have just started to get a bit more interesting. Can't we wait for the gateau?' Gareth begged.

Harriet was surprised Gareth wasn't panting like a dog he was so enamoured with that stupid girl. And a *girl* was precisely what she looked like. It was unlikely she was a day over 22. Far too young for Philippe to be lusting after. But then, he was used to groupies of all ages from his tennis days. A leopard never changes his spots, wasn't that the saying? His exploits with the opposite sex, which hit the press when he first arrived on the tennis circuit, were legendary.

Philippe could not believe that Harriet was here. It was terrible timing. The whole reason he had dragged Sophie up to the café was in the hope that they could have a private conversation, somewhere neutral, away from prying eyes.

The last thing he wanted was to bump into Harriet. She was bound to assume the worst. Not that it stopped those oafs flirting with Sophie. But what else could he do? He could hardly tell her the truth. With his car crash background already hanging around his neck, Harriet would write him off forever if she found out who Sophie really was, what she meant to him. There was only so much baggage that anyone could be expected to cope with. His hands were well and truly tied.

Ironic really, to trek halfway up a mountain only to find that Harriet and Jo were having lunch here, along with Harriet's male lapdogs who appeared to follow her wherever she went. Ignorant yokel farmers the lot of them!

How was it that his life, which seemed complicated enough two days ago, had suddenly exploded into complete chaos? He was furious with his agent. He had left strict instructions not to give his contact details to anyone, unless it was an emergency, although to be fair, Sophie could always be classed as that.

Even the hot chocolate wafting delicious smells in his direction could not calm the tension that pulled tight across his shoulders, making his neck ache.

She had arrived in the early hours of the morning, reeking of drink and hardly able to stand upright. What could he do but let her stay the night? He could hardly turf her out into a sleepy Wengen - God knows what havoc she would have wrought. She was completely wild, particularly in her drunken state.

They hadn't spoken yet, not properly. He had been too furious to trust himself to speak. At least in public he knew he would have to keep his temper under control.

'How the hell did you persuade Damion to give you my number?' Philippe demanded.

'I told him it was really, really urgent that I saw you,' Sophie whined. 'And it IS.'

Philippe absently sipped at the hot chocolate, barely tasting it. 'What is so urgent that it couldn't have waited until I came home?'

Averting her eyes from his, Sophie sighed. 'I'm in a bit of trouble.'

Typical! When wasn't she in trouble? Philippe ran his hand through his hair. He was trying to focus on what she was saying, working out how he could get her back to England into safe hands. It was nigh on impossible to concentrate. It was as if Harriet's eyes were lasers and they were burning into him.

'Do I really want to know?' Philippe asked Sophie. He watched as she drained her hot chocolate and beckoned the waitress over to order a second. He marvelled at the strength of her stomach, which could digest something that sweet on top of all the booze she had managed to chuck down her throat the day before. But then hot chocolate used to be her favourite drink before alcohol took its place. As she placed the empty mug back onto the table, he noticed that her hands were shaking. Nothing new there.

'You have to help me,' Sophie pleaded.

Philippe nodded. He could not refuse her anything. He never had been able to. From the day she exploded into his life, he had looked after her, and nothing would change that. Nothing.

'Come on, let's head back,' Harriet said, having forced down a few spoonfuls of Black Forest Gateau, which she was now regretting. Nausea flooded her system. She didn't know if this was from the rich chocolate cake or from watching Philippe in deep discussion with the blonde merely feet away from her. To think that she had given him a second chance. She had been completely taken in by him. She had actually thought he liked her and that he had left his old playboy days behind.

Out of nowhere a well of anger rose inside her. Well, she would show him that he wasn't the only one who could play that game. Leaning over to Andy she told him a rude joke, which one of her work colleagues had told her years ago. For some reason it had stuck in her mind. She wasn't a fan of crass humour, as a rule, but she was certain that it would evoke a reaction in Andy.

Andy's loud howl of laughter had heads turning throughout the café. Harriet bent in close to him, her giggles joining his laughter. Whilst her head was close to Andy's, her eyes were trained on Philippe's back. Sure enough, his head whipped around, his scowl prominent as he looked over in their direction. Harriet quickly averted her eyes, focusing her sole attention on Andy, who was still chuckling as he repeated the joke to his brothers, who were crowding closer to join in the fun.

This wasn't like her at all. She never played games or used manipulation. What had got into her? She felt tears starting again. Honestly, it was too much. She really had to pull herself together. If she wasn't careful, she'd become dehydrated with all the tears she was shedding.

'I've got to go.' Harriet reached blindly into her bag. She pulled out a bundle of francs from her purse and threw them onto the table.

'Harriet, wait!' Jo tried to extricate herself from the middle of the table, but she was pinned against the wall, with two of her brothers blocking her in with their chairs and Welsh bulk as they had gathered around to hear Harriet's joke. 'Come on! Shift!'

By the time Jo managed to squeeze herself out into the café, Harriet had already disappeared out of the door, and must already have made it a good way down the mountain.

As Jo stood, debating whether or not to go after her, Philippe hared past her, through the open door. With an impatient toss of her hair, Jo stared after Philippe in surprise. That settled it. If the speed with which Philippe had dashed after Harriet was anything to go by, Harriet might well need a shoulder to cry on.

Before Jo had a chance to set off after Harriet, she watched in despair as her brothers' attention zoomed in on Philippe's blonde.

95

'Would be a shame to leave a damsel in distress all on her own, wouldn't it now?' Gareth motioned towards Sophie.

'I'd love one of those liqueurs,' Jo could hear Sophie practically purring. 'Well maybe two as we might be here a long time.'

Enthusiastic grunts of assent echoed around the café. Chairs were scraped back and before Jo could say or do anything to keep her brothers under control, Sophie was surrounded. Not that she seemed to mind one jot. She just didn't seem to know which brother to flirt with first.

Jo shook her head. She would definitely be more use to Harriet than she would to her brothers. They were enjoying their freedom away from the farm a little too much, and there was nothing she could do about it. They were being led by pretty faces and quantities of beer in equal measure. Anyway, they were old enough to look after themselves . . . weren't they?

Harriet's head was pounding. Her pace was starting to slow. Just as she thought she was home free, a loud voice bellowed behind her. 'Stop! Harriet, stop!'

She glanced back to see Philippe careering down the mountain towards her. What was it with Wengen? She seemed to spend her time running down the mountain, with Philippe in hot pursuit.

Her calm and ordered life had morphed into a soap opera that she no longer recognised. And the worst thing of all, she seemed to have taken on the role of Chief Drama Queen in all this. Ed would be horrified: from Ice Queen to Drama Queen in a matter of months. It didn't bear thinking about.

Chapter 11

After his initial burst of energy, and with Harriet finally in sight, Philippe ground to a halt. What was he doing? This was too much like déjà vu. The last time he had caught up with Harriet on this same mountain path, she had made her feelings quite clear. It was obvious she did not want a relationship, and more to the point, neither did he, so what was he doing pursuing her, yet again?

He felt torn in too many directions. Every fibre in his body wanted to close the gap between them, to take her in his arms, and yet . . .

Indecision kept him frozen to the spot. He looked at the mountains in the hope that they would provide him with some inspiration. The whistle of two birds of prey carried in the breeze, competing with the incessant chatter of what sounded like hundreds of crickets. He took a deep breath to steady himself. This could not be about him and what he wanted. After all Harriet had been through, the last thing she needed was to complicate her life further by getting involved with him.

Philippe's sigh was long and heartfelt. He took one last look at Harriet, whose eyes had not left him the whole time he had been standing there. He was just about to turn back up the mountain when Jo came flying around the corner, panting hard.

'Have you seen her?' Jo asked, her face flushed.

Philippe motioned with his head to where Harriet was standing a little way down the path. 'Look . . . I need to get back to Sophie.'

'Of course you do,' Jo said, a hint of sarcasm lacing her words.

It was impossible for Philippe to shake Harriet from his mind. Every step he took back up the mountain towards Sophie was leading him a step further away from Harriet.

He stopped briefly, lowering himself onto the grass, trying to bring his breathing under control. A vibrant red and orange paraglider floated across the sky next to another boasting a green and purple canopy. Even they reminded him of Harriet. Although the idea of being away from his responsibilities and worries, gliding like a bird through the air, seemed very appealing at that precise moment.

His leg was aching again. He cursed out loud. He hated the fact that he limped, that his body would not let him lead the life that he had worked for since he was old enough to stand upright and hold a mini racket.

And then, there was Sophie.

Sophie! He pushed himself upright and started climbing back up the mountain to the café. He hadn't been gone more than 20 minutes. Surely she can't have got into much trouble in so short a time?

Once Philippe had left, Jo gave Harriet a big hug and asked her if she wanted some company or to talk. Harriet shook her head. It would be impossible to put any of her whirring emotions into words. Jo told her to come and find her if she changed her mind. They had a final hug before Jo turned back the way she had come. She set off up the steep slope dreading what mischief her brothers had caused in her absence.

It took over an hour for Harriet to get back to the chalet. Instead of hiding out in her room as she had planned, Harriet wiped a tissue roughly across her eyes, ran a hand through her dishevelled hair and straightened her T-shirt. What she needed now was a strong coffee and a distraction.

Harriet wound her way through the little paths that criss-crossed Wengen. After a short distance, she found herself in front of Der Hausenbaum. This would do nicely. It was out of the way enough for her not to bump into anyone she knew. Walking through their elegant restaurant, Harriet made her way to the outside terrace, which overlooked Männlichen to the left and Jungfrau to the right.

She was about to take a seat in the corner when she heard someone calling out her name.

'Coo-ee! Harriet! Over here!'

Harriet looked in the direction of the voice. There, sitting with a large pot of coffee and a bowl of ice cream in front of her, was Elspeth.

Strangely, she was the only person Harriet wanted to see. There was something special about her. Whether it was her calm intuition or her upbeat sense of humour she wasn't sure, and frankly it didn't matter. She was an oasis in the desert she had somehow wandered into.

Harriet slid into the seat next to Elspeth. She gave Elspeth a brief smile.

'You look like you need to talk.' Elspeth waved her hand to attract the attention of the waitress. 'Coffee and ice cream?'

'I'm not sure I could stomach ice cream-' Harriet started to say.

'Nonsense! Ice cream is exactly what you need on a sweltering day like this. And you, my dear, look as though you could do with some cooling down.'

Harriet nodded. Maybe she could manage a bit. She hadn't eaten more than a few mouthfuls of her lunch.

The terrace was dotted with guests. An elderly couple were buried behind newspapers. A group of young hikers were chatting quietly over cold beers, the odd burst of laughter breaking through. Two children dressed in identical bright yellow and green shorts and T-shirts were playing hopscotch up and down the far end of the terrace, their parents looking on, taking full advantage of the relative peace and quiet.

'I come here a lot. It's my private get away.' Elspeth smiled. 'I can stretch my legs a little and be anonymous. And they do serve the most delicious walnut ice cream.'

As with many of the buildings in Wengen, Der Hausenbaum was made of wood, chalet style, with window shutters and window boxes overflowing with riots of light blue flowers. Yellow tablecloths fluttered in the breeze. The matching yellow chair cushions transformed bare garden chairs into reasonably comfortable seats.

Once the waitress had brought over Harriet's coffee and ice cream, Elspeth reached across and took Harriet's hand in hers. 'You don't have to say anything, my dear. We can simply sit here and admire the view. But if I'm not very much mistaken, you have a few things you would like to get off your chest. If you don't mind me saying, you look wretched. And I strongly suspect there's a young man involved?'

A shy smile graced Harriet's lips. 'No, you're not mistaken. Not about any of it.'

Elspeth started to spoon dollops of fast-melting ice cream into her mouth. She closed her eyes as she savoured the ice cold flavours. 'Mmm, scrumptious!'

Harriet's mind was whirring. She didn't even know where to start. What she did know is that she could do with airing all of it, to try to make sense of her life. She blew hard on her coffee before taking a sip. She winced as the burning liquid slipped down her throat. 'Ouch! Too hot!'

'Quick, ice cream!' Elspeth picked up Harriet's spoon and fed her a couple of mouthfuls.

'That's better. Goodness, this really is yummy,' Harriet said, smiling.

'Right, I'll let you eat your ice cream and then you must tell me all. I miss the days when I worked. People were always coming to me with their troubles. It was one of my favourite parts of the job.'

Dabbing her mouth, Harriet looked over at Elspeth. 'What did you do?'

'Have a guess.'

'Nurse?'

Elspeth shook her head.

'Carer?'

'No.'

'Doctor?'

'Uh uh.'

'Counsellor?'

'You'll never guess. Nobody ever does.'

Intrigued, Harriet insisted Elspeth tell her.

'I was a zoo keeper.'

It was impossible not to laugh imagining Elspeth, who was elegant and beautifully dressed, in a monkey enclosure surrounded by squealing, jumping animals as she fed them fruit and nuts. Or cleaning out the rhino cage. Or letting snakes slither around her before dropping dead birds into their cage, or whatever it was they ate.

A faraway look clouded Elspeth's eyes. 'I loved my job. It was my whole life. Apart from Duncan.'

Harriet was about to ask more. Like, who was Duncan? About whether she was married. Which zoo she worked in. And . . ., but before she could utter another word, Elspeth's shrewd blue eyes locked onto Harriet's.

'Right young lady. Enough about me. Talk!'

They sat together for well over two hours. Harriet explained everything. She told her about her mum, about her job, about Greg and even about Toby. Elspeth asked a few questions, nodded, and from time to time, touched her arm. The shadow of Philippe hung between them. Harriet closed her eyes.

'And then there's Philippe.'

'The "frog"?'

Harriet nodded.

Never one to beat about the bush, Elspeth asked Harriet outright: 'Do you love him?'

'Love? No. No. Not at all. Love was what I felt for Greg, or at least that was what it felt like at the time. I was all set to marry him. And look how that turned out. I loved, no still love, Toby, and now he's gone. Love? No. More being swept away. Infatuation. Rebound, possibly. Anyway, I've only known him for a matter of weeks.'

'D'you know how long it took me to fall in love?'

Harriet shook her head.

'One day. One day was all I needed. Duncan proposed after a week. We were married within a month. Everyone said we were insane. That it would end badly. We celebrated 50 years of marriage before he died.'

'Wow! 50 years. That's remarkable. And you knew, after one day?'

The waitress appeared by their table. 'Can I get you anything else?'

'We need a refill of coffee please,' Elspeth ordered. 'Or would you prefer tea? Hot chocolate? Something cold?'

At the mention of "hot chocolate", Harriet winced. 'No, coffee would be great, thank you.'

After the waitress had left, Elspeth turned to Harriet. 'You have to push all your preconceptions aside. Ditch what's gone before. Tell your fears to get lost. Listen to your heart. That's the best advice I can give you.'

'I don't think my heart can take another break,' Harriet said in a quiet voice. Philippe leapt into her vision. The way his eyes crinkled at the sides when he smiled. The way his hair flopped over his eyes and he had to keep sweeping it back with his hand. The way he touched her cheek . . .

'Don't bury yourself away, Harriet. Life is about risking.'

For the next hour, the two of them sat chatting about this and that, discussing the weather and the other guests at the hotel, some of which, Elspeth included, stayed for the whole season.

All of a sudden Harriet jumped out of her chair and screeched.

'Oh my God, I'm so late!' She bent over and kissed Elspeth's cheek. 'Thank you so much Elspeth. You've done me the world of good. Here, let me get this.' Harriet went to pick up the bill, but not before Elspeth's hand got there first.

'My treat Harriet. Now go! I don't want you to get into trouble.'

Harriet shouted thank you as she raced back across the terrace and through the hotel.

Elspeth watched her retreating back. Whilst she didn't like how much old age had slowed her down, she was eternally grateful she wasn't young again. Poor Harriet, she had so much on her young shoulders. Moving stiffly, Elspeth raised herself out of her chair. She would go and see Frau Tanner, explain to her how she had bumped into Harriet and insisted that Harriet join her for an early tea. That should stop her from getting into trouble.

When Philippe walked back through the entrance of the café, he could not believe his eyes. Standing on the table, waving a scarlet napkin around her head, was Sophie. The louts from Wales were crowded around her, cheering her on.

'What the hell!' Philippe stormed over to the table. He shoved Gareth and Andy roughly out of the way.

'Get down from there this minute!'

Sophie pouted. 'You always spoil my fun! I'm having a great time. Why don't you join me up here? I can see forever.'

Philippe reached over and lifted Sophie bodily off the table. She was wild with fury, kicking her legs and waving her arms around.

'Enough!' His voice was low but his pitch had changed. It was altogether more serious. Philippe meant business.

Sophie sensed as much and allowed herself to be lowered to the floor. Somehow she found her footing, despite the large number of liqueurs she had managed to down in a very short space of time.

Andy and Tom melted away. 'Come on,' they called to Gareth, who had not moved an inch. 'We'd better get going.'

'I'll see you later.' Gareth picked up Sophie's hand and brought it to his lips.

Sophie moved towards Gareth, giggling like a school girl. She was just about to throw herself into his arms when Philippe's hand caught her wrist.

'Oh no you don't!' Philippe glared at Gareth. In that one stare, Philippe let him know, in no uncertain terms, what would happen to him if he went anywhere near Sophie again.

'You're such a spoilsport.' Sophie wound one of her blond curls around her finger and stared coquettishly at Gareth.

Reluctantly, Gareth sloped off. He wasn't going to give up, but he would wait until Philippe had cooled down, or at least until he could get Sophie on her own.

The waitress presented Philippe with an extortionate bill. Philippe gave her his card. 'I'm so very sorry about the, the disruption.'

'It's okay,' she smiled. 'It's more fun than we've had in here for ages!'

It took a long time to get Sophie down the mountain. She kept collapsing in giggles or sat down on the ground and point blank refused to walk another step.

'I feel dizzy!' she complained. 'Can't you just let me sleep?'

In response, Philippe pulled her up by her arms. 'You can sleep when we get back to the chalet.'

Philippe let her into the room next to his suite. Frau Tanner had kindly sorted this out for him when Sophie had turned up out of the blue. He could not have her in his room. She was too much of a distraction. Somehow he had to finish writing his novel.

The difficulty, however, with her being next door was that he couldn't keep an eye on her 24/7. Goodness knows what she would get up to. But he could not be her jailer. He had tried that once before and it had not turned out well. No, somehow, he had to step back a bit. Give her some freedom. For both their sakes.

However, freedom and Sophie strung together in the same sentence was terrifying. From experience, giving her any freedom at all inevitably led to chaos: chaos that he was left to sort out. It was one of the many reasons why he had escaped to Wengen. And now she'd caught up with him. Hell!

Once he had persuaded Sophie to get into bed, he shut her curtains. She had fallen asleep by the time he reached the door. Should he lock her in? No, heaven knows what she would do if she found herself unable to get out. He shuddered as he remembered the last time.

He settled himself in front of his laptop, but there was too much tension knotting his muscles. The blank screen stared back at him. How could he string together anything creative when his past kept creeping up on him? He couldn't hold back the memories that were flooding in, not with Sophie here.

And yet, despite all that had happened with Lauren and Sophie and with his career, it was Harriet who was constantly in the forefront of his mind. He could hardly bear the thought of her coping alone with the pain of her past. Worse than that, he kept imagining any one of those Welshmen stroking her hair back from her forehead or kissing away her tears.

He banged his fists down on his desk. Unable to settle, he stood up and started to pace up and down his room. In an instant, words flooded into his mind. Words he could use in his novel. Within seconds, he was sitting at his desk, typing word after word. If he couldn't be with Harriet, then at least he could take advantage of the creativity that she was inspiring in him. It was ironic that he had at last found his muse, and yet she was off-limits to him. Life sucked!

Chapter 12

'Better watch out. Herr Tanner's in a foul mood this evening,' Jo warned Harriet under her breath.

Before Harriet had arrived, Herr Tanner had made Jo and Becky check out every cover in the restaurant. If the cutlery wasn't shining bright enough to see your face in, if the napkins weren't folded just so, if the glasses weren't sparkling like crystal, Herr Tanner came down on them hard.

'Oh, by the way, he's swapped you with Becky.' Jo raised her eyebrows at Harriet before smiling at two guests as they ambled into the restaurant.

In the middle of tying her white apron around her middle, Harriet's head shot up. 'What d'you mean?'

'He's given you Becky's section and Becky's got yours.'

They never changed sections. Frau Tanner liked to keep the same waitress on the same section so they could build a rapport with their guests. Each waitress got to know the guests' likes and dislikes. Hardly able to take this in, Harriet could only stare open-mouthed at Jo. Eventually she croaked out: 'But why?'

Before Jo could answer, Herr Tanner scowled at them across the restaurant. Both of them sprang into action. Jo walked across to her first two guests and poured water into their waiting tumblers, asking them how their day had been. Harriet scampered across into unfamiliar territory.

It was horrible not to be serving the guests she had got to know over the past couple of weeks. She hated the fact that she would have to get to grips with Becky's table numbers, but most of all she hated the fact that she would have to serve Philippe and his, his blond floozy.

Fortunately, several of her tables filled up simultaneously so Harriet didn't have time to dwell on the unexplained change of section. She whizzed between the restaurant and kitchen, ferrying in starters and offering freshly made bread rolls.

The kitchen was as hot as ever. Herr König was puce in the face, and not just from the fierce flames emanating from the hobs, grills and ovens. Herr Tanner's black mood seemed to have infiltrated every area of the hotel. Even Fred and Hans, who were normally joking around in the kitchen, were silently carrying out Herr König's bidding, serious expressions pasted across their faces. Fred did wink at her once when he caught her eye, but on the whole, a subdued atmosphere had settled over the kitchen.

Fifteen minutes into service, Becky joined her at the pass, waiting for starters for two of Harriet's elderly guests who she had grown very fond of.

'Why have our sections been swapped?' Harriet demanded. Surely there must be some logical explanation for this. To her, it made no sense at all. Under normal circumstances, she would have tried to reason with Frau Tanner, but as Frau Tanner had this evening off, there was no way she was going to risk antagonising Herr Tanner further by questioning one of his decisions.

'If you think I'm serving that dim blond simpering all over Philippe, then you're very much mistaken,' Becky said. She grabbed hold of two bowls of steaming soup.

Harriet turned to Becky, hardly able to believe what she had heard. 'You mean you requested the swap because of that?'

'Of course,' Becky said. 'Obviously I didn't put it like that. I just explained to Herr Tanner that it was important that we all stayed fresh and alert and that by swapping sections we wouldn't get complacent.'

Before Harriet had time to formulate a coherent response, Becky disappeared out of the swing door into the restaurant, leaving an outraged Harriet standing beside the pass.

'Are you working tonight Harriet or are you just going to stand there like a statue all evening?' Herr Tanner's curt words roused Harriet out of her inactivity. 'Oh, and Elspeth has requested she move to your new section. I have seated her by the window.'

'Thank you, Herr Tanner.' Harriet picked up the bread basket and hurried over to where Elspeth had sat down.

Elspeth shook out her napkin and laid it over her knees. She positioned her reading classes on her nose and ran her eyes over the menu.

'What's got Herr Tanner all riled?' Elspeth asked as she selected a walnut roll from the basket Harriet was holding out for her.

'No idea,' Harriet replied, 'but I'm trying to keep my head down.'

'And messing about with the sections! How can he expect me to be served by that crass American girl? She's more interested in filing her nails and making eyes at all the men than actually serving anyone.'

Harriet grinned.

Piece by piece, Elspeth broke bits off her roll and began buttering each of the chunks in turn.

At that moment, Philippe strolled into the restaurant with a defiant looking Sophie following behind him. 'Any update about lover boy and that blond bit?'

The mask slammed down over Harriet's face, making her eyes unreadable. Harriet pursed her lips. She looked at Elspeth and gave a tiny shake of her head. She could not talk about it now. It was bad enough to have to serve him and her, but she did not want to talk about it.

Elspeth ordered smoked salmon followed by lamb. She patted Harriet's hand. 'I'll talk to you later, dear.'

Once Elspeth's order had been processed, Harriet planted a smile on her face and approached the dreaded table 13. Typical. If it had to be any table, why did it have to be 13? That didn't bode well at all.

'Yum!' Sophie said. She reached into the bread basket and came out with two bread rolls.

Harriet couldn't help noticing how Sophie's blue eyes sparkled as she chattered away to Philippe. He was getting one hundred per cent of her attention, whilst Harriet might as well have been a redundant third chair for all the notice Sophie was taking of her. Although, why shouldn't Sophie ignore her? She was nothing more than a waitress.

Without looking at Philippe, she filled both of the tumblers with water.

'What would you like to drink?' Harriet asked Sophie, keeping her eyes firmly on her order pad.

'Ummm, I would love a brandy. No, make that a double. And then a bottle of your house red. Is it a nice one? I don't like anything too dry.'

Before Harriet had finished writing down Sophie's order, Philippe's head jerked up. 'No! No you're not. We'll both have apple juice please. With ice.'

Harriet couldn't stop herself glancing down at Philippe. He was staring right at her. She felt her pulse quicken. Somehow she managed to drag her eyes away from him. She re-focused on her pad.

'You're such a spoilsport, Phillie,' Sophie whined. 'You always spoil my fun!'

Phillie? Harriet cringed.

Philippe's answer was said through gritted teeth. 'I think you demolished enough alcohol this afternoon to last you a few weeks. If you want to stay here with me, then you will drink apple juice.'

Despite a valiant pout from Sophie's direction, Philippe did not budge an inch. 'Can you give us a bit longer to choose our food?'

Whilst it was pleasing to witness Philippe putting the blond starlet firmly in her place, she was seeing another side to Philippe, which was not altogether pleasant. Greg used to try and control her exactly like that and because she had been so desperate to please him, she had allowed him to call the tune. That's where she had changed. She would never let anyone treat her like that again. Another reason to add to the rapidly growing list of why she had to stay well away from Philippe Myers.

Harriet nodded. She was struggling to keep herself under control. Despite all the evidence that Philippe was strictly a no-go area, she could not get her mind to toe the line. It was as if someone had turned her upside down and shaken her so that every molecule of her body was inside out and upside down. She only had to think about Philippe or hear his voice or sense his presence for her body and mind to go into orbit.

She had read plenty of novels where this phenomenon was described, but had always believed it was exaggerated. It had never occurred to her that one day she would be affected like this. And it definitely wasn't all it was cracked up to be. Ignorance, in this case, was bliss. But it was too late for that. She could not turn back the clock, and now he was in her section, she couldn't even avoid him.

How on earth was she going to get through the next few months? Especially with Little Miss Perfect pouting her Cupid's bow lips at him all the time. God, she hated her with a passion!

'I can't believe you were actually considering a drink?' Philippe looked at Sophie in amazement.

Sophie flicked her blond curls out of her eyes. 'Hair of the dog, Phillie, haven't you heard of it?'

With a sigh of exasperation, Philippe took a large gulp of water. He should tell her she couldn't stay. Send her back home. *Should* . . . but the trouble was he didn't know what she would get up to if she was left to her own devices. He could hardly dump her on her parents again. He knew that they were at the end of their tether with her. At least here he could keep an eye on her, not that he was doing a very good job of that so far.

'And you're really hungry?' A look of incredulity passed across his face. 'Most people with your hangover would be curled up under their duvet wanting to die.'

A smug smile crept over Sophie's lips. 'I'm not *most* people! You should know that by now.' She took a bite of her roll. 'Mmm, delicious. And anyway, you know what they say, practice makes perfect!'

'Well, you've certainly had plenty of that.'

Philippe's face grew serious. 'Right, Sophie. Exactly what sort of trouble are you in?'

'I might have slipped a few things into my bag without paying. Mum caught me . . . well, actually, so did the shopkeeper. He wanted to arrest me. Mum managed to sweet talk him. She made me put everything back. She's thrown me out.' Sophie hung her head.

Philippe's eyes widened. Audrey, who protected Sophie, who rescued her time and time again, who made excuses for her, she had thrown Sophie out?

Sophie squirmed on her chair. She refused to look Philippe in the eyes. 'I told her to "go to hell" and then I left.'

Philippe shook his head. 'Sophie, tell me you've let her know where you are, that you're safe?'

A tear trickled down Sophie's cheek, then another.

'Give me your phone. Now!'

With a petulant look on her face, Sophie extracted her phone from her bag and passed it to Philippe. It didn't take long for Philippe to dial Audrey's number. He spoke to her in a hushed voice for several minutes, his eyes never leaving Sophie's face.

After he handed the phone back to Sophie, he could hardly bear to look at her. She was unbelievably selfish. Audrey had been out of her mind with worry.

They sat in silence.

It was hard to take in. In fact, it was hard to take anything in. He tried to focus on the table cloth, but his eyes kept searching out Harriet. He had managed to keep his eyes from continuously following her when she had waitressed on the opposite side of the restaurant, but now here she was within easy reach. He felt as if a powerful magnet had taken control of his eyes, moving robotically to wherever Harriet was in the room.

'Ah! Now I see.'

'What?' Philippe's forehead creased into a frown.

'D'you know who you remind me of?'

Philippe shook his head. He tried to pretend he was more interested in studying the menu than listening to Sophie.

'Remember Peggy? When her puppies were taken away from her, she moped about the whole time, her puppy dog eyes all forlorn and full of yearning. Well, that's exactly how you look. You're pining!' There was more than a tinge of anger in her voice.

Sitting upright in his seat, Philippe cleared his throat. 'You're completely wrong. I've got a lot on my mind that's occupying my attention.' Not least you, he thought, but didn't say.

'I know, *that* waitress for starters.'

Harriet chose that moment to reappear with their apple juices. Philippe bit back the retort that hovered on the end of his tongue before he said something he regretted, and worse still, within earshot of Harriet.

'I don't want ice.' Sophie waved the drink away. 'Change it!'

Two bright red spots flushed Philippe's cheeks as he watched Harriet's face drain of colour.

Sophie faltered. She knew the warning signs. She could see that Philippe's temper was teetering on the edge and she did not want to push him over it. Before he could speak, she retracted her command.

'It's fine. As it is.' Sophie reached out her hand and retrieved the apple juice from Harriet's tray.

Herr Tanner chose that moment to arrive at the table. He shook hands with Sophie and wished her a pleasant stay. While he was exchanging some small talk with Philippe, Harriet took deep, slow breathes. In, out, in, out, in, out.

The second Herr Tanner moved onto the next table, Harriet took Philippe and Sophie's order, relieved them of their menus and escaped into the haven of the kitchen. She managed this without once catching Philippe's eye.

The restaurant was filling up. The evening morphed into a blur of orders and dishes and drinks and racking her brain to remember Becky's guests' names. On the rare occasion that Harriet looked over at table 13, the intimacy of Philippe and Sophie's heads huddled together made her flinch. Now and then Harriet could hear their laughter echoing across the restaurant causing her to grasp the plates she was ferrying backwards and forwards in a stronger grip than was necessary.

By 10.30pm, most of the guests had retired to the lounge to be served with coffees and liqueurs. Harriet was just shaking out a new table cloth when Philippe approached her, a worried look on his face.

'Harriet, I'm so sorry, I need to ask you a big favour.'

'You want to ask *me* a favour?'

'I know. I'm so sorry. If it was anything else . . .' Philippe's voice trailed off.

The dejection on his face was all it took.

'What is it?'

'It's Sophie. She went to the ladies 20 minutes ago and hasn't come back. I'm worried something has happened to her.'

Harriet was unable to contain her horror at being asked to search for *that* girl. Incredulous, she shook her head. 'You want *me* to look for *her*?'

'Please Harriet. I have to find her.'

With a deep sigh, Harriet threw the immaculate table cloth onto the table. She stalked across the restaurant and headed for the Ladies. Staff were not allowed in the guest toilets, but this was an exception. Herr Tanner could not object when she was acting on a direct instruction from one of the guests. Surely?

It took a while for Harriet to close her mouth. The toilets were luxurious compared to those provided for the staff. It was reminiscent of the Master and Servant quarters in Downton Abbey. They even had individual towels folded up in a pile for the guests to dry their hands on. What a big difference from the scratchy paper towels that refused to be released from the dispenser in the staff toilets without shredding into useless little pieces.

Once Harriet had drunk in every last detail of the cloakroom, she pushed open each of the cubicle doors in turn. Well, Sophie wasn't in here.

When she stepped out of the Ladies, Philippe was loitering in the corridor. He hurried over to her.

'She's not in there,' Harriet told him.

'I need to find her! God knows what she's up to.'

'She's not five!' Harriet heard herself saying.

Philippe's face fell.

Immediately Harriet regretted her words.

'If only she was. Five-year-olds would be tucked up in bed safe and sound.'

Harriet watched as Philippe rubbed his hand over his brow. The tension knotting across his back and into his shoulders was almost visible.

'I should've known this would happen. I should've sent her home the moment she arrived. She always leaves me with this dilemma. If I send her back to England, God knows what she'll get up to there, and yet I'm hardly doing a great job of supervising her here. She could be anywhere!'

Harriet frowned. Why did he stay with her if she was such a liability? It showed loyalty, but honestly, he was acting more like her mother than her boyfriend. She glanced at Philippe. His skin had turned a sickly shade of grey. He looked ill.

Harriet touched his arm. 'Give me five minutes to finish clearing up, then I'll come with you.'

Philippe hesitated for a second, and then nodded, before slumping in one of the armchairs. He put his head in his hands. 'Thank you.'

'I won't be long,' Harriet reassured him.

Ten minutes later, Harriet stood in front of Philippe. She had changed into jeans and a light green shirt, which picked out the colour of her eyes. With a few minutes to spare, she had run a brush through her hair and slicked on some pink lipstick. Frivolous, she knew, given the apparent gravity of the situation, but four hours of waitressing was not conducive to glamour of any kind.

The air was still warm when Harriet ventured out of the hotel. At the last minute, she threw a cardigan over her shoulders, just in case. Goodness knows how long they could be traipsing around Wengen and beyond searching for *her*. As Harriet rounded the corner, she found Philippe pacing up and down outside the main entrance.

'Where to first? I haven't a clue where to start?'

'Is she the type to wander into the mountains?' Harriet asked. She kept her fingers crossed that this girl would not be that stupid. Hiking up pitch black, narrow mountain paths in the dead of night was not something she fancied. Even with Philippe close beside her.

Philippe shook his head. 'No. The nearest bar's a better bet.'

'Right, let's start with the Tannenbaum. That's the closest.'

Lively music was blaring out of the open windows of the Tannenbaum. Smells of rich stews and fondues drifted into the night air, mingling with the less pleasant aroma of cigarette smoke and beer. By the time they reached the open door, Harriet's legs were aching. So much of this village, as quaint as it was, required an uphill or downhill walk. You'd have thought she would've acclimatised by now.

'I don't know your friend's name.' Harriet tried to stop her face from showing her jealousy.

'It's Sophie.'

Despite looking in every corner of the bar, it was clear she wasn't there. Harriet questioned the barman and he was adamant he hadn't seen anyone matching her description.

'How many bars are there in Wengen?' Philippe asked Harriet.

'I don't know exactly, but I suspect over 40.'

Philippe ran his hands through his hair. He leaned against one of the bar stools.

In the corner of the bar, a young couple was holding hands and gazing adoringly into each other's eyes. It was as if they hadn't noticed all the people and all the noise surrounding them. They were joined in their own cosy world of two, not needing anything else or anyone else to make it complete.

By the time Philippe turned back to Harriet, she was deep in conversation with one of the men at the bar.

When she re-joined Philippe, who was waiting impatiently outside the hotel, she filled him in on her conversation. 'That old chap I was talking to, he told me he saw a pretty blond girl walking towards the Sonnenberg Hotel about fifteen minutes ago. He wasn't sure whether she went in or not.'

'Damn! There must be hundreds of pretty blond girls in Wengen.' Philippe kicked out at a stone that rolled its way noisily down the path, disappearing into blackness.

Harriet couldn't tell whether he was angry with her or angry with Sophie. But one thing she was sure of: if he carried on being so irritable, she would head back to her room and leave him to search for his . . . for Sophie on his own.

'Have you got a better idea?' Harriet snapped.

They walked up the hill together in silence. It was torturous for Harriet having Philippe so close, but with so much distance between them.

Philippe glanced over at Harriet. 'I really appreciate you helping me. I'm sorry to be so bad-tempered.'

'It's fine.' Harriet kept her eyes trained on the path in front of them. This was as much a practical decision with what little light there still was fading fast, as a tactic to avoid Philippe's eyes.

All of a sudden, Philippe stopped dead. Harriet almost walked into his back. 'Can I ask you something?'

Philippe's common sense was urging him to keep his mouth shut, telling him that it was the wrong timing and inappropriate. Common sense was pleading with him not to ask the question that was hammering to be released. He shut his eyes. He must not ask her. He must not.

Curiosity took hold of Harriet. Her instinct told her to carry on up the hill. But she knew that if he didn't ask her, she would spend the next few days or weeks wondering what his question had been. 'Fire away.'

There was a silence for 10, 20, 30 seconds. Harriet could hear Philippe breathing. He was so close.

Before Philippe could stop them, the words flew out of his mouth, uncensored. They could never be unsaid. 'Are you still in love with your ex?'

Harriet's sharp intake of breath made Philippe step back a few paces.

'What gives you the right to ask me that? We had a wonderful day together at Männlichen and Kleine Scheidegg, well I thought it

116

was wonderful, and then not only d'you run out on me and completely ignore me as though it had never happened, but, but you go and turn up with—'

'You're not interested in me! You made that very clear.' Philippe's eyes challenged her.

Harriet glared at him. 'What *are* you talking about?'

'That day I kissed you, you shoved me away like I was some kind of monster.'

'That was weeks ago. You'd lied to me. You weren't who I thought you were. Greg sold me enough lies to last me a lifetime. The last thing I wanted was for you to kiss me.'

Philippe stared into the distance. 'Can we start again, Harriet? From scratch?'

Wide-eyed with indignation, Harriet stared at Philippe. 'What about Sophie? Tell me, Philippe, where does *she* fit in?'

'I don't know what to say.' How did he begin to explain about Sophie? Harriet would run a mile. And who could blame her.

Just as Harriet opened her mouth to tell Philippe what she thought of him, a loud giggling followed by the appearance of Hans, Fred, Becky and Tom caused Philippe and Harriet to jump apart.

'Ach so! And what do we have here?' Fred winked at Harriet.

'Come on, Fred, leave them alone.' Hans grabbed Fred's arm and pulled.

Becky walked right up to Philippe. She fluttered her eyelashes. 'My, my,' she breathed, 'aren't you a busy boy!'

The end of his tether, for Philippe, had just been reached. 'IF YOU'D JUST MIND YOUR OWN BLOODY BUSINESS AND STOP BEING SUCH A—'

Harriet interrupted him before he could say anything he might regret. 'You'd better go Becky. NOW!'

Becky did not need to be asked twice. With a furious flick of her hair, she stalked up to Fred and Hans. She strutted past them, wobbling slightly with the rough terrain and her three inch high Manolos.

Tom looked ready to punch Philippe, but the lure of comforting Becky pulled him, instead, down the hill towards her.

'Sorry,' Hans said. He pushed Fred in front of him as he left.

There was an awkward silence as Philippe tried to bring his emotions under control.

'We'd better get a move on.' Harriet placed her hand on Philippe's arm. Her eyes caught his.

Philippe nodded. What else could he do?

When Harriet removed her hand and set off in front of him, the imprint of her fingers was warm and tingly. He shivered.

The path ahead of them was steep and uneven. His leg was throbbing again.

Nothing, but nothing in his life was the same anymore, unless you counted his parents, which he didn't. And to top it all, he had gone and lost Sophie. Would he ever claw back an identity? Get to a place where he actually felt he fitted in his own skin? His own life? Whatever that now was.

And as for Harriet. What was he going to do about her?

Chapter 13

The Sonnenberg Hotel was huge. It stopped walkers in mid-stride. It was no ordinary hotel. It must have been at least twice the size of The Neueranfang. Every bit of wood looked as though it had been freshly varnished. Their window boxes, instead of the typical displays of brightly coloured flowers cascading from them, were planted with the strangest flowers, which would not have looked out of place at Chelsea Flower Show: large puff balls, which resembled white candyfloss; tall, electric blue, spiky creations, reminiscent of the 70s fluorescent period; light pink bulbous petals with fluffy yellow whiskers and a number of other equally crazy looking flowers. Harriet stopped to admire the window boxes, breathing in the heady scent emanating from them before Philippe urged her onwards along the length of the hotel to the entrance.

When they stepped into the hotel, a deafening sound assaulted their ear drums. Loud, raucous and out-of-tune singing filled the hotel, much to the disgust of the guests huddled over cups of lukewarm coffee in the neighbouring lounge.

'Oh dear.' Philippe hurried towards the noise, quickly followed by Harriet.

As he stepped into the bar the sight that met his eyes rooted him to the spot.

Standing on the table, in a bright green bikini, was Sophie. She had somehow managed to prise the microphone off the low key comedian who had been hired for the evening, and was taking full advantage of her acquisition.

Just to her left, an immaculately dressed and clearly distraught man was waving his hands about frantically. 'You must come down! You must come down now! I won't have this in my hotel. It is intolerable!'

Oblivious to his pleadings, Sophie was swaying to and fro as she belted out 'YMCA' at the top of her voice. Apart from a couple of young men who were drunkenly cheering her on, the rest of the extremely reluctant audience were gaping at her with a mixture of horror and disgust.

Within seconds, Philippe took control of the situation. He strode over to the table and grabbed Sophie. He yanked her arm, managing to dislodge her from the table. Fortunately, he caught her before she hit the ground.

After the initial shock, Sophie flailed about, thrashing her legs in every direction, trying to extract herself from Philippe's very firm grip. Her high-pitched screams were almost as unpleasant as her karaoke had been.

'Get the microphone!' Philippe signalled to Harriet with his eyes. His arms were fully engaged with Sophie.

Harriet hesitated. She looked from Sophie to the front door of the hotel, then back to Sophie again. Indecision twisted at her insides. Did she run out of that door and not look back or—

'Harriet please!' Philippe was clearly finding it hard to keep Sophie within his grasp.

How could she leave now? Harriet focused on the two of them. She chose her moment carefully, ducking under one of Sophie's arms. Somehow, she managed to grab the microphone out of Sophie's hand.

'Can you get us all a strong coffee?' Philippe asked the hotel manager, struggling to keep his hold on Sophie who was still squirming about like a captured eel, enraged at being deposed from the limelight.

Five minutes later, the three of them were seated around a table at the end of the terrace, as far away from the hotel as was possible. Sophie was curled up on the chair, her arms crossed tightly against her chest. She glared at Philippe and then at Harriet, in turn.

Philippe turned to Sophie. 'Drink your coffee. It will sober you up.'

'What if I don't want to be sober? What if I want to carry on drinking?'

'At this precise moment I couldn't care less what you want. You need to sober up so I can take you back to the chalet.' Philippe said, through clenched teeth.

'It's always about you, isn't it? Always! Why can't you think of me for once?'

If Sophie hadn't been drunk, she might have noticed the colour drain from Philippe's face and a steely glint flash into his eyes. Instead, she wrapped her arms around her knees and pulled them tighter to her chest.

It was awkward being the gooseberry. Harriet did not want to be here in the middle of it. Watching the interaction between the two of them was hard enough when they were arguing. She did not want to be around for the making up.

'If you don't need me anymore, I'll head back. It's been a long day.'

'I'm so sorry. To have put you through this. I couldn't have found her without you.' Philippe's eyes flicked over to where Sophie was sitting.

Sophie snorted in disgust.

'It's fine, honestly.' The words sounded hollow even to Harriet. It certainly wasn't fine, not by any stretch of the imagination. Did Philippe have no sensitivity or conscience at all?

Harriet stood up.

'Of course. You go. And thank you so much for your help tonight. Really.'

'I hope she's okay.' Harriet squeezed out the words, drawing on the politeness her mum had drummed into her before she could even speak, even though it was through clenched teeth. What Harriet wanted to say was: 'I hope the stupid cow burns in hell!', but she didn't have the energy for any kind of confrontation. Not tonight. In fact, not very much recently at all.

'Don't you DARE "she" me!' Sophie exploded. 'I have a name! It's Sophie! Anyway, who the hell do you think *you* are?'

'I'd better go.' Harriet could feel her anger rising. The last thing she wanted to do was make a fool of herself by stooping to the level of that, that . . . Harriet tried to bring herself under control. She must not start a slanging match with Philippe's . . . girlfriend. There, she had acknowledged it. At last. Philippe was a no-go area. She had to get out of there as quickly as possible. She could not bear to see them together for one more moment.

'You're NOTHING!' Sophie slurred.

That was one step too far. Despite all her resolutions, Harriet whipped around, her eyes blazing. She faced Sophie head on. 'At least I'm not a sad, shameless drunk!'

With that, Harriet marched back across the terrace, through the hotel and out onto the downward path. Inside, she was shaking like a leaf.

Silence descended on the terrace. Philippe watched Harriet until she had disappeared out of sight.

'Now look what you've done! How can I ever move on with my life if you keep screwing it up for me?'

'You've done that all by yourself!' Sophie scowled at Philippe, her left hand twisting her bracelet around and around her arm.

'Don't you think I know that? Don't you think I live with the wreckage every single day? Can you imagine how it feels? How could I ask anyone to take all that on?'

'But you've got me, Phillie.' Sophie reached out and touched his arm.

Philippe yanked his arm out of reach. 'That's just the point, Sophie. That . . . you complicate things even more.'

Tears started to trickle down Sophie's face. She put her hands over her face and sobbed.

It was no good. The tap that turned on her waterworks had to be rigged to the soft centre that was lurking inside him somewhere. When her tears switched on, any anger inside him melted away. In its place, compassion flooded through him, leaving him powerless to do anything other than give comfort. As he held her in his arms, she rested her head against his shoulder.

'You love me, Phillie, don't you? Tell me you still love me.'

Snowflakes were falling relentlessly onto the path in front of Harriet. The route she had been following was deep in snow within a matter of seconds and she couldn't see which way she had to step. To each side steep mountains fell away into valleys far below. One false move and she would be falling, falling . . .

Then, through the whiteness, she heard Philippe's voice calling out to her. Quietly at first, then more and more insistent. Panic engulfed her. She had to find him. He was in trouble. She couldn't let him down again.

Every direction she turned, she was faced with a blanket of snow. Philippe's cries were becoming louder and more desperate. It was no good, she couldn't just leave him out there. Reaching out her arms like a blind man without a stick, she started walking forward, her eyes flitting in every direction trying to see something, anything, through the whiteness.

A loud knocking to her right made her jump. What was that? Who was that? Where was it coming from? Was it hurting Philippe?

He was calling her name, over and over. The cold was wrapping around her, drilling down into her bones. Her whole body was shivering. At this rate, she was never going to find him.

As she shuffled forward, her foot lost its grip, she could feel herself falling, tumbling helter-skelter down the mountain, gathering snow as she went until she became a massive snowball with only her head peeping out of the top. Her mouth opened wide. She could hear herself screaming.

Harriet sat bolt upright in bed. She was drenched in a layer of sweat, her breath coming out in gasps. It took a while to orientate herself. Another loud knock made her heart almost leap out of her mouth and through the window. Jerking her head up, she stared at her bedroom door. She could still hear Philippe's voice calling her name.

Oh hell! She jumped out of bed. She wrapped her dressing gown around her nightshirt. It really was Philippe at the door. What was he doing here?

Harriet opened the door a crack. She peered around it, conscious that her hair must be sticking up in tufts or flattened tight to her head like a skull cap. Neither of these options was attractive. Not that she should be bothered about that - Philippe certainly wouldn't be. He had Sophie, and she was not going to get in the way of an established relationship.

'Can I come in?' Philippe whispered. He surveyed the corridor in both directions on the lookout for anyone who would spot them in this compromising position. 'I won't be long, I promise.'

Harriet was indecisive. What to do? What to do? Surely it couldn't hurt to let him in for a minute, just to find out what he wanted. I mean, it might be important. And she couldn't leave him hanging around outside her room. That would look highly suspicious. With a deep sigh, she opened the door. Philippe nipped in. Harriet closed it quickly behind him.

Philippe's tall frame seemed to dwarf her room. The air closed in on the two of them.

'Well?' Harriet kept her distance from him. She was extremely conscious of her breath. She hadn't even had time to slosh around some mouthwash.

'Sorry, look, I-I, well I wanted to explain. To thank you. And to explain.'

'Is that really necessary?' Harriet lowered herself onto the bed. What with the late night and her whirring head, she hadn't slept until the early hours, and the little sleep she had managed to get had been fraught with vivid dreams.

'Please.' Philippe leaned his back against the door.

Every single ounce of common sense was screaming: 'NO!', and yet despite that, she found herself agreeing. Before a minute had passed, Philippe had slipped from her room, having extracted the promise of a coffee in an hour's time.

A wave of heat hit Harriet as she opened the chalet door. Wow! Today was another scorcher. The sun burned down from a clear blue sky. As she walked up the hill towards the centre of Wengen, her summer dress brushed against her legs.

The little grocer's shop was already buzzing with people: tourists carrying out bags bulging with bottles of water and various items of food to load into their rucksacks for the day ahead; locals wandering up and down aisles to stock up their fridges and freezers.

For once, the tennis courts were quiet. Harriet wondered whether Philippe had played since he'd been in Wengen. He probably thought it would attract too much attention, and of course with that came the risk of being recognised.

They had agreed to meet at the local bakery, which sold a tempting selection of pastries and gateaux. Their apple turnovers were the best that Harriet had ever tasted, which made this bakery another of her favourite places in Wengen.

The décor was dated, as were the burgundy leather booths. Very little light filtered in through the front window. Fortunately, the weather in Wengen was such that during the summer most people chose to sit outside on the tables and chairs spread across the wide pavement. Large umbrellas advertising a wide assortment of beers shaded customers from the fierce sun, whilst still allowing them to admire the breadth and height of Männlichen and watch the cable car clanking its way up to the summit. Not that Harriet wanted to be reminded of that terrifying journey. Although being cocooned in Philippe's arms the entire time made the memory more bearable.

Only one table was occupied when Harriet arrived. There was no sign of Philippe so she sat down beside a table at the front, which had the best views of the mountains. The tennis courts were visible to the right and she wondered whether Philippe would be unsettled by this.

Butterflies fluttered in Harriet's stomach as she caught sight of Philippe's lithe figure ambling towards her. Over the weeks his tan had darkened in direct proportion to the extent his hair had lightened.

'Hi!' Philippe smiled down at Harriet, whose flowery summer dress was fanned out around her.

'Cute dress!' The words were out before he could sensor them.

A smile twitched at the corners of Harriet's mouth, but she acted as if she hadn't heard his compliment.

'Is this table okay?' Harriet, all at once, felt self-conscious and shy. She had to pull herself together. It wasn't as if this was a date. They were going to chat. That was all. Predominantly, she was here because of Sophie. She must not forget that.

Philippe pulled out a seat opposite Harriet, one that faced away from the tennis courts.

'What can I get you?' The waitress was as round as she was tall. She had a wide pigtail on either side of her head which was wound around her ear. It looked as if she was wearing ear-muffs. Harriet imagined her trekking through artic conditions and not needing a hat because of it.

'A white coffee and one of your apple strudels.' Philippe closed the menu, then looked at Harriet. 'Wasn't that the strudel you raved about halfway between Männlichen and Kleine Scheidegg?

When Harriet didn't reply, Philippe lightly touched her fingers.

Harriet jumped. 'Sorry, yes. You won't be disappointed, I promise.' She dragged her eyes away from the curled up pigtails and tried instead to focus on the waitress' face. 'I'll have the same. Your strudels are my absolute favourite.'

The waitress beamed with pleasure. Having collected their menus, she bustled back into the bakery, humming an out-of-tune song as she went.

'So,' Philippe picked up a beer mat and turned it over in his hands, 'where do we begin?'

'With Sophie,' Harriet replied. There was no time like the present. Until they cleared the air about her, there was nothing much else that could be said.

'Ah yes. Sophie. It's a long story and I'm not sure it's one you'll want to hear.'

'I know you may not believe it, but I doubt there's much that can shock me.' Harriet crossed her fingers under the table. 'I've got all day. I'm not working until this evening.'

'And you think my novel can wait that long?'

Harriet frowned. 'It's waited quite a few weeks already by the sound of it, surely a few more hours won't make a difference?'

'I'll have you know that a few hours can make the difference between an ending and being left hanging, and not in a good way.'

'For you, an extra-large strudel!' The waitress banged two plates down in front of Harriet and Philippe. Large whirls of cream balanced enticingly along its length. 'Coffee just coming.'

Harriet's mouth watered.

'So, let's see whether this lives up to its reputation.'

There was little opportunity for conversation as they tucked into their strudels. Groans of ecstasy emanated from Harriet, making Philippe smile back at her. The spices were delicious, and the pastry was crispy on top.

'I think,' Philippe patted his groaning stomach, 'that it is important to eat at least one of these every couple of days.'

'I can't argue with that,' Harriet grinned. 'Although daily would be better!'

'It's got to be good for you. It's at least one of your five a day.'

Harriet scraped the last of the cream into her mouth. 'And you're adding dairy to your diet. Vital for calcium, wouldn't you say?'

'I'll second that!'

A roar of applause exploded from the direction of the tennis courts. Both Harriet and Philippe's heads turned simultaneously. Philippe re-positioned his chair. They both watched the man serving to the petite blonde opposite him.

'Do you miss it?' Harriet asked.

'Well, I am itching to tell that man that if he just dropped his arm slightly and changed the position of his legs, his serve would improve one hundred per cent.'

'You're avoiding my question again.' Harriet ran her finger across the small dollop of cream melting on her plate. She raised her eyes to his, challenging him.

'I don't know, is the honest answer. I feel as if the courts are mocking me, daring me to play on them.'

'Why don't you give it a go?'

Philippe moved closer to Harriet. 'Because of my leg.' The only accolade he could expect from playing again was a large dose of humiliation and he had had enough of that to last him a lifetime.

No, he did not need to see the courts. Philippe turned his chair back to face Harriet, although it was impossible for him to zone out the whack of the ball on the racket and the sound of the ball as it bounced back and forth. These sounds were as natural to him as breathing.

'Isn't that just an excuse?'

'An excuse? My whole life was tennis and then it was ripped away from me. I felt like my life was over.' Philippe gazed into his coffee as he stirred in the sugar. 'Sometimes, I miss it so badly I feel as if my whole body is aching with the loss. Ah, that probably sounds a bit dramatic?'

'It does!'

Philippe's head shot up to see Harriet's eyes twinkle mischievously. He grinned. 'I asked for that!'

'You did step right into it. No, seriously you aren't being a Drama Queen. Not at all. I know it's different, but there are some days when I feel as if a bomb has exploded in my life, shattering it into unrecognisable fragments. Part of me is still grieving for my old life. There are times when I would do anything to magic myself back there. And yet . . . there have been times over the last few weeks when I've felt as if I could build a new life for myself. A better one. Although . . .' As Harriet looked at Philippe, Sophie sprang into her mind. '. . . that does come and go.'

Sipping the rich coffee, Philippe sat back in his chair. 'I'm not quite there yet.'

Itching to bring up the subject, Harriet kept her eyes firmly focused on her coffee. 'But you've got Sophie.'

A snort of mirth caused Harriet to look directly at Philippe. 'Sophie . . .' Philippe caught and held Harriet's eyes, 'is the bane of my life. It's like having an errant child, which I didn't ask for.'

'Then why do you stay with her?' Harriet asked.

'Oh Harriet. You think Sophie's my girlfriend?'

Harriet shifted uncomfortably on her seat. 'What else was I supposed to think?'

Both Philippe and Harriet sat with their heads down, in silence, for well over a minute. Harriet was the first to speak, 'Well, isn't she?'

Philippe sighed deeply. He had been afraid of this, but he had been more afraid of telling her the truth. Wasn't it bad enough that he was such a sad "has-been"? To then add to that a deep, dark, disruptive, embarrassing and ever present skeleton in the shape of Sophie in his cupboard. He ran his hand through his hair. He was petrified about telling Harriet the truth, certain that it would tip the balance, and she would run a mile.

'Tell me!' Harriet demanded.

He knew he could not put it off any longer. 'I'm so sorry I didn't tell you before.' Oh God, why was this his mantra with Harriet? First, not revealing himself as Philippe Myers and then keeping the truth about Sophie from her. How could he ever expect her to trust him?

Philippe reached across and put his hand over Harriet's. 'I thought you'd run for the hills. You know, one bit of baggage too many.'

Harriet yanked her hand from Philippe's. 'For goodness sake tell me!' Philippe's hesitation seemed to go on forever. The seconds ticked by. And then Philippe spoke, as quietly as if he was sitting next to a sleeping baby. 'Sophie's my sister.'

Chapter 14

It took a few minutes before Harriet could formulate any words. She stared at Philippe, open-mouthed. After a long pause, she squeaked, 'Your sister? Sophie's your sister?'

'She's my little sister. My alcoholic, nightmare of a sister. How could I tell you? What with my failed career, the groupies, the press hounding me and Lauren . . .'

'So you thought it was okay to leave me in the dark, did you? This scantily-clad blonde turns up and fawns all over you. Of course I thought she was your girlfriend or a bit on the side or . . . whatever!' Harriet picked up her teaspoon and stirred what little coffee there was left in her cup with more force than was required.

'I know. Harriet, I'm so sorry. But the thought of having to come clean about the family drunk, I've got enough shadows haunting me as it is.'

Philippe's hangdog expression, together with the surreal image of ghostly shadows hovering over him like death eaters, combined with the relief that Sophie was not another groupie or long-lost girlfriend, released the pent-up tension within Harriet as if it had been an overblown balloon pricked by a pin.

No matter how hard she tried to look stern, laughter spluttered out of her. She quickly covered her mouth with her napkin, concerned that her half-swallowed coffee would spurt out across the table. Hardly conducive to seduction . . . seduction?

Philippe leaned across the table and took hold of one of Harriet's hands. 'So, can we start again? Clean slate.'

'Maybe. But first, there is something I have to ask you.'

A shadow passed across Philippe's face.

Harriet tried to keep the expression on her face serious. 'Out of tune singing, Philippe, does that run in the family?'

The tension leached out of Philippe's face. The corners of his mouth started twitching. 'Sadly, yes. Our whole family is tone deaf. Is that a deal-breaker?'

'And you swear you'll never subject me to your singing?'

'What, not even a serenade?'

'No Philippe, not even that!'

Philippe clutched his hand over his heart. 'I duly swear never to sing in your presence, not even in the cause of romancing . . .'

Harriet grinned. She shook her head, unable to tear her eyes away from his. And then, all at once, the humour drained out of her face.

'But seriously Philippe, you have to be honest with me. No more withholding information. No more lies – promise?'

Philippe squeezed her hand.

'We can't have any of this canoodling in broad daylight.' Andy glared at Philippe.

Harriet whipped her hand out of Philippe's linking it primly with the other on her lap.

'None of the single girls are safe with him hanging around here,' Tom said. He patted Philippe on the shoulder. 'I don't suppose you're hiding Becky anywhere close?'

'Hardly! I don't think she is the type of person who makes a habit of going unnoticed.' Philippe wished he had a fairy Godmother who could banish these interlopers with one wave of her magic wand.

Tom chuckled, despite a deep frown continuing to dig rivets into his forehead.

Gareth, determined to get Philippe back for the bollocking he had given him over Sophie at the café earlier in the week, ploughed in. 'One blonde not enough for you, eh?'

Andy and Tom's eyebrows shot up in surprise. Gareth was normally calm and rational, but then he had never fallen in love before.

Philippe clenched his fingers tight, determined to keep a firm rein on his temper this time.

The three men dragged chairs over to the table. Andy sat as close to Harriet as the chair legs would allow. 'Jo'll be along soon. She knocks off at 11 'o' clock.'

131

'Where exactly is that other blonde of yours?' Gareth glanced around, his eyes searching in every direction.

Noticing a tiny muscle pulsing in Philippe's temple, and remembering Jo's warning words to all of them to: "stay out of trouble", Tom turned to Harriet, then to Philippe. 'Are you sure it's okay for us to be here? We've kind of invaded.'

Harriet nodded uncertainly. She looked from Philippe to the rabble circling them, and then back to Philippe again.

Feeling his blood pressure rising, Philippe's eyes flashed dangerously. These Welsh oiks needed to sling their hook. He did not want them sniffing around Harriet. He was about to tell them as much when Jo appeared.

'Here you all are. You could've waited for me.' Jo dropped into the nearest chair. 'I'm parched! Oh hi Harriet, I didn't see you there, squeezed in between my brothers.'

Philippe flinched.

'You've finished already?' Harriet asked, glancing at her watch.

'Yes, all the oldies went off walking early today, something about a planned trek.' Jo pulled her sunglasses off her nose. 'What does a girl have to do around here to get a drink?'

This was not Philippe's idea of fun. He was outnumbered by muscly men, even if they were from a Welsh Valley. At one time he wouldn't have given them a second glance, but since Lauren dumped him and Harriet rejected him after his impetuous kiss, his confidence with regards to romancing women was at an all-time low.

'Right! I'll leave you to it.' Philippe opened his wallet and dropped a couple of notes on the table.'

'Party pooper!' Jo grinned at him. 'Why don't you at least stay for a coffee?'

'Yes, Philippe, why don't you stay for a coffee?' Andy echoed, but with so much sarcasm that it was embarrassing.

There was an awkward hush. Philippe stood statue-still, torn between the desire to punch Andy's lights out and the sensible option, which would be to retain his dignity and walk away.

'Won't you stay for a coffee?' Harriet's eyes pleaded with him.

Reaching over and laying his arm along Harriet's chair, Andy met Philippe's eye. 'Don't worry, mate, we'll look after Harriet for you.'

That did it. Harriet was up and out of her chair.

Tinges of red infused Harriet's cheeks. 'Look, I don't need looking after, okay?' She shoved back her chair, nearly tipping Andy over in the process. 'Let's go Philippe.' And with that, she picked up her bag and walked over to Philippe. 'Leave these *boys* to their coffee.'

'You stupid oafs!' Jo ranted. 'Look what you've done now.' Jo took hold of Harriet's hand. 'I apologise sincerely for my brothers. They're more used to the company of sheep!'

'It's fine,' Harriet replied, 'it's not your fault. I'll see you later.' Philippe offered his arm to Harriet. A similar feeling to holding up a championship cup washed over him. Harriet had chosen *him*, and it made him feel like a million dollars.

They strolled, side by side, through Wengen in silence. Hikers strode purposefully past, swinging walking sticks in their wake. A couple of young children chased each other round and round one of the chairs in a nearby café shrieking with laughter. A light-hearted holiday atmosphere prevailed.

Glancing at Harriet, an idea popped into Philippe's head. 'How about a picnic?'

The thought of an intimate meal for two, stretched out on a blanket, with idyllic views all around, was tempting beyond belief. Yet somewhere deep inside Harriet the fear of intimacy, of allowing herself to get swallowed up by Philippe, with her feelings entirely at his mercy, terrified her. Particularly after the trauma that Sophie had put her through. She couldn't just bounce back from something like that.

'Could we picnic by the pool?' Harriet asked.

Philippe's smile waned slightly. 'I can't tempt you to dine somewhere more secluded?'

'The lure of cool water on a day like this is too much for me.' Harriet fanned her face with her hand.

'Okay. You're on! I'll organise the picnic and meet you outside the chalet at, say, 1pm?'

A little shiver tingled down Harriet's spine. What she hadn't considered by suggesting the pool was Philippe in nothing more than his swimming trunks.

The sun's rays shone down from a cloudless sky causing lights to dance and sparkle on the surface of the water. Harriet stretched out her arms and sighed with contentment.

'Ready for lunch yet?' Philippe's eyes meandered slowly down Harriet's body.

'I'm desperate for a drink.' Harriet sat up and propped her sunglasses on her head, squinting at Philippe who had dived into the picnic basket beside him.

'Champagne? Or would Madam prefer freshly squeezed orange juice?'

Harriet giggled. 'I think it's a bit hot for Champagne – it would go straight to my head.'

'Just the way I'd planned it!'

The picnic basket was wicker and looked like it had been plucked out of the back of an old fashioned car before the owners daintily swished into Ascot to watch the races. Philippe pulled out two plastic glasses. He gave her a cheeky smile. 'Anyway, would that be such a bad thing?'

'Not if you want me to feel sick and pass out! I'm a lightweight when it comes to drinking during the day. In fact, I'm a total lightweight with drinking full stop.'

'Orange juice it is then.' Philippe poured two glasses and handed one to Harriet.

'A toast,' he said. 'To the rest of the summer.'

Harriet raised her glass. 'I'll second that!'

They had already been in the pool twice since they had arrived an hour before. The water was warm, but felt cool against their skin compared to the fierce sun burning above them.

Philippe looked over at Harriet. 'D'you realise I hardly know anything about you.'

'That's the way I like to keep it.' Harriet smiled.

'What, an air of mystery?'

A loud splash caused both Philippe and Harriet to look over at the water. Hans and Fred were curling themselves into balls and throwing themselves headlong into the middle of the pool. A cool shower of spray splashed over their bodies.

'Lovely!' Harriet closed her eyes, basking in the heat of the sun combined with the refreshing relief of the cold water compliments of the hotel's chefs' splashes.

'So?' Philippe insisted. 'Tell me about yourself.'

That had to be the corniest question. It made Harriet feel as if she had been strapped to a swivel chair in an empty warehouse, with a bright spot light aimed at her face before she was interrogated. And it felt as if so many expectations were loaded onto that one question.

A shadow fell across Harriet's face.

'Sorry. Listen I didn't mean to pressurise you. I just want to know more about you.'

Harriet pulled her knees up to her chest and wrapped her arms around them. He was so close. His bare chest was still glistening with water droplets. She thought of wiping them away with her finger, with her . . . Harriet's mind went blank. Philippe was looking at her, waiting for an answer.

'Umm, I don't know where to start.' Harriet cleared her throat.

The sun was, if anything, getting hotter. Philippe reached over and poured some water into his cup, gulping it down as if he hadn't drunk for days. Holding it up, he offered some to Harriet.

'Yes please, I'm parched.'

Once they'd both finished the water, Philippe turned back to Harriet. 'Why don't you start with your job?'

This was safe ground. She would have no trouble telling Philippe about her job. It was the one area of her life where she had been a success.

Harriet told him about how she had started off as a secretary in the Human Resources department of Hardacres Ltd. In a matter of years, she had passed her Diploma in Personnel and Development with distinction and worked her way up the ladder to Human Resources Director.

'Ed was my mentor. He encouraged me every step of the way. I was very lucky.'

'I'm sure it wasn't just luck.' Philippe's eyes shone with admiration.

One thing Harriet found hard was to accept compliments. With her dad mucking up their lives, her mum working all hours juggling countless jobs just to keep them afloat, she didn't feel she deserved any credit for working one job, which paid more than all of her mum's jobs put together. No, her life had been a cinch compared with her mum's. Who was she to take credit for that?

'So you've taken a sabbatical?'

Flicking a far too eager wasp away from her face, Harriet shook her head. 'No, I resigned.'

Philippe cocked his head on one side. 'You worked your way to the top and then threw it all away?'

Harriet sighed. 'When Mum got cancer, it turned my world on its head. It made me question everything. All this time and energy I was throwing into work, and for what?'

The smell of smoke from a barbeque floated temptingly across from one of the nearby gardens. Harriet breathed in deeply. It reminded her of the barbeques her mum used to have in the summer.

'I tried to juggle both, at first. And then Greg left.' Harriet looked away. Tears welled in her eyes.

Within seconds, Philippe had moved closer to her. He folded her into his arms. At first, she froze. She willed herself not to cry again. But it was no good. The tears came, fast and furious. She allowed herself to sink into them, leaning her head against Philippe's shoulder.

She cried for her mum, she cried for Toby and she cried for the life that had been snatched from her. What took her by surprise was that she didn't cry for Greg.

As she cried, Philippe rubbed his hands up and down her back, telling her softly over and over that she was going to be okay.

After what felt like forever, Harriet pulled away from him. She hung her head as she searched her bag for a tissue. This was mortifying. How would she be able to look him in the eyes? She felt so pathetic. Vulnerability, particularly after Greg ran out on her, taking Toby with him, was not her strong point. To be honest, it never had been.

To save Harriet more embarrassment, Philippe reached into the picnic basket and with a flourish, shook out a deep blue tablecloth and laid it on the ground in front of their towels. He then proceeded to unload what seemed to Harriet to be a banquet to rival those Henry VIII used to throw when he entertained, minus the centre piece of a decorated pig's head, of course.

Harriet's stomach grumbled loudly.

'Have you raided the entire contents of Herr König's fridge?'

'I could tell you that I rustled this up myself but I doubt you'd believe me.'

Harriet shook her head.

'Hungry?' Philippe asked, laughing.

'You noticed.' Harriet smiled back at him.

They caught each other's eyes.

Harriet helped herself to a plate and proceeded to load it up with at least one of everything laid out in front of her.

'Thank you,' Harriet said, in almost a whisper.

'I only wish I could take credit for this. You'll have to thank Herr König or his underlings.'

'Not for the picnic,' Harriet said, 'but for . . .' How could she articulate how much it meant to her when he comforted her? 'Although this does look amazing. But I was actually talking about, you know, for earlier.'

Philippe reached over and squeezed her hand. 'Come on. Eat up!'

'Looks like we've got competition.' Harriet batted away another couple of wasps, which were already buzzing around the rolls.

There was a huge choice of food. Philippe picked up a salami roll and bit into it hungrily. 'We just need a couple of kids with sticky ice lollies to come and sit beside us. That would distract these pesky wasps.'

'You're terrible!' Harriet grinned as she munched on a brown roll packed full of salmon and cream cheese.

Philippe poured out some apple juice into both their glasses. He winked at Harriet. 'I wasn't a cruel elder brother for nothing, you know.'

'Talking of which, where is Sophie today?'

'Hmm, hopefully in her room. I read her the riot act. One more strike and I'm sending her back home.'

'Would you really?' Harriet asked.

'I honestly don't know.' Philippe looked beaten.

'So,' Harriet began in an attempt to lighten the mood, your mum also suffers from being tone deaf?'

'All I will say is that when she sang us lullabies as babies, we used to scream the place down! In the end, she resorted to music from tape recorders.'

Harriet giggled, picturing the scene Philippe had painted for her.

As their laughter subsided, Philippe took a deep breath. 'I don't know what to do with Sophie. None of us do. She's been in and out of treatment centres for the past two years. Each time we think she's got it cracked, she goes back drinking again.'

Harriet put down her sandwich. 'That must be so hard.'

'Mum's not coping well. The times I've retrieved her from hospital or police stations. Mum's at her wit's end. I mean, she must be if she threw Sophie out. That is unprecedented. She was beside herself with worry when I called her. Dad pretends it isn't happening.' Philippe shrugged his shoulders.

Should she mention this? It seemed insulting to suggest something so obvious. And yet, what if it helped? Hesitantly,

Harriet spoke, 'Has she tried Alcoholics Anonymous? A friend of a friend got sober a few years ago. Apparently, it completely changed her life.'

'She won't go. Completely refuses. Says it's for losers; losers who sit around in dirty coats tied with string.'

Harriet laid a hand on Philippe's arm. 'I can't imagine how difficult it must be for you.'

Pain washed over Philippe. His little sister; he loved her so much, and yet, he was furious with her for what she had put them through. What she was still putting them through. He covered Harriet's hand with his own and squeezed it. 'Thank you.'

Their eyes met and locked. Philippe touched Harriet's cheek. She leaned into him. His face hovered close to hers, so close she could feel his breath.

'Heh! You two! What are you doing hiding away here?' Jo weaved her way through the patchwork of towels, which covered the grassy area of the pool.

Harriet leapt away from Philippe as if she had been poked with a sharp implement. Philippe swore under his breath. Could they get no peace in this place? And, as if it couldn't get worse, following Jo like the children from the Pied Piper, were all of her brothers. They shouted out greetings as they threw themselves on the ground in very close proximity to Philippe and Harriet, as if tensions hadn't been raging outside the café only a few hours before.

How could this happen twice in one day? Clearly they were as sensitive as charging bulls. Even Jo didn't seem to care about gate-crashing their intimate picnic for two.

Philippe groaned. This was all they needed. Their intimate picnic invaded by those Welsh idiots.

'Right.' Philippe threw food and plates back into the picnic basket, 'Harriet and I were just leaving.'

Harriet gathered together her belongings at such speed, Jo raised her eyebrows at her. 'Oh Harriet, I'm so sorry. We've gate-crashed again, haven't we, shoving our size nines and 10s and 11s into your picnic? How stupid of us!'

'Well . . . It's just that . . .' Harriet could feel her face flushing.

'Look, you stay here. I'll drag my brothers over there.' Jo pointed to the furthest corner of the pool. 'Although, I can't quite believe you're leaving me on my own with these smelly men again!'

'Not entirely,' a voice rang out behind them. 'You guys have me as back up.'

Becky strutted closer, her stilettos hardly appropriate for lazing around a swimming pool. But then, Becky was anything but practical.

'Hey boys!' she waved, pouting at each of them in turn, although her eyes lingered longer on Tom, as if she couldn't quite drag them away.

Their jaws dropped as they took in her even tinier than normal fluorescent orange bikini. Each of them shuffled along, inviting her to join them. Tom, however, was the first to make some space, his eyes never leaving her body. Becky bent right over as she shook out her towel and laid it down next to Tom, giving all and sundry a prime view of her posterior.

Jo clicked her tongue, her mouth stretching into a straight line.

Once Becky had settled herself, she pulled up her sunglasses. Her eyes fixed on Philippe. 'So, you've settled for the home bird, have you? Don't go for glamour?'

Philippe's head whipped around. 'I had my fill of empty-headed mannequins when I was on the circuit. What I want now is a "real" woman.'

Scorn creased Becky's eyes into angry slits. 'If *that's* what you see as a *"real"* woman, then more fool you.' She flicked her head in Harriet's direction. 'Yes, you've fallen a long way, but to scrape the bottom of the barrel like that . . . well frankly, it's an epic fail.'

A shocked silence descended. Philippe struggled to control his temper. She wasn't worth it. With her brash American accent and her plastic features, it could have been Lauren spitting venom at him.

'Harriet,' he said through clenched teeth, 'is worth one hundred of you.'

Slinging the picnic basket over his back, he took hold of Harriet's hand. 'Come on, let's go. I can't bear to breathe her toxic air one second longer.'

As Harriet was led off in the direction of the entrance, she turned her head and mouthed 'sorry' to Jo. Jo gave her a rueful smile and raised her hand. Before Harriet could turn back, she watched as Becky handed her sun cream to Tom. The image of Becky's smug grin was imprinted on Harriet's brain as she followed Philippe out of the pool.

Jo looked over at Becky who was acting as if nothing had happened. She really was unbelievable. Forget *The Only Way is Essex*; Forget *Geordie Shore* or whatever it was called, *Becky the American Bitch* could have a programme all to herself and there would never be any shortage of dramas. Give her the uncomplicated women from the Welsh valleys as friends any day.

Jo turned her back on Becky and her salivating brothers. She buried her head in *Pride and Prejudice* and tried to ignore Becky's simpering giggles. As far as she was concerned, you couldn't beat a good romance to distract you from reality, not that she wanted to be distracted from all of her reality. Hans popped into her mind. A wide grin spread across her face. He had asked her out. And not just friendly drinks. A proper date. At last.

Chapter 15

Neither spoke as they made their way down the path back towards the hotel. The intimacy they had shared a matter of minutes before had been replaced by an awkward silence. Philippe was fuming. The arrogance of that girl!

He hated to think that he used to be anything like that, but his mum's warnings forced the word "hypocritical" into his mind. What had she said? "Too big for your boots"; "Ego as high as Everest"; "The old you, the real you, lost under layers of arrogance and self-importance".

At the time, he had allowed himself to believe it was sour grapes. She had been a superb tennis player in her youth, playing for her county, although it was hard to imagine. Her life now was all about baking, cosy kitchens and the WI.

It had been her choice to give up professional tennis when he was born. He knew that whilst she didn't regret her decision, as such, there was no doubt part of her that always wondered: what if? The instinctive drive to play tennis, however, had taken longer to leave her. In amongst nappies and school runs and other child-led commitments, she had still found time to bat a ball across a court at least once a week with some of the other sportier London mummies. Once she moved to Bradfield, however, it hadn't taken long for her oven gloves and mixing spoon to replace her racket, which was now hidden in the loft, gathering dust and providing an ideal playground for a host of spiders.

How had he been so ignorant, so blind? When he had first started out, he had sworn that he would never morph into an empty-headed star who was driven by money and fame, and yet that is exactly what he had become.

Harriet walked in silence, her footsteps matching Philippe's.

They were both deep in thought as they rounded the corner and started walking towards the hotel. There was a large group of people clustered around the entrance. Before either of them had time to wonder what was going on, loud cries rang into the air and the crowd of men and women stormed towards them.

Bright flashes from large-lensed cameras temporarily blinded Harriet. She jerked back, covering her face with her arms. Within an instant, Philippe had covered the distance between them. He grabbed her arm and pulled her behind him, shielding her bodily from the hoard of press closing in on them.

How the hell had they found him? Surely his agent wouldn't have been stupid enough to let it slip, although if Sophie had persuaded him to release his whereabouts, it would have been a cinch for a persistent, well-hardened journalist.

Philippe held up his hand to halt the stampede. 'Enough! Far enough!' The press skidded to a halt. They all started shouting things at once, pointing microphones in his direction. 'Who's the blonde?' 'Why did you choose Wengen?' 'Is your career really over?'

Philippe could feel Harriet shaking behind him. He was not having this! He would not allow Harriet, his lovely, gentle Harriet, to be dragged into this world, into his old world. Reaching back and holding Harriet's hand to reassure her, he geared up his lungs and shouted as loud as he could, 'QUIET!'

A hush gathered over the melee of reporters and photographers. Philippe was astonished. It had been a long shot. Normally nothing stilled a mob like this when they were hot on the heels of a scoop.

'Okay, so this is my deal. We can go into the hotel. I will give you half an hour. I will answer all your questions. But that's on the proviso that you will go away and leave me alone . . .' Philippe's humour kicked in. 'Come on guys! I have a book to write.'

There was a loud chuckle.

'What about the blonde?' One of the reporters piped up.

Philippe quickly released Harriet's hand.

Harriet started shaking. Her eyes flicked back and forth across the intimidating crowd of reporters and photographers who were inching forwards, ever closer.

'Leave her out of it! She's nothing to do with me. She just works here. I will do this on my own.'

Harriet flinched as his words hit her hard.

'Not quite on your own Philippe,' a sultry voice piped up.

Philippe's head shot up. The crowd parted and there in front of him stood Lauren.

Lauren? Here? Question upon question battled for supremacy in his head. How had she found him? What was she doing here? She looked, well she looked amazing. Maybe there was something to be said for "fake".

'Well aren't you going to say something?' Lauren sashayed over to him, swinging her hips. Her violet dress looked as if it had been spray-painted onto her body.

Cameras were flashing in every direction. Lauren was lapping it up, pouting and smiling, tossing her hair and calculating how many glossy magazines would splash her across their covers.

Harriet's breathing was coming out in panicky gulps.

Whilst the mob's attention was focused on Philippe and Lauren, Harriet tip-toed back the way they had come. She slipped through the side entrance of the hotel, which was reserved solely for staff. Once she was safely through the door, she leaned against the wall and let out several shuddering breaths.

Meanwhile, the paparazzi were milking the moment for all it was worth. They salivated at the thought of the headlines: 'MYERS BACK IN THE SWING!' or 'TRUE 'LOVE' FOR MYERS?' or 'GAME, SET AND MARRIAGE FOR MYERS' with their by-line in pride of place under it.

And what an incredible couple. They were like a God and Goddess, far outshining even "Posh and Becks" for the top spot. This was going to be such a hit. Pound signs glimmered in their greedy eyes.

Lauren giggled as she gazed up into Philippe's eyes. She linked her arm through his as though the last year hadn't happened. She was behaving as if she hadn't publicly humiliated him by marrying another star a matter of weeks after his motorbike accident; as if he hadn't been the last to know and to find out by picking up a newspaper.

Anger rose up in him. Roughly he tore her arm away from his. 'What the hell d'you think you're doing?' he hissed into her ear.

'Come on darling, don't be so touchy.' Lauren placed her immaculately manicured talons on his arm. Her voice was so soft and syrupy it was hard to believe that behind the façade there was nothing but pure venom.

The effort that Philippe needed to muster to prevent himself from screaming at her or bodily shoving her away from him was monumental. Conscious of the paparazzi sharpening their reporter's claws, desperate to capture a drama, Philippe took several deep breaths.

'Guys, give me ten minutes, then I promise you an exclusive. I'll be yours for 30 minutes, but then you need to leave. Deal?'

The reporters nodded. Half an hour was better than hanging around with nothing more than supposition and rumours to go by.

Without waiting a second, Philippe grabbed Lauren by the arm and led her, protesting loudly, over to the chalet and up into his suite. He could hear the clicking of shutters as he pulled Lauren in through the door.

With his attention 100 per cent bound up with Lauren, he had no idea that Harriet was watching his every move from the restaurant window. She saw Philippe and Lauren disappear into the chalet, no doubt en route to room 208. And understandably, her heart plummeted through the floor.

'I was just starting to have fun!' Lauren pouted. 'You always were a spoilsport.'

Count to ten, count to ten, Philippe chanted to himself. He had forgotten how often he had had to use this technique when he and Lauren were together.

'Sit!' Philippe walked over to the mini bar. He pulled out two Cola Lights and poured them into glasses. To Lauren's, he added a shot of vodka.

'You still remember my tipple, Phillie!'

'Cut the crap, Lauren!' Philippe snapped. 'What the hell are you doing here?'

Lauren wound her legs seductively under her. Never taking her eyes of Philippe, she drew on all the feminine wiles she had honed over the years. She stuck out her perfectly sculpted chest, the precise size and shape that she had instructed her plastic surgeon to create. Next, she fluttered her eyelashes, which were extended with falsies and heavy with mascara. Then the infamous pout. In the past, Philippe had never been able to resist her pout.

Philippe paced up and down the lounge area in front of Lauren. 'That's enough of your games, Lauren! I'm not interested.'

'But, baby—'

The words were hardly out of her mouth when Philippe swung around, glaring at her. 'Don't you DARE "baby" me, Lauren! You lost that right the day you married someone else.'

'Hush, babe. Will you just chill out? I admit I made a mistake. I mean we all do, don't we? But it's all going to be okay. I'm back now. Back for good.'

Philippe could not believe what he was hearing. 'So you think you can simply waltz back into my life and pick up where you left off?'

The bewilderment on Lauren's face said it all. She honestly believed it would be as simple as that. Well, she was wrong. Maybe, just maybe, if she had turned up a few months ago, he would have fallen back into her arms. He had been in a desperate place. He had lost everything and didn't know how to put himself back together again. She was the one piece of the jigsaw that still had a chance of being fixed, unlike his leg and his career.

But now the fog was lifting. Spending time in Wengen had opened his eyes to himself. There was so much more to life than the narrow world of appearances and kudos. And then there was Harriet . . . Harriet! Oh dear God, Harriet. He had been so shaken by Lauren turning up out of the blue, he hadn't given Harriet a second thought.

'But why not?' Lauren's voice had a distinctly petulant ring to it.

146

Philippe stood in front of her and looked her straight in the eyes, 'Because you dumped me for another man and didn't bother to tell me. Because you married him so fast the dust hadn't even begun to settle. Because you left me when I had lost everything, when I was still in hospital, for God's sake!'

The frustration that crossed Lauren's face was covered up in a flash. Instead, Lauren's lip quivered. She turned her baby blue eyes up to meet Philippe's. 'I am so very, very sorry, Phillie. I made such a silly, silly mistake. How can I ever make it up to you?'

The light was starting to fade as the sun worked its languorous way around to the other side of the chalet. Lauren was sitting on the edge of the sofa, half of her face in shadow. A few tears glistened in the corner of her eyes. How she had perfected that art over the years. Time and time again, whenever they argued about something, she would turn on the water works. And invariably, he would pull her into his arms and forgive her anything. But not this time.

Philippe moved his face close to Lauren's. 'You don't get it do you? I *never* want to see you again, Lauren. Not ever. We're finished. Over.'

The colour drained out of Lauren's face. She shook her head. 'No! No! You can't mean that. I've said I'm sorry. We can start again. It'll be like old times.'

It was difficult to gauge who was more shocked by the next words that came out of Philippe's mouth. 'Lauren, I'm in love with someone else.'

Philippe's head jerked up. Where had that come from? In love with someone else? He loved Harriet?

A primeval screeching noise made Philippe hold his ears. Lauren threw herself off the sofa. 'You. Complete. Bastard! I came all this way especially for you. I even got the press to come along. We could have recorded our reunion for posterity. You loser! D'you realise what you're throwing away?'

Watching Lauren morph into hysterical fury, his mind wandered back to Fatal Attraction. He could just see her dunking his pet, if he had one, into a pan of boiling water.

147

'It's over, Lauren. I want you to leave and take as many of those blood hounds with you as you can.'

Heat suffused Lauren's cheeks. Her eyes were granite-hard. 'You'll regret this. You will so regret this. Without me, you are NOTHING!' And with that, she stormed out of the door, leaving a stunned silence and the overpowering aroma of Poison perfume.

It felt as if a tornado had spiralled through his suite. His brain was having trouble processing what had just happened.

As he stood there with a blank look on his face, the door swung open. Oh no! Not Lauren again. He didn't think he could face any more haranguing.

In the room above Philippe, Elspeth leaned on her stick. It was unusual for her arthritis to play up here. Back in the UK the damp weather played havoc with her joints, but here she was mostly pain-free.

Assuming it was room service with her afternoon tea, Elspeth picked up a couple of francs from the dresser and made her way slowly to the door. Most days she took tea on the terrace, but today she wanted the comfort of her suite.

'Harriet?'

'I am so sorry to disturb you, Elspeth. It's just . . . well you did say . . . I mean, if it's not a good time, I can come back.'

Elspeth pulled the door open wide and moved aside to let Harriet in. 'Of course not, my dear. Always a delight.'

As Harriet crossed the threshold, Frau Tanner arrived at the door bearing a tray laden with cakes and scones, sandwiches and a large pot of tea. Frau Tanner glanced questioningly at Harriet.

'Oh I hope you don't mind Frau Tanner, but I invited this delightful girl to join me for tea. I do so miss my grandchildren, and she's the spitting image of my eldest.'

Frau Tanner instantly recovered herself. 'No of course not, Mrs Beecham. I'll bring you another cup.'

This was weird. She couldn't let Frau Tanner fetch and carry for her. Taking a step forwards, Harriet started to offer to take over, 'Shall I?'

'No. No, stay where you are. It's more important you keep our guest happy.'

Within a matter of minutes, Elspeth and Harriet were sitting opposite each other, an impressive spread set out in front of them.

'Jo's with her brothers. I didn't know who else to talk to.' Harriet twisted a tissue between her fingers.

'Don't be silly. You know I like your company. And d'you know what I like even more than that?'

Harriet shook her head.

Elspeth stirred the tea around, grumbling that foreigners didn't know how to make a decent cup of tea. 'A bit of gossip. And I suspect that's exactly what you're going to give me.'

Holding her hands around the cup, Harriet recounted the antics of the past 24 hours.

'Reporters and photographers clamouring to capture our very own tennis star! Well I never. And it would have to be the very day I'd chosen to hole up in my room.'

The array of cakes and gateaux were displayed on a three-tier stand. Harriet eyed them hungrily.

'Come on. Tuck in!'

Cream spurted out of a lemon slice as Harriet bit into it. Pastry crumbled over the napkin that Elspeth had handed her. 'Mmm, this is delicious,' Harriet mumbled between mouthfuls. She was surprised she could eat. Emotions normally squashed her appetite. Her friends, who had turned to chocolate when hard times hit, were jealous of this particular trait.

'So what was she like, this false-boobed bimbo?' Elspeth asked.

Harriet choked.

'Very plastic,' Harriet answered, a smile twitching at her lips.

'Barbie plastic?'

'Extremely.'

'Empty headed?' Elspeth was enjoying herself immensely now.

The giggles were about to explode out of Harriet. The word, 'vacuous,' came out as a squeak as Harriet burst out laughing, swiftly followed by Elspeth.

Tears of laughter streamed down Harriet's cheeks. She wiped them away with the tissue that Elspeth pushed into her hand. 'Oh my tummy, you have to stop now!'

With the odd hiccup, Elspeth and Harriet managed to bring themselves under control.

'How do you do that, Elspeth? Five minutes ago I was ready to throw myself under a bus, and now I can't stop laughing.'

Elspeth poured a second cup of tea for both of them, offering Harriet another cake.

'I can't resist,' Harriet admitted, picking up a thick slice of Black Forest Gateau. 'I'll be the size of a house after this, then I'll have no chance of getting Philippe back.'

'Do you want him back?'

That was a loaded question.

'Don't look so terrified. I'm not going to bite! It's just a question.' Elspeth blew on her second cup of tea.

Harriet grimaced, not knowing how to answer.

'Well, do you or don't you want him back? It's a simple question!'

'I wish it was simple. Lauren turns up out of the blue and the first thing he does is take her up to his bedroom. I don't want to get hurt again after Greg. After Toby.'

'Just because they were in a bedroom, it doesn't mean they were having sex.' Elspeth shifted position in her seat, plumping the cushion up behind her back. 'Now, my memory isn't what it used to be. Can you clarify? Greg's the bastard?'

'That's him,' Harriet said, a little grin curling the sides of her mouth.

Elspeth fixed Harriet with her probing blue eyes and then she asked the question that Harriet did not want to answer. 'And Toby's his son?'

Tears glistened in Harriet's eyes. Elspeth moved to Harriet's side. She put her arm around Harriet's shoulders. 'There, there,' she soothed. 'Life is rarely simple. I know you won't want to hear this, but the bumps make us stronger. And sometimes, things do have a strange way of working out.'

'I've had enough bumps for now. Can't it be someone else's turn?' Harriet's lips quivered.

Elspeth shifted position. 'I could think of a few people who would benefit from a bit of 'character building'. If only we could direct a few knocks in their direction!'

A tiny grin lit up Harriet's face, before she sank back into Elspeth's firm grasp, but still she refused to allow the tears to fall. She could've filled a couple of small inland lakes already with the amount of water that had flown freely from her eyes since she had set foot in Switzerland. She suspected that she had cried more than a new-born, for goodness sake! Talk about going from one extreme to the other.

How had she morphed into this weepy mess from the "Ice Queen" who was known for being tough and keeping a brave face; from someone who hadn't even been able to cry at her own mother's funeral; whose eyes remained dry when Greg left her; and who had not been able to shed one tear when Greg told her that she would never see Toby again?

Elspeth stroked her hair gently, reminding Harriet of how her and her mother's roles had been reversed when she was diagnosed with cancer. In the flip of a coin, Harriet had become her mother's carer, and was all at once the one comforting and nurturing her mother rather than the other way around.

Harriet pushed herself upright.

'What you need, my dear, is a good night's sleep.' Elspeth hobbled over to her dresser. Opening one of the drawers, she pulled out two camomile tea bags and a little bottle of lavender oil. 'A cup of this tea, double strength, and a couple of drops of this oil on your pillow, and I can guarantee you'll sleep like a baby.'

At the words 'sleep like a *baby*', Harriet closed her eyes. She had to stop doing this to herself. Toby was no longer a baby and he was no longer in her life. She had to find some way of moving on.

'If I can make it through this evening's shift in one piece.'

Elspeth guided Harriet over to the door. She pressed the herbal tea bags and the bottle into her hands. 'We'll speak tomorrow.'

'Thank you so much Elspeth. I . . .'

With a stern stare, Elspeth eased Harriet out of the door. 'Go on! Off with you!'

'Bye Elspeth. And thank you.'

'Sweet dreams!' Elspeth winked at her before she closed the door.

If only, Harriet thought as she made her way to her room to change into her waitress' outfit. If only.

Chapter 16

The door to Philippe's suite swung open, but no-one came through it. There was a loud crash outside the door, followed by a clatter. Well if it was Lauren returning, she sounded a little the worse for wear. Or maybe it was one of those journalists becoming too impatient to wait until he returned.

So it was with trepidation that Philippe stepped outside into the corridor. With a high-pitched giggle, Sophie flew at him, collapsing in a hysterical heap by his feet.

Philippe sighed. With practised ease, he hooked his arms under her shoulders, dragged her into his room and somehow managed to heave her up onto the sofa.

'I need a good man.' She waved her arm around and grinned up at him.

'No Sophie, what you need is a strong mug of coffee and a treatment centre.'

Sophie pouted. 'I hate those places. They are strict and horrible. You have to sit in stupid circles and everyone talks about *feelings* and more *feelings* and more *feelings* and —'

'What torture. You mean, instead of drowning their feelings with booze like you do?'

Philippe walked into the little kitchen area and flicked on the kettle. He put two mugs on the counter, grabbed the jar of coffee and practically threw two spoonfuls of coffee into each mug, followed by two heaped spoonfuls of sugar. After the day he had had so far, he needed this, and from what he could see, Sophie did too. The press would just have to wait another five minutes.

'You're such a spoilsport.' Sophie's head peeped over the back of the sofa. 'I told those nice people what a spoilsport you were.'

With the kettle held static in mid-pour, Philippe's head whipped around to where Sophie was lying. 'Which "nice" people would that be?'

'You know Phillie, those people who came to see you. They asked me to pose for some photos. I'll be famous just like you!'

Dread hit him like a lorry impacting at over 100mph. What the hell had she told them? And what compromising positions had they persuaded her to pose in for their filthy photographs? An inebriated Sophie at the hands of the gutter press? That didn't bear thinking about. Picking up the tray, he set it down on the table in the lounge area.

What to do? What to do? He raised his mug to his mouth, gasping as the burning liquid hit his throat. 'Damn it!'

'What's up, bruv? You really need to chill.'

Before Philippe could think through his actions, he had closed the distance between him and Sophie. He positioned his face up close to hers. His eyes were as dark as a stormy sea. He spoke clearly and loudly. 'You, little *sis*, need to grow up! Now drink your coffee and you do *not* leave this room. Do you hear me? When I get back from sorting out another of your messes, you and I are taking a train to Interlaken. And you, young lady, are going to the treatment centre there. You are not coming out until you can swear to me you have stopped drinking. For good.'

Sophie blanched. 'You can't send me back there! You don't understand how awful it is. It will send me back to drink, not stop me from drinking.'

'Can't you think of mum and dad for once?' He knew he was hitting her Achilles heel, but what choice did he have? It couldn't go on like this. They couldn't go on like this.

Sophie hung her head before curling herself into a ball on the sofa. She wouldn't look at Philippe or talk to him.

Once Philippe had added cold milk to both coffees, he drained the mug before handing the other to Sophie. 'Drink!' He commanded.

Sophie's reaction almost made Philippe laugh. Her face was so bolshie, it reminded him of when she was going through the terrible twos. In fact, there were some days when it felt as if she had never left them.

Rewarding Philippe with an exaggerated huff, Sophie pushed herself upright. She held the mug up to her lips and took a sip. She would have preferred another brandy, but at least it was liquid. Her tongue kept sticking to the roof of her mouth it was so dry.

Not sure whether he was doing the right thing, Philippe hesitated before turning the key as he left. But the last thing he needed when he met with the press was for Sophie to show up again and start drunkenly rambling about God knows what.

He shut his eyes and tried to block out the many times in the past when Sophie's revelations had been splashed across the less salubrious newspapers. On each occasion and for several weeks afterwards interviewers had focused more on Sophie and his feelings about what she had said than about tennis and how his matches had gone. It had infuriated him. Fortunately, over the years, her hair had changed in colour and style as many times as most people have a haircut, so she was rarely recognised as his sister.

A slight chill crept over him as he stepped out of the chalet. Several clouds skittered across the sky, blocking out the sun. He took a deep breath of the fresh mountain air, knowing that he could not delay it any longer. He had to face the reporters. The longer he left it, the more ferociously they would be snapping at his heels.

Philippe couldn't help glancing at the terrace as he walked towards the hotel's entrance. A few weeks ago, he was alone with his laptop, without the press, without Lauren and without Sophie. How had his haven so quickly become hell?

He watched as Becky strolled amongst the tables, picking up the odd dirty cup and sticking it on her tray. It was obvious that she would rather be anywhere else, but then serving others was a real come down compared with her former jet-setting lifestyle.

It was only then that Philippe remembered Harriet. His heart missed several beats. The last time he had seen her, Lauren was standing in front of him, looking to all intents and purposes like a cat about to pounce on her prey.

A large part of him wanted to turn back to the chalet and seek Harriet out. He had to put her straight, to tell her that he hadn't known Lauren was coming, that he didn't want her any more. But then, within throwing distance, that distasteful pack of hyenas was no doubt pacing the hotel, trying to sniff out any gossip, which might make the front page. If they got a whiff of his feelings for Harriet, they would make her life hell, as well as his.

No, there was nothing else for it: the hyenas had to come first. Gearing himself up, he headed for the hotel, wishing he was back in the café on the mountain drinking hot chocolate, with only the view and the pages of his novel to occupy him.

An hour later, Harriet was clearing dishes on the terrace. Her heart was feeling as leaden as her aching feet.

'Harriettttttt!' A pale streak, his brown curls dancing in the sunshine, flew across the terrace ready to launch himself onto an astonished Harriet.

Harriet's hand was poised in mid-air about to clear a pile of used dishes onto her waiting tray. This had to be a dream. It could not be happening. She squeezed her eyes shut and opened them wide just as Toby threw himself at her.

'I've missed you so much, Harri. I kept asking about you and dad said you'd gone and I cried. And I cried so much last week that dad said he'd take me to see you. And we went on this train right up the mountain. And it was SO cool, Harri. Do you work here now?'

How she had missed his untethered verve for life. As she hugged his little body to hers, a hundred different emotions raged within her. She found herself laughing and crying at the same time.

'Harri, you're crying.' Toby pulled away to stare at her tear-streaked face. He reached out a finger and wiped away one of her tears, only making her cry more.

His top lip quivered. 'Aren't you pleased to see me?'

'Oh Toby, of course I'm pleased to see you. This is the best surprise ever! It just made me realise how much I've missed you and it made me feel sad.'

'But I'm here now.' Toby grinned. 'And guess what? We're staying for three whole days!'

A shadow fell across them. Harriet looked up. Adrenalin coursed through her. Greg hovered behind Toby. It was unlike Greg to be anything but super-confident, and yet, his neatly cropped hair, for once, looked dishevelled. There were dark rings under his brown eyes. The five o'clock shadow across his jaw and his slightly rumpled clothes were far removed from the normally immaculate businessman she remembered.

'Toby was desperate to see you.' Greg's eyes pleaded with her.

After all this time, after discarding her like a used tissue, leaving her to shoulder the burden of a cancer-riddled mother alone, after ripping Toby from her without any warning, that was all he could say?

'Where are you staying?' Harriet's voice was ice-cold. She noticed Greg flinch. Well good! After what he had put her through, let him suffer.

At that moment, Becky appeared. She would! She seemed to have an in-built male-radar that alerted her whenever they came within strides of the terrace.

'And who do we have here?' Becky eyed Greg up and down, doing nothing to disguise her appreciation.

True to form, Greg's social persona automatically flicked into place. All at once, he reached out his hand and clasped Becky's, staring her straight in the eyes, once again oozing confidence and charm. This was the Greg that Harriet remembered.

Harriet watched Becky swoon as Greg introduced himself. She couldn't help but raise her eyebrows skyward. Did that girl have no scruples?

'Can I have a hot chocolate, Harri? Please?' Toby bounced up and down beside her, his eyes around with anticipation.

'Greg?'

Greg nodded, much to Toby's delight.

'Come on.' Harriet took hold of Toby's hand. 'You can watch me make it and if you're very good, you can squirt cream on top.'

Loud squeals of delight echoed across the terrace. Elspeth, who had left her room half an hour before, silently watched this interchange. Harriet caught her eye. Elspeth sent her a questioning look as if to say: 'Are you okay?'

With an imperceptible shrug of her shoulders as her answer, Harriet was about to lead an excitable Toby into the bar area when Becky shouted after her. 'I'm knocking off now, Harriet. Would you bring me and Greg a strong coffee?' She said it as if she had known Greg all these years.

'Get it yourself!' Harriet turned her back on Becky and Greg, and escorted Toby inside.

An hour or so later, when Toby had downed two large steaming mugs of hot chocolate overflowing with cream, Harriet sought out Frau Tanner. She rose to the occasion magnificently by granting Harriet two days off in lieu of working the following weekend.

Two whole days with Toby, it would be heaven, even if it meant spending two days with Greg. She just hoped he would let her and Toby go off together on their own.

If she was honest, the last thing she wanted was to spend time with Greg anywhere near her. All the hurt and anger of what he had done to her was simmering frighteningly close to the surface. She was pretty certain that if she spent too much time in his company, sooner or later, it would erupt.

And yet, she couldn't totally bury the attraction, which she had felt for Greg all those years. When he had appeared a matter of hours ago, a jolt of . . . well, of something indefinable hit her. She wasn't certain whether it was anger or whether an element of lust was still lingering inside her.

As Harriet walked back to the table where she had left Elspeth being entertained by an excitable Toby, she glanced over at Greg. He and Becky had their heads together. They were deep in conversation.

'Bitch!' Harriet swore under her breath. Darts of jealousy took her by surprise. She shook her head at her insanity. They were welcome to each other.

'I think,' Elspeth whispered, 'that's what's called "unfinished business".'

'No! Absolutely not!' Harriet shook her head. '*That* is very much *finished* business.'

Elspeth pushed back her chair and looked down at Toby. 'Would you like to taste the best ice cream in Wengen?' She held out her hand to him.

Toby looked at Harriet and then at Elspeth. Harriet nodded. 'I'll have a quick chat to your dad and then I'll come and join you. How does that sound?'

'Brilliant!' Toby jumped to his feet and raced over to Greg. 'Dad! Dad! That nice lady's taking me to have the best ice cream in Wengen! She's a friend of Harri's. Wanna come?'

Before Greg had time to answer, Harriet intervened. 'You can take your dad there tomorrow. We have a few things to talk over.'

A look of disgust crossed Toby's face. 'Grown up things? BORINGGGG!'

'I suppose . . .' Becky placed her hand over Greg's, '. . . you want me to leave you to it? Shame. We've had a blast hanging out.'

Plenty of time for that when I've finished with him, Harriet seethed, noticing that Greg took a few seconds longer than was appropriate to withdraw his hand. Bastard! He had not changed one bit. She was furious with herself for even considering the notion that they might get back together, even if that was driven by the thought of being permanently reunited with Toby.

Philippe was worn out. Forty-five minutes of intense grilling was more than enough. In truth, it was too much. He marvelled that this had been his life, day in day out: dealing with the press and photographers; having interviews; signing autographs; and countless other public "duties".

This time, however, he had managed to dodge any questions about his love life. They seemed to buy the story that Harriet was just one of the waitresses who he had bumped into as he walked back from the village. He passed her off as "nothing". It hurt him to deny her as it was so far from the truth, but he had to keep her out of this media circus.

Then there was Lauren. The questions fired at him poked and prodded that still-tender patch of hurt and betrayal. But with the ease of slipping on comfortable slippers, he smiled and joked, churned out text book answers and gave nothing away.

He managed to glean from the shouted questions and banter that Sophie had stretched herself along a table to be photographed, but was miraculously fully-clothed the whole time. And the only thing she would say about Philippe was that he was a complete and utter spoilsport for rationing her booze. If nothing else, his chat with the press had been worth it to set his mind at rest about that.

One by one the crowd of press left the room, ushered out, on request, by a stern-looking Herr Tanner. The reporters could tell from his stance alone that he would not tolerate any objections. It was time for them to leave, and leave they would.

Just as Philippe's shoulders sank with relief, he heard raised voices by the door. 'I'm his fiancée! You have to let me in!'

'I don't think so, young lady, I've been instructed to escort everyone off the premises.'

'That,' she said, looking disdainfully down her nose at Herr Tanner, 'does not apply to me.'

Herr Tanner looked across at Philippe for direction. He should have known that Lauren wouldn't give up that easily. Once she had the bit between her teeth, she was immovable.

'It's okay,' Philippe said. 'But thank you.'

With a curt nod of acknowledgement, Herr Tanner stood aside to allow Lauren through. He pulled the double doors closed behind him.

Lauren surveyed the lounge with its homely sofas huddled in groups, allowing guests to chat about their day's activities. She turned up her nose at the blown-up photos of mountain scenes hanging around the walls. With a look of disdain on her face, she walked over to the large window that overlooked the valley below. 'Very. Domestic. Well I suppose it has a view. That's something.'

'Lauren, what *do* you want? Why are you *really* here?' Philippe paced up and down the length of the lounge, not wanting to engage with her. It was pathetic how she thought she could wind her spell around him and reel him in without even trying. Despite the humiliation she had put him through.

'I.' Lauren stepped into his path, 'Want. You. Back.'

Okay, if she was going to play this game, he could too. 'Why? Tell me why, Lauren.'

Confusion would have creased Lauren's brow, had several syringes of Botox not been pumped into it a week or so before.

'Why wouldn't I?' She stepped towards him, fluttering her eyelashes and pushing her pneumatic chest out towards him.

Philippe could feel his heart rate increasing. Every sane thought scattered. All he could feel was the pull of lust that was tugging hard at him. It was pathetic.

At that very moment, however, two images flashed into his mind. One was of Lauren wrapped around her new husband a matter of weeks after his accident, splashed across every newspaper worldwide. The other was of Harriet with her head thrown back and her green eyes glinting as she laughed at something he had said.

Taking both of Lauren's wrists in his hands, he made her look at him. 'I would not take you back, Lauren, if you were the last person on this earth. What part of that don't you understand?'

Not one to miss an opportunity, Lauren pressed her lips against Philippe's and kissed him. Several flashes lit up the room as the paparazzi who were, despite their promises, still sniffing around the hotel, and no doubt briefed by Lauren, caught the moment for posterity through one of the large picture windows.

Philippe shoved Lauren roughly from him. But it was too late. The photos were taken. The damage was done.

'Get out of my life, Lauren! You've ruined it once. I won't have you ruining it again!'

'Going to run after little Miss Hilly-Billy, are you? The press might have swallowed your lies about that blond waitress, but I wasn't born yesterday.' Scorn dripped from every word. 'Well she's welcome to you, Philippe. You've changed. You're no longer the man I was engaged to.'

Through gritted teeth, Philippe answered her. 'That's the problem here, Lauren. You haven't changed one bit, and I have. You're still a spiteful nobody. You'd use your own grandmother if you thought it would get you photographed. Well you can tell those scum out there that if they so much as imply that this happened or print that photo, I will come after them. Personally.'

Lauren's eyes narrowed. 'You don't have a leg to stand on. Oh sorry, I forgot. You do. Pity it's crippled.' And with that, she swivelled on her dizzyingly high wedges and stormed out of the room, banging the door shut behind her.

What a day! Philippe sank onto the nearest sofa. He circled his neck a few times to try to relieve the tension knotted at the top of his spine. Could things get any worse?

A knock at the door heralded the arrival of Herr Tanner. 'Mr Smith. I am sorry to disturb you, but, your sister . . . there's been an incident.'

Chapter 17

The sound of laughter rang in the air as the terrace began to fill up with returning walkers eager to rest their weary limbs and indulge in cool drinks or piping hot coffee.

Jo brought Harriet and Greg a tray of coffee. She squeezed Harriet's shoulder as she passed by. The atmosphere crackled between them.

Before Greg's bombshell, when he finished their four-year relationship by text, she would've done anything for him and forgiven him anything. Somehow, she always managed to ignore the countless times he had been late or stood her up. She turned a blind eye when he left her with Toby and gallivanted off to do goodness knows what, under the pretence of important business meetings or deals.

Because, compared with her good-for-nothing father who had gambled away their savings and left her mother with sky-high debts and a five-year-old to look after, Greg was wonderful. That is what she kept telling herself.

And before Greg, her choice of boyfriends wasn't much better. She did not understand how she kept attracting life's no-hopers. You would have thought she would've learned that lesson by now. But no, it appeared she had a large, but invisible signpost on her forehead that read: 'Treat me mean and I'll stay keen'. She marvelled at how little self-respect her destructive choices demonstrated when it came to men.

And yet, Greg had been different. Greg had brought Toby with him. From the first time Toby wobbled his unsteady way over to her, she was lost. A long-buried maternal instinct rubbed the sleep out of its eyes and latched itself onto this adorable little boy. Greg had left Toby's mother six months before and the mother, in turn, had left without Toby.

All at once, at the tender age of 24, Harriet had a ready-made family consisting of a mum (her), a dad (Greg) and a child (Toby); something she had yearned for throughout her childhood and beyond. It had filled the aching void that her father had left. That was, until Greg exploded everything wide open.

'Why are you here?' Harriet demanded. Her insides were undulating faster than that of a boa constrictor. If only he wasn't so handsome. If only he didn't come with Toby. It complicated things. How could she stick to her decision to stay away from Greg when he came with Toby? They were one inextricable unit.

'I've made the biggest mistake of my life.' Greg gazed into Harriet's eyes as he reached across to take Harriet's hand, which she quickly withdrew out of his reach.

Harriet poured coffee into the waiting cups, more out of nerves than any great desire to drink it.

'Toby misses you, Harri. I miss you.'

How easy words were to say. 'Do you miss *Jessica* as well, Greg?' There, she had said it: the name of the woman who had devastated her life. The woman, who had not only taken Greg from her, but the woman who had succeeded, in the space of a few months, to achieve something Harriet had failed to for four years. She had somehow got Greg to put two rings on her left hand.

'Come on, don't be like that, Harri—'

'Don't call me that! My name is Harriet.' She scowled at him wanting to hate him, wanting to stay strong.

Harriet reached behind her and pulled her cardigan around her shoulders. The evening chill was starting to nibble at her bare arms.

Chairs scraped across the terrace as people huddled in groups dissecting their treks across the mountains and chatting with excitement about their plans for the following day's adventures. Harriet envied them. If only her conversation with Greg could be that straight-forward.

'I made a mistake. A stupid mistake.' Greg ran his hands through his hair.

'And you think that by turning up with Toby I will forgive you everything and fall back into your arms?'

At least he had the grace to blush. Of course he had assumed that. His inbuilt arrogance was not something that would disappear in a matter of months.

'Toby misses you, Harriet. Every day. Jessica wasn't really cut out for, well, for children. Her flat was too, too perfect. She didn't like chaos. It was . . .' Greg's words tailed off.

A vivid picture of Jessica leapt into Harriet's mind. The cascading blond curls that waved their coiffured way down her back. How Jessica's baby blue eyes had, she remembered, followed Greg's every move. How naïve she'd been not to guess there was something going on between them. Yes, she knew they worked together closely, as work colleagues do. She knew they had to go away for long weekends on conferences. And she had accepted it. She had wanted to trust him. More fool her!

'Please don't send us away, Harriet. Please. It would destroy Toby.'

Blind fury bubbled to the surface. Harriet leaned in close to Greg. Greg flinched. 'Don't you DARE use Toby in whatever game you are playing. Don't you DARE!'

Before Greg had time to reply, Harriet gathered together her things. 'I'm going to join Toby and Elspeth. I'll bring Toby back later. Please don't follow me.'

Greg's face was a picture. His mouth hung open with shock. Well, let him suffer! He may not be used to this new and improved, assertive Harriet, but this was the way it was going to be from now on. This worm had well and truly turned and the sooner he got used to it, the better.

With a slight spring in her step, Harriet was just rounding the corner of the hotel when someone ran straight into her, knocking her flying.

'Watch where you're going!' Harriet rubbed her elbow, which had borne the brunt of her fall.

'Harriet?' Philippe, breathless from running, stooped down. 'I'm so sorry. Are you okay? Here, take my hand.'

As Philippe's hand wrapped itself around Harriet's, all thoughts of Greg and Toby, of Jessica and Lauren, of her aching elbow, of her decision to keep clear of Philippe and his relentless past, vanished from her mind.

Philippe helped her up onto her feet. He slid one arm around her shoulders, without letting go of her hand.

His grey eyes held hers. Words weren't needed. All the doubts, all the question marks, all the tension melted away. Harriet closed her eyes as Philippe's head lowered towards her waiting lips.

'Herr Smith! Come quickly. The doctor has arrived.' Herr Tanner was panting from his dash across the courtyard. He was a man of absolute decorum; decorum that did not, under normal circumstances, involve rushing and certainly not running.

Philippe and Harriet sprang apart.

'What's wrong?' Harriet asked.

'It's Sophie. I have to go.'

Harriet stood undecided. Should she follow Philippe and offer him some support? But that would mean neglecting Toby, and he was only here for a couple of days. She had already wasted precious time by being foolish enough to listen to Greg, to believe he would have something to say that would be worth hearing.

Within seconds, Philippe rounded the corner, heading for the chalet garden. How could he have been so easily side-tracked? Sophie was in trouble and yet somehow Harriet had managed to stop him mid-flight. Just like that. As soon as her eyes had latched onto his, every thought of Sophie had been snuffed out like a burning candle. It was ludicrous.

Though to be fair, he had been running to rescue Sophie all of his life. From the time she'd "flown" out of the treehouse and broken her arm, having seen Peter Pan fly effortlessly across the stage in London's West End; to the drunken brawls he had dragged her out of; covering up her naked body with a rug from the floor to stop the paparazzi from winning the jackpot.

And now. Now this.

'I'm Juliet. Are you my Romeo?' Sophie giggled as the local doctor examined her swollen ankle.

'If you kiss me, I promise I won't tell!' she slurred, followed by another shriek of raucous laughter.

166

The "what ifs" crowded Philippe's head: what if I'd remembered to lock the balcony doors? What if I'd missed the press conference and stayed with her? What if I'd dropped everything and taken her straight to the treatment centre? Sophie always rattled the "what ifs" within him.

Sophie held out her hand towards Philippe. 'Phillie, why d'you look so sad?'

He bit his tongue. It had taken him years to learn that arguing with a drunk was useless. They were about as much in touch with reality as someone high on speed. It was completely and utterly pointless.

Since the doctor's English was not up to medical discussions, Herr Tanner translated for Philippe. She had a sprained ankle. It would be sore. The best treatment was rest, and possibly a cold compress to bring down the swelling. It would take time to heal.

The words bounced off Philippe's brain. He'd heard it all before, perhaps in a different guise or from a different medical professional, even from the police. It was time to be tough. He had to make a decision, and make it fast.

'Herr Tanner, can I have a word?' Philippe asked.

The two of them huddled together for several minutes, speaking in hushed, urgent tones. Herr Tanner nodded and set off in the direction of the hotel reception.

'You, young lady, wait here,' Philippe instructed.

'I can hardly run off!' Sophie laughed. There was still enough alcohol in her system to numb the pain in her ankle. And she did not realise how close she had come to breaking her ankle.

The doctor picked up his bag. He looked as if he was about to leave. Philippe knew it was wrong to take up any more of the doctor's precious time, but there was something he had to do, and he couldn't leave Sophie on her own. Philippe asked the doctor in his faltering German if he would mind waiting with Sophie for five minutes. The doctor gave a curt nod, no doubt wishing he was moving on to his next patient or heading back home to his wife and children.

Philippe tried to hurry back to his suite, but his left leg was stiff and sore. He had been using it too much over the last couple of days and hadn't taken care with its placement. Any uneven surface jarred the bone and aggravated the pain.

As soon as he stepped through the door, he pulled out a bag from under his bed. He let himself into Sophie's room. It didn't take long to throw Sophie's clothes, make up, toiletries and countless other items into the bag. Why, oh why did women never pack light?

By the time Philippe returned to Sophie, with the bag slung over his shoulder, she was sound asleep, her arms flung out either side of her. She reminded him of her younger self. As a toddler, that is exactly how she slept: on her back with her arms stretched out in a cross. But back then, she had been as innocent as she looked. Now it was a totally different story.

Well over an hour later, the hotel's electric wagon rolled its almost silent way towards them. A man and woman climbed out and introduced themselves to Philippe. After a brief exchange of words, they stowed the bag Philippe handed them in the wagon before moving across to Sophie. With one either side of her, they lifted her up and carried her into the wagon. As she was being lowered onto one of the seats, her eyes sprang open.

'What the hell?' Sophie looked at Philippe, then at the two people who had slotted themselves beside her.

'Where are you taking me?' she demanded. 'Philippe! What have you done? Where are you taking me?' With each question, her voice became more high-pitched.

Philippe walked over to the wagon and took one of her hands. 'They're going to look after you, Sophie. They'll make you better.'

They were too close. Philippe was never any good at concealing things from Sophie. She knew where she was going, and it was as effective as a good old-fashioned slap across the cheeks. It sobered her up on the spot. She snatched her hand away from his. 'You BASTARD!' she screamed. 'YOU CAN'T DO THIS!'

As if this was the cue for them to leave, the wagon slipped out onto the road. Philippe struggled to contain his emotions. If this was what it felt like to be a father, he didn't know if he was cut out for it. Doing the right thing was sometimes the hardest path to choose.

He watched until the wagon disappeared out of sight and Sophie's screams were no longer audible. Instead of retreating into his suite, as usual, he headed towards the terrace. Given Sophie's exploits over the years, one thing Philippe stayed clear of was alcohol. But tonight, for once, he could empathise with her need for drink. Tonight, he was going to get plastered.

By the time Harriet joined Elspeth and Toby, chocolate was smeared around his mouth, but even that couldn't conceal the beaming grin, which greeted her.

'Guess what, Harri? I ate the whole thing! Elspeth said I couldn't, but I could. Couldn't I?'

Elspeth nodded. He was enchanting. Even his pronunciation of her name made her feel special. Toby had managed to awaken her maternal instinct, which had been buried for many years. Ever since the countless rounds of invasive and often degrading tests, the two or was it three, IVF sessions? It was too much heartbreak all at once. The only way she could cope was to bury the pain and continue on with life as though nothing had changed. The animals in the zoo became her babies and she nurtured them as if they were her own.

The waitress took Harriet's order. Toby smiled up at Harriet and asked if he could possibly have another hot chocolate because they were so very yummy. Elspeth settled for a mug of mint tea. It would hopefully soothe her stomach after all the ice cream that Toby had persuaded her to eat.

'Can I help you make the hot chocolate?' Toby asked the waitress.

Unable to resist his pleading eyes, shining with excitement, the waitress checked with Harriet for approval. Harriet nodded before Toby was whisked away behind the counter, chattering away as if he had known her all his life.

'How are you?' Elspeth asked. 'I am assuming that's the blighter who deserted you in your hour of need?'

169

Harriet nodded. 'He thinks he can waltz back into my life and pick up the strands as though nothing has happened. He's unbelievable!'

'And he brings Toby with him as leverage?'

'He has no scruples. I can't believe I didn't see through him years ago.'

'Well, they do say love is blind.' Elspeth paused. She pinned Harriet with her shrewd blue eyes. 'Do you still love him?'

Did she? At this precise moment in time, she didn't know. Her emotions felt like they had been shoved in a blender and liquidised at high speed. The triangle of men: Greg, Philippe and Toby. How was she supposed to make sense of it all?

'Look what *I've* made!' Toby crept his way, slowly and carefully, towards their table. He held out the biggest hot chocolate that Harriet had ever seen. It was overflowing with cream, marshmallows and curls of chocolate.

'Willy Wonka himself would be proud of that creation!' Harriet blew on the strong coffee, which the waitress had brought over. 'Are you sure you're not going to go the same way as Augustus Gloop?'

Toby fished out several marshmallows, sucking them off his sticky fingers. He looked up at Harriet with a mischievous grin. 'Don't be silly, I'm not fat like him and there isn't a chocolate chute or a chocolate river anywhere near here!'

The selection of biscuits that Toby had arranged on a plate were irresistible. Elspeth chose a shortbread and dunked it into her tea.

'Lucky Jessica isn't here. She'd smack your hand and tell you that you are *uncouth*.' Toby paused. 'What's "*uncouth*"?'

Neither Elspeth nor Harriet answered. They sat silently staring at each other. Until, at last, Elspeth spoke. 'Fiddlesticks to "uncouth"! You take the chocolate one and let's see how many times you can dunk it before the biscuit breaks off in your drink.'

'Cool!' Toby picked up the chocolate biscuit and waited for Elspeth to start dunking hers. Hysterical laughter followed as bits of biscuit broke off and floated on top of their drinks as Harriet refereed, counting the number of dunks.

An hour later, full to bursting, Toby took Elspeth's hand on one side and Harriet's on the other. They walked together down the hill to their hotel, with Toby maintaining a running commentary as they went.

It was almost ten when Toby hugged Elspeth goodnight and allowed Harriet to lead him into the hotel lounge, yawning as he went. Greg's face was like thunder. He motioned to his watch and scowled at Harriet over Toby's head.

At one time this would have sent Harriet into full-blown panic. Her excuses and apologies would have tumbled out of her mouth as fast as an acrobat turning somersaults. But not this time. Instead, she ignored Greg. She bent down and opened her arms. Toby ran straight into them and he squeezed her tight and tighter.

'Are you coming up to sleep with us? Like before?' Toby asked, his eyes pleading.

'Not tonight, Toby. How about I pick you up first thing in the morning? I know this brilliant café. We can have breakfast together.'

'Can I, Dad? Can I? Please.'

'And guess what?' Harriet continued. She knew she was pushing her luck. Greg was already furious with her.

'What? What? Tell me, Harri!'

'They serve the absolute BEST hot chocolate ever.'

'What better than the one I made just now?' Toby's eyes rounded with incredulity.

Harriet put her head on one side. She did not care if she was being manipulative. All she was doing was playing Greg at his own game. 'D'you know, the only person who can judge that is you.'

'Dad pleasssse. I *have* to go. Or I'll never know which hot chocolate is the best!'

The choice had been firmly lifted out of Greg's hands. He knew as well as Harriet that he could not deprive Toby of an opportunity like that, not without Toby hating him for weeks.

'We'll all go.' Greg tried, but failed to conceal his smirk.

He had hardly got the words out before Toby's loud whoops of joy caused heads to whip up from all around them. And for once, the lounge was heaving with people; almost every chair was occupied. Normally it was the bar with its comfy chairs and sociable atmosphere that attracted most of the residents later in the evening.

Several loud tuts from around the room geared Greg into action. 'Right, it's bedtime for you, young man.' He turned to Harriet. 'Shall we meet here at nine?'

Harriet knew that she had been backed into a corner; she had been well and truly outmanoeuvred. She nodded and waved goodbye to Toby, watching as the lift doors slid closed behind them.

She was just about to escape back to her room when Jo ran up to her looking frazzled. 'You need to come. Now!' she said urgently. 'I need your help.'

Chapter 18

Even before Harriet reached the bar, she heard an out of tune voice screeching horribly from the far corner. Not surprisingly, the normally cosy and buzzing bar was almost deserted. It sounded as if someone had trodden on the tail of an alley cat and said cat was protesting wildly.

The last person Harriet expected to see standing on the table with a champagne glass acting as a microphone in full throttle, halfway through YMCA, was Philippe. The only upside was that he wasn't attempting the actions; in his inebriated state, teetering on the edge of the table, it would have been precarious to say the least.

What was it with him and his sister? Was bad karaoke and YMCA in their genes? And how come Hotel Neueranfang even had that in their repertoire?

'You see why I need your help?' Jo said, frustration lacing her words. 'He won't come down. I have tried everything.'

'Even Herr Tanner?'

'He's out with his Frau. Karina told me she should've knocked off an hour ago and that it was my problem.'

'Probably best that Herr Tanner doesn't witness this, although I can just imagine the complaints he'll get in the morning. As for Karina, she's just a "job's worth".'

Harriet reached across the bar and switched off the music, hoping that would still Philippe's caterwauling.

A few more lines of the song followed. Without the music to half-drown out his singing, the noise was even worse.

Harriet giggled. 'He was right when he said he couldn't sing.'

This elicited a little grin from Jo. 'It's been a nightmare. The guests have been giving me so much grief, but I couldn't get him to stop.'

'How long has he been, um, *entertaining* the guests?'

'Only about three songs, but that is more than enough, I can assure you. I don't think my eardrums will ever recover.'

Harriet laughed. At that very moment, Philippe realised the music had stopped. He turned in the direction of the bar. His voice trailed off as he spotted Harriet.

'Thank God for that!' Jo whispered. 'Look, I'm going to apologise to all the guests and get them free drinks. Will you be able to get him back to his room on your own?'

Philippe looked incredibly cute, even in his drunken state. His hair flopped in every direction and his cheeks were flushed. He looked like a naughty school boy who had raided his parents' drinks cabinet.

'I'll sort him out,' Harriet said, hoping that she would be able to persuade him to return to his room.

As soon as Jo had left the bar, armed with her order pad and a determined expression on her face, Philippe raised the champagne glass to his lips. He opened his mouth. A very alternative version of 'Three Times a Lady' filled the bar. He was just getting to the "and I love you" part when Harriet strode up to him.

'ENOUGH! Will you STOP SINGING!' Harriet yelled at the top of her voice, feeling her vocal cords straining with the effort. 'NOW!'

Fortunately, it had the required impact. Philippe stopped singing and stared at Harriet with a mixture of hurt and bewilderment.

'Philippe.' Harriet reached up for his hand. 'Let me take you to your room. You're drunk and you are disturbing the guests.'

A look of mortification flooded Philippe's face. 'But I was entertaining them. They all looked a bit bored. Needed livening up.'

It was impossible to contain her laughter. He looked so hangdog. The fact that he actually believed that the horrible noise he had been making could entertain anyone, well it beggared belief.

'Don't laugh at me, Harriet,' Philippe pleaded.

'Sorry. I'm sorry.' Harriet brought her laughter under control, even though her lip quivered each time she thought of Philippe's misjudged attempt at entertaining the guests.

'Come on, you have to come down from the table. Jo needs to set up for tomorrow and I need to go to bed.'

Philippe's eyes lit up. 'Take me to bed, Harriet,' he said, before sitting down on the table with a thud.

Harriet reached over and took the champagne glass out of his hand, having visions of him accidently cutting some part of him and bleeding all over the table and the floor.

Philippe half-climbed, half-fell off the table. Harriet took him by the elbow and led him out of the bar through the terrace doors. Anything to keep him away from the other guests who did not need any reminder of the battering their ears had experienced that evening.

'Lauren came here.' Philippe slurred his words as he weaved his way across the terrace, lurching from side to side. It was obvious that his leg was giving him trouble as he stumbled each time he dipped too far to the left. Harriet supported him as best she could, but she was much slighter and quite a bit shorter than him.

'I saw her.' Harriet wondered where this conversation was going.

'She wants me back.'

That destructive green-eyed monster that hid inside her waiting for an opportunity to pounce, kicked her in the stomach, almost winding her.

Harriet stuck her hands on her hips and glared at him. 'Well, Herr Myers, if you are stupid enough to take her back after what she did to you, then you're welcome to each other!'

As she said the words, Greg came into her mind. She pushed the image aside. That was completely different. Greg came with Toby and she loved Toby.

'There's no need to be cross.' Philippe looked wounded. 'I wouldn't go near her again Harriet. She's poisonous.' It took a few attempts for Philippe to articulate the last word. Poisonous contained too many s's, which weren't conducive to drunken pronunciation.

Harriet relented. 'Come on. Let's go.'

It took them three times as long as normal to get to Philippe's suite as they weaved a zigzag path to the chalet door. Then they had the stairs to negotiate, and that was without factoring in the five minutes it took for Philippe to locate his room key.

Harriet led him straight through to his bedroom. He fell back on the bed, his arms outstretched. She helped him off with his shoes and loosened his shirt. She wondered if she should undo his belt, but thought better of that particular idea. His shirt had ridden up and she could see a couple of inches of his tanned and firm stomach. She resisted the impulse to run her finger along the gap.

Stop it! She told herself. Here she was on the cusp of taking advantage of a drunken man. Now that would be a turn up for the books.

Philippe closed his eyes. This gave her the opportunity to examine his face in detail. She hadn't realised how long his lashes were until they fanned out blond against his tanned face. And his lips, they were . . . pulling herself together, she reached over to cover him with the duvet. She was so close. Her heart leapt around inside her chest.

Harriet jumped as Philippe's hand grabbed her arm. His eyes sprang open. 'I'm sorry, Harriet. I'm so sorry.'

He looked so woeful, she could not stay cross with him. 'It's okay. You don't have to apologise to me. But I think you have a bit of ground to cover with the other guests.'

Philippe put his hand on his forehead and groaned. 'Was I that bad?'

'You were terrible!' Harriet smiled.

'Remind me never, ever to drink alcohol again. I swore I'd never get drunk. Not like Sophie.'

'Look, it was only once. There's no damage done,' she paused, 'apart from to the guests' eardrums!'

Philippe propped himself up on his elbow. He placed his hand on Harriet's cheek. She moved her face closer, feeling the warmth of his touch ripple down her body.

Despite her mind screaming: 'No!' Harriet lowered her head. When their lips touched, a tingle snaked down her body. His lips were soft. Their kisses initially slow and tender. She melted into him, pushing herself closer and closer. His hand stroked her hair.

He repeated her name softly over and over. Harriet was losing herself in him.

Seconds later, Philippe rolled her over so he was lying above her, the length of him pressing down on her. Their kisses were becoming more urgent. Harriet's breath puffed out in short bursts. As Philippe's hand fumbled with the buttons on her shirt, an unwelcome wave of common sense hit her. Images of Toby and Greg flew into her mind. Pictures of fans and the press and Sophie and Lauren jostled for space. That, combined with the fact that Philippe was drunk. No, this wasn't good. As right as it felt, it was all wrong. Wrong timing. Maybe even wrong man. She just didn't know any more.

How Harriet found the strength, she would never know. She drew on every ounce of self-discipline she possessed, which was rapidly leaching from her. She braced her hands against Philippe's chest and pushed him off. This was starting to become a bit of a habit. Rolling to one side, she stepped off the bed. She was shaking.

Harriet couldn't look at Philippe, knowing the hurt and bewilderment that would be staring back.

'I'm sorry. I'm so sorry.' Harriet ran across the bedroom, through the lounge and out into the corridor. She leaned against the wall, breathing hard.

This was madness. Complete and utter madness.

The next morning, Philippe's groan echoed through his room as he was startled awake by a loud crash outside his window. He pulled the pillow over his head and wriggled back under the covers trying to regain the oblivion of sleep. He squeezed his eyes shut. But try as he might, sleep would not take him. The state of his head wasn't helping: it felt as heavy as lead and throbbed painfully. His mouth was dry and furry; he could hardly swallow, as if his tongue had swollen up overnight to twice the size.

Bit by bit, he lifted the pillow from his face. Sunlight shot through the gap in the window shutters and pierced through his eyelids like lasers. He groaned, squinting. If he hadn't craved copious amounts of water, nothing would have induced him to leave the sanctuary of his bed.

Bent over like an old man, he groped his way across his bedroom and located the fridge. He pulled out a bottle of water, and without bothering to find a glass, tipped the cool liquid down his rasping throat. Whilst the cold made him flinch it relieved, to some extent, the swollen passage to his stomach.

He lowered himself into a chair. One hand reached for his sunglasses, which were lying abandoned on the table next to him. Tentatively, he opened one eye, then the other. Ah, that was better: the world through a tinted lens. If only he could keep these on indefinitely.

What had happened the night before? He searched the recess of his fuzzy mind to try to piece together the events of the day before, but found it impossible to concentrate. His head felt as if it was exploding inside his skull. Painkillers? Did he have any? He wasn't prone to headaches. The last time he was hung-over was on his 18th birthday. Today was a great reminder of precisely why he had left it so long.

A loud rapping at the door elicited another groan. He didn't know if he was steady enough on his feet to answer the door.

'Come in.' His voice sounded as if he was a 50-a-day smoker. He only hoped that whoever it was had a key.

The door opened and Becky appeared. 'Wakey! Wakey! My, my, you don't look too bright this morning.'

Becky's loud American drawl grated through his head.

She set the tray down on the table and moved across to the shutters. Before Philippe had time to protest, she flung them wide open causing a searing pain to shoot into the back of Philippe's eyes as sunlight flooded the room, blinding him. Even his sunglasses weren't powerful enough to protect him from that.

Becky smirked. 'Harriet instructed me to bring you pain killers and strong coffee. Had a rough night did we?'

'Close those damned shutters or —'

'Or what?' Becky taunted. 'Or you'll complain to Herr Tanner? I think he's had enough complaints to deal with this morning. In fact, the guests were fairly queuing up in reception when I walked past, all eager to add their complaint about last night's antics in the bar.' Becky gave him a knowing look.

'What *are* you talking about?' Philippe's complete bafflement caused Becky to shriek with laughter: an extremely high-pitched laughter, at that. Philippe moaned as his head splintered into shards of pain.

'You can't remember, can you? Oh dear. Poor, poor Mr Smith. Well, no doubt you'll find out. Herr Tanner will be after your blood by the time the guests have finished with him!' And with that, Becky blew Philippe a kiss. She walked out of the room, making sure she banged the door hard, causing Philippe to flinch, yet again.

With concerted effort, Philippe managed to get himself over to the table. He poured himself a strong black coffee, his hands shaking as he lifted the heavy pot, hot liquid in danger of spurting everywhere except into the waiting mug. He popped out two painkillers and knocked them back with the large glass of water, which had also been provided, before falling back onto the chair.

Harriet? How had she known he needed painkillers? He couldn't remember anything after he had watched Sophie disappearing out of sight in the hotel's wagon. Even the events directly before that were blurry.

He wracked his brains. Vague recollections of the hotel bar swam into focus. Oh yes, at some stage during the evening he was pretty certain he had had a drink or two in the hotel bar, but after that everything was sketchy. In fact, it was far more than sketchy: it was totally and utterly blank. Vanished. Gone.

If this was how Sophie felt every morning, he had to admit a certain twisted respect for her tenacity and courage at tolerating such abhorrent consequences time and time again. Once every twenty or so years was more than enough for him. He actually felt as if he was going to die.

Harriet, Greg and Toby were all dressed in T-shirts with cardigans wrapped around their waists. Even this early in the morning, the sun was already warm. Toby, bouncing along between them, was oblivious to the chilly atmosphere between Harriet and Greg. He was ecstatic. He was finally with Harriet again, and better than that, they were spending time together as the only complete family he had ever known. Apart from six months living with Jessica, but that didn't count. She was horrible.

He always imagined her as the wicked witch in Hansel and Gretel. From the outset he had been terrified that she would stick him in a cage and ask him to poke his finger through the bars to see if he was fat enough to eat. Any time Jessica forced him to eat everything on his plate, he would know with absolute certainty that this was her cunning plan.

'What's that ringing sound?' Toby asked. 'Ting a ling! Ting a ling!'

'It's cow bells.' Harriet pointed to a field part-way down the valley. 'Look, you see the cows down there? Well they have large bells around their necks so they don't get lost.'

'Wow! They must be heavy. Maybe I need a 'boy bell' so you don't lose me! Like that time in town when I couldn't find you in that shop.'

Harriet remembered only too well. One minute Toby was by her side, the next he had disappeared. She could still feel the intensity of her panic, even now. She had searched ever more frantically, calling his name and asking everyone if they had seen a four-year-old boy, tall for his age, with brown curls and brown eyes. Each time they shook their heads, with pity in their eyes, she became more desperate.

It took an announcement over the tannoy and every member of staff in the large department store being alerted before they found him. He had taken up residence in one of the play houses in the toy department, which he had spotted on the way in. He was completely engrossed in his land of make-believe, unaware of the drama unfolding in the wider store. There were more important things to do: pouring tea for a couple of teddies; for a tiger, which was almost as large as him; and for a rag doll, which looked similar to "Rosie" from *Rosie and Jim*.

When Harriet found him, she squeezed herself into the play house. She hugged Toby to her, sobbing.

'I'm sorry.' Toby's bottom lip quivered. 'I should've asked you to tea.'

Harriet grinned. 'D'you know Toby, a 'boy bell' would've been an excellent idea.'

Greg marched on in front of them both. He knew he had to make an effort if he wanted to woo Harriet back, but he was still fuming about the way she had spoken to him the day before. If he had wanted a woman to answer him back, he would have stuck with Jessica.

Still, he had to find some way of persuading Harriet to come home, even if he had to swallow his pride for a few days. Looking after Toby on his own was exhausting. It was demanding. It was untenable. Harriet had been brilliant with Toby. He hadn't realised how brilliant until they moved in with Jessica.

And as for all this *fresh* mountain air, he could do without it. This place was hopeless. Even the five star hotels in Wengen had nothing like the same facilities as those in London. Eating out was a joke – this place had clearly not heard that the rest of the world had moved into the 21st century.

'How much further?' Greg moaned, starting to drag his feet as the path became steeper. Give him a treadmill any day. He was almost regretting wearing his smart shoes. Harriet had offered to find him a pair of walking boots, but he wouldn't be seen dead in a pair of those, not unless they were branded, of course. It was unlikely that any of the bumpkins who lived hereabouts had heard of "brands", let alone owned any.

'Wow! Look at that mountain. It's covered in snow! How come it's not melting?

'Because it's very, very cold up there.'

'But it's hot down here.'

181

'That's because it looks near, but it's actually way, way higher up than we are, and the higher up you go, the colder it gets.'

'Cool!'

'"Cool" is the right word, Toby!' Harriet laughed. 'And they even have ice caves in the mountain.'

'WOW! Can we go, Harri? Can we go? Pleassse!'

Harriet marvelled at Toby's enthusiasm for life. It made her see everything from a different perspective, as if the whole world had been painted with a fresh coat of paint.

By the time they reached the café, Harriet was exhausted from the zillions of questions that Toby had asked about anything and everything. After his initial spurt, Greg had continued to drag his feet every step of the way. He complained about the uneven path, about the gradient of the incline, in fact, about everything. He was behaving more like a child than Toby. If this was his effort at winning her back, she did not think much of it.

They managed to find a table with a clear view down into the valley. It was just as beautiful here as she remembered. Houses dotted the mountain side, flanked by clusters of trees. Sprinklings of wild flowers added bright splashes of yellow, purple and white amongst the green of the grass. Harriet turned her face up to the sun, which shone down brightly.

Toby was fully engrossed with his drink when Greg finally spoke. 'He misses you Harriet. I miss you.'

'You have a funny way of showing it. You've hardly spoken to me since we set off.' Except to moan, she thought.

'It's been hard seeing you again. You've changed.'

Yes, I'm no longer your doormat. Harriet allowed herself the luxury of a tiny grin. Funny how it was so hard for him when he had been the one to dump her and take Toby away. It always went back to Greg. How had she not noticed that before?

'The house isn't the same without you,' Greg persevered.

Filthy, no doubt. She had always been the one to clean, wash up and everything else.

'Come on, Harriet, work with me here!' His pale blue eyes pleaded with her. If only he wasn't so heart-stoppingly gorgeous, it would make this so much easier. And if only he didn't come as a package with Toby. Could she bear to be parted from Toby again?

The waitress brought over thick slices of lemon cake. Toby's eyes lit up as he picked up his fork and tucked in with gusto. It made Harriet think of Philippe. Her heart somersaulted. How come Philippe still did that to her? Despite the deception about his past, despite Lauren, despite his drunken antics.

As if her thoughts had conjured him up, the door opened and in walked Philippe.

Chapter 19

A couple of hours earlier, Philippe had been holed up in his suite feeling ill. His head continued to pound long after Becky slammed the door of his suite behind her. He finished several mugs of strong coffee in succession, but could not face any of the food that was loaded onto his breakfast tray. Despite standing under a hot shower, he was still not able to wash away his stinker of a hangover.

When Jo arrived to retrieve his tray, she told him that one or two errant journalists were still prowling around the neighbourhood, despite his threats, and that Herr Tanner was waiting to talk to him. What she did not elaborate on was what exactly had happened the previous evening to set Herr Tanner on the warpath.

He was not normally one to run from trouble. And yet, with a hangover as hellish as the one he was nursing, coupled with Herr Tanner and the journalists, and probably a number of disgruntled guests hunting him down, the mountainside and fresh air beckoned. Even though, he had to admit, the thought of hiding under a duvet all day was equally compelling. A duvet, however, would not shield him from Herr Tanner for long.

So with a deep breath to steady the rising nausea, he closed the door of his suite. As he ascended the mountain path, a good deal more slowly than normal, he tried to recall the missing pieces of the night before. The thought of what might have happened was, he hoped, more terrifying than the reality. He just needed to find someone who knew the score, and from what Becky had implied, he suspected Harriet would be able to enlighten him. As things stood, he did not have the courage to go looking for her until at least some of the dust had settled.

Thoughts of Lauren and Sophie and of the insidious journalists played on his mind as he trudged up the mountain. He stopped for regular breathers to rest his leg, which ached worse than ever. Flashes of his vacuous life before his accident and his new life, which at times he felt he was teetering on the brink of actually enjoying, flew through his mind. He couldn't help but compare the two lifestyles.

Philippe smiled at himself. For someone as hung over as him, he was getting into pretty treacherous waters with his meandering mind. And despite the feeling of superiority, which came from knowing he could no longer be classed as yet another fame-crazed clone, his life was hardly straightforward.

With Lauren still hot on his heels, even though he had already sent her packing twice; with Sophie being carted off to a treatment centre, having caused enough havoc in a few short days to keep the gossips going for months; and Harriet . . .

Harriet, who he wanted to pull close to him and never let go; Harriet, who had seen him with Lauren and those reporter blood hounds; Harriet, who pushed him away the first time he kissed her, and Harriet who had abandoned his bed . . . Philippe blanched.

Bed? Harriet had been in his bed? He closed his eyes concentrating on that image. How had they got as far as his bedroom? What had happened between Sophie leaving and Harriet running out on him? For Harriet to have been in bed with him said a lot, but for her to abandon him again? He had to know what had happened. Given that he was almost at the café he would have a quick cup of coffee before heading back to Wengen to track her down.

Philippe spotted Harriet the moment he walked into the café. She was sitting with her head bent over a young boy. As he watched, she tenderly tucked one of his unruly locks of hair behind his ear.

Harriet had a son? That she hadn't told him about? She couldn't have, could she? Wouldn't she have told him? Nausea rose in his stomach like a wave.

Greg grabbed Harriet by the arm and shook her. 'My God! That's Philippe Myers! What's *he* doing here? I'm going to ask for his autograph.'

The hairs on Harriet's arms stood up as if she'd walked into a wall of static.

185

Hell! How could Harriet have forgotten that Greg was an avid tennis fan? Probably because she was trying hard not to think much about Greg at all. And when she said "fan", she meant "*fan*". If Greg had appeared on Mastermind with his expert subject as "tennis", he would have thrashed the lot of them hands down.

Wasn't it typical that Greg was one of the few people who recognised a cleanly- shaven-Philippe miles away from his home country. If only Greg had let her watch the tennis matches with him, she would then have had a fighting chance of working out who Philippe was from the outset. And *that* would have prevented the misunderstandings between them, or one of them, at least.

But, oh no, Greg would not tolerate any interruption when he was watching his beloved tennis. This meant that she and Toby were kicked out of the house to 'go and amuse themselves', whilst Greg's eyes never left the screen for hours at a time.

Harriet lowered her eyes and tried hard to concentrate on Toby. She was conscious of her heightened colour. Her awareness of Philippe made everything else recede into the background.

Philippe was just about to escape out of the door when a loud voice called out his name.

'Philippe, you must join us. I've been a fan since forever.'

Slowly, Philippe turned towards the voice. He saw Harriet's startled eyes meet his for a second time before she lowered them quickly back to the boy. A bright flush stained her cheeks.

It was the man sitting opposite Harriet who had invited him over. He didn't need an astute intuition to realise that this must be Greg. Greg, who was far too handsome, and wore an air of authority, which he doubted few would challenge. The same Greg who had abandoned Harriet when she was at her lowest ebb. The man who, Philippe assumed, she'd had a child with.

The thought of Harriet sharing something so intimate and so binding with another man, it was almost too much to bear.

Philippe watched in slow motion as Greg approached him, hand held out in greeting. Without thinking, Philippe grasped his hand

and allowed Greg to shake it. He had to concentrate hard to hold back the glare that was straining to make itself known.

'Take a seat Philippe – I can call you Philippe? I'll get you a drink. What'll it be? A beer? Wine? Something stronger?'

At the mention of alcohol, Philippe blanched. 'Strong coffee, black,' Philippe replied, before slipping into the empty seat opposite Harriet. The very thought of anything sweet was making his stomach churn.

'What are you doing here?' Harriet asked. Her voice was laced with panic.

'Having a coffee? What about you?'

The shock of seeing Harriet with her ready-made family had thrown an unpinned grenade into his emotions. Philippe's clipped tones belied the urge he was suppressing to take her in his arms and show her exactly what he was doing here. Whilst at the same time, he wanted to push her as far away from him as possible and run. Escape to another country where everything was simple and straightforward.

The boy's head bobbed up. His eyes studied Philippe inquisitively. 'I'm Toby. Who are you?'

'Nice to meet you, Toby.' Philippe shook Toby's outstretched hand. 'I'm Philippe, a friend of your mother's.'

Philippe smiled, in spite of himself. Harriet's son was cute even if he did have a prize idiot as a father, and even if he could hardly bear to think of Harriet having created such a lifelong bond with another man.

Harriet tried to catch his eye, shaking her head.

'But she's dead.' Toby relayed this information in such a matter of fact manner, it made it all the more shocking. 'Did you know her before she died?'

'Dead?' Philippe repeated. His mouth hung open. 'Harriet's not dead.'

'No silly! Harriet isn't my real mum, but she is like my mum. And I do love her.'

Harriet watched the colour drain from Philippe's face. 'I'm so sorry. I should have told you. It's just, well I didn't think I'd see Toby again.'

'I know, we surprised you, didn't we?' Toby sucked his lemonade through the straw making slurping noises.

Harriet nodded.

Philippe took deep breaths in and out to steady his nausea. He didn't know whether the cause was the copious amounts of alcohol he must have consumed the evening before, the relief that Harriet wasn't Toby's mum or the emotions that this cosy little family scene was stirring up within him.

At that moment Greg returned with the drinks and turned on his charm offensive. He smiled and laughed in all the right places, asking Philippe question after question about his life as a tennis player, when he was a "somebody" rather than a "has-been".

Philippe's ego still enjoyed reliving his achievements on the court, even if this didn't extend to his vacuous life beyond. He fought hard with his fury at how two-faced and disloyal he was being by sitting and having a civilised conversation with the man who had treated Harriet so badly.

And yet, Harriet was the one playing "happy families", so who was he to spoil the pretty picture they had painted for themselves?

'Can you teach me how to play tennis, Philippe?' Toby asked. 'I'm not staying very long so we'd have to start this afternoon.'

Toby's little face grinned up at Philippe. More than anything, Philippe did not want to watch that hopeful smile droop at the sides. He did not want to let Toby down like Greg had let Harriet down. And it was obvious that Toby was very important to Harriet. But he couldn't do it. Even the thought of stepping onto a tennis court again filled his body with palpitations, sending his head into a merry-go-round spin.

'I'm sorry Toby, but I can't play anymore. You see, I hurt my leg when I fell off my motorbike.'

Toby spooned another huge mouthful of lemon cake into his mouth. He chewed a few times and swallowed quickly. 'You've got a motorbike? Cool? Can I ride on your motorbike?'

188

'Whoa, slow down.' Greg fixed Toby with a stern look. 'I don't think motorbikes are allowed in Wengen.'

'Oh.' Toby's face fell. 'That's okay. We can play tennis instead.'

Harriet sat silently, watching the conversation move backwards and forwards between them, as if she was indeed watching a tennis match. 'Toby, Philippe's leg is too painful to play tennis—'

'He doesn't *have* to play. He just has to show me how. Anyway, he walked up this mountain and he's not a mountain goat so his leg can't be *that* bad!' The tone Toby used simply underlined the stupidity of all adults in their refusal to acknowledge the obvious. It took a seven-year-old boy to explain life to them. He sighed deeply.

A smile played around Harriet's lips. She watched Philippe.

'Well, I'll have to see if the hotel has a racket the right size for you,' Philippe answered.

It had never occurred to him that one day he would identify with Alice in Wonderland when she drank the various potions and shrank to the size of a mouse and then grew as tall as a giant. However, the last 24 hours had turned his convictions and his misconceptions on their head, shaken them around vigorously and tipped them out in a completely different order. An order that he no longer recognised as resembling anything similar to his own life. Where everything was strange and muddled and where, if the Queen of Hearts had suddenly appeared with a tray of tarts, he would barely bat an eyelid.

Greg slapped Philippe on the back. 'That's my man! Might give you a bit of a knock around myself.'

'I'll give you "knock around",' Philippe muttered under his breath. Was it possible to detest this man more than he already did? Talk about getting on his nerves. What had possessed Harriet to give herself to a man like that? To a man who had no time for anyone but himself, someone who was driven entirely by his own ego? Philippe ignored his conscience, which prodded him hard with memories of how he used to be back in his star-studded days. That was different, he told himself, completely different.

The only reason that Philippe got through the next half hour or so it took for coffees to be drunk and cake to be eaten (excluding

189

Philippe whose stomach was way too tender to even contemplate something as rich and nauseating as cake) was due to Toby. He entertained them all with his off-the-wall comments and countless questions about anything and everything, from why cocktail sticks were pointed on both ends to how long it would take Harriet to run down from the top of the Jungfrau into Wengen. Philippe chuckled to himself as he watched Harriet visibly pale at the mere thought of it.

Every time Greg launched into one of his monologues, aimed solely at Philippe's tennis stardom, Philippe managed to bring Toby into the conversation or to ask Harriet's point of view. He could see that Greg was infuriated by this. What Greg wanted was to boast to all his friends about how friendly he and Philippe Myers were, and to show off by reciting all the personal facts he had gleaned from his alleged "best buddy".

Philippe learned early on in his career to spot this type of fan a mile off. He had developed an in-built radar in the name of self-protection. Since his accident, he was rarely recognised and did not normally have to dodge creeps like Greg. Pity he couldn't walk away, but there was Harriet and there was Toby. He had to play ball, but was not going to do it by Greg's rules.

'Come on, Dad. You promised you would give me a piggy back down that steep bit. You said, remember?'

'Lucky I haven't had a motorbike accident.' Greg stared at Philippe's left leg, which was stretched out in front of him.

Uh oh. Maybe he had pushed Greg a little too far. He had, he suspected, made himself an enemy. Not that he wanted Greg as a friend, but he had Harriet to think about. This would make things extra awkward for her, and that was the last thing he wanted. Damn that Greg! Why couldn't he have stayed away?

Greg was too busy getting an excitable Toby onto his back to notice Philippe's face tighten, his eyes flare or a hundred other emotions sketch themselves onto Philippe's face.

Harriet's eyes darted to where Philippe stood, rigid.

They both watched as Greg galloped off down the steep slope with Toby clinging onto his back, whooping loudly and telling Greg to: 'Giddy up!'

'Sorry,' Harriet said, as soon as Greg had galloped out of sight. 'I don't know what's got into him.'

'Why, Harriet?' Philippe asked. He could hardly bear the thought of this, this ignoramus being with Harriet, touching Harriet, making love—

'He isn't always like this. He can be kind.' Harriet shifted from foot to foot. 'Well at the beginning he was . . . charming. And then there was Toby. We bonded immediately. How could I leave him? He called me "Mum".'

Tears sprang into Harriet's eyes.

Philippe stepped closer, but before he could touch her, Harriet moved away from him. 'Y-y-you'll make me worse. And Toby will notice I've been crying. He always picks up on it.'

A couple of walkers glanced sideways at Harriet as they strode by, their map held out in front of them, their walking boots crunching as they ate up the ground before them like professionals.

Once she had dried her eyes with the back of her hand, Harriet gave Philippe a little grin. 'Thank you though.'

Philippe smiled back. 'Well, we'd better make headway or they'll wonder where we've got to.'

As they started walking slowly down the mountain, Harriet looked back over her shoulder at Philippe. 'I'm amazed you're even up. I thought you'd be comatose until at least mid-day.'

'Ah yes, that. I must admit the only thing that got me out of bed was the news that Herr Tanner was living up to his name. He was on the warpath: wanted to give my backside a good tanning by all accounts!'

A giggle bubbled out of Harriet. 'I'm not really surprised. You were very loud!'

'Oh no! What on earth did I do?'

Harriet stared at Philippe. 'You don't remember?'

'D'you really think I would ask you if I remembered? Come on, please, put me out of my misery.'

'All I can say is that you broke your promise; your voice is every bit as terrible as you said it was, and would give Sophie's a run for her money.'

'I didn't, did I?'

'Yup! About three songs, a couple of them with the actions, so Jo told me. You even made a champagne glass into a rather too effective microphone.'

Philippe hung his head. 'I'm mortified, particularly after watching Sophie's performance the other night!'

As they reached a bend in the path, Harriet's foot slipped on a loose rock. She stumbled as she tried to regain her balance. Just before she hit the ground, Philippe's arms came around her and pulled her upright.

'Thank you.' Harriet's pulse had quickened, and it wasn't just due to her near miss.

Moments passed and Philippe's arms stayed around her. Harriet twisted around so she was facing him. Her arms slid around his neck. One of her hands stroked his face, the other tangled in his hair.

All thoughts of Philippe's karaoke the night before, of Greg and Toby, and of her aborting their potential night of passion, went clean out of her head. Somewhere in the background, Harriet heard and ignored the sound of pounding feet coming closer. All she cared about was Philippe's head bent to hers, their lips meeting, their bodies close and —

'HARRI! PHILIPPE! COME QUICKLY! THERE'S BEEN AN ACCIDENT! DAD'S HURT AND oh . . .'

Philippe and Harriet quickly pulled apart, but not quick enough. Toby stood, panting from his fast dash up the path, a look of confusion written across his face.

Toby fixed them both with his enquiring eyes. He cocked his head on one side. 'Are you two boyfriend and girlfriend?'

Both of them shook their heads.

'But you were kissing?'

'Harriet was feeling sad, so I kissed her to cheer her up,' Philippe explained, crossing his fingers behind his back.

'Oh. Okay. Because Harriet needs to be my mum again so dad and her can be boyfriend and girlfriend and get married, otherwise we can't be a proper family, you see.'

A stunned silence fell onto their little group. In one sentence, Toby had covered them from head to toe in a heavy mantel: a mantel that forbade any further relationship between them.

It was Harriet who managed to speak first. She shook herself out of the shocked reverie that Toby's statement had put her into. 'Right Toby, let's go and rescue your dad.'

Philippe hesitated.

'Come on Philippe, we might need you,' Toby called as he careered at high speed back down the path.

It was only as Toby ran past her that Harriet noticed his elbows. They were scuffed and bleeding. Greg must have come a cropper with Toby still on his back. She sighed. Typical Greg! His only thought had been to prove his manliness compared to Philippe; Toby's safety had come way down his list of priorities.

As Harriet turned to follow Toby, she saw Philippe standing stationary, unsure whether or not to join them.

'We might need your strength.' Harriet was hardly able to look him in the eyes. Too much had been said, and yet not nearly enough. They were both flailing around in uncertainty as if the last few minutes had tumbled them into uncharted territory.

They heard Greg's moans before they saw him. His leg was twisted awkwardly beneath him and any colour that had previously graced his face had been white-washed with pain.

'We need to get him up,' Toby said, hooking his arms under his dad's shoulders.

'No, don't move him. We might damage one of his bones.'

'Oh! How d'you know that?' Even the trauma of his dad's accident didn't stop Toby's enquiring mind from wanting to know everything about everything.

'Playing tennis.'

Toby frowned.

'You wouldn't think it was a dangerous game, but I've seen some nasty injuries.'

'Harriet, my mobile's back in England. Can I use yours?'

Harriet shook her head. 'Mine's in a bin somewhere in Zürich.' It was uncanny how their lives mirrored each other's: both running away, both trying to sort out where their lives were going, both without their mobiles. Wasn't that serendipity?

Philippe raised an enquiring eyebrow.

'Well, that's a bloody stupid place for it. No wonder I couldn't contact you. I left hundreds of messages.' Greg's words were strained as he fought with the pain that was consuming him.

'Dad's got a mobile,' Toby piped up. 'Haven't you, Dad?'

Oh yes, Greg's notorious mobile. Harriet used to call it "his extra limb" the amount of time he spent glued to its damn screen.

Greg patted his left trouser pocket. 'Could you?' he asked, his eyes pleading with Harriet.

Harriet slipped her hand into Greg's pocket, feeling disturbed by the intimacy of this act. She grasped his phone and pulled it from his pocket before handing it to Philippe.

'Password?' Philippe demanded.

'"Harriet".' Greg lowered his head.

Harriet stared in astonishment. Her name as his password? Really? So he must still have feelings for her? It wasn't just another ruse to lure her back as his unpaid housekeeper and child minder.

Philippe raised an eyebrow as he tapped Harriet's name into the phone. 'There's no signal. Not one bar.'

After moving up and down the mountain by a few metres to see if he could get any reception, he strode back to where the three of them were huddled. 'Right, you two stay here with Greg, I'll find the nearest house with a phone.' And with that, he set off down the mountain, as fast as his aching leg would allow.

Well over an hour later, the helicopter whirred its way into the sky, with Greg safely installed inside, prone on a stretcher, his leg in a temporary splint.

Toby watched the tiny orange blob way up in the sky. It looked more like a bright beetle than an emergency rescue helicopter. 'How cool was that?'

'That was a very cool helicopter,' Harriet agreed.

'I wish I could have gone with dad. I wouldn't have been any trouble. It would have been SO awesome. I could've told all my friends.'

'Well, we'll have to commiserate over some ice cream.' Harriet suggested.

'Commiserate is the word.' Philippe shot Harriet a knowing look.

'You saved him. You got down that mountain double-fast!'

Toby slipped his hand into Philippe's. 'You'll come with us? For ice cream?'

A tiny grin lifted the corners of Philippe's mouth. 'You try and stop me.'

Philippe smiled, first at Toby, then at Harriet. 'Although I bet I can eat more scoops than you.'

'No way, he can't, can he Harriet? I am the supremest ice-cream-eater in the whole of Wengen, no actually, in the whole of the wide world!'

'Yes, you really are.' Harriet nodded. 'His nickname is "Toby Tub-Tastic" because of the number of ice cream tubs he can consume in one sitting.'

'Yeah, you see if you can beat that!' Toby laughed. He started to pull both Harriet and Philippe down the mountain path, thoughts of copious quantities of ice cream already replacing his excitement about the helicopter and his concerns about his father's leg.

Chapter 20

Philippe was startled awake by a loud banging on the door. He was disoriented for a few seconds, having been jolted from a, for once, deep sleep. His eyes felt heavy. The knocking persisted. With a loud yawn, he sat upright.

'Come in,' he called, thinking it must be room service with his breakfast.

'I can't!' A high-pitched voice yelled at him, somewhat muffled through the wooden door.

Philippe cleared the distance between his bedroom and the door of his suite in a matter of strides. As soon as he opened the door, a flash of bright blue flew into the lounge, his brown curls dancing with the momentum.

'Guess what?'

'What?' Philippe glanced at the clock on his wall. 'Toby, it's 7am. What are you doing up so early? And more to the point, what are you doing *here* so early?'

'I had to show you. Look! Herr Tanner gave me *this*.' Toby pulled a tennis racket out from behind his back. 'Tada! It was his daughter's when she was my age and he said I could use it while I'm here, which means we can play tennis or you can teach me anyway.'

'And that couldn't wait until 9am?'

'No way! That would have been two whole hours.'

Philippe smiled at Toby as his words tumbled out, falling over each other to be heard. 'Do you ever pause for breath?'

In the middle of thrashing the racket from side to side, Toby looked up and giggled. 'Not really. I don't have time!'

Another loud rap on the door caught Toby's attention. He rushed over and opened it. 'It's Harriet. She's brought us breakfast.' Toby placed his treasured racket onto a side table, and then gambolled over to the terrace door. 'Let's sit out here.'

By the stunned look on Philippe's face, Harriet knew that "Toby Whirlwind" had had enough time to cyclone through his suite.

Harriet had done her best to stop him from disturbing Philippe quite so early, but then again, she had managed to restrain him a full hour before finally giving in. 6am would have been too antisocial for words.

As they tucked into puffy croissants and French bread smothered in thick strawberry jam, Toby fired questions at Philippe about tennis and how you played it and how you could win and what it felt like to win. When finally, he came up for air, Harriet suggested he wash his hands and fetch himself some more juice from the fridge. He had already drunk everything in the jug, purportedly for the three of them.

'So how, may I ask, did you know I have juice in my fridge?'

'Because I gave Becky the cartons yesterday to re-stock it for you, so unless you've been thirsty enough to drink six cartons, I figured there'd be enough left in there for Toby.'

'Ah.'

'Did you think I'd been spying on you?'

'With a few of the journalists still sniffing around, I'm finding it hard to trust anyone,' Philippe answered.

'Are you saying you don't trust me?'

Philippe watched Harriet's face fall.

'It's not you, Harriet. It's, well it's Lauren and it's the paparazzi and—'

'But I'm nothing like Lauren!'

'I know. I know, but isn't it similar to you thinking I'm going to betray you like Greg?'

'I don't know.' It was all too much to think about.

Toby chose that moment to hurtle back into the room.

'Go on then. Get dressed. I'm ready to go.'

Both Harriet and Philippe burst out laughing. Toby had found a sweat band. He was wearing it around his head like John McEnroe. On the rare occasions when Harriet hadn't been around to chaperone him, Greg had reluctantly agreed that he could watch some old Wimbledon footage with him, as long as he didn't speak. John McEnroe had featured regularly.

By 8.30am, the three of them had made their way to the courts. Herr Tanner had sorted out the formalities the day before and lent Philippe his own racket. 'Not up to the standard you're used to, but it's all I've got, so it will have to do. And by the way,' Herr Tanner cleared his throat, 'best leave off the karaoke for the time being. Not sure the old folk here can cope with it.'

Herr Tanner had then waved away Philippe's profuse apologies.

The court loomed in front of Philippe. He took a deep breath. He closed his eyes. He hadn't even stepped onto a court since his accident. A layer of sweat beaded on his forehead.

How was it that no-one else had managed to get him even close to playing tennis for all these months, and yet a seven-year-old boy, who he had known for less than a day, had somehow made him promise to teach him tennis?

'You'll be fine,' Harriet placed her hand on his arm and squeezed.

The warmth of Harriet's hand shot right up his arm. He ran his eyes up and down the length of her. She was wearing a pale blue summer dress with the waist cinched in by a yellow belt. A slight breeze ruffled her hair. She kept trying to tuck it behind her ears. Adorable, that's what she was.

'Come on!' Toby shouted. 'I'm waitinggggg.'

Why was it that his leg quivered at the thought of stepping back into the limelight? Okay, so this might only be a couple of amateur courts high up in the Swiss mountains, hardly high spec', but to him, each court had meant fierce competition, against himself and against his opponents. It had meant winning. It had meant impressing. If he played now and failed, would that be his enduring memory of the sport?

At least it was still early; there were less people around to witness his fall from grace. He watched Toby jumping around, swinging his racket to and fro. Okay, so he was behaving like a first-class idiot. This was an hour of his time teaching a seven-year-old boy the basics of tennis. Why had it suddenly become all about him? Was there no end to the size of his ego?

'Come on then, Toby. Let me show you how this is done.'

Toby squealed with excitement. Harriet sat down beside the court. She watched as Philippe bent over Toby, as he explained how to hold the racket, showed him how to swing it back and forth and where to put his feet.

It took several attempts before Toby finally managed to hit the tennis ball over the net. 'Hurrah!' he shouted, jumping up and down.

For the next hour, Philippe alternated ends. One moment he was sending the ball back over the net to Toby, the next he was by Toby's side demonstrating how Toby could improve his game. Each time Toby played a good shot, he looked over at Harriet, craving her approval. Harriet clapped and gave him the thumbs up.

At the end of the session, Philippe solemnly held out his hand to Toby. 'Great game!'

Toby shook his hand and then high-fived him. 'I loved it! Can we do it again tomorrow?'

'I don't see why not.' Philippe smiled.

Life constantly surprised him. This lesson, which he had dreaded ever since Toby mentioned it, had actually been fun. He had been concentrating so hard on helping Toby, he hadn't had time to feel self-conscious or to worry about his leg or to feel a failure. In fact, quite the reverse. He felt on a real high from being able to, hopefully, be instrumental in kick-starting Toby's love of tennis.

Just as they were about to walk off the court, Elspeth arrived.

'Elspeth, look! Look at me!'

Elspeth waved to Toby. She watched as Philippe and Toby hit a few balls back and forwards over the net for her benefit.

'Can I have your autograph now?' Elspeth asked, 'so when you're famous, I can sell it and make loads of money!'

'Only if you take me for an ice cream,' Toby replied. 'I think Philippe needs to rest. I was very hard on him!'

'Is that okay?' Elspeth asked. 'I'll bring him back to the hotel by about, what mid-day?'

Harriet caught Philippe's eye. She quickly averted her gaze and focused on Toby.

'Yes please because we're going to see dad in hospital this afternoon, aren't we, Harri? He's got his leg in plaster and it's going to be so cool. I'm going to sign it, aren't I, Harri?'

Philippe's face dropped.

'Yes Toby, we are. It'll be fun.'

When Elspeth and Toby left, Philippe glanced at Harriet. 'Fancy a coffee?'

'I would love a coffee. How about The Berg?'

Philippe picked up Herr Tanner's racket. He turned to Harriet. 'Lead the way!'

It wasn't until they were settled on The Berg's raised roof terrace that either of them spoke.

'That was lovely of you. Thank you so much. Toby had a brilliant time.' Harriet hesitated. 'Was it okay for you? You know, with your—'

'D'you know, I really enjoyed myself. I might even take up coaching when I get back to England. Give something back to the sport.' Philippe smiled.

'That's wonderful.' Harriet tried to focus on the range of mountain peaks opposite, but her eyes were drawn back, time and time again, to Philippe.

A young waitress, with her blond hair curled around her face, gave Philippe a flirty smile. 'Shall I pour your coffee?'

'No, thank you, I'll pour.' Harriet's eyes narrowed. Would this adoration from the female species never cease? She wasn't naturally jealous, or hadn't been before she'd met Philippe, but this, this was too much!

The waitress flounced off. A clear pattern seemed to be emerging here.

Philippe could not help giving Harriet a cheeky grin.

'Well, how rude! In front of me. Am I invisible?' Harriet asked.

'Not to me, Harriet. Quite the opposite.' Philippe laced his fingers around Harriet's and raised them to his lips. 'I would say,' he continued, as he kissed each of her fingers in turn, 'you are quite delectable.'

'Oh, I bet you say that to all the girls.' Harriet tried to pull her hand away.

He fixed her with his heavily-lashed grey eyes. She was left in no doubt about his feelings for her as they shone transparently out of them.

Harriet closed her eyes to cut off the connection. 'Philippe, I can't. What about Toby? What about his dream?'

'What about Greg? D'you love him?' Philippe asked, still holding fast to her hand, massaging her palm with his thumb.

That wasn't the point: whether or not she loved Greg. Toby was the point. The image of Toby pleading with her as he described his dream of them being a proper family flashed into her mind. She could not destroy his dream. It took every ounce of self-control to push Philippe away.

'Why d'you keep pouncing on me?' She yanked her hand away from his.

A wave of hurt clouded his eyes. 'What? You're making me out to be some kind of letch? You haven't exactly been unwilling.'

'What about the other night when I practically carried you back to your room? You jumped on me before I had time to think.'

'Oh no. I didn't . . . I didn't force myself on you, did I? I could never forgive myself if—'

Seeing the horror written across his face, Harriet relented. She wanted to put him off her, not scar him for life. 'It wasn't that bad. I-I-I just changed my mind. You were drunk and—'

'So I didn't—?'

'No, no you didn't. I pushed you off.'

'Oh my God.'

'No, it's fine, honestly, we were fully dressed.'

'Harriet, I'm so sorry. Truly. That's why I never get drunk. Well, normally.'

Harriet could feel herself weakening. She could not bear to put him through any more pain. He had been through so much already. Her resolve, such as it was, was melting faster than an ice-cube in the Sahara dessert.

Before either of them knew what was happening, Harriet was in Philippe's arms and they were kissing passionately.

There were a few disapproving tuts from a couple of aged walkers sitting on the surrounding tables, but neither Harriet nor Philippe noticed. They were making up for lost time.

After what seemed like an eternity, but in reality, wasn't long enough, they pulled apart, each flushed with the passion that had flared between them.

'We may need some more coffee.' Harriet chuckled. 'It's stone cold.'

'You've warmed me up far more than coffee,' Philippe said. 'Sorry, I know that was cheesy, but I couldn't resist!'

Philippe ran his hand over her hair, cupping her face. 'You really are gorgeous.'

'You're not so bad yourself.' Harriet grinned. A warm glow burned inside her. She knew it was corny, but she felt as if she had come home.

'What next?'

'I'm afraid that next I need to nip to the gents. As unsociable as that is.'

'Well, you sure know how to pour cold water onto passion.' Harriet smiled.

'I'll be back before you know it.' Philippe leaned over and kissed her lips, then kissed her again. It was five minutes before he finally left her side.

'Don't go anywhere,' he said.

'As if!' Harriet grinned up at him. 'I'll order us more coffee.'

While Harriet waited for the sullen waitress to bring another pot of coffee, she noticed a British newspaper lying on the table next to her. Smoothing it out in front of her she opened the first page. A gasp escaped her lips. She could not believe her eyes. He had promised her. And she, like a fool, had believed him. Well not anymore.

Harriet slung her bag over her shoulder and stormed down the two flights of steps, and out onto the road. There was only one thing for it. She knew what she had to do, and she had to do it fast.

Having got waylaid by the Maître D' of the hotel, who tentatively asked him some questions about his former life in the world of tennis, it was almost ten minutes before Philippe returned to their table. He was itching with impatience to see Harriet. Finally, there seemed to have been a breakthrough. Harriet's wall of protection had slipped, and now all he wanted was to be with her.

Denial was a funny thing. When he arrived back at the table to find Harriet wasn't there, he looked around the other tables, wondering if he had mistaken where they were sitting. No, his jacket was still hanging over the back of the seat. This was definitely it.

Maybe she'd visited the ladies or perhaps she had got fed up with waiting for him. He had certainly been gone a lot longer than he had expected. Lauren would never have tolerated being left alone for that long.

Philippe sat back down on his chair where he had a clear view of the other guests. There were a few staff from the Neueranfang Hotel who he recognised, all enjoying the luxury of a few hours off. One of the chambermaids gave him a shy wave, then blushed a deep red and looked away. She needn't have worried; Philippe's mind was trained solely on Harriet.

Where could she have got to? Philippe tapped his fingers impatiently against the table top. He pulled the newspaper towards him, intending to flick through the pages to kill the time before Harriet re-joined him. Immediately his eyes alighted on the full-sized photo splashed across the page in front of him.

'Shit! And double shit!'

Philippe shoved back his chair. He grabbed his jacket and the racket. He ran across the terrace and down the same steps that Harriet had raced down 15 or so minutes before.

It hadn't taken Harriet long to track down Elspeth and Toby. They were, of course, hidden away in Elspeth's Der Hausenbaum. She whispered urgently in Elspeth's ear and together they dragged a loudly-protesting Toby away from his ice cream and back to the Neueranfang Hotel.

Harriet's nerves were already torn into tiny, jagged pieces. She did not know how she found the courage to tell Frau Tanner, face to face, that she was leaving without giving even an hour's notice, let alone the required four weeks.

Frau Tanner was understandably furious. Harriet was leaving her completely and utterly in the lurch. But Harriet knew that it was either her or Philippe, and there was no way she could ask Frau Tanner to boot out a guest.

Harriet told Frau Tanner not to pay her, that she would return all her money. And that was when Elspeth stepped in.

'Frau Tanner, I know a lovely young lady who lives in Zürich. Last I heard, she was bored out of her mind. If you'll allow me, I'll make a quick call to see if she can help you out.'

'Well, that would certainly be very kind,' Frau Tanner said. 'Not that it won't take her a while to get up to speed.'

Harriet hated letting people down, but at this moment in time, it really was the lesser of two evils.

Once Harriet had thrown a few essentials into a bag for her and Toby, and had given her notice to Frau Tanner, Elspeth hugged Harriet hard. Elspeth told her to keep in touch.

Just before they left, Toby dashed to the kitchen to get a glass of water. Elspeth questioned Harriet as to whether she was doing the right thing. She asked her whether she could have been mistaken and whether she shouldn't at least give Philippe the chance to explain.

'A chance to lie more like,' Harriet retorted. 'No, he's had enough chances. Every man in my life has had more than enough chances.'

'So you're going back to Greg?' Elspeth raised an eyebrow.

'That's different. He has Toby.' As Harriet said the words, she knew it wasn't different. In some respects, Greg was worse. He had proved that he was untrustworthy, whereas Philippe? Well, he *was* the same. Photos never lied, did they?

Toby bounced back into the reception area. 'Will you visit us in England, Elspeth?'

'You try and stop me!'

'But do you have our address?'

'I have all your details, so there's no escaping me, even if you hide really well.'

Toby giggled. He pounced on Elspeth and cuddled her. 'You are like my granny. I don't have any grannies because they all died.'

Tears glistened in Elspeth's eyes. 'That's official then. I'm adopting you as my grandson.'

'Yay!'

Elspeth watched Toby and Harriet climb into the hotel's wagon. She watched until they had disappeared around the corner. Toby's squeals of excitement could still be heard, even when his waving hand vanished out of sight.

Toby's eyes glittered as they reached the station. 'Are we going to stay in a big hotel, Harri? Are we going to see dad in the hospital? Will we be a proper family again? Will you let me see Elspeth when she comes to visit you because I'm her grandson now?'

Harriet heaved the strap of her bag across her shoulders. She tried to smile, but her mouth would not cooperate. Her heart was still beating rapidly against her chest, no matter how many deep breaths she took.

'Look, here's the train.' Harriet took Toby's hand and showed their tickets to the Ticket Inspector.

At least now she wouldn't have to dodge the onslaught of impossible-to-answer questions. She knew that Toby would be distracted by a dozen other excitements the moment they stepped through the door of the train. Although her major relief was to get on the train before Philippe found them. She could not bear to even look at him, let alone risk him charming her all over again. That was her problem, she was a sucker for being romanced and could not spot a bastard even when they were an inch away from her nose.

As the train pulled away from Wengen station, a lump formed in Harriet's throat. Tears prickled her eyes.

'Are you crying again, Harri?' Toby patted her knee with his hand.

'Just dust.' Harriet ran her hand over her eyes.

'How long till we see dad? I can't wait!'

Harriet allowed Toby's chatter to wash over her. How different from her journey here when she was filled with a mixture of trepidation and hope. At the time, she had been missing Toby like crazy, had been grieving for her mother and unable to come to terms with Greg's betrayal. Life had weighed her down like an anchor.

Now she had a broken heart to add to that list. If only she had never met Philippe Myers or Philip Smith, or whoever the hell he was.

Chapter 21

By the time Philippe reached the hotel, he was out of breath. He careered into reception, panting hard.

'Herr Smith, is everything okay?' Karina asked in her clipped tones.

'No! No everything is far from alright!'

'Shall I get Herr Tanner for you?'

As if a soundless bell had alerted him, Herr Tanner strode out of the back office. 'Karina. What is happening here?'

'No more Karaoke I hope?' Herr Tanner, unusually, risked a small joke with Herr Smith, who was normally quite amenable to a little banter.

'Where's Harriet? I have to find Harriet.'

'Harriet?' Herr Tanner looked blank. 'Should I know this *Harriet*?'

Karina raised her eyebrows. Men were so dense. 'Herr Tanner, I think Herr Smith is talking about Harriet, your waitress.'

'Oh. I see. Well,' Herr Tanner cleared his throat, trying to preserve the unreadable and unshakable posture that a Swiss Hotelier was expected to maintain.

'Herr Tanner?' Karina prompted as she watched Herr Smith pace up and down the reception like a caged lion.

'Sorry, Herr Smith. No, I don't believe I have. Not since early this morning. Shall I help you look for her?'

'Yes, you search the hotel. I'll try her room.' Philippe watched Herr Tanner's disapproval cloud his face. 'Or maybe you could try her room and I'll start with the hotel?'

Herr Tanner and Philippe set off in different directions. Ten minutes later, they returned to the reception. Herr Tanner shook his head.

'Damn! Where the hell is she?'

'Karina, please fetch Herr Smith a coffee – we'll be in the lounge.'

Philippe started to protest. Every minute he spent chatting to Herr Tanner was time lost searching for Harriet. He couldn't bear her thinking the worst of him. Again. It had taken long enough to try and re-gain her trust.

Unless he was overreacting. Maybe she had had to leave The Berg for some other reason. Maybe Toby came looking for her and she didn't have time to pass on a message.

The large photograph of him and Lauren kissing in this very lounge was imprinted on his mind for posterity. No, it was too much of a coincidence. The newspaper left wide open on that page on their table at precisely the moment Harriet had vanished. And she had every right to be angry. Who wouldn't have misconstrued the photo when the evidence was right there in black and white in front of them?

He had told Lauren he would sue the pants off the reporters if they ever printed that photo. But what did he expect? He had put himself in the limelight. It wasn't their fault that Lauren had set him up. And to be honest, he didn't have the energy to throw himself into a law suit. He had more than enough to challenge him as it was.

'She can't have gone far,' Herr Tanner reassured him. 'You know what these women are like. She has probably gone shopping!'

Philippe grinned. If only it was that simple.

'Sugar?' Herr Tanner asked, poised with a spoonful of sugar hovering over Philippe's cup.

'Two, please.' Philippe watched the cream swirling around the black coffee.

Over half an hour elapsed before Philippe managed to extract himself from Herr Tanner's company. For once, the reserved Swiss Hotelier was on a roll. He told him about his ancestors and how they had built the hotel. He explained about the rules and regulations, which governed the industry. He spoke about his Irish wife, Frau Tanner, and how he had met her on holiday in what he described as "the country that serves pints of Guinness and has terrible signposts".

As Herr Tanner talked, Philippe fidgeted about on his seat. He kept searching for a suitable point during Herr Tanner's monologue to interrupt him. Eventually, Herr Tanner paused for breath.

Philippe made his excuses, and was up and out of the lounge before Herr Tanner could object.

Philippe was just walking through reception when Karina called him over. 'Frau Tanner knows where Harriet is,' she told him, without any preamble or niceties.

'Where is she?'

'Frau Tanner has returned to her house. She should not be long. She had something important to organise.'

Philippe's fists curled into balls. His muscles tensed around his shoulders and his neck.

Instead of pacing up and down, he decided to take some decisive action. He strode up the path towards the pool in case Harriet had decided to take Toby swimming. Given today was another scorcher, Philippe was hopeful he would find them there.

Disappointment flooded through him as his eyes scanned the poolside. It was unusually quiet. A couple of old ladies swam up and down the pool, their matching green caps decorated with yellow and white flowers. Along the side, various teenagers and couples in their early twenties read books, listened to music and sipped water to keep hydrated. Nowhere in sight was a child of around seven years old or a beautiful blond answering to the name of Harriet.

Philippe swore. He was about to leave when Becky tapped him on the shoulder. 'Coming in for a dip?' she asked. 'Now that your shadow has found a new home.'

'What are you talking about?' Philippe glared at her.

'Well, if you're going to be rude, then I don't believe I will tell you anything,' Becky moved on past him, eyeing up a young man stretched out on his towel on her way past.

Philippe grabbed her arm. 'Wait! Look, I'm sorry. Can you please tell me where I can find Harriet?'

Becky turned on him. 'It serves you right, Mr Myers. Why should you get a bloody happy ending with your girl next door? None of us do! Freddie hasn't called me once since he dropped me off in this dead-end place. He's a complete bastard!'

It was unclear whether Becky herself was more astonished by her outburst, or Philippe.

All at once, the shutters slammed down; Becky's face became unreadable. She poked Philippe in the chest with one of her talons. 'Harriet, it seems, doesn't want to be found. By you.'

· 'What the hell d'you mean?' Philippe's rag was almost at the end of its tether, and now this brash American was playing games with him.

'What I mean is she's gone, and I don't think you'll find a forwarding address.'

'Gone?' Philippe repeated.

'Well if you really run, you might catch them before they get on the train.'

The last few words were barely out of Becky's mouth before Philippe set off at a run towards the station.

'Shit and double shit!' His feet pounded on the pavement. His leg throbbed. He ignored it. His sole focus was reaching the station before Harriet, to stop her from getting on that train.

He heard the guard's whistle as he rounded the corner. Using every ounce of energy that he had left, he forged on towards the platform, willing the train to be delayed, if only by a few seconds. As he flew towards the platform, he watched helplessly as the train pulled away, picking up speed as it wound its way around the corner and out of sight.

Bent double, his hands on his legs, his breath coming out in gasps, Philippe's mind whirred frantically trying to think of how he could get down the mountain to cut her off at the next stop. But he knew it was hopeless. If he had been anywhere else apart from this infernal village, he could have hailed a taxi or flagged down a motorist, but here, in this remote area, the only way up and down the mountain was the funicular railway or the two legs he stood up on. And even without his dodgy left leg, there was no way he would make it down to Lauterbrunnen station on foot until Harriet was long gone.

Once the ticket collector had confirmed that the next train wasn't due for another 30 minutes, Philippe limped his way back to the hotel. He slammed the door of his suite and threw himself onto the sofa. Well, that was it. They were over: over before they'd barely begun. And it sucked.

The bees buzzed rhythmically as they lapped the nectar from the mass of wild flowers carpeting the grass behind Harriet. Their melodic tune was interrupted only by the odd yap of a dog bounding its way through the meadow, interspersed with loud splashes as it crashed in and out of the lake.

Today the water was emerald green, the day before it had shone a startling blue. Tiny ripples stroked the surface. Light particles from the sun high above danced and played. It never ceased to astonish her how one lake could change so dramatically from morning to evening and from day to day.

If only her insides were quite as serene as the scene before her. She rested her head on her hands. It had been a week since she had left Wengen. In some ways, her time working at Hotel Neueranfang seemed like a dream; it was only her memories of Philippe that made it real. Philippe, who interlaced her dreams, who invaded her every waking thought.

Even when Greg left it hadn't been like this. With Greg's departure, she had been consumed with a burning fury, which was tempered only by the enormity of her mother's cancer.

In contrast, Philippe had left a gaping hole, which ached more with every passing day. If it hadn't been for Toby, the pain would have been unbearable. Being with Toby stopped her resolve from weakening. It would've been so easy to get on the train from Interlaken and head straight back into Philippe's arms, that is, if Lauren hadn't already taken up residence there.

The thought of that over-made-up Barbie getting her claws into Philippe made her blood boil. Although, if she stopped to think about it logically, they deserved each other. She should simply move on with her life and leave Philippe to take up his plastic position as Ken to Lauren's Barbie. That thought made her chuckle, which surprised her. Laughter had been a long way from her mouth over the last few days.

'There you are, Harri. I've been looking for you!' Toby appeared with Giselle not far behind. The 16-year-old had adopted Toby, and from the moment they unpacked their meagre possessions in a small hotel in Interlaken, they had become inseparable.

Apart from taking Toby to see Greg each day and having dinner with him in the evening, Harriet had been granted some much-needed time to herself. If only that fateful morning at The Berg wasn't set on 'repeat' in her memory.

'Guess what?' Toby was jumping up and down.

'What?' Harriet smiled up at Giselle, who grinned back.

'We counted six different birds and we saw loads of little fish. I think there were about 30 or 40, weren't there, Giselle? And then a very wet dog jumped up at me. Look!' Toby held out his T-shirt. It did have extremely muddy patches covering the front of it. The formerly damp marks, however, had been evaporated by the sun within minutes.

'Harri, guess what? Giselle said she would take me out on a boat with her dad today if I am very careful and if I wear a life jacket. D'you think dad would mind if I saw him tomorrow instead?'

Harriet hesitated. She couldn't ever quite rid herself of the image branded into her brain of the time Toby nearly drowned in a lake when he was tiny. She knew she mustn't let her fears clip Toby's enthusiastic wings, but it wasn't easy.

It also meant that she would have to visit Greg on her own. However, all things considered, including the words "life jacket" and a responsible, experienced adult accompanying them, she couldn't deny Toby such an exciting adventure. 'Of course, Toby. You go. Anyway, we're taking dad home tomorrow so you'll be able to see him all the time.'

'Hurrah! Thank you, Harri.' Harriet was bowled onto her back as Toby launched himself at her, giving her the biggest hug. As she held him tightly to her, she reminded herself that Toby was her priority now. Toby needed her. Toby would not let her down.

The question she tried not to ask herself was whether or not she would be able to fulfil Toby's dream: whether she was willing to give Greg a second chance.

An hour later, Harriet arrived at the hospital. She knew the route to Greg's ward by heart. Everywhere was bright and clean and smelled of efficiency and cleanliness. The building was so luxurious there were moments when she imagined she was in a five-star hotel. What a difference a large budget made. The comparison to hospitals she had passed through in England was a bit like the before and after photos on programmes where run down properties were given a makeover. She knew it wasn't very patriotic to feel so judgemental, but there it was. Although, to be fair, at least the National Health Service in the UK was free. Goodness knows what the Swiss paid for this level of luxury.

Greg walked towards her on his crutches. His scowl was deeply entrenched. He had been made to stay until the physiotherapists were happy that he could move himself around safely, without assistance. Needless to say, he was not amused by being holed up in the ward all this time. Patience was not one of his redeeming features. Come to think of it, what redeeming features did he have?

Harriet shook away her negativity and fixed a smile onto her face. 'How are you doing today?'

'How d'you think?' Greg lowered himself onto a chair.

'You're doing great with the crutches,' Harriet tried.

'That's alright for you to say when you can stride in here on your own two feet.'

If he was anyone else, Harriet would've told him where he could stick his darned crutches. But he came with Toby, so instead, she took some deep, if shaky, breaths.

'So where's Toby?' Greg's eyes searched behind her.

'Giselle's taken him on her dad's boat and —'

'What? You let a 16-year-old take a seven-year-old on a boat? Are you insane? How irresponsible can you get? And you think you're up to being a mother?'

Harriet tried counting to ten. She tried biting her lip very hard, but was a wimp with pain so stopped as soon as it started hurting.

213

She tried distracting herself by watching a nurse chatting to a family outside the room.

'WELL?' Greg's face was puce with fury.

Who the hell did he think he was? He was acting as though she had physically shoved Toby in a bag, weighted it down with boulders and thrown it into the lake herself.

'CAN YOU HEAR ME?'

That was one prod too many. Harriet's eyes flared as she whipped around to face him. Her voice was low and dangerous.

'How *dare* you speak to me like that? I love Toby. Do you hear me? I *love* him. And I wouldn't do anything, not *anything* to hurt him. And if you think that I'm going to let you treat me like a piece of dirt, then you are very much mistaken. It's your choice Greg. You carry on like that, and I'll walk out of that door and you'll never see me again.'

'Y-y-you wouldn't.'

'You just watch me!' Harriet picked up her bag and headed for the door.

'Harriet, wait!'

Harriet tossed him a look over her shoulder.

'Please.' Greg put his head in his hands.

Harriet moved back into the room. She perched on the edge of the guest chair, surveying him coldly.

Greg arranged his face into what he imagined must be regret. 'Harri, I'm so very sorry. I-I don't know what's got into me. The accident and the pain and well, I just lost it. It was wrong of me to take it out on you.' Greg reached over and touched her hand. 'Can you ever forgive me?'

Chapter 22

The first thing Harriet noticed when she stepped out of the taxi was the cold air. It had been so hot in Wengen she had almost forgotten that British summers weren't as predictable. Pulling her jacket tightly around her shoulders, she paid the driver and lugged her suitcase up to her front door.

'Harriet, you're back! Have you been on holiday?' A cheeky face peered at her through her over-long fringe. Alice was the seven-year-old who lived next door.

'Sort of,' Harriet said.

'And did you fly in a plane?'

'Alice, leave Harriet alone. The poor woman hasn't even got in through her front door yet!' Beth smiled at Harriet over Alice's head.

'But Mummmmm!' Alice protested.

'No "but mums" young lady, we've got to get you to school.'

Beth turned to Harriet. 'We've kept an eye on the place. It all seems to be as you left it.' A look of guilt flashed across Beth's face. 'And, well, I owe you an apology. Greg turned up with Toby a couple of weeks ago. He said it was an emergency. That they had to get hold of you. Toby begged me to tell him where you were. He said his heart was broken.'

'It's okay, really. It's been amazing to see Toby again.'

'You're not the only one who was thrilled to see him - Alice didn't stop talking about him for days afterwards. I'm surprised Greg managed to drag those two apart after I'd given him your details.'

'Thank you so much for keeping an eye on the house. We must get together for a coffee. I'll fill you in on all the gossip!'

'Yes, like why you returned my bikini to me!' Beth grinned. 'And why you're back so early . . .'

'It's a very long story,' Harriet told her.

'Fortunately, I'm a very good listener.' Beth took Harriet's hand and gave it a squeeze.

'Mum! We've got to go now. We'll be late!'

Beth called goodbye to Harriet who smiled as Alice dragged her by the arm in the direction of school. She had spotted one of her friends a few yards ahead. Harriet was now a distant memory and certainly no longer worth delaying for.

Harriet remembered her excitement the day she moved into her home. It was bright and modern and it was all hers. Her mum had been so proud of her. They had celebrated with takeaway fish and chips eaten out of the newspaper, leaning on piles of packing boxes. She had worked hard to raise the deposit.

When Greg came along and swept her off her feet, she had insisted on keeping her own house, much to his annoyance. He had imagined the size of house they could have lived in if they had pooled their resources, not to mention how convenient it would have been to have a live-in babysitter. Thank God she had stuck to her guns, on that issue anyway.

The house smelt musty. It was smaller than she remembered and could do with a bit of a makeover. She ran her fingers over the sunflower stencils, which she had painted into one corner of the lounge when she first moved in. At the time, she'd been thrilled with her creativity. Now she hardly cared.

Greg and Toby had headed back to their house in Pangbourne. They had more space there so it was better for his crutches. Toby had pleaded with her to come back with them, but she had made an excuse. After the emotions of the past couple of weeks and the journey back from Switzerland, which had been fraught with delays and was excoriatingly stressful despite the Valium, she just wanted to go home.

She wanted the familiar. She wanted a bath in her own bathroom with candles and soft music. She needed time to think, to work out where her life was going and whether she wanted it to go in Greg's direction. She also wanted to lick her wounds: Philippe was never far from her mind.

As compact as it was, she had missed her home. She missed it when her mother was ill and she nursed her day and night in her mother's bungalow. She only popped back home briefly to stock up with clothes or pick up something she needed. Or to throw on some washing when her mother's machine gave up the ghost, a few weeks before her mum followed suit. And she missed it for the couple of months she had spent in Wengen.

But, compared with the pain of missing Philippe, homesickness was like a sore gum compared with the full blown toothache of loss, which consumed her daily.

To re-orientate herself, she walked into every room, looking in drawers, adjusting curtains and opening all the windows to let in some fresh, if chilly air. In the corner of her bedroom was a sack of her mother's things. She had been in the process of sorting them out when she'd broken down completely. After hours of sobbing uncontrollably, for the first time since her mother's death, she'd known she had to get away: away from work and away from Theale; away from everything and everyone. Reminders of her mum ran through the whole of Theale like veins, and combined with the memories of Toby and Greg, it had all been too much.

So this is where it had all started. Little had she known then that when she returned to Theale she would be experiencing more rather than less grief than when she had left. It was ironic really. Vivid images of Philippe with his head bent, kissing Lauren passionately, threw itself into her mind. Each time she recalled the photo in the paper, she was jolted with a blast of disbelief, betrayal and jealousy.

And to think she had actually thought he was different. She had truly believed that after a succession of bastards, she had stumbled across her knight in shining armour. The knight who was going to whisk her to the altar, make an honest woman of her and they would gallop off happily into the sunset. Okay, so that was a bit far-fetched, but she had bought into this image. As it turned out, it would be impossible for him to make her an honest woman when he himself was such a, such a . . .

Harriet walked into the kitchen, filled up the kettle and flicked on the switch. Good, at least the water was working and she had electricity. You heard so many horror stories about what happened to people's houses when they were away.

217

She reached into the fridge for some milk. Empty. Of course. Well she would just drink black coffee until she had the energy to nip around to the Co-op for some milk.

After rummaging in the cupboard, she managed to find a couple of wrapped biscuits, which weren't too far away from their "best by" date. Sinking into her sofa, she dunked one of the biscuits into her coffee, closing her eyes as the burst of melting chocolate and crumbling biscuit dissolved in her mouth. There, you see, she *could* carry on her life without him.

What she had to do now, she knew, was put Philippe right out of her mind. To shove his grey eyes and his blond hair out of the fire exit of her mind and not let him come in again, no matter how many times he knocked.

Her future was with Toby and with Greg. At least, that was her most obvious option. What she had to decide now was whether that really was the path she wanted to tread.

It was no good, she had to get some fresh air. Abandoning her now sludgy-with-biscuits half-drunk cup of coffee, she picked up her bag, checked she had her front door key and set off for the High Street.

Walking through Theale was like relaxing in a warm bath, despite how fresh the air was. She had moved here with her mum when she was five years old, not long after her dad abandoned them, leaving them with monumental debts. When she was growing up she always told people that Theale was the village where "The Borrowers" (a family of tiny people) were filmed as the "Big People" (the human family) drove down the High Street to their new house just off Englefield Road.

She had been to both the primary and secondary schools and knew a lot of the residents. And if she didn't know them personally, the chances were high that they had known her mum. It was the sort of place where shopkeepers stopped to have a chat and knew you by name. Normally she valued this aspect of village life, however today she wished was as tiny as the Borrowers. She didn't want to speak to anyone.

Talk about tempting fate! Harriet rounded a corner and bumped straight into Joyce. Joyce, who used to live next door to them before she moved onto "greater things", as she always delighted in reminding them.

'Still in the same bungalow?' Joyce would ask her mum each time they met. That was until the day her mum bit back.

'Yes, it's very homely, thanks,' her mum replied, a smile plastered on her face. 'We currently have lovely neighbours.'

That had put Joyce's nose out of joint for a good few weeks, until the next piece of compelling gossip was too good to allow resentments to spoil being able to pass on. It did, however, succeed in silencing the one-up-man-ship. From that day onward, she never again mentioned their meagre bungalow.

'I hear you've been mingling with the rich and famous?' Joyce's beady eyes probed deep into Harriet's.

'Sorry?' What was the old bat talking about?

'You, in Switzerland with that man, now what's his name? You know, that tennis player, the one who had the accident.'

Harriet shook her head. How did Joyce know about that? She hadn't spoken to anyone back home or sent a postcard or anything. News couldn't have travelled on the grapevine from Switzerland already. Could it? Or maybe Toby said something to someone in Pangbourne who knew someone in Theale, but they had only got back less than an hour ago. Surely the Bush-Telegraph out here hadn't turned supersonic in her absence?

'Ah, you can't have seen the papers today.' Joyce nodded knowingly.

'What papers, Joyce? What are you talking about?'

'The Daily Mail, Express and I might have seen something in one of the others as well. As for those broadsheets, they're more interested in real news aren't they?'

'Sorry Joyce, I've got to go. Say hello to Harold.' Harold was Joyce's long-suffering husband. He was a lovely man, if frightfully hen-pecked. There was no way she was going to give Joyce the satisfaction of breaking down in front of her or showing Mrs Chief

Gossip precisely how shocked she felt by the revelations that her face was splashed across UK newspapers.

Harriet managed to nip into the Co-op, throw one of each newspaper into her basket, and as an afterthought remembered milk and bread, without meeting anyone else she knew. That would have to do. All she wanted was to get home to find out what the vultures had written about her. She had no doubt that her source was correct; Joyce was as astute a gossip as any she had encountered.

'You're quite our little star, Harriet.' Janice grinned at the number of newspapers crowded into her basket as she bleeped them through the till. 'Everyone's been talking about you. And he is dishy. I mean, really. How did you manage to—'

'Janice, look I'm sorry, but I only got back from Switzerland an hour ago. I need a decent cup of tea and some sleep. Can we talk about this next time?'

'Sure, honey. I'm sorry. I got carried away with all the excitement. We even had a few journos in here this morning trying to get us to dish the dirt on you.'

Seeing Harriet's horrified expression, Janice quickly added that of course she hadn't said anything. 'Only that you were very friendly and that you had lived here for donkey's years. I didn't want to put my foot in it like that chap at that shop in Goring when he bad-mouthed George Michael, and was directly quoted in all the papers. Imagine having to sell him his daily after that, heh? Talk about awkward!'

Somehow Harriet managed to make it back into the sanctuary of her home with nothing more than a hurried wave across the street.

Harriet dropped everything onto the table. One by one, she pulled open the newspapers. She didn't have to look hard. Staring out of the pages were photos of her and Philippe walking through Wengen, another of them laughing outside a coffee shop, and one of them kissing on the terrace of The Berg. And in the background of that particular photo, she could just make out a newspaper on the table behind them; the very newspaper that had exploded her hopes and dreams into a million shattered pieces.

So much for her incognito escape to Switzerland. Now, not only was she more confused than ever, but the whole world knew her business.

The papers sat her mugshot side-by-side with Lauren's and compared them in minute detail. Lauren was this, whereas Harriet was that, and Lauren's background was this, and hers was - oh my God!

They had rooted around in her history and dug up tasty little morsels of dirt on her background. Details of her dad and his gambling past had been sensationalised. She could hardly bear to read further. But like a spot that itched and you couldn't stop scratching even though you knew it would make it worse, she read on and on.

By the time she had read all of the stories in all of the papers, you would be hard pressed to believe she was the same person. How she was portrayed depended on their slant and the pieces of information they chose to include and highlight. In some, she was the home-wrecking slattern who had split up Greg and his wife, leaving their little boy, who wasn't even two-years-old, motherless.

In another, she was the victim of a good-for-nothing, gambling father. The story read a bit like Cinderella where she was abandoned by her father as a child, lost her mother through cancer and then the charming Prince Philippe hiked his way fearlessly into her heart under the pink morning glow of the Jungfrau.

One of the more clichéd headings splashed across the top of the article read: 'Love Triangle – Will it be Forty-Love to Philippe?' Three rackets were held up, each with a face peering dubiously out of them: one of her, one of Lauren and one of, of Greg? Wow, he would not be happy about that. He loathed that particular photo. His company had used it in one of their brochures. At the time, she had never heard the end of it: His 'hair was too long,'; 'his shirt the wrong colour'; 'if only he'd been told it was corporate photo day,' etc, etc. And the best bit, flying between the three rackets was the ball, out of which grinned a photo of Philippe. For goodness sake!

Who made up all this crap? Did they sit behind their desks and wonder which fairy-tale to tell their hapless readers next? And how did they know all this stuff about her anyway? She felt as if Big Brother was indeed watching her, and she hadn't even applied for the stupid programme.

Oh no. Toby! If he saw these pictures or was questioned by a journalist, what would he think? The last thing she wanted was for him to be dragged into this media circus or for these articles to explode his one dream of "happily ever after". She had never had any dealings with the press before, apart from requesting advertising space when they were recruiting. And this was in a totally different league. What a God-awful mess!

For two days after Harriet left, Philippe sat at his desk, with the windows flung open, hoping for inspiration. The deadline for completion of his novel was creeping closer and closer. All the ground he had made up when his creativity had taken on a life of its own, had been lost. His creative well had effectively run dry and there was nothing, it seemed, he could do about it.

It was the last few chapters he was battling with, and according to his diary he only had just over a week before the first draft was due on his Editor, Sebastian's desk. As they always worked to tight timelines, he knew that Sebastian would throw his weight around if he missed their deadline by even one day.

Harriet was haunting him again. Every time he sat down in front of his laptop, her green eyes would stare back at him. How was a man supposed to concentrate on writing when that was all he could see in front of him?

He wondered time and time again whether he should have got on the next train and followed her. Greg had been taken to the hospital in Interlaken so it was likely that she had been heading there.

The magnetic pull to go to her had been fierce. There were three things that stopped him: one was the fact that she had clearly chosen Greg; the second was Toby; and the third was him.

He was hardly a great bet for her. The baggage he brought with him was too heavy a load to expect someone to carry, especially if you cared about that person. And Toby, he was a good kid. He deserved his "happy ever after" even if it was at the expense of Philippe's.

The "buts" drove him demented: *but* Greg was an idiot who, he was certain, wouldn't nurture and love Harriet like she deserved; *but* she didn't know that the photo with Lauren was a set-up; *but* she didn't know that the only feelings he had for Lauren now were contempt and pity; *but* she didn't know that Lauren had launched herself at him and tipped off a photographer to capture what she would have loved to have been their reunion. And speaking of Lauren, it was highly likely she had received a generous pay-out for that one photo if she had sold the rights worldwide. Not that it would be enough to keep her extravagant lifestyle going.

That's what puzzled Philippe. Why would she come after him when he was no longer a highly-paid star with countless advertising deals under his belt? Unless, ah yes, of course, she must have read all the hype about the absurdly high advance it was rumoured he had received for a three-book deal after the success of his first crime novel. *That* was why she had hunted him down. It made sense now.

Frau Tanner, when he had finally caught up with her, told him that Harriet had asked her to forward all their belongings, including Greg's and Toby's, back to England. Harriet was shipping out.

Frau Tanner, who had initially been extremely put out by being deserted mid-season, was enchanted by Stefanie, Elspeth's friend's daughter, who was apparently charming all her guests.

Elspeth! That's who he had to talk to.

Closing his laptop, he picked up his wallet and banged out of his suite. He knew exactly where Elspeth would be. Everyone knew that her one weakness was ice cream, and apparently in Der Hausenbaum's ice cream parlour, she had her very own seat. As today was one of the hottest days this summer, he felt confident that he would find her there.

He wasn't wrong. Sitting at the back of the terrace in the shade, Elspeth was tucking into what looked like double chocolate chip ice cream, covered with caramel sauce and topped with swirls of piped cream and curls of chocolate, just in case it wasn't rich enough.

'Philippe,' Elspeth greeted him. 'I wondered when you'd track me down.'

'I didn't have to try too hard.' Philippe kissed Elspeth on the cheek. He had become fond of her over the last couple of months. She was intriguing. As grandmotherly as they came, but with a wicked sense of humour and an impropriety that you would normally find in less salubrious joints than the Neueranfang Hotel. Most telling of all though, Elspeth had a good heart and wisdom, which befitted her years.

'Try some!' Elspeth scooped a generous helping of ice cream onto a spoon and offered it to Philippe. He hadn't felt like eating much over the last few days and certainly anything sweet was the last thing he wanted. But today, his stomach finally grumbled hungrily at the thought of the cool, sweet richness being offered to him.

'Mmm, that's delicious.' Philippe picked up Elspeth's coffee spoon and reached towards Elspeth's bowl for a second helping. His hand was smartly slapped away.

'I'll order you one.' Elspeth laughed at the astonishment on Philippe's face. 'I'm afraid no-one gets more than one taste of my ice cream. I'm very protective of my stash.'

'It makes you sound like a drug addict.' Philippe smiled back at her.

Elspeth groaned. 'Don't I know it! I've never taken to the strong stuff. Oh, I've smoked my fair share of dope.' She paused. 'No need to look so shocked, young man. I was young once, you know. It just happens to be rather longer ago than I'd care to remember.'

'Anyway, as I was saying. So no, I never went for booze in a big way. In fact, after a couple of glasses of Babycham, I was anyone's!'

Philippe raised an eyebrow.

The waitress took Philippe's order. She didn't seem at all fazed when he asked for a coffee and "one of those" pointing to Elspeth's rapidly melting ice cream concoction. 'Are you trying to shock me, Elspeth?'

'Sorry dear, I can't resist a little teasing! What I'm trying to say is that ice cream is my drug, just like smoking or drinking or shooting up heroine—'

'There you go again!' Philippe shook his head. 'I can see why Harriet and Toby took to you so quickly. You're a one-off Elspeth. Truly.'

'I'll take that as a compliment.'

'What amazes me is how you keep your figure so trim indulging in all that ice cream.'

News of Philippe Myers staying in Wengen had spread as quickly as a bush fire in a high wind. His previous anonymity was well and truly blown. So when a group of girls came into the café, the first thing they noticed was Philippe. They started to giggle loudly. One of them pointed to where Elspeth and Philippe were sitting.

'I think you've been spotted,' Elspeth whispered. 'Don't look now, but they're coming over.'

The girl with the wavy ginger hair fluttered her eye lashes and opened her baby blue eyes as wide as she could. Next came the pout. 'Could I, like, have your phone number? Oh!' Giggle. 'Pardon me, I meant your signature.'

A sharp voice startled the girl. 'Young lady, can't you see he's with me? It is extremely rude to encroach on our time together. If you want a piece of him, you'll have to pay up, just like I have. And you'd better have a Gold credit card because, my dear, I can assure you, he doesn't come cheap!'

Shocked gasps echoed through the girls, although none of them looked as shocked as Philippe.

Seconds later, the girls melted away, whispering loudly amongst themselves and throwing backward glances in their direction.

'There!' Elspeth brushed her hands together smugly. 'That told them.'

For once, Philippe was silenced. He could just see her words splattered across tomorrow's papers. What a headline that would make.

'From Courts to Courting – Myers now *comes* at a Cost!'

At that moment, the waitress brought over his bowl of ice cream. Somehow, he found he had lost his appetite.

'Right, Philippe. Are you going to talk to me?'

Philippe hesitated. He knew that once he started voicing any of it, an avalanche would cascade out of his mouth and there would be very little he could do to prevent it. Even if he did temporarily manage to stem its flow, it would only be prolonging the inevitable. But, if there was anyone he could trust with his innermost thoughts, it was Elspeth. He knew that she wouldn't call the nearest journalist and sell his story. Trust was a rare gift, and he was not going to throw that away.

'I'll have to get you another ice cream,' Philippe said, 'because I think we could be here rather a long time.'

Once Elspeth's second ice cream had arrived, Philippe took a deep breath. He started talking. To his surprise, everything came out: the accident; Lauren's betrayal; teaching Toby tennis; what he thought of Greg; and finally, the photo of Lauren kissing him in the paper.

Elspeth was an intent listener. She nodded here and there, patted his hand, and inclined her head. When Philippe stopped talking, she fixed him with her shrewd eyes: 'So, do you love Harriet?'

Philippe thought hard before speaking. 'I can't stop thinking about her. She makes me feel whole. And the thought of Harriet going back to that creep, well, it makes me furious. I have to see her again.'

'Then you love her. And if you love her, why didn't you follow her? Why did you hand her to Greg without a fight?'

'It's complicated. There's Toby to consider.'

'Poppycock! Greg is using Toby as his trump card. He's manipulating Harriet.'

'But, they're like a family. How can I tear them apart?'

'Well, you tell me. You were about to do that, I understand, before Harriet saw the photo of you and that bimbo.'

Elspeth was right, and yet . . . Philippe fell silent. He didn't know what to think any more.

'Look, I know it's not straight forward, but you love Harriet. Isn't she worth fighting for?'

'But what if she leaves me, like Lauren?'

'Yes, but what if you miss out on the love of your life because of what that plastic wannabee did to you? Harriet is nothing like Lauren.'

Philippe sat in silence, deep in thought. After a few minutes, he stood up. He took Elspeth's hand in his. 'Thank you, Elspeth. You really are one in a million. I knew you'd sort me out.'

A large smile lit up Elspeth's face. She squeezed Philippe's. 'Go get her! And remember, she has to kiss you before you turn back into a prince!'

Chapter 23

Philippe's mum insisted on collecting him from the airport.

'Mum, there's no need, honestly. Harry will pick me up.'

'You're coming back in a taxi? I don't think so!'

'Harry isn't exactly a taxi.'

'I don't care what posh car he drives; a taxi is exactly what he is.'

Philippe smiled to himself. Having an account with 'Harry's Executive Cars' was one of the perks of his former stardom that he couldn't quite let go of.

'So, you'll cancel Harry?'

'I'll see you at the airport. And thank you.'

Audrey greeted him effusively at arrivals. Her Anais Anais perfume wafted around like her signature aroma. Her greying hair was swept back off her face by a blue velvet Alice-band, her Laura Ashley dress swirled around her. Her familiarity and predictability warmed him through. But it was the love that shone out of her and the hug she gave him that made him feel as if he had truly come home.

Nostalgia wound tightly around him as the car bumped down the gravel drive. There had been a time when he couldn't wait to be out of the clutches of his parents, but coming back now made him realise how much he valued their solidness. They had always been there for him, through everything.

Their house had all the charm of Beatrix Potter's cottage, but was substantially larger. Wisteria threaded its way around the walls, reaching for the roof. Inside, varnished wooden floors were scattered with red and cream rugs; the same colour scheme that featured throughout most of the inside of the house. The only exception was the kitchen; the canary yellow walls combined with the sky-blue ceiling made you feel as if you had walked into a sunny day.

'Entry not recommended with a hangover', his dad told Philippe one morning, aged 18, when he was looking particularly green around the gills.

Philippe had already been in the house for a couple of hours before his dad, Jack, appeared from his man-cave. He wandered through the house in search of a missing piece of some experiment he was working on. A former professor at Reading University, he was always cobbling together pieces of broken household appliances and coupling them up with a garage full of scrap salvaged from various sources to make robots.

Toy Story mutations had nothing on what his dad had come up with over the years: headless monsters, which rolled across the floor, allegedly sweeping up dust; one armed, semi-human contraptions, which were designed to stir cups of tea, but ended up breaking the majority of Audrey's best tea set; the spider-like monstrosity that scuttled like a crab in the name of 'spying'. The latter robot moved so quietly that Audrey had banned it from the kitchen, having tripped over it more times than she could tolerate. And many, many other inventions. The majority of them would have given children nightmares for years if they ever reached the general public. Thankfully, none of them had progressed further than their initial prototype.

Jack shook Philippe firmly by the hand, clapped him hard on the back and told him he would catch up with him at lunchtime 'old boy'. Having mumbled something about a pressing problem needing his attention, he ambled off in a different direction altogether.

Audrey raised her eyebrows and focused on assembling the beef and ale pie: Philippe's favourite. And boy, was she a great cook, at least she was now. When they lived in London, her cooking consisted of microwaved meals from Marks & Spencer or takeaways at the weekend. Moving to Bradfield had changed her unrecognisably, at least in the culinary department. His mother was, in fact, a *Women's Institute* convert.

When Philippe was still at primary school, they moved to the "suburbs" from central London. Audrey had initially turned up her nose at the very mention of the "WI", picturing a gang of feminist women proudly bearing lip hair with nothing better to do than bash their cooking pots together.

After a couple of months of twiddling her fingers in between playing game after game of tennis at the local club, she learned that a couple of Lady So-and-So's were major players in the local WI, with not a moustache between them.

She was dragged to her first *Women's Institute* meeting by the Captain of the Ladies Tennis Team, an action that the Captain would live to regret. No-one was more surprised than Audrey how much she enjoyed her first meeting. Not that she was a snob, not at all. It just made her realise that the net that captured women for the *Women's Institute* reached far wider than she had ever imagined.

It also ignited a love of baking, which started, rapidly, to overshadow her former addiction to tennis. So the Ladies Tennis Team lost one of their best ever players almost before she'd begun to win matches for them, and the family gained a prolific cook, who would rival Mary Berry any day.

Whilst she barely tolerated the large quantity of Jack's junk, which trickled constantly into their home, every single last little bit of it had to be contained in their double garage. Any stray wire or hub or spring or hinge that she came across outside of this remit, was swiftly and brutally dealt with: generally dumped into the wheelie bin, rarely seeing the light of day again. It had taken a few months for Jack to learn the drill, but after that, he rarely brought any of his precious trash outside of his inventing domain even when Audrey was out at one of her "Women's meetings".

'Your sister beat you home.' Audrey dropped this into the conversation as casually as if she had just told him that she had baked cottage pie for supper. She slipped it in between: 'Mrs Parsons ran off with the butcher's wife' and 'Ted Simpson won First Prize for his carrots for the third year running; it was obvious to everyone that the whole stupid, alleged competition was fixed'.

'Sophie's back?' Philippe closed his eyes. Not even a whole week. She was incredible, but not in a good way. This was the fifth time she had ducked out of a treatment centre early and each time, within hours, she had well and truly fallen off the wagon. 'And you let her stay?'

'She's better.' Audrey shot Philippe a tentative look.

How many times had he heard this before? He had to give his mum her due, she was certainly optimistic, if a little misguided.

'I suppose she's out partying?' Philippe warmed his hands on his third coffee. All of a sudden, they had become icy right to the tips.

Audrey poured the meat mixture into the pie case before lifting the rolling pin over the top, smoothing down the pastry as she went. Once she had crimped the edges to her satisfaction, she brushed egg wash over the top and placed it into the oven.

'There's no need to be like that,' Audrey sighed.

Philippe bit back all the inappropriate retorts hovering on his tongue. Maybe now was the time to disappear up to his old room and get cracking on his novel. Now that he was back in England, and it wouldn't take long for that news to hit the grapevine, his long-suffering publishers would be on his back.

'How long are you staying?' Audrey asked. 'We don't see enough of you.'

'Couple of days', Mum, just until I get the first draft sorted.'

'Ah, so you want board, lodging and laundry?'

Philippe pulled her into a hug. 'You're the best.'

'Don't push your luck.' Audrey laughed before shooing him out of the kitchen. 'If you leave me in peace, I might even rustle up an apple crumble!'

Normally the word "crumble" would instantly turn his mood around. But the news that Sophie had absconded from Switzerland, combined with pining for Harriet, meant that his mood was far too morose for even one of his mum's crumbles to lift.

Following his recent conversation with Elspeth over ice cream, he had been fired up, ready to track Harriet down the moment he stepped onto English soil, ready to declare his undying love for her. He knew that it would only take one call to his agent and he would be handed the number of a discreet Private Detective, who would in turn have her address in his hands before he laid his head on the pillow that evening. Okay, so he could have asked Elspeth for Harriet's address as she was bound to know, but he didn't want to put her in that position.

However, as soon as he stepped onto the plane, the "what-ifs" began. They crowded into his head as if they were paying customers out for a bargain and it was Black Friday between his ears. By the time he landed at Heathrow, his brain had conjured up a dozen reasons why tracking down Harriet was the worst idea ever. They, in turn, fought with the compelling arguments for declaring his undying love to Harriet, which Elspeth had laid out in front of him. The result was not only a killer headache, but had left him more confused than ever. He was at an impasse and hadn't a clue what he was going to do, or not do.

Before Philippe had time to exit the kitchen to pace-off some of his frustration, Sophie appeared at the doorway. Normally she would bounce in and take over whatever conversation they had been in the middle of. She would swallow up their words, twist them around and go off at any tangent that came into her mind at the time.

Today was different. Today, she hovered in the doorway. She twirled a lock of her blond curly hair around and around her finger, her eyes examining her toes.

Philippe looked at her suspiciously. He wondered what game she was playing or about to play. Had she changed her tactic to try to wheedle her way around him? She knew he would be furious that she had ducked out of treatment, yet again.

Sophie slunk over to the nearest chair and slouched into it. She still didn't raise her eyes above knee level.

'So?' Philippe fixed her with one of his most steely looks. 'What was it this time? Too much food? Not enough? Horrible people who forced you to confront yourself? Lumpy beds, oh sleeping beauty?'

'Sorry.' Sophie's voice was barely audible, contrasting dramatically with her normal foghorn and brash tones.

Philippe was used to the drunken Sophie; he couldn't remember the last time he had seen her properly sober. He had lost the lovable and shy Sophie when she hit her early teens and got into a hard-drinking and hard-partying crowd. To be honest, he hadn't thought he would ever see her sober again.

And yet, here in front of him was a different Sophie: a Sophie who had just apologised quietly, and seemed to mean it. Previous apologies were said sarcastically with a sting in their tail or they were said manipulatively because Sophie wanted something or to get out of something.

As he watched her, Sophie's bottom lip started quivering. One by one large tear drops rolled down her face. Within seconds Philippe was up out of his seat. He held her tightly in his arms as she sobbed, her whole body shaking. What was it with him at the moment? Every female he came in touch with seemed to break down into floods of tears on a far too regular basis.

'I'll make us all a nice cup of tea.' Audrey bustled around the kitchen, switching on the kettle, popping tea bags into mugs. She didn't really do emotion, especially when it came to Sophie. They had lost hope years ago that Sophie's life would ever be anything approaching normal, and it was just too heart-breaking to think about. The hope that had surfaced time and time again into Sophie's late teens had been knocked out of Audrey as promises were broken and dramas continued apace. And yet, if she didn't have hope to cling onto, she had nothing.

'So, mum's let you back in again, even after that shop lifting incident.'

Sophie's lip quivered.

'It's okay. That was all sorted out at the time. I spoke to the shopkeeper and sorted out the misunderstanding. The police weren't involved.' Audrey's tone was flat and despairing.

Philippe nodded. He couldn't speak. There was too much he wanted to say, but very little that was appropriate. He could feel both his mum and Sophie teetering on the edge.

Once they were settled with their tea, Philippe asked Sophie if she wanted to talk about it.

'I can't. Not yet. Sorry. I'll never stop crying if I do.'

'That's okay.' Philippe rested his hand on her shoulder.

'I do want to get well though. This time. I can't do it anymore. Not any of it.'

Hope fluttered in Philippe's heart. He knew he shouldn't let it spread wings within him only to have it dashed yet again against the rocks, but this time it felt different. This time it might actually be a new start for Sophie. He wasn't religious, but nonetheless he sent up a pleading prayer. It would mean *everything* to him. Everything. A picture of Harriet swam into his mind. Well, maybe not everything, but almost.

Half an hour later, Audrey sent them both out of the house armed with a shopping list.

Sainsbury's car park, just across the M4 motorway from Theale, was busy. Sophie used to turn up her nose at this store, flanked by Next, Sports Direct and Boots. Waitrose, M&S and Designer boutiques had been more her style. If she hadn't managed to twist her dad around her little finger to indulge her spending sprees, she would latch onto some city boy and allow him to spoil her lavishly.

'I feel a bit queasy,' Sophie said.

She did look pale. Philippe looked at the list in his hand. Audrey would not be happy if he returned without at least every item carefully packed in the reusable shopping bags she'd given him. There was a Starbucks. But to be honest, he was terrified about leaving her on her own for one minute, let alone the 30 or so it would take him to get around the store. It would take one moment of weakness for her to grab a bottle of something, bleep it through the tills and—'

'I'll be okay, Philippe. I'm not going to drink.'

The sincerity in her voice matched the sincerity on her face. Something had definitely shifted in her. She looked completely beaten. And whilst that gave him hope, he had seen her in this defeated state a handful of times over the years. On each occasion, however, the pull of the booze had been too great and after a few days of recovery from whatever hellish hangover or situation she had got herself into, back she went into the fast lane, back to the crazy drunken lifestyle that Philippe was convinced would kill her.

'Look, call me alright. If you feel that, well, you know. I've got my mobile on me.' The same mobile that had a long queue of voicemails still to be listened to, whose text In Box was full to the brim and whose missed call log stretched for pages.

Sophie nodded. She settled herself into one of the free seats, which looked directly out onto the store. She would have preferred to have been tucked into the back of the seating area, but it was already buzzing with shoppers grateful for a few minutes' reprieve from the trolley battles that challenged them as they made their way down aisle upon aisle, working through gargantuan lists.

She watched as Philippe strode off, pushing the trolley in front of him. His limp was hardly noticeable anymore. He didn't see the improvement, but she could.

If only the lights weren't so bright and the noise level so high. Screaming kids whined and moaned and protested about being dragged around a boring shop without even being allowed to spend time browsing the DVDs or playing with the array of toys that lured them closer.

Women, with their heads bent, dissected their lives in minute detail whilst indulging in pastries and cupcakes, washed down with steaming hot drinks fresh from the baristas.

Sophie clutched her peppermint tea. Her stomach wouldn't tolerate coffee. Even the smell of other people's drinks was making her feel sick. She had been warned that she would feel rotten for a few weeks and that withdrawing from years of booze and the odd tablet and joint would not be pleasant. And they had been right.

Previously, she had got to this point and thrown in the sobriety towel. That was the whole point of the drink wasn't it? To drown out emotions, feelings, pain. Yet, the reality that she hadn't seen so clearly until now, was that these substances lied. What they actually did was to exacerbate the pain, but at the same time they ripped you apart inside, bit by bit, whilst pretending to be your best friend.

Sophie looked out at the mass of shoppers wondering how many ankles Philippe would collide with in his desperate bid to get around the store superfast in case he came back to find her comatose on the floor or standing on the table singing karaoke with her clothes discarded beside her.

She was deep in thought when someone tapped her on the shoulder. Sophie jumped, her nerves already strung out as tightly as guitar strings. A blond lady looked down at her.

'Sophie?'

Sophie stared at her. She experienced a vague hint of recognition, but she couldn't put her finger on where she had seen this person before. To be fair, though, most of her past was hazy.

'I'm Harriet. I worked in Wengen at Hotel Neueranfang. I know your brother.'

Ah, the blonde: the one Philippe was all gooey over, although he wouldn't admit it. This was an interesting development. Something she could focus on rather than her throbbing withdrawal and sobriety acclimatisation.

A memory of her standing on the table in very few clothes in that café way up the mountainside flashed into Sophie's mind. She remembered seeing Harriet at one of the other tables. How mortifying. All she wanted was to leave that life behind her, but everywhere she went and everyone she met reminded her of her less than salubrious past.

Harriet watched as a blush spread across Sophie's cheeks.

'What are you doing here?' Harriet asked, not only to distract Sophie from her embarrassment, but also curious as to how Sophie had ended up within 10 minutes of her house. It was a bizarre coincidence.

'My parents live in Bradfield,' Sophie told her, 'what about you?'

Harriet's mind careered into a spin. Philippe's parents lived in Bradfield? That close to Theale and she hadn't realised?

'D'you mind if I sit?' Harriet's legs had become shaky. She didn't want to collapse in the middle of Starbucks.

'Be my guest, although, I couldn't ask you to get me another peppermint tea first, could I?' Sophie fished in her pockets, coming out with a few coins and a condom. She shoved them quickly back into the depths of her coat. Yet another unwelcome reminder of the different life she had been living just a few short weeks ago.

'I'll get it.' Harriet said, relieved to have a few moments to herself to digest this information.

Sophie couldn't let Harriet buy it for her. She hardly knew her. Now she was sober, or getting sober, she wanted to do things differently. She didn't want to sponge off people like she had done all her life, and yet here she was, having asked for a drink, she now couldn't pay for it.

'I can't let you —'

'Of course you can. Would you like anything to eat?'

Sophie shook her head. The thought of eating anything sticky or gooey or sweet made her stomach churn.

As Harriet stood in the queue, she glanced over at Sophie. This was a completely different girl from the one she had known in Wengen: the wild party animal. It was clear she had the hangover from hell, either that or she was unwell.

Guilt prodded Harriet. She knew the only reason she was standing here buying Sophie a drink was because she was a link to Philippe. Philippe, who she had thought she would never see again.

Maybe a peppermint tea wasn't such a bad idea. It was more likely to still her churning stomach than a coffee or even a milky tea.

Harriet set the mugs down on the table and settled herself on the seat opposite Sophie. 'How are you feeling?'

'Like rubbish,' Sophie admitted. At Harriet's suggestion, despite her reservations, she tipped a sachet of sugar into the tea. The sweetness of the sugar combined with the zing of the peppermint was a surprisingly good combination. She felt it warming her all the way down.

'Hard night last night?'

'No. Not last night.' Sophie studied Harriet. There was something about her, which instilled confidence. She raised her eyes to Harriet's, 'the last 10 years . . .'

'That bad?'

Sophie felt tears threatening. She didn't want to cry again, not in such a public place. It reminded her too acutely of her drama queen outbursts, the tears that she had switched on and off like a tap and the rages she had flown into. She had to change the subject.

'How about you, Harriet? Why did you leave Wengen?'

A thousand excuses peppered Harriet's brain. She could hardly say: 'Because your brother's an arse'. She would have to tread a safer path, but still stick to the truth.

'My ex broke his leg and his son, Toby, well, he was like my son for four years and . . .' Harriet trailed off. Sophie's attention was elsewhere. She was waving to someone behind her.

Turning around, Harriet's heart missed a beat. There, in front of her, pushing a loaded trolley and looking as shocked as she was, was Philippe.

Chapter 24

At first Philippe and Harriet just stared at each other as if they could not believe what they were seeing.

'What are you doing here?' Philippe and Harriet's voices rose and fell together in complete synchronicity. As harmonious as any well-versed choir sufficiently rated to sing in Westminster Abbey.

Sophie looked from Philippe to Harriet and from Harriet to Philippe.

'I live in Theale.' Harriet's voice simmered with anger.

Harriet watched Philippe's grey eyes flicker with emotion.

'You ran out on me!' The words were out of Philippe's mouth before he could stop them.

A woman trailed by four children tapped Philippe on the shoulder. 'Sorry, could you move your trolley. I'm trying to get past.'

The interruption gave Harriet the chance to swallow down the anger that was bubbling to the surface.

'Um, Philippe, why don't you get us all a drink?' Sophie said. 'And I think my appetite's coming back. I'm sure I could manage one of those muffins.'

Somehow, Sophie's measured tones snapped Philippe out of the defensive mode that he had slipped into. Why was he effectively interrogating Harriet when his many pleas to the world, to the universe or to whatever was actually out there, had been answered?

Here, in front of him, was Harriet. He could hardly believe it. And to add to this being a great day, Sophie was still sitting in the same place, drinking peppermint tea, and still sober. Okay, so he had to iron out a few issues with Harriet, but at least now he had a chance.

'Harriet?' Philippe's voice was softer. His eyes searched hers. 'Would you like a drink?'

'Yes. Um. Coffee please. Strong.'

Philippe manoeuvred the trolley so it was out of the way of other shoppers and joined the long queue.

Harriet dragged her eyes away from Philippe and focused instead on Sophie. 'D'you live in Bradfield as well?'

Sophie drained the last of her now cold peppermint tea. 'For the moment, although I've been a bit nomadic recently, not really settling anywhere for long. Philippe lives in London, but he's staying with us for a few days to be pampered by mum. He's got to finish his first draft. I don't think it's going that well.'

Sophie and Harriet chatted about the local area and about their families. Harriet was about to plug Sophie for more information when a man loomed behind Sophie.

"Sophie! It is you, I thought it was.' A dapper elderly gentleman greeted Sophie warmly. He looked as if he'd walked out of Pride and Prejudice: musty, but dignified. Sophie stood up and allowed herself to be embraced by him.

'Am I glad to see you!' Sophie grinned from ear to ear.

'Oh, sorry. Tim, this is Harriet, Philippe's friend. Oh, and Philippe is in the queue—'

'Actually, Philippe is standing right behind you with a heavy tray.' Philippe slid the tray onto the table and eyed the man in front of him. What now? Had Sophie gone and got herself a sugar daddy? Was this her replacement therapy for the alcohol?

Tim stretched out his hand and shook Philippe's.

'So how do you two know each other?' Philippe's voice had a cool edge to it. His dad wasn't here to give Tim the once over, so he would have to take on that role. Although to be fair, his mum was more likely to step into those shoes. He very much doubted his dad would do more than wave as he went past, no doubt ruminating on some tricky connection problem with whichever robot he was working on at the time.

'Well, um, well, we met, um, through some friends.' Sophie's face turned an unsightly beetroot-red.

'Look,' Philippe demanded. 'What is going on here?' There was no way he was going to welcome goodness knows who into their lives when Sophie was so recently off the drink and at her most vulnerable. For all he knew, she could have met him at the local pub. They could be drinking buddies, although to be fair, Tim did not look the type.

'Tim, d'you mind if I tell him?' Sophie asked.

Tim nodded.

Harriet watched the scene playing out in front of her. There were so many undercurrents swirling around, it was reminiscent of being in the middle of the River Thames during a violent storm.

'I met him at the meetings. You know. At Alcoholics Anonymous (AA). He's been helping me. Him and his wife.'

Philippe had the decency to look ashamed. 'Look Tim, I'm so sorry. It's just that—'

'I completely understand,' Tim said. 'Completely. I got sober first, 20 years ago. My wife didn't follow me in for three years. It was hellish. I was suspicious of everyone and everything. It was a nightmare.'

Harriet's eyes widened, but she kept quiet. Instead, she observed the interactions between the three of them, although to be honest, most of her attention was focused on Philippe.

While the others chatted, Harriet located her coffee, grateful now for the "personal service", which Starbucks offered by writing a name on each cup.

It wasn't long before Sophie stood up. With a shy grin, she slipped her mobile number to Harriet on a scrap of paper, before waving goodbye. She and Tim left together to meet up with Tim's wife and to do some, apparently, much needed "sharing".

Philippe sank down into the chair. Pity it wasn't a squashy sofa; he could really do with that now. He chuckled to himself - that made him sound like an old man. I mean he was getting on in years, but he had only just passed 30. Hardly drawing his pension.

'Are you okay?' Harriet asked.

The dark shadows under Philippe's eyes and the millimetres of stubble grazing his face were impossible to miss.

'I worry about her. If she drinks again, I don't know if mum could take it. I'm not sure I could. It's been like a merry-go-round, which we never wanted to get on, but one that you can't ever get off, not until the person controlling the ride decides to stop.'

Harriet swallowed hard. 'It must be so difficult. When you love someone, and yet are powerless to get them well.'

'Was it like that with your mum?'

Harriet nodded.

All Philippe wanted to do was to comfort her, but there was this unseen barrier between them, which made any form of physical contact impossible. His thoughts went back to Sophie. 'It's the hope that's the worst. You get used to coping with the drama, but when you believe that everything's going to be okay, you relax. And when it all goes wrong again, well, it's hard to pick yourself up from that when it happens time and time again.'

Before Harriet realised what she was doing, her hand was covering Philippe's. The warmth of his hand penetrated deep into her as his fingers tightened around her palm. All at once they were connected at a deep level.

Whenever they touched, Philippe was overwhelmed with a sense of having come home. It was as if he and Harriet were both two halves of the same whole, which had been cruelly wrenched apart some time in history. This had left them wandering the planet aimlessly not even knowing that what they were really searching for was each other. That was, until they had met.

His hand cupped her face. Their eyes found each other's. A level of emotion and feeling that a million words could not have achieved passed between them. Harriet's lips were asking to be kissed. He was just leaning forward when . . .

'Harriet! Oh my God it *is* you! And this must be the, yes, Philippe Myers. You sly devil, you!'

Philippe and Harriet jumped apart.

This was unbelievable! Harriet closed her eyes. In the space of a couple of days, she had been spotted twice by Joyce, Theale's most notorious gossip. And once Joyce started talking, she would embed herself as effectively as they had in the trenches in France. Why, oh why couldn't she just be rude and send Joyce away?

'Joyce, this is Philippe. Philippe, Joyce.'

'So lovely to meet you, finally,' Joyce said, as if she had been privy to their relationship, if you could call it that, in Switzerland.

Within seconds Joyce had pulled up a chair and was just about to sit herself down on it when something deep within Harriet rose to the surface. She was fed up with being rail-roaded and taken advantage of. A bully always knew how to target a vulnerable victim.

Well, she had had enough! She knew she had it in her to be assertive: she had had no trouble slipping on the iron gloves at work. In fact, one of the staff had nick-named her "iron balls". This had made Ed laugh out loud. So why was it that when she slipped off her metaphorical uniform and walked into her own life, her so called "iron balls" turned to jelly?

Drawing on all her courage, Harriet fixed Joyce with what she hoped was a cold stare. She geared up her voice box to something assembling an assertive tone. She took a deep breath and spoke, hoping that the quavering in her voice wouldn't let her down. 'Sorry Joyce, but we are having a private conversation.'

Joyce leapt out of the chair she had been about to lower herself into as if she had been stung by a very angry hornet. Her eyes widened. She stuck her chin in the air. 'Well if you don't want my company, that's your loss!' And with that, she tossed her red curls over her shoulder and marched away.

It had been *that* easy? All these years, with very few exceptions, she had allowed people to make mincemeat of her in her personal life, and it turned out that being assertive outside of the workplace was actually not that hard. And it felt amazing.

'What?' Harriet demanded as a smile stretched across Philippe's face.

'You,' he replied. 'You were impressive.'

As Philippe moved towards Harriet to continue where they had left off, Harriet stopped him. 'We have to talk.'

He sighed. 'You're right. But not here. It's too noisy. Not private enough.'

'D'you fancy a walk by the canal?' Harriet asked.

Philippe nodded.

'Philippe! Philippe! Can we have your autograph? Pleassse!'

Two giggling girls dressed in dangerously short skirts were practically fainting over Philippe. Now that his cleanly-shaven photo had appeared in all the British papers, he no longer enjoyed the anonymity that he had been able to hide behind in Switzerland for the last few months. He had already been stopped four times in the store and a few people had clapped him on the back.

Before leaving with their precious autographs tucked safely in their bags, they glared at Harriet.

'Sorry. The press must have been busy printing photos of me without my beard.'

Harriet grimaced. 'Not just of you.'

'About that,' Philippe paused. 'Lauren set me up. You have to believe me. I had just finished the interview with the journalists. She came in and begged me to reconsider. Then she launched herself at me. A photographer was outside the window. She must have arranged the whole thing.'

'But why? Why would she do that?'

Philippe shook his head. 'Who knows what goes on in her mind? Maybe she thought that if the world saw we were back together, it would put me under pressure to make it happen. I honestly don't know. I am so very sorry.'

'I thought—'

'I know. And I understand. Papers twist reality every day. Millions of people are taken in by the nonsense they read. You have to believe me, Harriet. I pushed her away, as soon as it happened, but the photographer was one step ahead of me. He had the photo before Lauren had even connected with me.'

Harriet hung her head. 'I, I didn't give you a chance to explain. I just assumed.' All that wasted time and energy because, yet again, she had run away rather than staying to face the situation.

A loud ringing made Harriet pause. She looked around her. Where was it coming from?

'Is that your phone?'

'Oh yes, of course it is.' Harriet dived into her bag and rooted around until she located her ancient mobile, which was tiding her over under she got around to buying a replacement for the mobile she impetuously dumped into a bin at Zürich airport. Just as she pressed the accept call button, the phone went dead. 'I'm not used to having a mobile, not after Switzerland.'

'I know the feeling.' Philippe patted his pocket.

A text bleeped. Harriet opened the message. 'Oh. It's Toby. I need to go.' Harriet stood up.

'Give me your number, Harriet. Please. We need to talk.'

The sensible thing to do, she knew, would be to walk away. The worst thing she could do would be to take Philippe's phone number. She had Toby to think about, and Greg. Philippe would only complicate matters. And yet, she found herself punching Philippe's number into her phone and reeling hers off to him. It was as if her mouth and her body had a mind of their own and she had absolutely no say in their behaviour.

They stood facing each other, the humdrum background noise of shoppers hardly registering. Philippe moved closer. Harriet's heart started beating wildly. He laid his hand on her shoulder, his fingers sizzling into her skin. Her lips parted. She closed her eyes. His lips brushed her cheek, and then he was gone.

Harriet felt giddy, as if she had just got off a ferocious roller coaster. She opened her eyes in time to see Philippe striding through the doors and out into the car park. The impulse to run after him was powerful. She clenched her fists tightly at her side. No! Toby was her priority now. She had to get to him. And fast.

Chapter 25

Harriet had always loved Pangbourne. Before the cancer had confined her mum to bed, they had spent many afternoons walking along the river bank, throwing bread to the ducks and coots. They had laughed like children as they watched the various birds fighting each other for the biggest morsel.

Afterwards, they rested their legs in their favourite coffee shop, which served homemade pastries and cake. Toby often came with them, especially when Greg was away working. Greg wasn't a great fan of the open air, preferring swanky restaurants for refreshments and a gleaming gym for his exercise.

Try as she might, Harriet was finding it hard to push away the doubts that kept assailing her. The cavernous differences between her and Greg kept spoiling the image she wanted to nurture of her and Greg and Toby living happily ever after as a proper family, just like Toby dreamed. And then, of course, there was Philippe.

Harriet pulled up at Greg's Victorian house, wondering what could be so urgent. The tenderness of Philippe's kiss haunted her, along with a sense of loss at having found and lost Philippe within the space of an hour.

Greg had bought this house shortly after they got together. Before that, he had complained constantly that her house was too small for the three of them when they stayed with her at the weekends. And yet, even when he moved to Pangbourne, you couldn't take the city bachelor out of him. Greg still preferred his London flat, even though most of his work had transferred to the local area when he moved.

She wasn't quite sure how he managed to buy this house, as well as keeping his London flat, but then chartered accountants raked in the cash. Not that you would know it, Greg was always pleading poverty. He insisted she pay her way whenever they went anywhere, which meant half of everything, except once a year on her birthday when he paid the bill as long as she left the tip.

She had her pride and always offered to pay her way, but sometimes it would have been nice if he had offered to treat her on days when it wasn't her birthday.

Then, a little over four years after they had met, his 'Dear John' text had arrived. He ditched her for a work colleague, changed his mobile number and told her that Toby was too upset to see her again.

It was like a computerised scoreboard in her mind, clicking up results by the second. One moment, all the numbers pointed to the fact that a future with Greg was impossible, that she was meant to be with Philippe. The next moment, she pictured Toby's face, alight with hope, as he told her and Philippe that all he wanted was for Greg, Harriet and him to be a proper family. The scoreboard then changed in a flash, and once again pointed to how impossible it would be not to spend the rest of her life with Greg and Toby.

As Harriet knocked on the front door of Greg's house, it swung open. She could hear classical music playing and Toby giggling, being shushed loudly by his father.

Intrigued, Harriet found her way to the lounge. She pushed open the door. Her mouth hung open at the sight of Greg and Toby dressed in identical suits and ties. A long banner had been strung up behind them. It read: 'WILL YOU MARRY US?'

Greg and Toby approached Harriet. Greg was hobbling, which slightly spoiled the effect. They both got down on one knee - Greg with great difficulty - in front of her. From behind their backs, Toby pulled out a deep red rose and offered it to her. Greg whipped out a royal blue box and flipped it open. A diamond the size of a small marble sparkled brighter than any star in a coal-black sky. He took her hand in his.

'Harriet, will you do me the honour of becoming my wife?'

Toby took her other hand, his eyes shining with excitement. 'Harriet, will you do me the honour of becoming my mum?'

Harriet's heart lurched as she looked into Toby's trusting eyes, which pleaded with her to make his dream come true. The dream, that she herself had chased all her childhood days as she had watched her mother half-kill herself to provide for the two of them, and as she had watched her friends joking with their fathers around the dinner table. Her mother had done her best. She had tried to be both parents all at once and yet, when parent's evening came and only two chairs were needed for her and her mum, whilst the other stood empty, it was a stark reminder of how incomplete their family was.

Tears sprang into her eyes. How could she say 'no'? How could she abandon Toby when it would shatter him? And as for Greg? Well, they could make it work. Couldn't they?

Harriet took the ring and held onto Toby's hand. She smiled down at him. 'I would be honoured to be your mum, Toby. Honoured.'

Toby flung himself into her arms and whooped with joy. 'Hurrah! Hurrah! Dad said you wouldn't be able to resist both of us! Hurrah!'

Harriet glanced at Greg, who had the decency to look sheepish. So this was his idea, was it? Pull on her heartstrings by using Toby as his weapon, knowing how she felt about him. Could she really spend the rest of her life with a man like that? And more to the point, did she want to? At that moment, Toby hugged her tight and laid his head against her tummy.

'You've made me the happiest boy in the whole world.'

'Champagne?' Greg asked, holding up the bottle. 'Cost me a fortune. We may as well drink it.'

Sophie came home just before dinner, her whole face glowing. For one moment, Philippe worried that it was alcohol making her shine, but given she wasn't slurring her words and she wasn't behaving erratically or giggling insanely, maybe it was actual happiness. This was something he had not seen in his sister for years, unless it had been artificially manufactured by alcohol.

Audrey bustled around them both like a mother hen whose precious chicks had flown home to roost. She had already laid out a banquet along the length of the table, which was positively groaning with roast duck with orange sauce and all the trimmings, together with the pie she had made earlier, just to make sure they didn't go hungry.

Philippe's phone bleeped. His heart started racing as Harriet's name popped up. He clicked on the text.

I am so very sorry. Toby needs me. I can't let him down.

What the hell did that mean? That Toby needed Harriet tonight? Forever? That she couldn't see Philippe again? That she was now with Greg? He swore under his breath, before slipping his phone back into his pocket.

The smell of food was starting to make Philippe's stomach churn. He wasn't sure how much he could eat. The emptiness in the pit of his stomach had nothing to do with lack of food. He tried not to imagine Harriet snuggled up on a large squashy sofa with Greg and Toby either side of her. There was that damned sofa image again! The "happy family" picture he kept conjuring up was too painful. But, he had to get used to the reality that Greg had the trump card, and he didn't have anything in his armoury to match that.

They were all tucking into plates piled high with homemade pie, steaming duck and mounds of vegetables, although Philippe was simply going through the motions so as not to upset his mum. Suddenly, Audrey pushed back her chair and reached for something on the sideboard.

'Oh, I completely forgot to show you this.' Audrey spread the newspaper out on the table to her left, where there happened to be a free space without any dishes on it. 'Are you going to tell us who this young lady is?' Audrey asked. 'Or is she another of those over-eager fans?'

The colour drained out of Philippe's face. How the hell? A number of photos of him and Harriet in Wengen stared back at him. Sophie strained her neck to get a better look. 'That's Harriet. I met her today. She lives in Theale.'

'Theale? What? She followed you here?'

Audrey fixed Philippe with an "I'm not moving from this table until you tell me everything" stare.

Philippe sighed. He knew that when his mother was in this mood, there was no point trying to fob her off. She would be like a dog with a bone, picking away until she had stripped every last bit of news from him.

'She was a waitress at the hotel in Wengen. It is complete coincidence that she lives in Theale.' Philippe began.

'Pfff, coincidence? No such thing. That's fate.' Audrey shifted in her chair. Her back was playing up again.

Philippe ignored his mum's comment. 'She, I, well, we spent some time together. It was only a kiss.' There he was denying Harriet once again, brushing her aside. Guilt consumed him. But, he dared not let on to his mum how much Harriet meant to him or she would no doubt march into Theale, and not rest until she had found Harriet and dragged her back to their home, forever.

Philippe watched the over eager expression spark on Audrey's face. Ever since Lauren had dumped him, she had been doing her best to set him up with every single suitable and equally unsuitable female within a 50-mile radius, despite his protestations that he was not interested, that he needed time to lick his wounds.

'It's over mum. In fact, it never really began, not properly. Harriet's ex has a son. They both came to see her in Wengen.' What else could he say? That he didn't know where he stood? That he didn't think Harriet knew what she wanted. No, the sooner he put a stop to any of Audrey's romanticising of this potential coupling, the better.

'Fiddlesticks!' Audrey said. 'You're just going to stand by and let her slip through your fingers?'

'What can I do? Drag her away from Toby? She loves him.'

'Well he must be her ex for some reason?' Audrey persisted.

'Toby is the son. He's seven years old. He's adorable.'

Audrey was silent while she chewed on a mouthful of duck, her mind whirring. 'Surely she can see Toby without marrying the father?'

How could Philippe explain the look on Toby's face that day? His whole face had lit up at the thought of Harriet joining them so they could be a "proper family". What sort of man would he be to destroy that dream? The sort who had kissed Harriet more recently than he cared to admit, his conscience prodded.

'I taught him to play tennis.' Philippe knew that once those words had left his mouth, he could never take them back; that this would be his new reality. But more than anything, it was the one thing that would distract his mum from her quest to get him together with Harriet.

Audrey's knife and fork clattered onto her plate. 'You played tennis?'

'Not played. I gave Toby one lesson.'

Audrey's eyes filled with tears. Within seconds, he was in her arms.

'Does anyone want to know about my day?' Sophie piped up. Okay, so she was sober, but she still wanted the world to revolve around her.

Philippe grinned. 'Tell me Sophie. How was your day?'

For the next half hour, Sophie raved about Tim and his wife Lisa; about how they had been sober for years and years; about working the steps and having a sponsor; about meetings and sharing; about chairs and chips for length of sobriety; about how everyone was so lovely; about a new life; about being given a second chance.

'And there's a programme for you guys as well,' Sophie told them. 'It's called Al-Anon. You see, it's a family illness. Alcoholism affected all of you as much as it affected me.'

At that point Philippe wanted to add: 'If only you knew how much.'

'So you'll come? To a meeting?'

Philippe couldn't imagine why they would need a meeting in order for Sophie to recover, but he didn't care. If it took him going to a few meetings to help Sophie stay sober, well, he would do anything.

'Heh, where's dad?' Philippe asked. They were so used to their mum sneaking a tray of food into the garage for their dad because he was at a "crucial point" in his current invention that they barely noticed when he was absent. But all this talk about being a proper family and all of them going to an, what was it, Al-Anon meeting, made him think.

251

'Oh dear, oh dear!' Audrey clapped a hand over her mouth. She pointed to the tray on the sideboard.

'Don't worry Mum, I'll take it.' Philippe picked up the tray. It was unlikely that Jack would touch a morsel of it when he was deeply engrossed in a project. But even if he didn't, it was the thought that counted.

It was pitch black in the garage and too quiet. 'Dad?' Philippe parked the tray on one of the few surfaces that was clear of debris. He reached for the light. Nothing. Blackness. Within seconds, he was back in the house. He rummaged in the cupboard under the stairs and came out with a torch, which for once, not only had batteries with some charge left, but was also in working order.

Philippe stepped back into the garage. He shone the torch back and forth, searching for his dad.

It didn't take long to find him. He was lying in a crumpled heap beside his workbench.

'Dad!' Philippe ran to him. He picked up his wrist and felt for a pulse. Yes, it was there. Faint, but there.

As quickly as he dared, given how cluttered the garage was and how little light came from the torch, he dived back into the house. He yelled to his mum to call 999 and ask for an ambulance.

Audrey flew past him, sobbing.

'Mum! Mum stop!' Philippe grabbed her arm and pulled her to him, holding her close as her whole body shook with sobs.

'Sophie, call 999 now and ask for an ambulance. Dad's collapsed. He still has a pulse. The lights aren't working. He may have fused the lights.'

Sophie ran to the phone and punched in the numbers. Philippe could hear her talking. Taking Audrey's arm, he led her into the garage, shining their way with the torch.

Audrey knelt down beside Jack, her hand stroking his forehead, murmuring his name over and over, her tears splashing down onto his forehead.

Jack groaned and moved slightly.

'Oh Jack. Jack. It's okay. Jack, there's been an accident. You have to stay still. The ambulance is coming.'

Jack groaned again.

Sophie came into the garage holding two large candles, their flickering flames adding to the already surreal atmosphere.

'You both stay with dad. I'll wait outside for the ambulance. Show them where to come.'

The ambulance took over 30 minutes to arrive. Every second felt like an hour. Philippe's brain was numb. All he could think about was his dad, and what if he died, and what his mum would do if he died. And, he thought of Harriet.

From the time the paramedics came into the house and Jack was taken to the waiting ambulance on a stretcher, it was a complete blur. Philippe vaguely recalled completing various forms and asking his mum for information when he wasn't sure of the answer.

Audrey's face was as white as freshly fallen snow. The paramedics agreed that Sophie could go with Audrey in the ambulance. Philippe would follow in his car. All Sophie could think of was thank God she wasn't drunk. Thank God she could be there to support her mum just like her mum had supported her hundreds of times over the years. Thank God she wasn't making a bad situation worse by being as much of a worry to her mum as her dad was now. Thank God for sobriety.

Philippe watched the ambulance drive away. He had been asked to put together a few things for his dad and to meet them at the hospital.

He ran around the house, throwing together clothes and shoving items into his dad's wash bag. In his anxiety, he almost forgot to lock the front door, but thankfully habit took over and he jumped out of the car to turn the key. He prayed that he wouldn't get to the hospital too late. What if his dad had already died?

The ring sparkled on Harriet's finger. It seemed unfamiliar and out of place. As Harriet took the first sip of her champagne, Greg announced that he was very sorry, but he had an urgent job to sort out in London and would she mind staying with Toby until he got back.

Toby leapt onto Harriet's lap. 'We can go to the park and then I can have a sleepover at your house. Can I, Harri? Can I?'

Harriet swallowed down the anger that had risen to the surface. That was typical of Greg! Even on the day of their engagement, albeit their second one, he couldn't even prioritise her. But she couldn't stay cross for long as Toby's enthusiasm was infectious.

'Your old room is ready for you,' Harriet told him, thankful that she hadn't changed anything in it since Greg had left her. Instead, she had closed the door and pretended it was a normal spare room, like anyone would have, not the room of a then six-year-old boy, with an impressive wardrobe of clothes, none of which would probably fit him now.

'I'll leave you to pack, shall I?' Greg said. He ruffled Toby's hair and grabbed his briefcase. He paused at the door. As an afterthought, he limped over to Harriet and pecked her on the forehead. He picked up his crutches. Without a backward glance, he disappeared out of the lounge. Harriet heard the door slamming and the powerful roar of whatever high class taxi he had called to take him to wherever he was going.

'Hurrah! Just you and me, Harri! Hurrah!'

Toby sat in front of the TV while Harriet packed a bag for him.

'Can I bring Penguin?' Toby asked, his eyes still glued to the screen.

Oh yes, Penguin. When he was younger, he couldn't sleep without Penguin. She remembered having a very long night on one occasion when Greg had forgotten to pack him.

Harriet searched Toby's room, the lounge, the kitchen, in fact every room in the house, except Greg's study. As extraordinary as it seemed to her now, she had never set foot in this room, not once. It was Greg's domain and he had made it very clear that no-one was allowed in, but him. However, in this case, she had no choice.

Curiosity filled her as she pushed open the door. Oh yes, this was very "Greg". Expensive walnut furniture smacking of the austerity of a Barrister's chambers filled the room. An expensive-looking computer sat in the middle of his large desk. Thick, dark red brocaded curtains hung from the window. The curtains, combined with the dark red paint on the walls, made the room seem dull and gloomy.

In the process of looking for Penguin, Harriet knocked a pile of papers off the desk. As she was shuffling them together, the words "Confirmation of your International Role" jumped out at her. She knew she shouldn't read Greg's letter, but she couldn't resist a peak. She quickly scanned the letter. Her eyes narrowed. What the hell was Greg playing at?

'I've found him! Harri, I've found him!'

Harriet shoved the letters back onto the desk in what she hoped was the same state that Greg had left them. Closing the door behind her, she came face to face with Toby, holding up Penguin in triumph: a very clean and fluffy Penguin, at that.

'I forgot. Marcia put him in the wash. He was in the airing cupboard.' Toby hugged him tightly.

'Marcia?' Harriet asked.

'She's our housekeeper. She comes here every day and sometimes she stays the night. I think she stayed last night. Yes, she did, because she made me pancakes for breakfast. They were yummy. Daddy said that she has to stay over sometimes because there is so much extra work for her to do.'

Stayed the night? Last night? Greg's house had three bedrooms: Greg's; Toby's; and a third that was currently a dumping ground and crammed full of furniture and files.

Harriet's legs had turned to jelly. This was too much. Way too much.

Chapter 26

It was two in the morning and Harriet couldn't sleep. After tossing and turning for what seemed like hours, she finally pulled on her dressing gown and padded down to her tiny, but functional, kitchen to make herself a drink.

Armed with a camomile tea, she sat at her dining room table and flicked open her laptop. She had been meaning to reply to a recent email from an old school friend ever since she had opened it a couple of days ago, but hadn't yet put fingers to keyboard.

While her laptop whirred, she sipped her camomile tea. She had heard that smells and tastes remind you of the past. At that moment, she was transported straight back to Wengen. After drinking the mug of Camomile tea that Elspeth had given her to help her to sleep, she had bought a whole box of the tea bags. It had become her nightly tipple. Vivid images of her time in Wengen flashed through her mind, but it was Philippe, not Elspeth, who featured in most of them.

As her "In Box" sprang into life, new messages flashed their way down the screen. If she received half as many personal emails as she did junk emails, she would be very happy. Quite a few of her friends had, understandably, drifted away. When they were together, Greg liked to see his friends; hers had been shoved to the periphery. And what astounded her now was that she had acquiesced.

And in addition to that, she had been completely wrapped up, first with Toby and then with her mum, neither of which were conducive to having much time to keep up with old mates.

Greg's friends, well, when they weren't talking about how high up the career ladder they were and how much further they intended to climb, they were discussing stocks and shares and investments. The girlfriends and wives were as bad. Their conversations revolved around the latest fashions, where they got their nails and hair done, and the "in" places to be seen. Harriet shuddered. Did she really want to welcome that life back into hers again?

At least Beth had remained faithful to her, although it wasn't exactly hard to keep in touch with her, seeing as she lived next door.

The first thing she noticed was that Jo had written to her. Harriet beamed. Jo had been so much fun. She had even managed to keep her sane when Becky was lording it over them all. No doubt Jo had a few morsels of gossip to pass on.

Intrigued Harriet clicked into her email and started reading:

My dearest Harriet,

What a shock we all got when we heard you'd done a "Cinderella" on us! If only you'd let me be your Fairy Godmother. I'd have sorted out your going away carriage and a few good-looking mice! Honestly Harriet, it's always the quiet ones ☺

Thanks so much for the note you slipped under my door. It was good to know that you were okay, but it still doesn't quite explain why you snuck away like a thief in the night . . . although it was actually a daytime flight in your case! I'm pretty certain there's more to it?

Becky, of course, was ecstatic! She thought you'd left the path clear for her to seduce Philippe, only to find that he wasn't far behind you. Any attempts she made to woo him before he left were firmly rebuffed. Good on him!

But you'll never guess what's developed since then? Becky's fiancé turned up! He was a strange little man. And old. He came to take back his ring. Would you believe it? Becky was quite upset (furious as well, in fact more furious than upset) - not sure if it was the loss of the ring or having to give up all that cash! I'm pretty darn certain it wasn't his character (pig ignorant) or body (scrawny) she was mourning.

The boys have gone home, well two of them. It's really quiet without them hanging around, albeit driving me mad. But Tom has stayed on. Dad is furious. Him and Becky have been getting on like a house on fire, would you believe it? Can you imagine having her as a sister-in-law? Honestly, I think I'd rather shove my head into a bee hive!

Elspeth's sort of niece, Stefanie, who swooped in from Zürich to save your bacon, she certainly gives Becky a run for her money, which is well worth seeing! She's a total breath of fresh air. We have a real laugh together – pity you aren't here as well. You'd like her.

Frau Tanner stomped around for a bit when you first left, grumbling under her breath, but now Stefanie has stepped up, I think she's forgiven you.

And you're probably not that surprised, but Hans and me, well, we've got a bit closer. He makes me laugh a lot. I adore him. You don't have to buy a hat quite yet, but who knows?!

Anyway, enough of me. How are you doing? You're certainly a dark horse. I saw all those photos of you and Philippe in the paper. I also saw the ones of Philippe and Lauren – just make sure he's not a player, although he seemed decent enough, not the type to do the dirty. And you know what the press are like, Harriet, they'll twist anything.

Oh, by the way, Philippe left his precious mug here. I know how sacred it is to him. Not sure if you will be in contact with him at all, but happy to send it to him if he lets me have his address. I don't like to bother Frau Tanner with it – she's always so busy.

Okay, so here's the question: Are you or are you not going to give that Greg a second chance? Toby's a sweetie, but Greg . . . make sure you're sure, Harriet. Marriage is a big commitment. Not that it's any of my business. And really how can I judge? I only met Greg a couple of times. All I would say is that you need to follow your heart, Harriet. Life's too short not to.

Oh, by the way, did you know that "Neueranfang" means "new start" – I'll keep my fingers crossed that it's true for both of us.

Anyway, must go, my shift starts in 10 minutes and I haven't even had a shower!

Loads of love, missing you.

Jo xxxx

Harriet smiled. It was wonderful to hear from her. She felt nostalgic for Wengen. Yes, it had been a bumpy journey, mostly because of Philippe, but they'd had a lot of laughs in between times.

And an email from Elspeth. It was very brief. Just to say she was moving back to the UK, and she hoped that Harriet was okay. That was surprising. Elspeth was not normally short on words. If she was honest with herself, she felt a bit hurt at the lack of news and how impersonal the email was. But then to be fair, Harriet hadn't emailed her once, so she could hardly talk.

Picking up her mug, she sipped her drink; the liquid warmed her insides as it went down. She put her hands to the keyboard and started typing. She would reply to Jo first and then Elspeth.

But before that, she would text Philippe and let him know about his mug. Her previous text to Philippe stared back at her. It had been hard to type. It seemed so final, and yet she couldn't keep stringing him along. Focus Harriet, she told herself. If she didn't do it now, she knew she would forget; once Toby was awake it would be all systems go.

The thought of Toby was followed by images of Greg and Marcia, whoever the hell she was. Maybe Toby had been mistaken? Maybe there was a logical explanation? And maybe pigs did fly.

Yes, and maybe she was a total pushover who was happy to lie down and let Greg walk all over her. Again. To sleep with someone else and propose the next day, surely that was the lowest of the low? Where was her self-respect? How much was she prepared to sacrifice for Toby?

Then there was the letter about the "International Role" he had accepted. What did that mean? Would he expect her to drop everything and come with him without even warning her? Surely he would discuss it with her when he got back from London? Surely?

Harriet picked up her phone. She tapped out a text to Philippe and then deleted it. She changed the words and then deleted them as well. Why was it so hard to write one text? All she had to tell him was that he had left his mug in Switzerland and could she have his address so Jo could return it. The trouble was, she knew that there was so much more she wanted to say. In the end, she kept it simple:

Jo emailed. You left your mug in Wengen. Do you want her to post it? Hope your sister is doing okay. I hope you are. Harriet x

The kiss was also a dilemma. One kiss or two? Or maybe she shouldn't put any. But that would seem cold. In the end she opted for one as the compromise. One little cross that was so heavily weighted with emotion. If only he knew.

Philippe paced the corridor of the hospital. His father was still very groggy, but was being closely monitored. It was most likely, they'd said, that an electric shock had caused his dad to fall backwards and knock himself unconscious. The doctors were hopeful that he would make a full recovery, but needed to observe him for at least 24 hours to make sure there was no lasting damage.

His mother was asleep in the waiting room, as was Sophie. Philippe couldn't settle. He headed for the entrance to get some much-needed fresh air. As he stepped outside, his phone beeped. Who was sending him a message at this time of the morning? He prayed it wasn't Lauren.

Harriet? What was she doing up in the middle of the night?

Philippe hardly read her text. Instead he messaged her:

Dad collapsed. At the hospital. Why are you up?

He tried hard not to picture her in a negligee. It would be too inappropriate to be lusting after Harriet with his dad lying in hospital. And, for all he knew, she was lying next to Greg. That thought was unbearable.

Harriet's phone bleeped. A text from Philippe? Her eyes widened as she read it. She replied instantly:

I'm so sorry. Is he going to be ok? Are you?

She couldn't help noticing that there were no kisses, so she resolutely sent the message as it was without going anywhere near the 'x' button. Then she waited.

'Philippe, the doctor's arrived. A nurse just woke me. He wants to talk to us,' Sophie called from the doorway.

Without a second thought, Philippe slipped his mobile back into his pocket as he hurried after her, back into the hospital.

'Harri! Harri where are you?'

Harriet's eyes sprang open. She must have dozed off in the armchair in the lounge. Her mobile was still clutched in her hand.

'Can I have pancakes for breakfast? Pleassssse!'

It was going to take her a while to adjust to the pace of a seven-year-old, especially in the morning when her eyes still wanted to be glued together. Especially after such a disturbed night's sleep.

'Can I help you make them? Can I? Marcia let me. I can show you how.'

At the mention of their alleged housekeeper, Harriet flinched. When Greg came back, she had a few things she wanted to say to him.

By noon, they had eaten piles of pancakes, played football on the green opposite her house, read a couple of chapters of *Harry Potter and the Philosopher's Stone* and Toby was now asking for lunch. She had forgotten how much energy he had. He was like a Duracell battery, whereas she, in comparison was the low budget value version who was struggling to keep up.

While Harriet made sandwiches in the kitchen, Toby settled down to watch television. The kettle had just boiled when the doorbell rang.

'I'll get it!' Toby yelled. He jumped to his feet and careered to the door, although to be fair, there wasn't that far to career as her house was so small.

'Elspeth! What are you doing here? Have you brought me some ice cream from Switzerland?'

Elspeth? Elspeth here? Surely not? Toby must be mistaken. Harriet dried her hands on a towel and walked into the sitting room. There, standing at the door, a small overnight bag in her hand, was Elspeth.

'I hope you don't mind, Harriet, dear. I was going to head home, but then I realised I would drive right by your door on my way to Swindon. So I decided to pop in. It was a spur of the moment thing.' Elspeth said. 'You know it was very quiet in Wengen without you.'

'And without me?' Toby grabbed hold of Elspeth's hand and guided her into the lounge.

'Particularly without you, Toby!' Elspeth smiled.

Harriet tried to wipe the silly grin off her face, but she just kept on grinning. Elspeth was definitely her Guardian Angel, always turning up when she needed her. And at this precise moment in time, Elspeth was exactly what she needed. Her mind was so tangled up with Greg and Marcia, with the ring that sparkled on her finger, with Toby and of course with Philippe, that she didn't know whether she was up or down or sideways. And, more importantly, she didn't know what to do about any of it.

Once Toby had settled back in front of his programme, Elspeth joined Harriet in the kitchen where she quickly briefed her on what had happened over the last couple of days.

'My goodness girl, your life is like a full blown drama all on its own. Although I have to say that there's no shortage of that back in Wengen. You heard about Becky, I presume?' Elspeth sighed as she took a gulp of her PG tips cuppa, loaded with three heaped spoonfuls of sugar. 'They can't make tea like us in Switzerland. Must be something in the water.'

'Becky? That she was ditched by her sugar daddy?' Harriet buttered some more slices of bread. She popped a couple of pieces of cheese into her mouth: Emmental was her absolute favourite.

Elspeth shook her head. 'Oh, no! That's old news. Becky got married. Yesterday.'

Married? Well that was a turn up for the books. Having shown off her ring for weeks, she had finally tied the knot. But, thinking about it, that made no sense at all. Becky's wedding would have to be as huge and as spectacular as Princess Diana's, even though it would no doubt end up being as tasteless as Jordan's. So what had happened? Had her fiancé had a very sudden change of heart?

'Yesterday? What to the sugar daddy? Did he come back?'

'No, no. He's long gone. She married Tom, Jo's brother.'

'Well, I didn't see that one coming, although Jo did mention they'd been spending a lot of time together. I thought their bank balance had to be bottomless to make them worthy of anything more than a plaything. But marriage! Really?'

'I know! No-one could believe it. You should have heard the gossip it caused. And I, for one, would like to see her on a sheep

262

farm in the middle of Wales.' Elspeth chuckled. 'Perhaps she was drunk at the time! Although, they were behaving like a couple of lovesick teenagers, so maybe there is something more to it.'

'It would have to be something pretty special for Becky to make so many compromises. I'm not sure the beauty salons or fashion boutiques in the middle of the Welsh valleys will be up to her normal standards. What does Jo think about it?'

Elspeth grimaced. 'Let's just say, I think it will take her a while to get used to the idea!'

'I'm hungryyyyyyy!' Toby bounded into the room. 'After food, can I show Elspeth the park?

Half an hour later, just before they left, Elspeth ordered Harriet to: 'take her butt to the hospital and to give that Philippe some support.'

'But Elspeth, he might not even want me there. I'll feel like an intruder. I—'

'Poppycock! Honestly woman, are you "man" or "mouse"?'

Harriet hesitated. 'What about my . . .?' Reluctantly she held out her hand, the ring hung heavy and unnatural on her finger.

'It's not a done deal until you sign on the dotted line,' Elspeth replied. She then refused to leave the house until Harriet promised faithfully that she would at least call Philippe.

Harriet waved goodbye as Elspeth and Toby walked down the street towards the park.

For the next few minutes, Harriet started dialling Philippe's number over and over again. On each occasion, she ended the call before it connected. She glanced from her ring to the phone and back to her ring again.

If she hadn't promised Elspeth, she didn't think she would have the nerve to call him. But she had given her word. Harriet took a deep breath and dialled Philippe's number. She breathed a sigh of relief when he didn't pick up. This was followed by a crash of disappointment. As the tone beeped, having invited her to leave a message, she found her mouth had gone dry and nothing but a high-pitched squeak winged its way down the line. She hung up.

Let's hope that if he listened to her message, he would assume the screeching was a technical fault, not her.

Right, she'd kept her promise. Now, she could get on with normal things, like changing the sheets on Toby's bed for Elspeth. Fortunately, Toby was heading back to Greg's later that day, otherwise she and Toby would have been top to tail on her double bed. Whilst in principle, this sounded fun, he was a real wriggler. In the past when they had shared a bed, she had hardly caught 10 winks of sleep, let alone 40.

She knew she would have to keep herself busy until Toby and Elspeth came back to stop herself from obsessing about Philippe. The urge to drive to the hospital was tempered by indecision: by the vision of Toby's excitement at their engagement and by the ring cutting into her finger. Anyway, despite the promise she had made Elspeth, she could hardly just turn up and gate crash their family crisis. As it was, the hospital had countless wards and never-ending corridors. She would never find him.

She was just tugging a Dr Who pillow case off one of Toby's pillows when her mobile rang. Philippe's voice was as deep and as sexy as ever, although she could detect a weariness that hadn't been there before.

'Harriet. I didn't get back to you, did I? I'm sorry.'

'Please don't worry, Philippe. You've had other things on your mind. How's your dad doing?'

'He's a lot better this morning. Not quite his old self, but they're pleased with his progress.' Philippe paused. 'Look, you don't fancy that walk by the canal that we didn't take yesterday?'

The words: 'Don't you want to be at the hospital with your father?' came out of Harriet's mouth before she could censor them.

Philippe ran his hand through his ruffled hair. 'I need a break, Harriet. I've been here all night. I need some fresh air to clear my head.'

'Yes, of course. Sorry. Shall I meet you at the car park by the lock?'

Philippe nodded, forgetting she couldn't see him.

'Philippe?'

'Oh, yes. Sorry. Good idea.' As if Philippe's brain had begun to pick up momentum, he changed his mind. 'Actually no. Why don't I pick you up? You live in Theale, don't you? I have to drive through Theale to get to the canal.'

Harriet gave Philippe her address before dashing upstairs. She ran a brush through her hair, covered the dark shadows under her eyes with concealer and applied the lightest of make-up. She looked as pale as a ghost today, and without a brush of blusher, her pallid sheen was not a good look.

Standing in front of the mirror, she surveyed herself. She had stripped off her rather past-its-best T-shirt and pulled on a bright pink top. At least it would detract from her insipid face! Shame it wasn't warm enough for shorts; the tan on her legs was already beginning to fade. She wouldn't have many more opportunities to show them off.

Harriet shook her head in irritation at her vanity. She then pounded down the stairs in time to see Philippe's silhouette outside the door. Bracing herself for the impact she knew he would have on her equilibrium, she flung open the door.

She tried and failed to smother her gasp of surprise, clapping her hand to her mouth to quell the squeal that escaped.

'Greg?'

Chapter 27

'Well! Are you going to stand there gawping or are you going to let me in?'

Greg's face looked like thunder. He pushed past Harriet and limped into the lounge.

'Well, *now* I know what's been going on. Behind my back. And you took my ring after, after *this*!'

Harriet wondered what she had missed. How had her previously charm-personified husband-to-be turned into a furious fireball?

'Greg! What *are* you talking about?'

Greg flung his briefcase onto the table, flicked it open and pulled out a newspaper. '*THIS*!' He jabbed his finger at the photos of Harriet and Philippe. 'So much for Mr fucking Philippe Myers! What a jerk!'

The blooming cheek of him! Talk about the pot calling the kettle black.

'So Greg. Tell me about Marcia.'

From the set of Harriet's face and the harshness of her voice, there was no doubt that she meant business.

It was with great satisfaction that Harriet witnessed raw panic flicker across Greg's eyes. Well what did he expect? Toby was bound to have mentioned something.

Like the smooth cover-up expert that he was, Greg brushed it aside. 'What about her? You don't expect me to do my own cleaning, do you?'

Harriet clenched her fists. She answered him silently in her mind: 'No, but you'd expect me to do it.' He was such a shmuck!

'What, in your bedroom overnight, Greg? All those cobwebs to brush away?'

At that moment the doorbell rang.

'Leave it! Whoever it is will go away.' Greg glared at Harriet.

Harriet's eyes flicked over to the door. If she didn't answer it, Philippe was bound to knock on the window, and who knew what hell would break loose then.

'It's my house, Greg. I'll get rid of them.'

Despite the fact that her porch was tiny, it had a door between the entrance and her lounge/diner, which she shut firmly behind her. She pulled open the front door, her heart beating loudly in her chest. Philippe's hair was sticking up in all directions. His face was pale and drawn. The events of the last 24 hours had taken their toll, and now she was going to have to send him away at the very time she should be supporting him.

'Harriet, I—'

It was no good. She could not, no, would not do it to him. Greg's bad mood and the way he had dodged her question about his cleaner made up her mind.

Harriet pushed a finger to her lips and widened her eyes, trying to impress on Philippe the importance of remaining quiet. Philippe looked puzzled, but did as she asked.

She slipped her feet into her shoes, lifted her jacket off the hook and picked up her keys. Thank goodness she had, for once, hung them on the key rack.

'Where's your car?' Harriet asked under her breath. She pulled the front door to as quietly as she could.

She needn't have asked. There in the driveway lounged a sleek black Porsche.

'Very nice,' she whispered.

Philippe held the door open for her and inclined his head, grinning. She slipped easily into the comfort of the passenger seat and buckled up.

Within seconds, Philippe had started the engine and they roared off down the street. A sigh of relief burst out of her. She had dodged Greg for a few hours. Yes, he would be furious when he caught up with her, but she could not face the inevitable showdown, not quite yet.

'Dare I ask?'

'Sorry about that. Greg turned up. He saw the photos. Of us.'

Philippe swung the car out onto Theale High Street, keeping to the 20mph speed limit. 'I'm so sorry, Harriet. The paparazzi are worse than locusts once they get the sniff of a story. That's the last thing you need.'

'Don't worry.' Harriet sighed. 'Greg's as bad. Toby told me some interesting facts about his housekeeper.'

If only she could rewind back to Wengen, to lying in the sun relaxing with Philippe. But then, without the complication of Greg, she wouldn't have the joy of Toby. And to be frank, it had hardly been straightforward back in Wengen.

'Housekeeper?'

'It's a long story!'

Philippe reversed into a parking space and pulled on the handbrake. He glanced over at Harriet and smiled. 'Fortunately we have a long walk ahead of us!'

The sun had forced itself out from behind the clouds and shone brightly down on the canal. A slight breeze ruffled the water causing droplets of sun to twist and turn amongst the ripples. Several ducks flapped and quacked, showing each other who was boss.

'How's your dad?' Harriet touched Philippe's arm as they strolled along the canal path towards Newbury.

'He's doing well. Thank God. It was terrifying. I thought he was going to die.'

Harriet rooted around for his hand. When she found it, she slipped hers into his.

Philippe glanced at Harriet. All he wanted to do was show her how much she meant to him. But first, they had to sort things out. This pushing and pulling and coming together and parting was tearing him apart. They could not carry on like this. Something had to give, and he hoped it wasn't him who would be losing out and going home alone.

He squeezed her hand and then reluctantly let it go. It was too tempting to feel flesh on flesh, too distracting for him when they needed to talk. Properly. Work out where they were going, if anywhere.

'I know he's on the mend because the poor nurses only have to monitor his blood pressure for him to launch into his theory on experimental cures for various diseases. I swear most of them give him a wide berth now.'

Harriet smiled. 'I'd like to meet him. He sounds like a real character.'

'Oh he's that alright.'

'And your mum?'

'Baking!'

'Baking?'

Philippe chuckled. 'Yes, whenever she gets emotional, she bakes. That's her "cure all". As a child I was always up to mischief so she had plenty of excuses to bake with me around.'

'What you?'

'Yes me! You ask mum, she'll tell you. Honestly, I fell out of enough trees to make the most fearless mum a nervous wreck. So to soothe my wounds and her terror, she fed me: cupcakes, cookies, peppermint creams, biscuits. You name it, and she has probably baked it for me at least once. I'm surprised I'm not the size of a house.'

'So you threw yourself out of trees on purpose to get a good feed?'

'Well, what's a boy to do?' Philippe grinned, feeling himself relaxing.

'Toby would love that. He's got such a sweet tooth.'

Philippe groaned. 'Don't! If she even got a whisper of Toby, the oven would be on and her mixing bowls in action before he had even stepped through the door. And then I would never hear the end of it. She's desperate for grandchildren. As I'm the oldest and Sophie has been, well, out of action, you can imagine the pressure I've been under.'

A cyclist rang his bell loudly as he raced up to them from behind. Philippe pulled Harriet out of the way as a blur of tight yellow Lycra flashed past. Harriet was so close. It would be too easy to lift up her chin, to lower his head and, no! He must stay strong.

Harriet's breath was sticking in her throat. Philippe's body was pressed against hers. She raised her eyes and caught him staring at her intensely. Her lips parted and . . .

'Come on. If we make it to the pub, I'll treat you to a coffee.'

Harriet's face fell.

Half an hour later, Harriet and Philippe were seated at a table with hot coffees and glasses of water.

'Nuts or crisps?' Philippe dropped several packets onto the table.

'Nuts please! Dry roasted are my favourite.'

I adore you. Philippe couldn't control his thoughts, but he made sure that the words were left unsaid.

'Oh, I forgot to ask, how's Sophie doing?'

Two dogs barked ferociously at each other on the neighbouring tables. Owners yanked leads and shouted commands, which the dogs pointedly ignored.

'Oh the bliss of the peaceful countryside!' Harriet laughed. 'Sorry, Sophie? Is she okay still?'

'Miraculously, yes. I keep waiting to smell fumes on her breath or for her to morph back into the loud and dramatic drunk who I've known for years.'

'That's wonderful. Let's hope it lasts. I liked her. Well, sober anyway.'

'We all prefer her sober,' Philippe smiled. He breathed in the fresh air. So different from his life in the city. He had barely lived in his flat for the last six months. Maybe it was time to put it on the market and find something closer to home.

Philippe pulled open a packet of crisps. 'You know, it makes you re-think life, doesn't it? Sophie nearly killing herself with alcohol. Dad collapsing. It makes you realise how we are all on borrowed time. Puts everything into a different perspective.'

Harriet nodded. A shadow passed across her face. She looked at Philippe and then down at her hand. Greg's ring sparkled in the sunlight.

'So tell me about the housekeeper.' Philippe pulled out a handful of crisps and began crunching on them.

When Harriet spoke, her voice was so quiet he could hardly hear her. 'She stays over at Greg's. She stayed over the night before last. Toby told me. Said there was so much work to do, that was why. She made pancakes for breakfast.'

'I'm sorry, Harriet.' Philippe's hand had hardly covered Harriet's before he whipped it away as if he'd been bitten. The indent of her ring had imprinted itself on his palm.

'You're engaged? To Greg? After everything that's happened? After the housekeeper?'

Harriet hung her head. 'It's Toby. How can I leave him? I've only just got him back.'

'Harriet, he lives in the next village. You can still see him any time you want. I'm sure Greg would encourage it?'

In a voice that was so quiet, Philippe had to lean forward to hear her, Harriet voiced the thoughts that had been haunting her ever since she had read the letter. 'He's moving away. Abroad. An international role. What am I supposed to do?'

Philippe pictured Toby running up and down the court, throwing everything he had into trying to hit the ball. He saw the devastation written across Harriet's face. How could he ask her to walk away from Toby, even if it meant leaving her with that jerk?

And ask her to put up with the paparazzi, who had become part of his life. If she chose him, they might never leave her alone. What if their children were hounded? What if . . .

They finished their drinks in silence. Harriet kept glancing over at Philippe. His eyes were trained on his drink. He didn't look up once.

Even though they walked back along the canal together, they could not have been further apart. Neither of them spoke when Philippe pulled up outside Harriet's house. There was nothing left to say.

The smell of baking hit Philippe the moment he walked through the front door. Flour coated every surface as well as a fair amount of the floor. Broken egg shells lay discarded in empty egg boxes, and tray upon tray of cakes sat cooling on every spare surface.

'Going for the Guinness Book of records, Mum?' Philippe planted a kiss on his mum's forehead.

'Grab a cuppa love, I've iced the first three trays. Take your pick.'

A rainbow of red, yellow, blue and green icing shone out from the first three trays. Goodness knows how long she'd been at it.

'Are you taking them to the hospital?' Philippe asked.

'Good Lord no! I'll stick them in the freezer for a rainy day.'

There would have to be a very large number of rainy days for all these cakes to be consumed. Especially as he had to go back to London within the week, and he very much doubted Sophie would hang around for long. She never did.

'I might put a few in a box for the nurses,' Audrey said. 'They've been excellent.' Hardly pausing for breath, Audrey fixed Philippe with a shrewd stare. 'Have you seen that girl? The one from the photos?'

How did she do it? Half the time she seemed to be away with the fairies, but very little passed her by.

There wasn't much point lying to her. 'Yes, Mum. And she's just got engaged.'

'Engaged? To another man?'

'No Mum, to an alien from outer space!' Philippe knew he shouldn't take his frustration out on her.

Audrey donned some oven gloves and carefully pulled open the oven door a fraction, peering in carefully. No, not quite brown enough. A few seconds longer should do it.

'Well, you can never be sure these days, can you? It could be a civil partnership for all I know.'

'Mum, she was kissing me!'

'Well bi-sexual then. That's what they call it when they swing both ways?'

'Look, can we change the subject?' More from habit than hunger, Philippe picked up a lurid green cake and began unwrapping it. As he bit into it, the soft sponge melted in his mouth. 'Up to your usual standard.'

Audrey started to fling dirty utensils into the sink and began the mammoth task of tidying up. At least wiping down what little surface was free from cooling trays didn't take long, not until the cakes had been safely stashed away in cake tins or in Tupperware boxes in the freezer.

'So, d'you love her?' Audrey asked him the question without looking up from the sink.

The only sound in the kitchen was the clock on the wall ticking away as if its life depended on it and the whirring of the fan in the steaming oven.

'Well?'

'Yes, Mum. I love her.'

'And you've told her, I presume.'

'How can I? She's engaged to another man.' Philippe stared at the ceiling. He had known this Spanish Inquisition was on the cards ever since Audrey had seen the photos in the paper. If he weathered the storm of his mum for a few more minutes, hopefully it would blow over.

'Only because you are sitting on your bottom in my kitchen instead of trying to win her back. Are you just going to let him steal her from under your nose?'

Philippe pushed back his chair and got to his feet. 'Haven't you heard a word I've told you? What about Toby? How can I ask her to leave him?'

'Have you asked her? Isn't she old enough to make that decision herself?'

'Yes, but she has, hasn't she? She's wearing Greg's ring for goodness sake!'

The minutes ticked by. Audrey pulled off her rubber gloves and lowered herself onto one of the kitchen chairs. 'Sit!' She pulled out a chair for Philippe. 'I have a little story to tell you.'

Mum and her stories! If her usual ones were anything to go by, he could be here a very long time.

'Don't forget, we promised to see dad later.'

Audrey threw the dishcloth at him. 'You'll find this one relevant.'

'When I met your dad, I was engaged to Pete.'

'Engaged? To another man?' This was the first he'd heard of it.

'Yes, well he was a bit rough around the edges, but we'd been going steady for a good few years. And he had a dog. I loved that dog, probably more than Pete. We went everywhere together.'

'And your point is that Toby is like a dog?'

Audrey ignored him. 'Your dad and I, we met at the park. He was walking your nan's dog, under duress initially, I might add. You see, it took him away from his precious inventing, even at that age.'

Philippe smiled. It didn't surprise him in the least.

'We fell in love. But I refused to believe it. My future was already mapped out: me and Pete and Chocolate.'

Philippe raised his eyebrows. Imagine calling your dog to heel and everyone thinking you were hungry or begging . . .'

The timer beeped. Audrey pulled out another two trays of cakes, sliding them one by one onto a spare cooling tray. 'Jack was a very moral chap. He wouldn't say anything that would have compromised my engagement, not at the time, anyway.'

'So what happened?'

'Chocolate died suddenly from a heart attack. I was devastated.'

'So you were free to marry dad?'

'Not quite. Well yes, technically, although I was still engaged. Your dad was the most amazing support to me. He was the one who got me through, not Pete. I was completely torn: loyalty towards Pete, particularly after losing Chocolate; I didn't want to put him through another trauma. But it was your dad that I loved. I just didn't have the courage to make that leap.'

How come he didn't know this? He was 30 years old and he had only just learned a whole new element to his mum and dad's relationship. Philippe tried to picture Jack being supportive, but it was a stretch too far. It was rare these days for him to be out of his garage for long enough.

'I know what you're thinking. It was different then. He was different then.' Audrey had that faraway look in her eyes.

'Don't keep me in suspense, Mum. How did you two get together?'

'Don't ask me what got into your dad, but one day he showed up on my doorstep. Thank goodness Pete was out. Dad was wearing a dinner jacket, complete with cummerbund and bow tie. It was a little on the small side for him, but I didn't care. He had champagne in one hand, a rose in the other and a ring in his pocket. He got down on one knee and asked me to marry him. I accepted just like that. And here we are 40 years later.' Audrey smiled. 'I'll never forget that day.'

Philippe had a horrible feeling she was going to pluck a couple of roses from the garden, produce a bottle of champagne she had been chilling in the fridge and offer him one of her old rings, before booting him out of the door to find Harriet.

'Philippe. You love her. Tell her you love her. What have you got to lose?'

Chapter 28

Harriet steeled herself before pushing open her front door. She breathed a sigh of relief to find her house was empty. No Greg.

A note had been left on her dining room table: "~~HOW DARE YOU~~! WE NEED TO TALK. WHERE THE HELL IS TOBY? CALL ME."

As if on cue, Toby tumbled in through the door. Judging from the grass stains on his trousers and the flush in his cheeks, he and Elspeth had had a great afternoon. If only she could say the same.

'Harri, it was AWESOME. We found some trees and played hide and seek and then we played football and then we went to the park. Elspeth can push me as high as the sky and back again!'

Harriet smiled. 'That sounds amazing fun. I bet you could do with a drink. What would you like?'

'A long weeeeee!' Toby shouted as he careered upstairs.

'I bet you're whacked, aren't you?' Harriet asked.

'Physically yes, but my word they keep you young. I don't think I've done as much exercise in years, not of the running around variety in any case.'

As soon as Harriet had made them all drinks, Toby shouted down the stairs that he was going to change his clothes otherwise dad would tell him off for getting dirty.

Elspeth clicked her tongue. 'Dirty my foot! Isn't that what children do?'

'Not children of revered accountants like Greg,' Harriet replied.

Elspeth's eyes scanned the table. 'You haven't got any biscuits, have you? I'm feeling rather peckish after all the energy I've expended.'

'You're in luck, I bought some Kit Kats and custard creams yesterday.'

Harriet opened the packets and tipped them out onto a plate. 'Dig in!'

'So Harriet, did you see Philippe?'

Harriet gave Elspeth a brief description of what happened 'So you see. I'm more confused than ever. I don't know what to do.'

'I think you do,' Elspeth answered. 'I just don't think you're brave enough to do it.'

'But what about Toby?' Harriet asked.

The biscuits were making Elspeth's mouth water. She pulled the plate towards her and nibbled on a custard cream. 'Toby is not attached to Greg night and day. You can still see him.'

'But what if Greg forbids it?'

'What? Free babysitting and taking Toby out of his hair? I doubt it.'

'But that's exactly what he did last time.'

'Yes, but last time, I seem to remember, he had Jessica to fill that role?'

Harriet sighed. 'But they're moving abroad. What on earth will I do?'

Reaching across for a Kit Kat, Elspeth peeled off the wrapper. 'You will do what every other separated parent does, you will share him. He can come and stay with you during the school holidays.'

Harriet could detect a hint of impatience slipping into Elspeth's voice. And no wonder. She was impatient enough with herself.

'Look, Harriet. I don't want to talk about this. Not anymore. It's not helping you. But, what I can tell you is: if you lose Philippe, you may regret it for the rest of your life. Boys grow into men and move away. Just think about that.'

Harriet stared into the distance, not seeing anything. Why couldn't life be straightforward?

A loud thundering echoed around the house as Toby descended the stairs in record time and shot into the lounge. 'I am SO thirstyyyy. Can I have a drink before I go back to dad's? Please.'

'Wow! You look a lot cleaner, Toby. Apart from that splodge on your nose.' Elspeth said, leaning forward.

'What splodge?' Toby frowned. He could have sworn he wiped his face clean with the flannel. He had even checked it in the bathroom mirror.

'That splodge just there!' Elspeth dabbed his nose with a blob of chocolate from her half-eaten KitKat on the end of her finger.

'Elspeth! You did it!' Toby cried, giggling. 'She's worse than you, Harri!'

An hour later, Harriet left Elspeth settled in front of the TV with the remote control in her hand. 'I'll just catch up on the news,' she told them. 'See you soon, Toby. Thank you for a fun day.'

Toby hugged her tightly. 'You really are like my granny,' he said.

Harriet could see Elspeth welling up. 'Right you, off we go. Let's take you back to Pangbourne.'

As the car ate away the miles, Harriet's heart thumped against her ribs. She had no idea what kind of reception she would get from Greg, but she guessed it wouldn't be a warm welcome. As long as Toby was spared the animosity between them, then she would survive. She crossed her fingers on the steering wheel.

Harriet pulled into Greg's driveway. Greg hobbled out of the front door, one crutch under his arm. He moved to her side of the car. He opened the car door and put his arm around her as soon as she had stepped out.

'Sorry, Harri,' he whispered in her ear. 'Forgive me?'

Having braced herself for WWIII, Harriet was completely thrown by his 180-degree about-face. He had returned to the adoring, charming, husband-to-be wooing her and making her feel special.

Toby put his hand into one of Harriet's and the other into Greg's. 'We're a real family now,' he said. 'Just like Harry and Jake's. They can't call me "divorcee kid" anymore.'

Shocked, a look passed between Greg and Harriet. "Divorcee kid"? That was outrageous. The school would be hearing from her the moment the doors opened after the summer break. "Divorcee kid" - Really?

Greg had made a monumental effort. The table was laid with a white tablecloth, freshly out of the packet by the exaggerated seams running in squares along it. New candles sat in their elegant silver holders and three crisp, white napkins were rolled up in silver

278

rings. The aroma of a casserole filled the air, mingling with the perfume of scented candles.

Toby's eyes widened. 'Wow Dad! Is this for us? All of it?'

Greg nodded. He pulled Harriet and Toby closer to him. 'For you and Harriet. My family.'

Oh no! Oh no! Oh no! A fight she could have handled. A fight would possibly have given her the strength she needed to cut the strings that bound them together. But this? This romantic, "we're a devoted family" scenario that he was creating for her? *This* was a nightmare.

She could not stay. She just could not. It would further scramble her already scrambled brain. 'Listen, I'm so very sorry, but I have to get back to Elspeth. She's expecting me.'

Greg punched the door hard, wincing at the impact. Toby's howl of disappointment sliced right through her. But what the hell was she supposed to do? Go through with this, this charade.

Harriet watched Greg as he struggled to bring himself under control. 'It's fine. We have all our lives to plan evenings like this. You can be my guest of honour tonight, Toby, and you can eat all of Harriet's profiteroles.'

Toby's face lit up. 'Ok then. And Elspeth would be lonely if you left her at your house all on her own.'

Harriet kissed Toby goodbye. He wrapped his arms around her neck and held her in a bear hug for over a minute. She swallowed as all the churning emotions threatened to break through her carefully constructed dam of self-control. It was tempting to stay, but flashes of Marcia with Greg and of Philippe's face when he found her engagement ring, spurred her on.

At the door, Greg grabbed her. Before she realised what was happening, his lips were pressed down hard on hers, as if he was stamping his ownership onto her. She was *his* now, this kiss was saying: *his* fiancée; the future step-mother of *his* child.

Harriet waited to melt into his arms. She waited for the zing and the tingle. She waited for her body to respond to his. She waited. Nothing happened. Zilch. Zero. Not even the smallest of twinges.

Her libido, where Greg was concerned, was as dead as the proverbial Dodo.

Harriet and Elspeth spent the evening watching films on Netflix, and giggling like school children. Elspeth was such a hoot! The tales Elspeth told her of her childhood and some of the jobs she dabbled in would make most people's hair stand on end.

By the time they stirred from their beds at mid-morning the next day, they prepared a large brunch before Elspeth packed her things ready to return home. They promised to keep in touch, and Harriet knew, without question, that they would be friends for life.

As Harriet closed the door, Elspeth's words: 'you may regret it for the rest of your life' hovered in her mind. Images of Greg's functional kiss compared with Philippe's movie-style-swoon-making-smacker flashed in and out of her thoughts. This competed with the look of utter joy on Toby's face when she agreed to marry him and Greg, coupled with painful memories of the huge, gaping hole left in her heart when Greg ripped Toby away from her. All these conflicting emotions chased each other around her head, like a dog chasing its tail in never-ending circles, but with none of them coming out on top.

She could not carry on in this excruciating indecision. It was too painful.

Harriet sent a text and was rewarded with an immediate answer. With her car keys in one hand and her umbrella in the other, she made a quick dash to her car. She flicked on her windscreen wipers, reversed out of her parking space and drove off down the road.

It took a while to find the house. The lanes were wiggly and narrow, and most of the houses were set right back from the road. After a frustrating 10 minutes of reversing and turning around and stopping to ask pedestrians the way, she finally pulled into the driveway of "The Poplars".

The garden certainly lived up to its name as tall poplars stood sentinel around three sides of their plot of land. Their cottage looked as if it had been plucked straight out of the Cotswolds or from the pages of one of Enid Blyton's novels.

Harriet hesitated with her hand on the knocker. Should she be doing this? It wasn't as if she had made a decision. But wasn't that the point? Wouldn't it help her clarify everything? Or would it confuse her further?

Fed up with her washing machine mind, Harriet knocked loudly on the door. A homely woman, with a bun of grey hair tied up behind her head, opened the door. Her mouth creased into a welcoming smile. 'Do come in,' she said, holding the door for Harriet. 'Please excuse the apron. I'm baking.'

'Mmm, I can smell,' Harriet sniffed the air appreciatively. 'Lemon?'

Audrey nodded happily. 'Yes chocolate chip and orange and lemon, and I think I might do some lemon drizzle as well. They are Jack's absolute favourite, well, along with spinach and coconut.'

Harriet tried not to screw up her face at the thought of such a bizarre combination. A quick change of subject was called for. 'Oh yes, sorry, how is Jack? Is he feeling better?'

'Almost as right as rain. I saw him this morning. Driving the nurses mad. He's desperate to get back to his inventing. He has already filled dozens of sheets of A4 with the ideas that have been pouring out of him ever since the accident. He thinks it's the electricity. It kick-started something in him.'

Harriet pulled up the chair that Audrey pointed to. 'That's great news. I know Philippe was worried about him.'

'Fancy a cuppa?' Audrey asked. 'I'm completely parched. Been at it for hours.'

While Audrey fussed around popping tea bags into mugs and arranging a dozen or so newly iced cupcakes onto a plate, Harriet surveyed the kitchen in amazement. It was like a production line. She had never seen so many cupcakes in a domestic kitchen, or indeed anywhere.

'You're like a cottage industry all on your own. You'd even give Mr Kipling a run for his money!'

'Well yes. I love it too much really. Jack had to buy me a couple of chest freezers to store them in. They're in the outhouse – Jack wouldn't let me keep them in his garage. I've nearly filled them to the brim this week.'

'Wow!'

Audrey perched on the chair opposite Harriet before sliding a mug of tea across the table, along with a sugar bowl and a tablespoon. 'Sorry, all the teaspoons are in the dishwasher.'

Harriet smiled. 'That suits me. I've got a terribly sweet tooth.'

'Eat up then,' Audrey encouraged. 'Try the orange and lemon. They're really rather good.'

The soft sponge crumbled in her mouth as she bit into the cupcake; the tangy icing melting on her tongue. 'These are incredible!' Harriet said. 'Truly incredible.'

Audrey beamed. There was nothing she liked more than to feed someone her home-baked cupcakes. To be frank, it made her day.

'So you're Harriet?' Audrey asked.

'Oh sorry. How rude of me! I haven't even introduced myself.'

'Don't worry, dear. I saw the photos.'

Harriet wished the ground would open up and swallow her whole. She put down her cupcake. 'Oh.'

'No, no! Don't get me wrong. It's wonderful. Philippe has been miserable ever since that, that woman did the dirty on him. Although she had no taste at all. She didn't even have one mouthful of any of my cupcakes, can you believe it? Not even a crumb. And she could've done with fattening up; she looked like a rake. Honestly, if I could get my hands on her . . .'

'Me too,' Sophie agreed as she wandered into the kitchen. 'Glad you found it. My instructions were a bit vague. I always miss out a couple of turns.'

'So I noticed!' Harriet gave Sophie a tentative hug. She asked how Sophie was, but didn't need to hear her answer. Sophie's eyes were bright and shining. Her hair bounced and shone. Her make-up was tasteful and her foghorn voice had dissipated to a gentle melody.

'I've honestly been transformed,' Sophie gushed. 'Although some people say that it's my "pink cloud". That the relief of not being in the hell of alcohol means that you go into a kind of euphoria. And that after a few weeks, reality hits and feelings hit and the pink cloud dissipates. But other people say they never get off their pink cloud! I mean, the meetings are amazing. My sponsor is amazing. The steps are amazing. It's all amazing. Although there are times when I feel overwhelmed. So many emotions. Too many. Sometimes it's like being on a little ship in a raging storm. Isn't it, Mum?'

Audrey nodded. She pulled up a chair for Sophie. 'I'm so proud of you,' she said, her eyes shining with tears.

'Yummy! Can I try the orange one? Mum makes the most delicious cupcakes.'

'I know,' Harriet agreed. Her mouth was too full of a rich chocolate chip cupcake for conversation, so a burst of crumbs flew out over the table. 'Oops! Sorry!' Harriet swallowed a large mouthful of tea to try and wash down the rest of the cupcake.

Sophie laughed. 'Don't worry. Philippe does that too.'

At the mention of Philippe's name, she could feel herself blushing.

'He should be back soon. They've promised to come with me to an open AA meeting this evening.'

Harriet frowned. 'Open meeting. Are the others closed?'

The clock clanged the hour.

'No, silly! Open to people who aren't alcoholics. Why don't you come along too? It will be fun.'

"Fun" wasn't a word that would have sprung to mind at the thought of attending a meeting for alcoholics. 'I don't want to intrude,' Harriet replied quickly.

'The more the merrier!' Audrey answered. 'Oh there you are Philippe. We've been entertaining your visitor.'

Philippe stopped in his tracks. Harriet here? In their kitchen? With his mum? This was too weird. He tried to focus off her face. She

283

looked stunning. Her white floaty skirt matched with an equally floaty light blue T-shirt gave her the look of a vulnerable waif who needed protecting from the big bad wolf – Greg – and of course, he was the man to do it.

It took one look before his resolve to stay strong and give her space to choose between him and Greg started to melt. He could hardly order her out of the house.

Audrey looked from Philippe to Harriet. Moving a tray of cupcakes out of the way, she addressed them casually over her shoulder. 'Why don't you three go into the lounge? I'll bring you some coffee.'

'I've got some writing to do. Step 1, you see. About how I'm powerless over alcohol. I'll see you later.' Sophie disappeared up the stairs.

Harriet stole a look at Philippe, but neither moved.

'Come on. Out! Out!' Audrey flapped at them with the dishcloth she was holding. 'I've got cakes to bake! How can I concentrate with you lot lounging around here?'

Philippe looked at Harriet. 'Come on. If we stay in here, she'll get us baking as well and we'll be tied to the kitchen for months!'

'Out!' Audrey repeated.

The lounge was cosy. Old leather sofas, formerly a rich red, but now a shadow of their former selves, had grown squashy and worn with age. They provided the centre piece of the room. Faded floral curtains entwined with red roses were held back from the windows with matching tie-backs, frayed from years of being opened and closed and accosted by small children and animals. A large fireplace was full of scrunched up newspaper balls. A tower of logs to one side rose towards the chimney.

Three of the walls were a creamy yellow. Whether this was from age or the original colour of the paint was anybody's guess. Audrey had, of course, wanted them red, but for once, Jack put his foot down. To keep the peace, he allowed one of the walls to be deep red. However, to make up for Jack clipping her red wings in this manner, the carpet was a vibrant red, or it had been when it was new, 20 years or so ago. It had also faded over time, much to the relief of the rest of the family. Newspapers and magazines were strewn across the rectangular oak table, which stood in the middle of the room.

'It must be so cosy in the winter with the fire lit.' Harriet sank into one of the sofas, literally. 'And these feel as if they have been made to fit my body exactly.'

As the words left her mouth, she blushed.

Philippe found himself imagining them both curled up together in front of the fire, with steaming mugs of coffee waiting on the table and a dog curled at their feet. This room held a million different memories, both good and bad. He would love to make more memories with Harriet at the heart of them.

Family weekends in the past, before Sophie tried to drown herself in a sea of alcohol and his career and life were shot to pieces, were the best. The cards and board games they played; the films they snuggled up and watched, armed with popcorn and fizzy drinks to replicate a cinema; the laughter, which resounded around the room. And then Sophie found alcohol. And dad retreated further into his garage and his mum, well, she baked.

Videos of the past started to run through his mind: of Sophie staggering into the lounge, throwing up on the carpet and then passing out on the sofa; of Philippe in a put-up bed for days and days whilst his leg tried to heal; of hearing his mum sobbing at the loss of his career and fiancée, and the loss of her daughter to the bottle.

The light suddenly left Philippe's eyes.

'Are you okay?' Harriet asked.

'The trouble with having lived somewhere so long is that there are some memories you would prefer to forget.'

Harriet moved along to allow Philippe to sit next to her on the sofa. 'I do understand. Truly.'

Both sat, close together, awareness of each other fizzing between them.

'Err, so when's your dad coming back?' Harriet blurted out.

'He's coming home tomorrow. He's been told to rest for a week, but I don't think there's much chance of keeping him away from the

285

garage, not even for 24 hours. He'll want to start on his pad full of sketches, which he's been working on in hospital.'

'Won't your mum be able to persuade him?'

'She'll do her best, but I'm not sure how long she'll manage to restrain him.'

As if on cue, Audrey bustled into the room carrying a tray loaded down with a vast flask of coffee, two hand-painted mugs and a plate loaded to the brim with cupcakes.'

'Here Mum, let me take that.'

Philippe lowered the tray onto the table. 'Thank you.'

'Have fun you two. Must go. Baking calls!'

'I've never seen so many cakes. She's like a bakery all on her own the amount of cakes she churns out.'

'I know. I did warn you!' Philippe raised an eyebrow.

'Couldn't she sell them? I mean, there's hundreds of them. From what she told me the freezers must be groaning under the weight of all those cupcakes.'

'She can't sell them. They're too personal. She's put too much of herself into them. It would be like selling part of herself.' Philippe smiled fondly. 'She's been through so much.'

'I like her.' Harriet reached out and selected one of the strawberry cupcakes, which Audrey had just iced. 'And I can't resist these cakes. If I lived here, I'd have to go running every day to keep myself from blowing up like a balloon.'

'Are you saying, Miss Anderson, that I'm the size of a balloon, given I live here and don't go running?'

Harriet giggled. 'Well, maybe one of those long, tall balloons! You don't look round at all. I can't understand it.'

Philippe leaned in closer. 'Harriet, there are only so many cupcakes you can manage to eat day in, day out. After a while, one a day is more than enough. As delicious as they are.' He paused. 'Anyway, enough of cupcakes. How are you doing?'

'I don't know, Philippe. Truly. I feel as if my world has been put in a cocktail shaker by an over-enthusiastic barman and I don't know which way up I am!'

The cream spiralled around the coffee as Philippe stirred it in. 'I know the feeling,' he said, looking up at her. 'What are we going to do, Harriet?'

At that moment Sophie burst into the room. 'We've got to go and get dad. He's about to leave the ward and walk home if we don't get there fast. He's discharged himself!'

'I'm so sorry, Harriet. Will you stay here? I won't be long.'

Harriet nodded. She watched as Philippe flew out of the room, Sophie following in his slip stream.

'You'll help me clear up, dear?' Audrey stood at the door. She handed Harriet a tea towel.

An hour later, the kitchen was once again spic and span. Most of the cupcakes were bagged and in the freezer.

'Well, that was a whirlwind.' Audrey dropped onto one of the kitchen chairs.

'Why don't I make us a cup of tea?' Harriet suggested. 'Philippe texted to say they should be back in about half an hour or so.'

'He texted me too. It's just like Jack, refusing to get into the car unless they stop at B&Q to pick up the bits he needs for his new inventions. Honestly, I swear that man was born half-robot.'

Harriet smiled. 'How long have you been together?'

'More years than I care to remember!' Audrey closed her eyes. 'I was so scared he was going to die, Harriet. I don't know what I'd do without him.'

While the kettle boiled, Harriet went over to Audrey. Audrey had tears in her eyes and her bottom lip wobbled. Harriet pulled a couple of tissues out of the box on the sideboard. She handed them to Audrey. She slipped her arms around her. Audrey's head sank onto Harriet's shoulder and she cried, her whole body shaking.

When Audrey finally raised her head, her eyes red-rimmed, Harriet patted her hand. 'You'll be okay, Audrey. You've had such a shock.'

Audrey nodded. 'Thank you. I needed a good cry.'

Harriet carried two mugs of tea over to the table and they sat, sipping their drinks and chatting about this and that. It was well past 4pm when Philippe's car pulled into the driveway.

'Needs a bigger boot!' Jack could be heard complaining as Philippe escorted him into the house. 'Totally impractical that car of yours.'

Audrey was up on her feet the second she heard the car crunching across the gravel. She welcomed Jack with a huge hug. He stood ramrod straight in her embrace and patted her awkwardly on the shoulder.

'I'll just unload the car, then we could all do with a cup of tea. A strong one!' Philippe disappeared back outside.

'I'll help you.' Harriet followed Philippe, passing Sophie as she came into the kitchen with her arms full of long metal strips.

When Harriet looked into the boot, she gasped. 'How did you manage to get all of that in there?'

'Not without great skill!' Philippe pulled out three bags and handed them to Harriet. 'Can you manage those? They're the lightest.'

Harriet reached out and took the bags. 'Are you calling me a lightweight?'

'Wouldn't dare! Just trying to be a gentleman. I can hardly give you the heaviest bags, can I?'

'I'll let you off just this once.' Harriet grinned. She followed Philippe through the house and on into the garage.

Harriet could not believe the amount of stuff that was piled high in the garage, a lot of it leaning against the large double doors, which would, at one time, have opened out into the driveway. 'Ah, now I see why you have to go through the kitchen.'

'Yes, we gave up on the garage door years ago. Mum wasn't pleased about it at first, but at least this way dad is forced to come into her domain whenever he wants to leave or enter the garage. Otherwise she'd never see him.'

The garage was crammed to the gunwales with a plethora of metal, screws, nuts, bolts, wires, material, wood, tools and many other unidentifiable artefacts. 'I think there's some space over here,' Philippe motioned to a corner at the far end of the garage.

'Is it safe for him to work here after the, well you know, with the electricity?'

'Mum has sorted it out. She made three different electricians look at every single connection. It took them hours.'

'I don't blame her. If it was you, I would want to be certain you'd be okay.'

Philippe turned to her. 'That's very touching. I knew there was part of you somewhere that cared about me!'

'I was merely thinking of the insurance.' Harriet's eyes sparkled.

'What the insurance money or how much the insurance premium would go up if you had to claim for my death?'

Sophie struggled into the garage with her arms full of long lengths of wood. Harriet and Philippe both grabbed a few pieces from her and together they carried them over to the corner.

'We have to eat as soon as we've finished unloading the car,' Sophie said. 'The meeting starts at 7pm. We need to get there at 6.30pm to grab a coffee and have a chat first.'

'Are you sure you want me to come?' Harriet asked. 'I don't want to intrude.'

'You won't be intruding. I'd love you to come with us.'

'Come on then, we'd better get this car unloaded.' Philippe led the way out of the garage, through the kitchen and back out onto the driveway.

'Food in 15 minutes,' Audrey yelled. She was thankful for the ready meals she had thrown into her trolley at the last moment. Generally, she didn't approve of anything that wasn't homemade, but the last few days had turned her world upside down, and any cooking that got in the way of baking cupcakes frustrated her. Hence the plastic trays that were now, one by one, whirring their way around the microwave before being slotted into the oven to keep warm.

Chapter 29

As the three of them approached the entrance to the church hall, Harriet noticed the air outside the venue was filled with laughter and cigarette smoke. Well, that figured. What did Sophie say on the way over here? Something about "the addictive personality".

Audrey had managed to duck out of their expedition pleading "Jack-sitting duties". As there was no way that Jack would stay away from his workshop without at least one of them staying behind to keep an eye on him, Sophie relented. However, she wasn't hearing any other excuses.

'Well you two *have* to come if mum can't,' Sophie had insisted.

'Sorry,' Philippe had whispered in her ear as they had walked to the car behind Sophie.

'You owe me!' Harriet had grinned at him.

There was a lot of kisses and hugs and shaking of hands going on, combined with good natured pats on the back. Generally, a welcome worthy of a Royal Visit, without of course the bows, curtsies and "ma'am's". It all seemed surreal to Harriet who had only heard of Alcoholics Anonymous via a friend's friend, and hadn't known what to expect.

Tim came over and introduced his wife. They chatted for a few minutes, before the couple were whisked away to speak to the constant stream of people who were arriving in the hall.

The first thing that surprised Harriet was the lack of hairy, dirty and bearded old men shuffling around in tatty macs with a piece of string holding together the two sides. Even though her preconception didn't make any sense because Sophie was polar opposite to that.

The people gathered in the hall drinking from large polystyrene cups brimming with tea and coffee, looked more like they were about to hold a committee meeting than recover from alcoholism. Everyone looked clean and they were clothed in a wide array of attire from meticulous to glamorous to casual to the odd inevitable shell suit.

What amazed her more than anything though, was the warmth that filled the room, and the laughter. Weren't alcoholics supposed to be angry and morose? Harriet thought back to Sophie's antics in Wengen. She had been a wild and embarrassing drinker then. But since she had got sober, she was changing in front of their eyes. She was calmer and nicer and easier to get on with. She had clearly left the drama queen in the same place as her abandoned bottles. Although Philippe had said that her histrionics hadn't completely disappeared, but at least they weren't now fuelled by alcohol, and she apologised afterwards.

Harriet lost count of the number of people who came up to shake her hand or kiss her cheek. So many people told her how lovely Sophie was and how well she was doing. Even though Sophie wasn't a relative, Harriet began to feel vicariously proud. Philippe was also surrounded and being given similar treatment. Harriet scowled, noticing one or two of the prettier women paying him particular attention.

Tim was sitting at a table at the front of the hall. He banged a mug down on the table a couple of times. Everyone, who had previously been milling around, found themselves a seat in one of the rows laid out in a half circle around the top table. Two long banners hung from the wall either side: *The Twelve Steps of AA* and *The Twelve Traditions of AA*. Were these the rules? Harriet wondered, but before she had time to start reading them, Philippe squeezed in front of her and sat down on the seat between her and Sophie.

'My name's Tim and I'm an alcoholic.'

Like a chant around the room, everyone, except for her and Philippe, echoed back: 'Hello Tim.'

Philippe raised an eyebrow and nudged Harriet, who then had to try extremely hard not to laugh.

Two notices stood on the table at the front. One was yellow and read: "Who you see here, What you hear here, When you leave here, Let it stay here"; the other: "God grant me the serenity to accept the things I cannot change, Courage to change the things I can and the Wisdom to know the difference".

Whilst Harriet wasn't religious, that philosophy made a lot of sense. How many times had she banged her head against a brick wall, railing because Greg wasn't behaving in the way she wanted him to? Even though, deep down she knew she couldn't change him. She had tried and failed often enough. And on other occasions, she would be incensed, for example, by how long a salesman had kept her talking at her front door, when all she had to do was to tell him she was busy and close the door. Hmm. She must remember those pearls of wisdom. So obvious now, but at the time . . .

Then people started speaking one by one around the room: 'I'm Pete and I'm an alcoholic and I've been sober for 36 years'; 'I'm Alison and I'm an alcoholic and I've been sober for three months and four days' and so it went on. It was fascinating looking at the different people and hearing how long they had been sober. So why did they keep coming after all that time? Surely they were fixed?

Harriet was so engrossed listening to the years of sobriety that when the room fell silent, Harriet looked around to see who was next. Philippe nudged her. 'It's you,' he whispered.

'Oh. Me. Oh. Sorry. Umm. Well I'm Harriet and I'm here with Sophie and I'm not an alcoholic and my last drink was, well, weeks ago now . . .' Her voice trailed off. She flushed with mortification.

A few people murmured: 'Welcome.' Harriet couldn't face looking up in case they were scowling at her for getting it all wrong.

'I'm Philippe and I'm a visitor,' he said, clearly and calmly.

Harriet rounded on Philippe. 'Smart Arse!'

'Sorry, Sophie just warned me. I didn't have time to brief you.'

'I'll bet!' Harriet crossed her arms in front of her.

A grey haired old lady sat next to Tim. She beamed at everyone. Harriet zoned out as different people read readings and a number of announcements and apologies were given. See, it was feeling more and more like a committee meeting.

Then the grey haired old lady announced herself as: 'Ann.' Ann was undeniably posh. Her twin set and pearls and her cut-glass accent left you in no doubt about which side of the bread her life had been buttered. Until, that is, she started talking.

Philippe stared at Ann in astonishment, having to work very hard at stopping his mouth from gaping. She described how she had been expelled from three boarding schools in the space of a half term. She talked about drinking whisky out of the bottle that she had bribed the caretaker to bring in for her when she was 14. She told them about how she had been kicked out of mummy and daddy's mansion and that the only way she had been able to make enough money to drink was by selling her body on the streets.

'Is she making this up?' Harriet's eyes were agog.

'I doubt it,' Philippe answered. 'Sophie's been banging on about self-honesty ever since she came back from Wengen.'

'Ssshh.' Sophie shot daggers at both of them.

'Sorry,' Harriet mouthed.

The rows of chairs were packed tightly together. The length of Harriet's arm pressed against his. It was becoming more and more difficult to concentrate on what was being said. He had to focus. This was important to Sophie and he wanted to support her. If AA could achieve what he had not been able to, despite his best and most concerted efforts, then they truly were miracle-workers.

After Ann had finished her story, Philippe put his hands together ready to clap. A rumble of "Thank you, Ann" rippled around the room, but no clapping. He was thankful he had waited before applauding.

Different people around the room announced themselves as alcoholics and then proceeded to tell the group a bit about their lives and explain which elements of Ann's story they identified with. Philippe could not help but feel moved at some of the heart-breaking dramas they talked about. Looking at the majority of largely happy, well-dressed people in the room, it was hard to believe they had lived through such horrors, and all because they couldn't stop drinking. Although if he thought about it, anyone who didn't know Sophie would be hard pressed to believe the nightmares she had lived through.

What surprised him the most was the humour that bubbled throughout the room. From what he had heard, there was precious little to laugh about with their near-death experiences, and the loss of family and friends, and dignity and jobs, which seemed to have blighted their lives. Flashes of the horror and dramas that Sophie had put them through over the years, flew through his mind. At this precise moment in time, Sophie's past seemed like a very bad dream, which somehow he had woken up from. Thank God.

A bag came around for donations. Philippe took out his wallet. As he opened it, a photo fell onto the floor. Three sets of eyes focused on the image captured for posterity: the mountains towering in the background; and a rosy-cheeked Philippe and Harriet, both grinning inanely.

Sophie smiled to herself.

Harriet felt a deep warmth glowing through her.

Without looking up, Philippe shoved the photo back in his wallet as if he had just given his entire hand of cards away in one single movement. With a frown plastered across his forehead, he snatched a bundle of notes out of his wallet. If these people were going to save Sophie's life, the least he could do was support them financially.

Just as he was about to push the bundle of notes into the bag, Sophie stopped him. 'You can't,' she whispered. 'We have to be self-supporting. Sorry.'

Well, that was just great! He couldn't get her sober himself and now he couldn't even contribute. What was it with these people?

After the meeting, everyone queued up for yet more coffee. Philippe lost count of the number of people who shook his hand and took time to chat to him. Every now and then he would catch Harriet's eye as she smiled at another person who had come up to talk to her. It was incomprehensible how one tiny grin from Harriet made him feel as if he was flying.

Watching Sophie in her element, more relaxed and happy than he had ever seen her, was the best gift in the world. Given the years and years of watching her destroy herself and her life, and being totally powerless to help her, it was hard to believe that this was actually happening. It was hard to have faith that she would stick to it. The crazy fads that she had tried over the years normally only lasted a couple of weeks. As far as he could tell, these meetings were her last hope.

Sophie chattered away non-stop on the journey back to Bradfield, her whole face illuminated with happiness. 'It was so lovely to have you at my meeting. What did you think of it?'

'Where were all the men in old overcoats?' Philippe turned and grinned at his sister. She nudged him back.

'I was surprised how many young people were there. I thought everyone would be older,' Harriet said.

'What, like me?' Sophie smiled.

The banter continued until they arrived back at The Poplars. As soon as they walked in through the front door, they were herded into the kitchen by Audrey, who fussed around making them drinks and urging them to eat more cupcakes.

'Dad's tucked up in bed,' Audrey told them. 'Would you believe it? I managed to keep him out of the garage all evening.'

'So you've just untied him then?' Philippe smiled at Audrey.

'No, I locked the garage door and pocketed the key.'

Audrey turned to Harriet. 'I've made up the spare bed for you. You can't go home now. I've left one of Sophie's nighties on the bed and a few wash things, which I keep here just in case.'

Harriet turned to Philippe and raised an eyebrow.

As if Audrey read Harriet's mind, she quickly added: 'I've kept them in stock for years now, but apart from some strange looking men who Sophie tried to bring home . . .'

'Mum!' Sophie protested.

'. . . who, by the way, I refused to let in, they've remained in their wrappers. So I'm thrilled that you will be christening them.'

'Well. I don't know . . .'

Harriet glanced over in Philippe's direction. His eyes sparkled. He gave her a little nod.

'That would be lovely. Thank you.' Despite the words of gratitude coming from Harriet's lips, tension played across her forehead and around her mouth.

Before Harriet could dwell on the wisdom of staying the night under the same roof as Philippe, Audrey beckoned to her. Together, they made their way up the narrow staircase. She showed her into a small but cosy room, covered floor to ceiling in red floral wallpaper and more frills than Harriet could ever remember seeing anywhere. If it hadn't been for the décor, the size of the room reminded her of her bedroom in Wengen, but without the window shutters.

After Audrey had left, Harriet sat on the edge of the bed. Should she go back down and say goodnight? Was she expected to stay up here now? Honestly, she felt like a shy 12-year-old who was totally out of her depth in the world of grown-ups.

There was a knock on the door so quiet that at first Harriet thought she had misheard. Then another.

'Come in,' Harriet called out.

Philippe stuck his head around the door and grinned at her. 'I've brought you a night cap.'

'Not literally, please! I've already got the winceyette nightie.' Harriet grimaced at the unflattering nightie, which was laid out on the bed. That can't have been Sophie's, not recently anyway.

'It's a bit of a passion-killer alright.' Philippe put down the tray on the bedside table and settled himself next to Harriet.

Her mouth had gone dry. Everything had slowed. All she was aware of was being in a bedroom with Philippe no more than a few inches away from her.

Philippe must've read her mind. He took her hand in his and brought it to his lips. His eyes searched hers. She reached up both hands and wrapped them around his neck, pulling him close. Philippe's lips found hers. The first few kisses were loving, tender. That was all it took for the spark to ignite between them. It was as if they were plants parched of water as their kisses became more passionate: kissing, touching, fondling . . .

A sharp rap at the door made them jump apart. 'Harriet dear, I forgot to give you a towel.' Audrey opened the door. Her eyes widened as she took in their flushed faces, their rumpled clothes, their hands still entwined.

'Sorry dears. I-I, shall I leave the towel here?' Audrey made a quick exit, closing the door behind her. She smiled to herself as she walked down the hallway. 'I told you!' she whispered to Sophie who was hanging out of her bedroom door waiting for the verdict.

Philippe groaned. 'I knew this was a bad idea. Nothing is secret in this house, not with those two women conspiring together!'

The mortified look on Philippe's face was enough to send Harriet into uncontrollable giggles. 'You look like a naughty school boy who has just been caught having a midnight feast.'

'Well it's nearly midnight Harriet, and I certainly wouldn't mind feasting on you.'

Before Philippe could show Harriet just how much, there was another knock on the door.

'Sorry,' Sophie said, hovering at the door. 'I just wanted to thank you both for coming with me today. It meant a lot.'

Sophie walked over and embraced Philippe and Harriet in turn. 'I like you way better than Lauren,' she whispered in Harriet's ear.

Harriet smiled at Sophie and squeezed her hand.

Just as Sophie was closing the door, Audrey flew into the room. 'Philippe, quick! I need you.'

Philippe jumped up and ran out after his mum. Harriet stood up, unsure whether to stay where she was or to complete the trail of people hurtling down the stairs. Curiosity got the better of her.

By the time she reached the garage, it wasn't hard to guess the reason for the hysteria. The garage door was locked and it seemed that Jack was the only person who had a key.

'Let me in, you big fool!' Audrey shouted through the door. 'You're meant to be recuperating! If you die in there, how d'you think that will make me feel?'

'Mum.' Philippe laid his hand on her shoulder.

'You're so pig-headed! Nothing means more to you than your bloody inventions. Come out of there right now!'

'Mum,' Philippe repeated. He took hold of her arm and steered her away from the garage back into the kitchen.

'But Philippe—' Audrey started.

'But nothing, Mum. There's no point forcing him out of there. You know what he's like: as stubborn as twenty mules.'

'It's all my fault. I hung the key back up on the hook. I thought he was asleep.'

'You mustn't blame yourself.'

Harriet hovered in the background. Sensing she could be of some use, she stepped forward. 'Shall I put the kettle on?'

'I could do with a strong coffee. Would you mind?' Audrey gave her a brief smile.

'And me,' Sophie said.

'I'm scared he'll do himself another injury. I couldn't bear it if, if . . .'

'Mum, he's 65. It's useless trying to change his mind. He's stronger than he looks, you know and the electricity in this house is safer than it's ever been. And he's come through a good deal worse than an electric shock.'

Audrey nodded. 'D'you remember the day he spilt acid on the back of his hand?'

Sophie hugged her baby blue dressing gown tight to her and shivered. 'Is anyone else cold or is it the thought of dad's hand being dissolved in acid?'

'Sounds horrible.' Harriet grimaced. 'Shall I make a coffee for Jack? Would that entice him out?'

'It's worth a try,' Audrey agreed. 'Two sugars and no milk.'

It took several minutes to organise the drinks with all the different requirements: tea, coffee, hot chocolate, milk, no milk, sugar, no sugar. Eventually all of them, apart from Jack, were gathered around the kitchen table, sipping from their mugs and nibbling on yet more cupcakes, which had miraculously appeared. Harriet couldn't imagine ever getting fed up with them.

Each of them in turn, except for Harriet, tried to tempt Jack out of the garage, to no avail. In the end, they left a mug of coffee and a lemon cupcake beside the door. As if by magic, when they came back 15 minutes later, both had disappeared.

'So what do you do when you're not waitressing in Wengen?' Sophie asked Harriet.

'I used to work at Hardacres in their HR department,' Harriet told her.

'Let me expand on that. Harriet was the HR Director,' Philippe added.

'Did you have to tell people off?' Sophie grinned. 'I can't imagine you being very scary.'

'Don't you believe it!' Philippe whispered under his breath.

Harriet tried to kick him under the table, but only succeeded in stubbing her toe on the table leg. She yelped loudly.

'Are you okay, dear?' Audrey asked, patting Harriet's arm.

The grandfather clock in the hallway solemnly chimed midnight.

Audrey got to her feet. 'Well I don't know about you lot, but sometime after midnight I lose a slipper and my gown turns to rags.'

Harriet laughed. 'I'm going up too. I'm exhausted.' This wasn't strictly true, but she didn't want to be trapped down in the kitchen playing happy families with Philippe and Sophie, as much as she liked Sophie. What she wanted to do was to carry on exactly where she and Philippe had left off. Being in such close proximity to Philippe, but without being able to touch him, was excruciating.

Like follow-my-leader, one by one they traipsed back upstairs. First Audrey filed off into her bedroom, calling goodnight, followed by Sophie who disappeared into her bedroom. Then Philippe and Harriet reached the spare room.

Philippe stopped outside the door. 'I won't come in.'

Confusion washed across Harriet's face.

'You have a decision to make.' Philippe took her hand and twisted her engagement ring around her finger. 'I thought I could pretend it wasn't there. But I can't.'

Harriet hung her head. She didn't look at Philippe. She didn't say a word.

Philippe took a deep breath. He had to tell her. If he didn't tell her, how could she decide? But if he told her and she went back to Greg, he didn't know how he would survive it.

He slid his finger under her chin, forcing her to look into his eyes. 'Harriet, I love you with all my heart. I loved you from the moment I first saw you.'

A sob escaped from Harriet's mouth. Philippe's arms were around her before either of them had time to think. He crushed her mouth against his and kissed her as if this was their last chance to be together. Harriet's breath came out in gasps as she pulled him closer and closer.

'No!' Philippe pushed her away from him. 'Harriet I can't. Not yet. I'm sorry. Not with another man's ring on your finger. You have to make a choice.'

Harriet tried to blink away the tears.

'It's impossible. I can't win, whatever I do. Either I lose you or I lose Toby, and I-I can't bear the thought of losing either of you.'

The tears were streaming down Harriet's face. Philippe stepped towards her. Harriet dodged him. She picked up her bag from the dressing table and swept past him.

Philippe tried to grab her arm, but she managed to avoid his grasp and set off down the stairs. 'Harriet wait! You can't leave like this.'

Harriet crossed the kitchen. She heard Philippe's footsteps thundering down the stairs. As she unlocked the door, she could feel Philippe's breath on her neck.

'If you have to go, please drive carefully.'

Harriet nodded. She didn't speak and she didn't turn around. Philippe was like a drug, drawing her back to him, despite her body urging her to run fast in the opposite direction. One glimpse of those grey eyes imploring her to stay and she would be lost.

Philippe could not take his eyes off her as she ran down the path and slid into her car. He watched until the lights disappeared around the corner. This could be it: not just "au revoir", but "goodbye", forever. How could he bear it?

Chapter 30

Tears poured down Harriet's face as she drove the few miles from Bradfield to Theale. On the spur of the moment, instead of turning right towards Theale, Harriet veered left towards Pangbourne.

Yes, it was late at night and yes she should probably leave this until the morning when she had thought everything through, but then hadn't Greg always said that there was no time like the present? She was pretty certain he hadn't meant one in the morning, but there it was. She had, at last, come to a decision. If she waited until a civilised time in the morning to tell him, she might lose her nerve.

She pulled up outside his house and turned off the ignition. The house was in darkness, apart from a dim light shining from Toby's room. He never could sleep with the light off. He was terrified of the dark, bless his little soul.

Harriet wavered. The thought of waking up every morning without seeing Toby; the thought of not being able to take him to and from school every day and do proper mummy things; the thought of her waiting arms not being there for him when he was upset; was unthinkable. And yet, two minutes earlier, she had known with absolute confidence that she could not live without Philippe, even if it meant losing Toby.

'Damn!' Harriet thumped the steering wheel. Would she ever be able to choose?

Maybe if she spoke to Greg first. Maybe he would let her be involved in Toby's life, even if she was with Philippe. Maybe Elspeth was right, and Toby would stay with her during school holidays. Even that seemed like too big a sacrifice to make, to be a part-time mum, but it was more than she'd had three months ago when she didn't think she would ever see Toby again. That way, she could have Philippe and Toby. That *had* to be the way forward? Surely?

Harriet phoned Greg's mobile. It rang a few times before a sleepy voice answered.

'Yes?'

'Greg, it's me, Harriet.'

'Harriet? What the hell are you doing phoning me at this time of the morning? Is everything alright?'

'I need to talk to you.' Harriet was beginning to regret her impulsivity.

'Well, it'd better be important, Harriet. I've got work in the morning.'

'I-I I'm outside.' Harriet heard him grumbling before he disconnected their call.

Harriet waited, shivering as the cold air nipped at her skin. Greg hobbled down the stairs, a deep frown embedded in his forehead. He opened the door and stood back to let her in. He led her through to the kitchen.

'Well, you may as well make us a cup of coffee now you're here.' Greg slumped onto one of the kitchen chairs. He ran his hand through his hair.

Harriet filled up the kettle. He really was very handsome. He didn't look even a bit rumpled even at one in the morning. Shame his face was set in such a sour expression. Harriet knew that this conversation would not be an easy one.

'Well?' Greg demanded as soon as Harriet had perched on the chair opposite his.

'I'm not sure whether we're doing the right thing.' Harriet stared down at her coffee, anything to avoid looking him in the eyes.

A stony silence hovered between them. 'What exactly do you mean by *that*?'

'Um, well. Well, I just wondered, you see . . .' How could she tell him?

'You've woken me up at some unearthly hour of the morning to witter? Spit it out girl. For pity's sake!'

Carefully, Harriet slipped the ring off her finger and laid it on the table next to her. Her next words came out in a whoosh. They weren't the diplomatic ones she had expected to say, instead, she spoke straight from her heart. 'I don't think I can marry you.'

The chair scraped against the tiled kitchen floor as Greg shoved it back. He leapt to his feet. He put his arms onto the table in front of her. His face was contorted with fury. 'Oh you don't, do you? You've downgraded to a one-legged, ex-tennis champ have you?'

Harriet leaned back in her chair. She had never seen him lose control like this. She started shaking. The combination of lack of sleep, too much strong coffee and sugar, and the shock of Greg's reaction was too much for her.

'You've made your choice, Harriet. You will never see Toby again. Not EVER. DO YOU HEAR ME?'

Greg pushed his face right up to hers. Harriet jerked backwards. Her chair crashed back. A dull thud resounded around the room as her head cracked onto the tiles.

A shrill scream tore through Greg's ears. Before Greg could stop him, a blue and white blur flew across the kitchen and threw himself bodily onto Harriet who lay motionless on the floor.

'Harri! Harri! Wake up! Please, please wake up! I love you, Harri!' Toby pulled at Harriet's arm, shaking her. 'Daddy, she's dead. I think she's dead.'

Greg, who had been frozen to the spot, grabbed the home phone. He punched 999 and requested an ambulance. Somehow, despite his plaster, he managed to kneel down beside Harriet. He felt for her pulse. She was still alive. He tried to pull Toby away from Harriet, but he was like a limpet, and the rock he was clinging to for dear life, was Harriet.

By the time the paramedics arrived, Harriet was moaning with pain. Toby stroked her forehead over and over with one hand, holding one of her hands in his other. Greg stood on the outskirts, looking every bit an observer rather than a participant.

Even the over-sized cases that the paramedics lugged around with them, did not distract Toby from Harriet. Normally they would have been quizzed at length as to the contents and purpose of every item.

It took a while to persuade Toby to move back a little so they could carry out some tests on Harriet to 'help her get better'. When he was told he couldn't go with her in the ambulance, he had hysterics. This was calmed only by Greg's assurance that he would call a taxi and they would follow right behind the ambulance and he could see her as soon as she had been assessed at A&E.

Harriet's head was throbbing. Sounds merged into a muffled blur as if they were being forced through a long and echoing tunnel. By the time the sounds reached her, they didn't make any sense. She was pretty certain she heard sirens blaring and vaguely wondered if anyone she knew had been hurt. The sensation of being lifted and moved made her head feel swimmy as nausea overwhelmed her. All she wanted was to sleep; to close her eyes and disappear back into oblivion.

'Harri! Harri! Open your eyes! Please Harri.'

Someone must have glued her eyelids down. It took an almighty effort to prise them open even a millimetre. Blinding light scorched her eyes. She slammed them shut.

'Harri. It's me. Toby. Please, please open your eyes.'

It was as if a key had been turned in the lock that was sticking her eyelids together. They sprang open. She had to squint to stop the light from burning into her pupils. All she could see were white curtains and a stern looking man in a white coat. She tried to move her head, but groaned as a stabbing pain seared through it.

'Toby?' Her voice came out in a ragged rasp.

'You're alive. Harri. You're alive!'

Toby's dear little face appeared in her field of vision. He was blurry, but he was Toby. He reached for Harriet's hand and squeezed it. She managed to pulse her fingers, but couldn't seem to get her fingers to grasp properly.

'Water,' she rasped.

A nurse approached her with a plastic cup and a straw. Harriet drank a few mouthfuls feeling the cool liquid lubricating her dry mouth.

Her head was throbbing again. It was too much effort. It was all too much effort. Her eyes slid shut again as she slipped away, back into her world of pain relief-induced inertia.

Toby burst into tears. The nurse squatted down and took hold of his free hand. 'Your mummy has had a nasty bump on her head. She needs to sleep to get herself well.'

Uncertain, Toby searched her eyes. 'Are you telling me the truth?'

'I am,' the nurse answered. 'I promise that we'll look after her really well all night and you can come back and see her in the morning.'

Toby hesitated. He looked at all the equipment around Harriet's bed: at the machine's buzzing and whirring; at the chart; at the monitors. How could she be alright with all this stuff they were doing to her?

The doctor told Greg they would keep Harriet in overnight to observe her just in case, but they were hopeful that she would make a full recovery. Greg sighed with relief. Toby would never have forgiven him if he had been instrumental in killing or damaging her.

A glance at the clock on the wall told him that he would normally be getting ready for work. Not that he could go into the office today. But if he stuck Toby in front of a film, he could at least sort through some paperwork at home.

'Toby, come on! You look dead on your feet . . .'

'Don't say that, Dad! Don't say that! It makes me worry that Harri will die.'

'Enough nonsense, Toby. We need to go home. We'll come and see Harriet in the morning.'

'But what if she gets worse? What if I'm not here when she wakes up?'

The nurse stooped down to Toby's level. 'If your mum gets worse, we'll call your dad immediately. And if she wakes up, I'll tell her that you will visit her in the morning. How does that sound?'

Toby looked from Harriet to Greg, from Harriet to the nurse. Eventually, he nodded. Greg let out a sigh of relief. It had been a long few hours. They would have precious little time at home before he had to take Toby back to the hospital. Honestly, it was so inconvenient. Although, maybe it was a blessing. Maybe Harriet would have changed her mind. Maybe the crack on her head would have knocked some sense into her. If not, goodness knows how he was going to cope with all this international travel without Harriet to look after Toby. It would be a disaster! A complete disaster.

'Here's a nice cuppa for you.' Audrey set the mug in front of Philippe as he lowered himself onto one of the kitchen chairs.

'Rough night?' she asked.

Philippe had dark rings under his eyes, and despite the tan he had built up in Wengen, his face was pale and drawn.

'Didn't sleep much.'

'And Harriet?' Audrey asked.

'Gone. Last night.'

'What gone, gone?' Audrey resisted the impulse to pull him into her arms so she could comfort him properly like she had when he was small.

'Yes. I think so. I don't know.'

The smell of burning hit Philippe's nose followed by a stream of smoke pouring from the grill.

'Mum, the bacon!'

Audrey dived for the cooker and pulled the grill pan out from under the fierce heat. Despite the bacon being charred black, it hadn't, at least, caught fire.

'Sit down, Mum. I'll cook breakfast.'

'It's all been such a worry.' Audrey sat down, relinquishing control of the cooker to Philippe. 'Your dad didn't come up until gone four 'o' clock this morning. I despair!'

Philippe scrubbed the grill pan in a bowl of hot soapy water. 'You know dad. You can't tie him down. He's only happy when he's inventing.'

Audrey nodded. 'I know, dear. I know. It's just that sometimes I wish I was an interestingly shaped piece of metal, which dad wants to shine, which he would treasure, which he would make good use of.'

The grill pan came out unscarred from its brush with fire. Philippe laid out the rest of the bacon and slotted it back under the grill. Next, he whisked up the eggs with salt and pepper and a dash of milk and tipped them into the buttered pan, which Audrey had already prepared.

'He loves you, Mum. You know that.'

Audrey nodded. 'I know. I only wish that he'd show me.'

Jack chose that moment to walk into the kitchen. Whilst his face didn't register that he had been listening, he had in fact heard the whole conversation. This, in itself, was unusual. It was normally only items from the garage that captured and held his attention.

'I thought I smelt bacon.' Jack took a seat next to Audrey.

'Fancy a bacon buttie, Dad?' Philippe asked, knowing his dad would ask him to deliver it to the workshop when it was ready.

'I could do with a bite to eat, son,' Jack answered. 'And what does a man have to do around here to get a cup of tea?'

Audrey stared at Jack. He never sat down at the table with them unless it was supper, and even then he would frequently make up an excuse not to join them.

'Shall I bring you one, Love?' Audrey asked. 'To the workshop?'

'Nope. I think I'll stop here for a minute.'

Philippe looked at his dad and then over at Audrey, who raised her eyebrows at him.

'Yum! Bacon!' Sophie padded into the kitchen, yawning as she went. She stopped in her tracks when she spotted Jack sitting at the table as if it was a normal every day thing for him to do. 'Dad! What are you doing in here?'

'Can't a man drink a cup of tea at his own kitchen table without being quizzed?'

'Sorry, Dad, it's just that . . .'

'Full works for you, Soph?' Philippe carried on stirring the eggs so they didn't stick to the pan.

'Don't mind if I do. I've been ravenous since I stopped drinking. If I'm not careful I'll blow up like the Michelin man.'

Audrey laughed. 'You're as thin as a twig. It'll do you good to put a bit of meat on your bones.'

'Mum, I'm not a cow heading for market.'

Audrey smiled.

'Put some toast on, Sophie,' Philippe ordered. 'I haven't got enough hands.'

'Men!' Sophie laughed. 'Can't multi-task, that's your problem.'

Philippe pretended to bash her with the spatula. 'I'll have you know I'm cooking bacon and scrambled egg at the same time.'

'What d'you want, Phillie, a medal? Anyway, where's Harriet? I thought she stayed over.'

'Nice girl that Harriet.' Jack fought the urge to escape into the garage to add the finishing touches to his most recent creation.

Philippe focused on dividing up the eggs and bacon onto the plates while Sophie buttered the toast. He didn't know what to tell them about Harriet.

There was a loud knock on the front door, then another.

'Bit early for the postman?' Jack sipped his tea. He made no attempt to answer the door.

Audrey rushed out of the kitchen and across the hall. A grey-haired lady with a kind face stood in their porch; her hair was being whipped about her face by the wind, which was howling around the house.

'Come in, come in.' Audrey pulled the door wide open. 'It's chilly outside for August, isn't it?'

'Indeed it is,' the guest agreed, stepping into the hallway.

'Now what can I do for you?' Audrey looked her up and down. *Women's Institute* enquiry maybe? They were always looking for new members. Or the local church perhaps? Or the village befriending scheme? She wouldn't mind doing a bit of visiting in the community. They might like a few of her cupcakes.

'I've come to see Philippe. Is he in?'

Audrey tried to hide her surprise. Fortunately, the good manners that her mother had instilled in her routinely over 18 years, kicked in. 'Of course. Let me take your coat and I'll show you through.'

The kitchen was warm and smelled of cooked breakfast. Philippe had just finished handing out plates of bacon and eggs when he looked up and saw Elspeth.

'Elspeth! To what do I owe this pleasure?' He walked over to her and planted a kiss on her cheek. 'It's lovely to see you. Harriet said you'd visited her.'

'Honestly, let the poor lady speak.' Audrey laughed.

'Look Philippe, I'm just going to spit it out. Harriet's in hospital.'

Harriet, in hospital? Why? How? What if she'd had an accident on the way back from his house? It would be his fault. His fault for rejecting her. She had been so upset.

Elspeth crossed the few feet to where Philippe was standing frozen to the spot. 'Sit! She hit her head. They've kept her in overnight for observation.'

Audrey sat down next to Jack, who took her hand in his. She had to smother a gasp that tried to creep out of her mouth at this unexpected gesture of affection.

'How?' Philippe asked, pushing away the plate of food that was rapidly congealing on the plate. Even the thought of it made him feel sick.

'That, I don't know. I thought I'd pop in this morning on my way back from London, but Harriet wasn't in and she wasn't answering her phone. So I called Greg and he told me the news.'

At the mention of Greg, every fibre in Philippe's body went on the defensive, before collapsing in despair. So, she had made her choice. She had gone straight from his house into Greg's arms. He had forced her there by making her choose.

An image of Harriet lying in a hospital bed wired up to monitors, her life hanging in the balance, invaded his head. Suddenly, nothing mattered except Harriet getting well and being okay. The thought of her being with that loser was preferable to her dying. Harriet dying was incomprehensible to him. It couldn't, wouldn't, mustn't happen.

'Will she be alright?' Philippe asked, his fists clenching together.

'I honestly don't know,' Elspeth said. 'I'm going to the hospital now. You'll come with me?'

Would she want him there? What about Toby? And Greg? Would he be intruding?

'Philippe?' Elspeth asked.

All eyes in the room focused on Philippe. Indecision tousled inside him.

'You've got to go,' Sophie urged. 'What if she dies?'

A vivid picture of Harriet lying cold and white on a stone slab crowded into his mind.

'Let's go!' he said. 'I'll drive.'

Chapter 31

Harriet had been lucky enough never to have experienced a migraine. She had, however, heard graphic accounts of the pain that sawed its way across your eyes and around the head, how nausea could be triggered by the slightest breath of air and how splintered vision would fragment objects right in front of your eyes. From the way her head was feeling this morning, she suspected that a migraine would not be that dissimilar.

She winced as loud voices rattled through her head. A moan escaped her lips. How come loud sounds could accentuate each of her senses? She closed her eyes tightly to try to block out the commotion merging horribly with the bright hospital lights.

'Sir! Sir! You can't go in! It's not visiting hours yet . . .'

Harriet half-opened her eyes and stared at the door in time to see the nurse hurtling into her room through the now open door. Following close on her heels was Elspeth, who was moving faster than she had ever seen her, even when she was playing chase with Toby.

Elspeth? What was she doing here? How did Elspeth know she was in hospital?

Someone took her hand. Slowly she moved her head to her left. There, standing next to the bed with a concerned expression on his face, was Philippe.

'Philippe?'

'I'm here now.' Philippe stroked her forehead. 'How are you feeling?'

'Groggy,' Harriet admitted, 'and my head feels like someone has been using it as a pin cushion.'

Concern wrinkled Philippe's brow. 'That sounds painful. My grandma used to sew. I couldn't tell you the number of needles she shoved into her pin cushion over the years, but it must have been thousands.'

Harriet flinched.

'You certainly look pale.' Elspeth moved around the bed so she was on the same side as Philippe to save Harriet from turning her head more than she had to.

'What happened?' Elspeth asked. 'You weren't trying that pole dancing in your kitchen again, were you?'

Philippe's head jerked up. His eyes flared with interest. 'Pole dancing, heh? Tell me more.'

'I'll have you know that my kitchen is barely big enough to swing a kitten let alone swing around a pole.' Harriet's eyes moved to Elspeth. 'Elspeth, behave! You're meant to be the one setting a good example.'

'I don't see why.' Elspeth replied.

'Plenty of scope for pole dancing in my flat in London.' Philippe raised an eyebrow.

'Will you two stop with this pole dancing lark. If you must know, I fell backwards off a chair.'

The nurse was still hovering by the door, hands on her hips. 'I really must insist that your guests come back later.'

'Can't they stay a few more minutes? Please.'

'Right, five minutes and that's your limit. If the doctor catches them in here, he'll haul me over the coals.'

Philippe nodded. 'Thank you.'

Once the nurse had slipped out, Elspeth sank down onto one of the uncomfortable plastic chairs reserved for guests. Perhaps that was a ruse to discourage visitors from loitering for longer than was necessary. 'You'll be okay, Harriet?'

'I'm waiting for the final prognosis when the doctor does his rounds, but apart from a headache from hell, I'm pretty sure I'll be fine.'

Harriet's face was almost as pale as the sheets she was lying on. In the space of a few hours any colour that had formerly graced her face had been sucked clean out of her. She looked as frail as a baby bird. Even her hair seemed to have lost its oomph.

'You'll need to recuperate.' Philippe laid a hand on Harriet's shoulder and squeezed gently; his other hand was still entwined with hers. 'Mum said to tell you that the guest bedroom is yours for as long as you want it. She's already made a start on making it pretty for you.

Harriet grinned back at him.

'Or I can be your live-in housekeeper, nursemaid, companion and whatever else you would like?' Elspeth suggested. 'Normally it's you young 'uns looking after us old 'uns but with you, I'm prepared to make an exception.'

The loud roar of an aeroplane assaulted Harriet's ears. Seconds later, Toby dived into the room, his arms outstretched like a fighter plane. 'Look at me Harri, 'I'm a Red Arrow shooting across the sky. Watch me, Harri. Watch me!'

'You'll be breaking the speed of light if you're not careful.' Elspeth stepped to the side to avoid being crashed into by a human Red Arrow.

The plane halted its noisy descent. 'Elspeth. What are you doing here? Have you come to see Harriet? Oh Philippe. And you? I thought you were still in Switzerland.'

'And breathe.' Elspeth took a deep breath and winked at Toby.

Toby giggled.

'Well, *this is* cosy.' Greg stood stock still, his body framed in the doorway, taking in the scene in front of him.

Philippe let go of Harriet's hand and stepped back from the bed.

'You're SO popular, Harri.' Toby jumped onto the edge of the bed sending shooting pains across Harriet's temple.

Elspeth got to her feet. 'You wouldn't happen to know where the nearest vending machine is, would you, Toby? I'm sure everyone could do with a drink.'

'And some sweets,' Toby added. He jumped to his feet and bounced up and down on the spot. 'I know! I know! It's just around the corner, isn't it, Dad?'

Greg nodded.

Elspeth looked to Greg for his authorisation. He nodded again, curtly this time. His eyes were cold and hard, flicking between Philippe and Harriet, and back again.

Once the door had closed behind Elspeth and Toby, Harriet closed her eyes. Wishful thinking: that if she couldn't see them both standing there, it wouldn't really be happening. A show down between the two of them when her head felt as if it was exploding was not something she was looking forward to.

'I don't know what you think you're playing at,' Greg addressed Philippe, 'but that's my fiancée you are toying with.'

'"Was", I think, is the word you're looking for,' Philippe retorted. It was the first thing he'd noticed. Harriet wasn't wearing her engagement ring anymore. He hoped it hadn't been removed for practical purposes when she'd been admitted.

'I know what you famous people are like. A different woman each night. Well, I won't have you tampering with Harriet. She's mine!' Greg's crutches clicked as he advanced towards Philippe, a menacing look on his face.

Philippe stood his ground. He was not going to be intimidated by the immaculate suit and highly groomed exterior.

'Oh, for goodness sake you two!' Harriet managed to raise herself up on her elbows.

Philippe reached over and pushed an extra pillow behind her back to give her some support.

'I'm not some chattel you can fight over. Has it not occurred to either of you to ask me what I want?'

Philippe looked ashamed. 'Sorry Harriet. You're right. Of course. What, who, do you want?'

'Why the hell would I ask you?' Greg glared at Harriet. 'You haven't a clue half the time what's best for you. You are engaged to me, and just because we had a slight disagreement, it doesn't mean you have to get all dramatic on me. Honestly, sometimes Toby has more common sense than you do!'

Adrenalin was a remarkable pain relief. As fury coursed through Harriet's veins, the pain in her head miraculously receded into the background.

'How DARE you!' Harriet's words were clipped and cold. 'I DO know my own mind, and one thing I know for certain is that I sure as hell don't want to spend another minute in your company. I must have been mad. You think you can sleep with other women and drag me abroad without even having the decency to discuss your plans with me?'

'Now, come on, Harriet. You're being unreasonable. That is totally unfair.'

'Unfair! You'd think we'd gone back to the cavemen days the way you treat me. You may as well be dragging me around on my back by my hair for all the respect you show me!'

Philippe stood watching this heated exchange, hope welling up inside him.

'You just don't know when you're onto a good thing.' Greg persisted. 'You're more of a fool than I thought you were if you've fallen for that, that philanderer's line.'

Harriet watched a muscle twitching on Philippe's temple, his fists clenching by his side.

'I meant what I said Greg.' Two bright red stains infused Harriet's cheeks. 'We're over. Finished. I never want to see you again! Not EVER!'

No-one heard the door opening until a loud sob resounded through the horrified silence.

'NOOOOO!' In a flash, Toby shot out of the room. Harriet could hear his footsteps pounding along the corridor.

'Quickly! Someone! Go after him!'

Harriet had barely finished her sentence before Philippe was out of the door like a hare. He raced passed Elspeth carrying a tray of drinks, who stared after Toby and then Philippe in astonishment.

Greg stepped closer to Harriet, waving his fist at her. 'Now look what you've done. You stupid cow! How could you?'

Elspeth placed the tray on Harriet's table. She strode over to Greg. She laid her hand on his shoulder and to his complete surprise, turned him towards the door. 'You need to leave. NOW!'

Greg glared at Elspeth. He turned towards Harriet. 'And don't think you'll ever see Toby again.'

With that, Harriet burst into tears. Her head was pounding with a new level of pain.

Elspeth frog-marched Greg out of the room just as the nurse reappeared. 'What has been going on in here?'

'All under control,' Elspeth reassured her. 'Although I think your patient could do with a bit of TLC.'

The nurse hurried over to where Harriet was sobbing. She handed her a box of tissues and began carrying out some tests, conscious that the doctor was doing his rounds at any minute. He would not be happy to be faced with a hysterical patient. And this wasn't any old doctor, this was Mr Meticulous, "jump when I say jump, or preferably before, and hang on my every word as if I am God" type doctor. The last thing she needed was for him to find out that she had allowed a crowd of visitors to come into the ward well before visiting time upsetting his patient.

Whilst Nurse Elaine did her best to soothe Harriet, Philippe ran down the main hospital corridor, stopping now and then to peer through doors. He wondered whether Toby would have ventured into the eye clinic, but decided against it. When Harriet got a tiny grass seed lodged in her eye in Wengen, Toby had been extremely squeamish.

As he passed countless doors, he realised how much this was like searching for a needle in a haystack. Toby could easily have dashed through any one of them in his bid to hide away from them all. And who could blame him? The thought of a lifetime without Harriet was enough to make him want to run away. Harriet was the closest person Toby had to a mum. Having already lost her once, of course it was too much for Toby to think of losing her again.

Philippe pounded down yet another corridor. As he ran past a couple of abandoned hospital beds, a loud sob stopped him in his tracks. He scanned the corridor. He couldn't see anyone. Another sob came from the direction of the hospital beds. Philippe bent down. There, curled up on the floor under one of the beds, was Toby.

'GO AWAY! Toby shouted: "Go Away!" I HATE you!'

Philippe sighed. He slid down the wall and sat on the floor so he was more or less eye-level with Toby.

'You've taken Harri away from us. I'll never see her again. NEVER!'

'I'm sorry Toby. Really. I never meant to take Harriet away from you.'

Toby sniffed, rubbing his eyes with his balled fists. Philippe reached into his pocket and pulled out a handkerchief. He handed it to Toby. Toby hesitated, and then snatched it out of Philippe's hand, rubbing at his eyes with it.

'I tried not to fall in love with her. I tried to stay away from her so she could be with you. But I love her too much.'

There wasn't much room under the trolley. Toby uncrossed his legs and stretched them out as they were starting to get pins and needles.

'But she's my mum,' Toby said. 'Have you got a mum?'

Philippe nodded. 'Yes. I have a mum and a dad.'

'And you'd be sad if your mum left you and never came back, wouldn't you?' Toby turned to Philippe. His large brown eyes stared up at Philippe's like a sad puppy.

'I would be heart-broken.' Philippe felt as if his heart was breaking now watching Toby go through so much pain.

'Does Harri love dad?' Toby asked.

'I don't know, Toby. I think you'll have to ask Harriet yourself.'

'Will you come with me?' Toby crawled out from under the trolley.

Philippe nodded. He pushed himself to his feet. He was incredulous that Toby could go from hating him in one breath to asking him to come with him in the next. For a seven-year-old, he was unnervingly philosophical.

As they approached the room Harriet was occupying, they saw Elspeth hovering outside.

'You have to wait a few minutes,' she whispered. 'The doctor is in with Harriet at the moment. Why don't we go and get a drink at the café? We can see her straight after that.'

'I'll have a large Pepsi!' Toby said, beaming. 'And we'll get one for Harri too. She looks like she could do with some cooling down.'

Twenty minutes later, three heads peered into Harriet's bedroom to find the bed empty.

'She's gone!' Toby squealed. 'Harri's gone! She might have died. Has she died?'

'I'm here.' Harriet appeared from behind the door.

'You must be a ghost!' Toby flung his arms around Harriet and squeezed her hard.

Harriet squeezed him back. 'If I were a ghost Toby, your arms would go right through me.'

'Cool!' Toby said, pulling away.

Harriet swayed on her feet. Philippe rushed over to her side and steadied her with his arm. He guided her to the seat next to her bed.

'What did the doctor say?'

'He's discharged me with some painkillers for my head, although he has said that I mustn't be alone for at least 24 hours.'

'Well, that settles it, you must come and stay with us,' Philippe said.

Elspeth noticed Toby's stricken face. 'Or maybe Toby and I could look after you at home, if Greg is okay with that.'

Toby walked over to Harriet. For once he looked serious. He took her hand. 'Harri, do you love me?'

Harriet's eyes filled with tears. 'Toby, I love you very, very much. You are like a son to me.'

Silence filled the room as Philippe and Elspeth watched the two of them.

'And do you love dad?'

Everyone held their breath. Harriet closed her eyes. Toby's face pleaded for her to say yes. The thought of him collapsing in tears if she told him the truth was almost too much for her to bear. How could she explode his world so callously?

She opened her eyes. Toby's serious face wracked with worry stared up at her. It was almost enough to inspire her to call the vicar and get the ceremony between her and Greg over and done with. Then she could focus her whole life on being the best possible mum to Toby. But, hovering above, mocking her with the intensity of a brewing storm, were vivid images of Greg and Jessica, of Greg and Marcia, of Greg telling her she didn't know her own mind. Something inside her had snapped. She knew that she couldn't go back there. Never again!

Harriet picked up Toby's hand and held it tightly in hers. 'Toby, I am so sorry, but I don't love your dad. Not anymore.'

Toby's eyes filled with tears. 'Couldn't you try harder?'

'It doesn't work like that. I'm so sorry. But I still love you very much. And I'm going to speak to your dad and see if you can visit me a lot. Would you like that?'

'But you won't be a proper mum.' Toby turned his face away and started sobbing.

'I can't be with you every day, but I'll try to be the best part-time mum ever. Your dad might even let me pick you up from school sometimes, and we can have sleepovers and lots of treats.'

Okay, so Greg had told her she would never see Toby again. But this time, she'd fight. She wouldn't let Greg simply walk away again, taking Toby with him. Not this time.

Toby's whole demeanour changed. He looked up at Harriet between his eyelashes. 'What sort of treats?'

'Take away pizza in our pyjamas? Hot chocolate and marshmallows watching a film? Or homemade popcorn? Legoland maybe?'

The boy who had, a few minutes before, looked like he would have to be carted away by the National Society for the Prevention of Cruelty to Children (NSPCC), shrieked with joy and bounced up and down in the air as if he was a pogo stick.

'I'll have to join you both,' Elspeth said, 'sounds far too tempting for the two of you to keep this all to yourself. What about you, Philippe?'

Before Philippe had a chance to answer, Toby butted in. 'You can teach me tennis. I want to be world champion like you.'

Philippe looked over at Harriet. Her eyes shone with love for the little boy standing in front of her.

Harriet caught Philippe looking at her. Her smile widened. The love that flowed from her to Toby didn't dim when she held Philippe's eyes. Philippe's heart thumped loudly in his chest.

'There you are!' Greg's voice barked out across the room. 'Come on, Toby. We're leaving. Now!'

Toby threw his arms around Harriet and clung to her. 'I'm staying with Harri. I love Harri. She's my mum and you're trying to take her away from me.'

The whole room rang with Toby's words. Greg visibly blanched. He stepped towards Toby. 'But Harriet doesn't want us.'

Deep colour infused Toby's face. 'SHE WANTS ME! HARRI DOESN'T WANT YOU, BUT SHE WANTS ME AND YOU CAN'T MAKE ME LEAVE HER!'

Greg's face was like thunder. He stalked towards Harriet. He shoved his face right up close to hers. 'LOOK WHAT YOU HAVE DONE NOW!'

Philippe watched Harriet as she struggled to contain her anger. He saw Toby's eyes flitting between the two of them. He stepped forwards and placed his hand on Greg's shoulder. 'Let Elspeth take Toby for lunch, and then we can all sit down and talk this through.'

Greg was about to launch into another tirade, when Philippe added: 'Toby is the most important person here. We have to make him our priority.'

No-one spoke. Everyone looked at Greg. He turned away from Harriet. He shoved Philippe out of the way and then tried to stalk towards the door, which proved to be impossible whilst attempting to negotiate a pair of unruly crutches.

Toby raced after Greg. He grabbed him by the arm. 'Dad! Please don't leave. Please talk to Harri. Please.'

Greg stopped. He looked at Toby's upturned face, tear stains running down the length of it. 'Okay.'

'And promise you won't make Harriet go away.' Toby's eyes implored Greg.

Greg nodded, keeping his fingers crossed behind his back. Some old habits from childhood were hard to break.

Ten minutes later, Greg, Harriet and Philippe were sitting around a table in one of the hospital's many cafés. Greg hadn't wanted Philippe there. He said it was between him and Harriet. But Philippe had insisted. Eventually, Greg conceded. 'You may as well hear what I have to say.' Greg had said. 'That should put you off her good and proper,' he had then added under his breath.

Just as Greg was about to launch into his diatribe, Harriet spoke. 'I love Toby with all my heart. It would tear me apart not to see him. I can help out, Greg, don't you see? He can stay over when you're working late. He can go to school when you're away. We can make this work, Greg, truly we can. Unless, unless, you're taking him abroad with you? But he can still stay with me during school holidays, can't he?'

Harriet's eyes flicked over to Philippe's. He gave her an encouraging nod and a slight smile.

Several minutes of silence passed. The tension was building. Harriet could hardly bear it. 'Greg?'

Yet another internal battle raged within Greg. His dented pride at being abandoned by Harriet fought with the convenience of allowing Harriet to be a part of his life, or Toby's at any rate. It would save him some enormous headaches, particularly with this new role, which would necessitate him visiting different countries a couple of times a month. He thought back to the last few months with Jessica. She didn't do anything with or for Toby. It had been a nightmare sorting out childcare, having to cut meetings short, getting told off by the after-school club for arriving late, yet again.

And Toby had begged. Yes, it hurt him to agree, but he didn't see he had any choice, not if he wanted an easy life, and not if he wanted Toby to behave. When he banished Harriet from their lives, Toby turned into a tyrant. It had been months before he could do anything with him. No, he could not go through that again.

'Okay, but on one condition: that *he* stays out of Toby's life.' Greg glared at Philippe.

A few people from surrounding tables glanced over at the raised voices.

'That is blackmail,' Harriet's fury hissed through her teeth. 'How *dare* you!'

'*How dare you*?' Greg mimicked. 'You mess around with Mr High and Mighty here, you throw my ring back in my face, you want half of my son and then, then you have the audacity to think you can parade Philippe around in front of Toby like some kind of trophy. Well, you are very much mistaken if you take me for that much of a fool.'

An old lady hobbled slowly along, supporting herself with a Zimmer frame. She accidentally knocked into Greg's chair as she tried to get to her table.

'Watch where you're going, can't you!' Greg shouted. He spun around to confront the person who had jogged his mug. Hot splashes of coffee stained his beige trousers and white striped shirt.

The old lady started trembling. Greg swore under his breath. Stupid old people. Honestly, they shouldn't be allowed out in that state. Look what the coffee had done to his clothes. Who was going to foot the bill for that?

Greg mopped at his trousers and his shirt ineffectively with a paper napkin. All he managed to do, however, was to spread the stain further.

'Greg! You need to move. She can't get past.'

Philippe stood up and gave the old lady his arm.

With great reluctance, Greg got up and moved his chair, muttering to himself. 'Bloody old woman! Bloody hero superstar!'

Once Philippe had guided the old lady past their table and set her on her way, she shuffled slowly towards her table where a man, who looked like a body builder or boxer, was sitting. What must have been 6'5" of him stood up and made his way over to where his mother was shakily moving towards him.

Once he had settled her at the table, he strode towards Greg. 'Next time you want to pick a fight mate, pick on someone your own size!' He shook his fist at Greg. Greg flinched. He shoved Greg on the shoulder. 'Leave old women alone!' With those parting words, he re-joined his mother.

Greg tried to bring himself back under control, but he couldn't think straight. Why had his life suddenly taken on a mind of its own and started defying him at every turn?

Chapter 32

Before anyone else could speak, Harriet clutched her head and swayed on her chair. 'I think I'm going to . . .'

Philippe lunged forward and caught her before she reached the floor. 'Right! That's enough! You're coming home with me.'

Harriet's head was throbbing. She couldn't think straight. She vaguely heard Philippe telling Greg to let Toby know that he could visit Harriet any time he wanted and to tell him that Elspeth knew the address.

'Toby's not going anywhere near Harriet, not until you sling your hook!'

Philippe ignored Greg. He was focusing all his efforts on supporting Harriet.

Greg sat motionless. He didn't have the energy for fainting women. He watched as Philippe supported Harriet along the corridor as they headed towards the car park. On this occasion, Philippe was welcome to her.

Whilst some of his attention was focused on Philippe and Harriet's slow progress, his eyes flicked constantly back to the muscly man sitting on the neighbouring table wondering whether he was going to attack him again. Time to leave. He eased himself to his feet, slotting the crutches under his arms. Right. Now to find Toby.

After 30 frustrating minutes, by which time, his temper was on an even thinner thread and his ankle was throbbing, he finally spotted Toby and Elspeth in a café opposite one of the shops. Toby was chatting away to her, tucking into what looked like some kind of cheese roll.

'Daddy! Where's Harri? Can I see her? You'll let me see her, won't you?'

'Of course he will,' Elspeth answered. 'Your daddy is lovely, isn't he, Toby?'

With a solemn face, Toby looked over at Elspeth and then up at Greg. 'You would have to be a very mean daddy to keep their son away from a mummy who they love . . .'

This had been one hell of a day. He was being attacked from every angle. How could he tell Toby that he could only see Harriet when Philippe wasn't around? If Harriet stayed with that idiot, it would mean that Toby would never see Harriet, or hardly ever. And that would mean massive complications for him in so many ways. He couldn't make a success of this international role without anyone to look after Toby. And as it was, Toby had been banging on about tennis lessons practically non-stop.

Well, there it was. He had been backed into a corner. The die had been cast. He may as well swallow his pride and take full advantage of it. Harriet wanted to see Toby; well, she was welcome to him. At least with Harriet in Toby's life, he could come and go from work and fly between countries without Toby standing in his way.

As for Philippe, he was a complete loser. He couldn't understand why Harriet would choose such a lightweight over him, but . . . Greg sighed. Okay, so he had lost that battle as well, but at least he could get on with his life. There were plenty of other women out there, and to be honest, Harriet had become far too opinionated. Philippe was welcome to her.

Greg's silence was correctly interpreted by Toby as capitulation.

'Oh, Daddy, thank you. Thank you so much! I can stay with Harri and have sleep overs and she can take me to school when you're away, can't she? And Philippe can teach me tennis, can't he?' Toby bounced off his seat and threw himself into Greg's arms.

Greg glared at Elspeth over Toby's head. He'd been backed into a corner and was trying to make the best of it, but his hurt pride was throbbing. It was obvious that Elspeth had been chief conspirator in all this. He wasn't going to let *her* off the hook so easily. Elspeth smiled back at him, unable to stop a certain smugness from creeping in.

'You're the best daddy ever!' Toby hugged Greg tightly to him.

The gravel scattered in every direction as Philippe's car swung into the driveway. He was out of the car and at the passenger door even before the engine had finished turning over. Harriet's deathly pallor had returned. Philippe reached across her to unlock her seatbelt. Gently, he lifted her into his arms and carried her into the house.

Audrey opened the front door and went ahead of him up the stairs.

'I'm okay really,' Harriet protested. 'Just a headache.'

'You, young lady, will do exactly as you're told. For once.' Philippe laid her carefully on the spare bed.

The light streaming in through the windows made Harriet squint and cover her eyes with her arm. Her headache had returned with a vengeance. Seeing Harriet's discomfort, Audrey hurried over to the window and swept the curtains across, coating the room in shadow. 'Better?'

Harriet winced again as she nodded. It was becoming harder and harder to keep her eyes open.

Audrey fussed around her, plumping her pillows and covering her with the duvet.

'Mum, would you get Harriet a glass of water.' Philippe lowered himself onto the edge of the bed.

Once Audrey had left the room, Philippe turned to Harriet. 'How are you doing?' He brushed a stray lock of hair away from her face. He couldn't resist stroking her hair, wishing that he could brush away her worries, her tiredness and her pain.

Harriet forced open her eyes. They were so green, they reminded him of the next door neighbour's cat that used to spend most of its time curled up by the fire in their kitchen.

'My head hurts,' Harriet whispered. She groped near him with her hand until she found his. Her fingers curled around his.

'You sleep, Harriet.' He wanted to add: 'my darling' but didn't quite dare. She was too bruised in too many ways. He had to give her time to recover.

Audrey placed the glass of water on the bedside cabinet and tiptoed out of the room. She squeezed Philippe's shoulder before she left.

Philippe sat holding Harriet's hand until her breathing became slow and even, until her eyelids lowered and her eyelashes fanned out on her cheeks. He let his eyes wander around the room. This was his mother's favourite. The reds and ruffles and flowers were enough to imagine Barbara Cartland taking up residence. How Sophie had hated this girly, over-the-top indulgence. But it made his mum happy and at the end of the day, surely that was the only thing that mattered: happiness.

It made him happy just being with Harriet, even when she was sleeping. He could study her face without her enquiring eyes challenging his.

Philippe shifted position and yawned. He knew he should be making the finishing touches to his novel, but he couldn't bring himself to leave Harriet, not even to collect his laptop. But, Monday was D-Day and the publishers hadn't yet received confirmation from him that he was going to meet their deadline. Probably because he wasn't certain he would. Even though he had been burning the midnight oil; in fact, the early hours of the morning oil, most nights this week, when he wasn't at the hospital, it was still touch and go whether his manuscript would be in a presentable state by Monday. The recent dramas had thrown out his schedule, hopefully not irreparably.

And that was the last thought he had until Audrey shook him awake. 'Philippe. I thought you might like a drink,' she whispered.

Disorientated, Philippe looked up to see Audrey hovering over him with a laden tray. He jumped up and took it from her. One glance at Harriet told him that she was still sleeping soundly. He motioned over to the door, which they both crept through. Audrey closed it softly behind them.

Back in the kitchen, Sophie was singing away at the top of her voice to a song that contained the word "happy" on more than a few occasions.

'Ssshh!' Audrey reached across and turned down the volume. 'Harriet's still asleep.'

Sophie scowled, but remembering that she was trying to be a better daughter than the drunken, argumentative one she had been for years, she forced a smile. Anyway, she really was concerned about Harriet. She had grown fond of her surprisingly quickly. 'How is she?'

'She *was* fast asleep . . .' Philippe took the mug of tea that Audrey handed him.

'I see you've still got that stupid mug I painted for you when I was, what, five?' Sophie threw herself down on the seat next to Philippe. Secretly she was quite pleased he hadn't thrown it out.

'Yes, some kind person named Jo, was it? she posted it back to Philippe.' Audrey offered around her new creation: cherry and lemon cupcakes with pistachio icing.

'Posted? Don't tell me you took it to Switzerland with you?' Sophie stared at her brother in astonishment.

'Might have.' Philippe looked sheepish.

'Do I smell tea?' Jack peered through the garage door, his hair sticking up in tufts.

Audrey looked at him, love shining out of her eyes. 'I don't know how you do it. The moment the teabags start brewing, you appear!'

'As if by magic . . .' Sophie quoted, remembering "Mr Ben" who used to go into a fancy dress shop, put on an outfit, walk through an enchanted door and have exciting adventures before the shopkeeper arrived to take him back to the changing room.

'. . . the shopkeeper appeared!' Philippe finished off, grinning. 'D'you remember how many episodes you watched back to back on our ancient video player?'

There were mixed reactions to the new brand of cupcake. It was a hit with Sophie. She polished off her own and Jack's hardly eaten cupcake. Philippe tried to like it, but couldn't manage more than one mouthful, whereas Audrey hailed them as a great success. She told the men of her family to be more adventurous.

'What like Mr Ben?' Sophie joked.

'How's the girl?' Jack asked.

'"The girl", as you put it, has a name.'

A ginger cat flew through the open back door and darted into the garage.

'Pesky cat!'

'That's Marmalade from next door. Remember? She only wants to hide in your garage.'

'Marmalade or not, that cat has no right to be in my garage.' Jack shot up out of his chair and chased after Marmalade, closely followed by Sophie.

'What is happening with you two?' Audrey asked.

'It's complicated.'

Audrey waited.

'Greg won't let her see Toby if I'm around. There's no contest. Before, there was always a chance that Harriet could still see Toby, even if we were together. But now . . . how can I destroy a seven-year-old's dream? Or Harriet's for that matter?'

Audrey busied around, wiping down surfaces and slotting cutlery into the open dishwasher. 'But, you do love her, don't you? And yet, you're not going to fight?'

Philippe watched his mother bustling around. How could he fight? Greg had been deadly serious. If he stayed around, Harriet would never see Toby. He couldn't do that to either of them. It was unbelievable that, after so much chasing around, here they both were, back at square one.

And if Audrey got involved, who knew what would happen then. He had to find some way of throwing her off the scent. He could sense that her much-frustrated match-making skills were about to kick into play big time, and he knew that neither of them would get a moment's peace.

Lying wasn't something he did regularly, but when it came to his mother on the prowl, it was the only way. All things considered, the best plan would be to pack up his belongings and return to his flat in London to focus on his writing. Now was the time to make a complete break. He needed to get on with his life and let Harriet get on with hers, as unbearable as that thought was.

Philippe swallowed and looked down at the tablecloth as he replied. 'No, Mum. You couldn't be more wrong. For a moment, I confused infatuation and the challenge of the chase with love. But she was just a passing phase. Honestly. I don't love her. I mean, she's a great girl, and she needed my support, but she's just not my type.'

Harriet covered her hand with her mouth to stop herself from gasping out loud. She had to push herself back hard against the wall so she didn't collapse. It had taken every ounce of energy she possessed to get down the stairs.

Philippe didn't love her. She was a "passing phase". She was just not his "type". But how? Why? He had seemed so convincing, so loving, so caring. He'd even told her that he loved her. Bloody, bloody men!

How she got herself back up to the bedroom without passing out, she had no idea. It must have been the thought of Philippe or Audrey catching her there, knowing she had heard every word. She didn't think she could have borne the humiliation. All she wanted to do now was leave; to get away from here as fast as possible. Unfortunately, this time, a midnight dash was out of the question. Somehow, she would have to make it through to the morning.

Harriet's emotions swung backwards and forwards like the pendulum of a grandfather clock. He didn't love her, and yet the way he'd looked at her, the way he'd stroked her hair. She hadn't imagined that, had she?

But of course, this was *the* Philippe Myers, the "darling" of the tennis world. He was well-versed in romancing and schmoozing with his public. And yet, it was so hard to believe that she meant nothing more to him than someone who had needed a helping hand.

She had certainly fallen for his charms, over and over again. She had believed that his feelings were genuine. But she could not un-hear the words that had, a minute or so ago, slipped naturally and convincingly out of his mouth, denying her. She felt as betrayed as if it was Judas shooting her down. Not that she could of course come anywhere near likening herself to Jesus . . . no beard for starters. A tiny smile tried to wind itself around her mouth, but both the physical and emotional pain she was feeling froze the attempt in mid-flow.

Harriet took another couple of pain killers, curled up on the bed and was eventually, after a lot of tossing and turning, rewarded with the oblivion of sleep.

It was midnight by the time Philippe reached his flat. As he walked in through the door, memories flooded back: Lauren, the whirlwind of matches and adoring fans, of interviews and training, of a different life.

He flicked on the lights. This place seemed more foreign to him than the suite he had occupied in Wengen. Lauren had paid a high-end interior designer to brush the flat with a minimalist look. Well they had succeeded: cold flagstone floors; bright white walls; a few pieces of curved, uncomfortable furniture; and some bleak pieces of art, which would no doubt be revered in the Tate Modern.

The cleaner had been in once a week, even when he was away. There wasn't a speck of dust or a trace of life to be found. He almost wished a spider would dangle itself from the ceiling. It was more like a mausoleum than a home.

The first thing he did after dropping his case onto the floor was to head through to his office, which had little to differentiate it in style from the rest of the flat. Honestly, as soon as this novel was packaged up and out of his hair, he was going to make some big changes. He could not live in this cold and clinical environment, not anymore. The last few months had changed him. He was no longer Philippe Myers, Tennis Champion. He was Philippe Smith, writer. All he wanted to do now was to shrug off the last few remaining vestiges of fame, which still hung heavy in his life like a thick winter coat during a hot summer, except the 'pe' on the end of his Christian name, of course. He was keeping that.

He was certain he didn't want to live in London. Having spent months in the fresh air of the mountains and a week or so back in Bradfield, the city had lost its appeal. He wanted to sink into a sofa, pad across a carpeted floor and open his French windows wide to let in the perfume of flowers and the fresh air of the countryside.

Maybe he should sell up and let someone else take London by storm so he could make his dream a reality? The only thing he was sure about was that without Harriet, his dream was likely to be as bland and as lifeless as the sparse décor running throughout his flat.

With a deep sigh, he opened his laptop. Today, he had to get this draft to his publishers or they would be threatening all sorts of horrible clauses and court action. Harriet or no Harriet, he had to get this finished. His fingers hovered over the keys. Within seconds he was lost in the complex plot of the drawn out crime that was about to be solved.

Discovering that Philippe had already left for London was a shock. Harriet knew that it was for the best, but the thought of never seeing him again was, well it was unthinkable.

'Are you sure you'll be alright on your own?' A frown creased Audrey's forehead. 'You know you're welcome to stay as long as you like.'

Harriet forced a smile. Audrey had been lovely to her, but she couldn't stay here a moment longer. Being "here" meant Philippe, and the last thing she needed was more reminders of him. 'Elspeth's going to look after me. I'll be fine. Honestly. I just need to be at home. Anyway, I can't put you to anymore trouble. You've been wonderful to me.'

'It's nothing.' Audrey waved Harriet's gratitude away. 'You're welcome any time, you know that.'

Sophie bounded in through the door. 'Your carriage awaits, madam!'

Harriet grinned. 'Why thank you, Jeeves. As long as you don't think you're getting a massive tip at the end.'

'On the house, madam.' Sophie bowed low.

Audrey pushed a tin of cupcakes into Harriet's hands once she was settled in the front seat. 'Just chocolate and lemon. I didn't think you were quite up to one of my experiments.'

'Lucky you!' Sophie grimaced. 'Mum, can you pretend I'm unwell and only give me normal cupcakes?'

'Get away with you! If you keep on like that I'll bake those egg and bacon cupcakes again . . .'

Sophie made a gagging noise and grinned at Harriet. Audrey tapped on the car, closing the door as she did so.

'Get well soon,' Audrey shouted as the car made its way slowly down the drive towards the gate.

Harriet waved out of the window. 'Thank you, Sophie. I really appreciate the lift.'

'Are you running away?' Sophie's eyes might have been focused on the road ahead, but her words hit their target hard.

'What d'you mean?'

'Philippe?' Sophie said. 'You love him, don't you?'

Harriet sighed. She wasn't surprised that Sophie had noticed. The light that shone in her eyes whenever Philippe was near her, it must be as obvious as if she had a neon sign on her head advertising the fact. Sophie must also know that Philippe didn't share her feelings, and what she didn't need right now was pity.

'So tell me Sophie, how's it going at your meetings?' If there was one thing that could distract Sophie, it was her AA.

Just at that moment, the car swerved suddenly to avoid a bus that took the corner of the lane too sharply, narrowly missing Sophie's bonnet.

'IDIOT!' Sophie shouted. 'These pig-ignorant bus drivers! They think they own these roads.'

By the time Sophie dropped Harriet at her house in Theale, they had discussed the pros and cons of women drivers, self-driving cars and whether a man's car was a true reflection of his manhood, and of course, AA. Any thought of Harriet's feelings for her brother had gone clean out of Sophie's head.

'Surprise!' Toby opened the door, a beaming smile plastered across his face. 'Dad had to fly to Germany so I'm staying with you and Elspeth for three whole days.'

'Come on young man, let Harriet through the door. Why don't you flick the kettle on like I showed you? We can make Harriet a nice cup of tea.'

It was good to be home and even better to see Toby, but her head was still delicate. Any inventor out there who could create a dimmer switch for a noisy, ebullient seven-year-old would, she decided, be a very rich man.

Although, at least she knew she would be too distracted by Toby to be able to nurse her heart that, at the thought of never seeing Philippe again, felt as though it was being physically wrenched in two.

Chapter 33

The next few days whizzed by. Toby consumed a large proportion of Harriet's time and energy, although Elspeth took him to and from holiday club to allow Harriet to recuperate. Harriet would have had Toby with her all the time, but Greg had booked Toby into the club before they travelled to Wengen. As a large number of Toby's friends also attended, he was up and raring to go well before the doors opened.

Harriet felt she should be the one taking Toby. Elspeth brushed aside these protestations stating that Harriet had the rest of her life to devote to Toby; that for now she needed to concentrate on getting better.

By the time Greg came to collect Toby, Harriet was feeling physically back to normal, but emotionally shot to pieces.

Greg barely said two words to her as Toby squeezed her hard and promised to come back very, very soon. 'And we can paint my room black, can't we, Harri? You said, didn't you?'

'As black as coal,' Harriet replied, hoping the 'black' phase wouldn't last as long as the sunny yellow that had graced his walls since his first visit.

'Right, young lady,' Elspeth said, once Harriet had closed the door behind Greg and Toby, 'you need to sit down and tell me what's going on with Prince Charming. You've had a face that would've rivalled my grandmother's for the past few days, and I can tell you, that's saying something!'

'Precisely nothing is happening, Elspeth. Prince Charming has turned out to be that rotten, slimy frog that I accused him of being back in Wengen. He can go take a jump into the nearest mud hole and sink without trace for all I care!' Harriet crossed her arms over her chest.

'Oh dear Lord! I clean forgot to tell you that Greg will let you see Toby even if you're with Philippe. Philippe doesn't know, does he? That's why he's staying away.'

Tears gathered behind Harriet's eyelashes. She had been determined not to cry yet again. It was as if a whole dam full of swirling, writhing water was heaving and jostling for release. Once a crack appeared, the whole lot whooshed through the inept barriers of her eyelashes and cascaded in a never ending stream down her face. It was infuriating!

'He doesn't love me.' Harriet said the words so quietly that at first, Elspeth couldn't believe that she had heard them right.

'Doesn't love you?' Elspeth repeated. 'What nonsense! Of course he loves you. Any fool can see that.'

'No. No, truly he doesn't,' Harriet clenched and unclenched her fists folded neatly in her lap. 'He told his mum. He made it very clear.'

A dog barked loudly outside the house. Harriet vaguely wondered whose it was. No-one in their cul-de-sac owned a dog, at least they didn't as far as she was aware. Not that she was very up on the neighbourhood at the moment, given the weeks she had spent in Wengen.

Elspeth lowered herself down onto the sofa next to Harriet. She put her arm around her. 'I'm sorry Harriet. I must have completely misread the signals. I would have wagered a large stake on the two of you getting together. Honestly, men are a complete mystery.'

'Tell me about it.' Harriet fought to keep her emotions under control.

'Shall I make us a nice cup of tea, and maybe the last of Audrey's cupcakes?'

Harriet groaned. 'My diet is terrible. I've spent the last few days eating cupcakes, drinking hot chocolate and dunking biscuits.'

'Don't forget the ice cream.' The first thing Elspeth had done before Harriet got home was stock up her freezer with a wide variety of Ben and Jerry's.

'How could I?' Harriet smiled. 'D'you know Elspeth, I think you must be 50% human and 50% ice cream!'

Elspeth nodded her head. 'That suits me fine, my dear. How perfect that would be.'

'Yes, until you go out in the sunshine. We don't want you to go the same way as the Wicked Witch of the West!'

Elspeth laughed. If only she could feel as light-hearted as Elspeth.

Two hours later, Harriet waved as Elspeth's car drove past the Green and along the windy road back to the High Street. All she wanted to do was to hide under her duvet and not emerge for anything or anyone ever.

And yet, it was too much like déjà vu. She had been here before, less than a year ago, when Greg had left her. It seemed to be a repeating pattern in her life and she knew she couldn't go through it again. No, from now on she was going to be an independent lady. Men, as far as she was concerned, were dead to her. And this time, she *actually* meant it.

All those months ago, the day Greg's "Dear John" text had arrived, Harriet sank into a deep black hole. Thankfully, her mum's neighbour stepped into the breach and cared for her mum until Harriet emerged from what had effectively become her jilted person's lair.

After a week of doing a great "Bridget Jones" impression, bizarrely minus the tears, she had surveyed the tip that her house had become with abject horror. Take-away debris littered every surface, competing with mugs half-full of cold, coagulating coffee and glasses stained with the remnants of red and white wine.

Her body had fared as badly. Dark ringed eyes with red rims from lack of sleep and too much alcohol stared back at her from the mirror; the same pair of light grey jogging pants she had worn night and day for over a week looked like they had been subjected to several over-enthusiastic contemporary artists splattering their marks on her attire with loaded paint brushes.

She remembered, as if it was yesterday, the total despair and shame she had been buried in after Greg abandoned her. Well, this time it was going to be different. Even if it took every ounce of her self-control, she would skip the remainder of the drowning in misery and self-pity phase, and head straight for the "re-invent my life" section without passing "Go" and without collecting £200, without escaping abroad and without, this time, collecting more baggage en route.

What she needed was a job. If she was working part-time and spending her remaining leisure hours with Toby, there would be little room for dwelling on Philippe. Anyway, that was her plan. She knew it wasn't fool-proof, but what choice did she have? Bridget Jones on a bad day or Jessica Ennis on a good one? She knew who she would choose. Although, at the present moment in time, she didn't know whether she possessed the energy to gear herself up for the latter.

Four weeks after Philippe handed in his draft manuscript, miraculously within the deadline, he was back at his laptop making the finishing touches to the changes that his editor had suggested. Fortunately, this time, there weren't many, which meant that very little re-writing was required. As his focus on the novel had been so fragmented during his time in Wengen, he was both surprised and relieved at this unexpected development.

It took every ounce of his will power to stay focused on the task in front of him. His mind wanted to pull him back to Harriet. If he wasn't on his guard, he would either be whisked back in time to relive moments spent with her or his life would be fast forwarded into a different world where they were reunited. In some ways, these daydreams kept him going, however, it made the reality of life without Harriet more difficult to come to terms with.

Although to be fair, it was hard to separate the two worlds: the story winding its way through his novel and the way his life had played out over the last few months.

A loud knock at the door forced Philippe out of his seat. Who on earth could it be at this time of the morning?

'Come on bruv, don't leave your little sis waiting on your doorstep.'

Philippe's instinctive smile turned into a frown. What was Sophie doing here? Was she pissed again? Turning up on his doorstep at 6am was something she used to do when she had been out on the rampage in London and had drunk herself into a catatonic state.

So it was with trepidation that Philippe pulled open the door.

'I slipped in the front door with one of your neighbours.' Sophie kissed his cheek and was about to walk through the door, when Philippe stopped her.

He skipped all the social niceties, fixing her with his steely grey eyes. 'What are you doing in London at six 'o' clock in the morning?'

Sophie raised an eyebrow. 'Nice to see you too!'

'Well?'

A hurt look flashed across her face. 'Look, I'm not pissed if that's what you're thinking.'

'Sorry Sophie, it's just that, for years . . . I worry about you. That's all.'

Sophie gave Philippe a big hug. 'I know you do. But I'm in recovery. I don't intend to go back.'

Once they were settled in Philippe's lounge, with plates overflowing with buttery toast, Sophie explained that she had been asked to speak at a breakfast meeting in London. She woke up early, so decided to pop in to see how Philippe was doing before it started.

'You look as terrible as Harriet.' Sophie noted the dark rings under Philippe's eyes and a fog of sadness that hung around him like a cloak.

Philippe brushed aside Sophie's concern. 'Burning the midnight oil. I need to get these revisions to the publisher by next week.'

'You're just like Harriet. She told me that it was the job hunting that was wearing her down.'

'Harriet's looking for a job?'

'Yes Philippe, it's what people do.'

'What's she looking for? Where's she looking? Locally? And she's okay, isn't she? She's not ill again?'

Only ill with the same condition as you, Sophie thought to herself. It was blatantly obvious that the two of them were head over heels in love. But for whatever reason, neither of them was willing to acknowledge it. They were hopeless, the pair of them.

Well, being a matchmaker was one thing she had never tried. In fact, quite the opposite. Whenever she had seen a happy couple together, she would flirt outrageously with the man. It was a challenge, admittedly a sick one, to see if she could lure the man's attentions in her direction. Sometimes she managed it, sometimes she didn't, but her aim was always to tear down rather than to build up.

Now she was in recovery, she wanted to be a positive influence on people's lives, not a destructive one. Therefore, it made sense to bring people together rather than to force them apart. The trouble was, in their case, she didn't have a clue how to begin to make this happen. They both seemed hell-bent on staying as far away from each other as possible.

'Whoa! One question at a time, Philippe. If you want to know all about Harriet, why don't you give her a call?'

'Look Sophie, just butt out, okay. Harriet has made her choice.'

One look at Philippe's face was enough to deter Sophie from pursuing the subject further. But it didn't mean that she was going to give up.

Many months later, the publicity machine began whirring to publicise Philippe's new novel. He was booked onto chat shows on the radio and television. His book-signing tour would have taken him right around the world if he had given his publishers free rein. As it was, he had been booked into venues around the UK on a tour, which would last over a month.

When his first book had been launched, he had managed to duck out of this promotional circus, pleading emotional scars from his accident, from Lauren and from the loss of his career. This time, however, it was non-negotiable. He was dreading it.

He knew that questions about Lauren, his languishing tennis career and maybe even about Harriet, would come up. This incensed him as this was meant to be about his book not an opportunity to delve into his personal life.

Sophie had shown an inordinate amount of interest in the interviews he had lined up. She had also insisted on reading his book before it was released. Whilst he should have been thrilled that she was, for once, demonstrating an active interest in his life, he was suspicious. He was certain that she was up to something, but he could not work out what.

Meanwhile Harriet, having trawled the local job agencies and having sat through a number of interviews at uninspiring companies, finally swallowed her pride and called Ed. She knew he would be furious that she had been back in the country for a couple of months and hadn't contacted him. He had been such a loyal friend to her, as well as the best boss you could ever ask for. So why had she held back from contacting him?

'I wondered when I'd hear from you,' Ed said.

'You knew I was back?'

'Of course! You didn't think you could keep that news quiet when I'm based within a stone's throw of your house did you?' Ed paused. 'And I read the papers!'

Harriet had to admit that, even without the newspaper coverage, Arlington Business Park was located on the other side of the dual carriageway from Theale. It had been naïve of her to make the assumption that Ed wouldn't have known she was back.

Most of the Business Park employees risked their lives dashing across three lanes of fast-moving traffic to swarm like bees into the various cafés, bakeries, takeaways and local shops to stock up on lunch or grab food for supper. Just because she hadn't bumped into anyone from Hardacres did not mean she wouldn't have been spotted.

'You'd like to come back to us?' Ed asked. He was always one to get to the point.

'To be honest Ed, I don't know. I need to do something, but I haven't quite worked out what. Which is one of the reasons I haven't contacted you.'

'Look Harriet, come back to us on a temporary contract. You can even work part-time if you want. I can't offer you your old role, but we could do with an extra pair of hands. It will give you a chance to work out where you want to be in the future.'

'Oh Ed, I could hug you.' Harriet smiled for the first time in ages. Yes, of course she smiled a lot when Toby was around, how could she not? But when left on her own, smiles were in very short supply.

A few weeks later, Harriet was slumped on the sofa with her feet up on the coffee table and a bowl of pasta balanced on her lap. She was relieved she had gone back to work part-time. If she had had to work full-time, there was no way she could have kept up the pace and looked after Toby at the same time, especially as he seemed to be with her more than he was away from her. She was so lucky. Ed was very supportive. He allowed her to work school hours on the days Toby stayed with her, but even so, she still seemed to spend her whole time playing catch-up. She honestly didn't know how single mums, who worked full-time, managed to juggle everything. She had nothing but admiration for them.

As she spooned pasta into her mouth, she flicked through the channels. Her phone beeped, announcing a text. She was just about to click into it, when the remote control dropped from her hand. There, on the screen, was a close up of Philippe's face. She knew that the wise thing to do would be to swap channels or turn off the TV, but like an addict, she found herself unable to do anything but drink in the sight of him.

He looked thinner. There was a haunted look about him, which hadn't been there before. She wanted to reach into the TV and smooth away the greyness. She wanted to run her hands through his hair and for those piercing grey eyes to be trained solely on her.

'So, this novel has quite a romance running through it,' Roger Bateman, the presenter, was saying. 'Can I ask if you were writing from personal experience?'

Philippe scowled his disapproval, various answers flying through his mind, most of which weren't suitable for day time or indeed evening viewing. He took a deep breath to calm himself. He had to play along with the press or both his publisher and his agent would be on his back, and he could do without that at the moment.

'I think we all have our own experience of love, don't we?' Philippe smoothly avoided the question.

'But this particular romance was based in Wengen, where I believe you wrote most of your book?' Roger persisted.

All Harriet's senses were focused on the screen, waiting for Philippe's next sentence.

'Are you suggesting that I can't write from my imagination and that everything has to be biographical?' Philippe raised an eyebrow. He looked as cool as a cucumber, even though his insides were churning like a food processor.

'Okay, so this romance that weaves its way from the initial crime, through the investigations to the conclusion—'

Philippe interrupted. 'I hope you're not going to give the game away.'

'So what I was wondering . . .' the presenter paused for effect, '. . . was whether this romance describes your relationship with a certain Harriet Anderson, who I believe you spent quite a lot of time with in Wengen?'

'Why would you think that?' Philippe wanted to tell this guy to get lost: to stop prodding around in his private affairs. He had created enough press fodder and media circuses in his tennis days.

'Let me take a liberty here, if I may, and read an extract from *Avenged*'. Without giving Philippe time to answer, the presenter lowered his head and started to read: *'The first time Inspector Reynard spotted her across the terrace, standing at her bedroom window, even at a distance she rendered him breathless. He couldn't move. He couldn't speak. He could hardly think straight.*

Her shoulder length, blond hair framed her stunning oval face; a smattering of freckles lifted her from attractive to adorable; her full lips ached to be kissed and her eyes, well she had the greenest of eyes. They sparkled like emeralds, which made Inspector Reynard want to jump into them headfirst.'

A photo of Harriet flashed up on the screen at the same time as a deep red flush infused Philippe's cheeks. Harriet watched the screen, entranced, her heart cantering in her chest.

Philippe's Agent tried to catch Philippe's eye. Danger vibrated out of him.

'So is Sally, who you so strikingly describe in this paragraph, based on Harriet? And does the ending in *Avenged* reflect how your relationship with Harriet has developed or how you would like it to develop?'

Hundreds of conflicting emotions raged within Philippe. He had been naïve to think that no-one would spot the likeness between Harriet and Sally, but he hadn't been able to write anyone else into the part, and he had tried, really tried. When he pictured Harriet, his words flowed; when he tried to replace her with someone from his imagination, the awkwardness and falseness of the words had him backspacing faster than typing onwards.

After several frustrating moments, his Agent managed to attract Philippe's attention by untying his tie and waving it at him across the studio. He then made slicing movements across his neck with his finger and feigned torture. Those drama classes his mum had forced him to attend aged eight, he had known they would pay off eventually.

Philippe's eyes settled on Roger. 'Well, I guess everyone will just have to go out and buy the book, and read to the end to find out.' A tiny grin nudged at the corners of Philippe's mouth. He would make an excellent politician: seemingly answering a question without actually answering any of it.

Roger laughed and moved onto details about the plot and his writing style. By the time he shook Philippe's hand and thanked him for coming on his chat show, Philippe's Agent breathed the biggest sigh of relief, not of his whole career, but almost.

Chapter 34

Even before the chat show finished, Harriet's mobile beeped with countless messages, all wanting to know more, all asking her whether she was, in fact, the Sally in Philippe's book. Ed's text made her smile: 'Fame at last Harriet, even if you are only a brief cameo!'

She only spotted Sophie's text telling her that Philippe was on the TV after the programme had finished.

Both Elspeth and Sophie phoned and left messages telling her to call them urgently. She turned off her phone and spent a sleepless couple of nights waiting in limbo until the book went on sale.

She asked Ed for the day off, mumbled something about an important appointment, which of course to her, it was, if not in the traditional sense.

The moment Waterstones opened, Harriet was the first through the door. She had been queueing since five 'o' clock that morning, along with a crowd of people as keen as her to get their hands on *Avenged*.

For the others, it was to immerse themselves in the heart-stopping twists and turns, which Philippe excelled at; for Harriet it was to see how the romance between Inspector Reynard and Sally panned out. Not that it would tell her much because only Philippe knew if he had been writing from his heart or as an author drawing on certain facts and weaving a story around it.

But still, she had to read the book.

Curled up on the sofa, an hour later, she was already at the end of Chapter Two. She could not turn the pages fast enough. To her surprise, her drive to continue reading wasn't just to know more about her alter ego and to see how the romance developed, but the story already had her gripped. She was desperate to know who had murdered the brash American in such a horrible way. How would Becky feel about her "double" being killed off in the first paragraph? Harriet smiled to herself.

The day passed by in a blur. She left the sofa only to grab a cup of coffee and a sandwich.

It was nine 'o' clock by the time she closed the book. The ending wasn't anything like she had expected. The curve balls inserted throughout the book had kept her guessing, incorrectly, both as to the perpetrator and also how the romance between Inspector Reynard and Sally would pan out.

If she was honest, she didn't know how she felt. A mixture of elation, sadness, excitement and uncertainty circled her like vultures hovering over their potential prey. Her eyes were dry and itchy from such a concentrated reading session. There was only one thing for it, she would have to sleep on it and see what the morning brought.

Philippe arched his back and stretched. He had been signing books at London's Waterstones for the last hour and the queue showed no sign of receding. His head was throbbing despite the paracetamol he had taken half an hour ago.

The noise level was exacerbating his headache. The crowd jostled as they chatted excitedly, waiting with his precious book in their hands to not only meet Philippe Myers, the tennis star and Philippe Smith the author in person, but ultimately to carry away a tiny part of him in the form of his signature.

He knew he was being a real book-signing bah-humbug, but he couldn't help it. The writing he enjoyed, mostly, but the promotion was something he could do without.

Although, there had been moments today when he found himself enjoying the conversations with some of his fans, as brief as they were, before they were whisked away by a member of the store. The wide range of people who turned up surprised him. Yes, you had the predictable young women who giggled and fluttered their eyelashes; you had the older generation who liked to lose themselves in the plot of a crime novel. But there were also gangly teenage boys; children as young as seven or eight, who made him think of Toby and Harriet; middle aged men and women; and in

London, particularly, a large number of tourists from a wide range of countries; and too many other variations to describe.

Philippe swallowed some of the ice-cold water that one of the staff had left beside him. He reached out his hand to take the next book, automatically opening the cover, pen poised above it.

'Err, to Harriet please, and perhaps you could, umm, say that you . . . ummm . . . miss her . . . umm . . . that's if you do . . . and . . . ?'

Philippe froze. Slowly he raised his head. There, standing in front of him, looking like she might skitter away from him at any moment like a terrified young deer, was Harriet.

Something inside Philippe snapped the moment his eyes locked with hers. He knew, without a shadow of a doubt, that life stretching into nothingness without Harriet would kill him. Whatever pain this decision caused Toby, whatever pain the loss of Toby caused Harriet, they would find some way through it.

It had been unbearable all these months. Without Harriet, his life played out in monochrome; without Harriet he was incomplete; without Harriet, he went through the motions of life, but couldn't connect, not properly.

Philippe bent over the book and wrote in slow deliberate letters: 'TO MY DARLING HARRIET. I LOVE YOU. I MISS YOU. I CAN'T LIVE WITHOUT YOU.'

Harriet's heart started beating wildly against her ribcage. She stood motionless watching Philippe's pen slide across the page. The words bounced off her brain as if they were too much, too significant, too incredible to process.

She was still standing motionless as Philippe walked around the table. The chattering of the crowd dissipated as everyone's eyes focused on the two of them.

Philippe reached up a hand and tenderly stroked her cheek. Their eyes found each other. Then his lips were on hers. He pulled her close, closer to him and kissed her with all the pent-up passion and all the unrequited love that he had been trying to squash deep within him ever since he clapped eyes on her. Harriet's arms reached up and entwined themselves firmly around his neck as she leaned into him. After too long in the wilderness, wandering alone, Harriet knew with utter certainty that, at long, long last, she had come home.

EPILOGUE

'Harri! Harri! It's Mother's Day at school next week. Can you come? I told them you are my mum because, well, because you are really, aren't you?'

Harriet's eyes misted over. 'Of course I'll come. It will be fun.'

Toby frowned as he studied Harriet's face. 'But I've made you cry. Don't you want to be my mummy?'

Within seconds, Toby was in Harriet's arms. 'I want to be your mummy more than anything in the world.' Harriet stroked his hair. 'Remember what I told you: sometimes people cry when they're very happy, as well as when they're sad.'

'Oh. Okay. Good. Can we hurry though because I've got my lesson with Philippe?'

Harriet smiled.

So much had changed in the last year. When Harriet and Philippe announced their engagement, Audrey and Jack were ecstatic. Sophie flew at them and embraced them as if her life depended on it. When she pulled away, she glanced up at them both.

'I have something to admit. That interview with Roger Bateman. Well, I might have called him beforehand and kind of hinted about Harriet, and that could have had something to do with the cross-questioning . . .'

Philippe did his best to look stern, but it was impossible to be cross with her. Without the grilling Roger had given him, Harriet might never have read the book, and if she hadn't read the book, she wouldn't have discovered how heartbroken Inspector Reynard was at losing Sally, how it was the biggest regret of his whole life. And Harriet might never have come to the book signing and well, it didn't bear thinking about.

When Harriet and Toby arrived at the tennis courts, Toby shot off to the changing rooms. Philippe strode over, a huge smile on his face. 'How's my beautiful wife today?' He leaned over and kissed her to a chorus of: 'Oooooo!' as a row of cheeky faces pressed against the wire of the courts waiting for their lesson to begin.

'So whose idea was it for me to take up tennis coaching?' Philippe laughed.

'I can't think.' Harriet kissed his cheek.

Audrey bustled over. 'Hello, dear.' She tied her apron around her waist. 'Now will you help me lay the tables? I'm a bit behind today as Jack needed a hand in the workshop.'

'A hand in his workshop? What, he actually allowed you to enter his domain and lay a hand on something?'

'I know. He's definitely mellowing, although I'm not allowed uncensored access like Toby. You should see the two of them together. They're in there for hours inventing goodness knows what. It's given Jack a new lease of life, I can't tell you.'

Tears sprang into Harriet's eyes. 'I can't thank you all enough. You've welcomed us both into your family as if we were your own.'

'Nonsense!' Audrey brushed it aside. 'You are part of our family now. We wouldn't have it any other way. And, you'll never guess the bombshell Jack dropped yesterday.'

Philippe's ears pricked up. A flicker of anxiety crossed his eyes. 'What now, Mum?'

Audrey laughed. 'He made me promise not to bake him any more spinach and coconut cupcakes. Apparently he only said he liked them so as not to offend me.'

'But that was years ago . . .' Philippe's voice trailed off.

'And you've been serving them to him ever since?' Harriet made a face.

'I'm afraid so. Silly old buffoon! He should've told me before.'

'Yes Mum, and you'd have sulked for weeks!' Philippe put his arm around his mum and hugged her. 'Thanks so much for providing refreshments. I think it's the only reason most of them turn up.'

'Granny! Granny!' Toby came flying out of the changing room, his laces untied and his top untucked.

Audrey opened her arms and swung him around. 'How's my second tennis star doing today?'

'Ready to thrash them all, Granny.' Toby grinned. 'Have you made the chocolate orange cupcakes with popping candy? You promised, didn't you?'

Audrey winked at Toby, her heart bursting with love for this little boy who had become her ready-made grandchild.

No-one had ever been so enthusiastic about Audrey's cupcakes. They concocted the wildest and wackiest flavours together, and the surprising thing was that most of them tasted delicious. Well, apart from the liquorice and coffee. Those had to go in the bin the moment Toby went home.

'Right Toby, are you ready to be put through your paces?' Philippe was proud of Toby. He had a natural aptitude for tennis and could hold his own against boys several years older than him.

'You're the best step dad ever!' Toby said before he dashed off to join the ever growing pack of children waiting on the court.

A well of emotion rose in Philippe. He slid his arm around Harriet. His other hand reached out and stroked her stomach. 'How's our little one doing?'

Harriet groaned. 'Training to be a footballer from the bashing he's giving my ribs!'

'I love you, Mrs Myers.' Philippe kissed her gently on the lips.

'I love you too.' Harriet squeezed his hand. 'Now you'd better go or the mums will be out for your blood. You're already a couple of minutes late.'

'Well, we can't have that! The thought terrifies me.' Philippe jogged towards the tennis court to whoops of delight from the line of children assembled there.

'Where would you like these cupcakes?' Elspeth appeared from the kitchen with a plate loaded with green and red cakes. She had recently bought a cottage about 10 minutes away in Padworth. She and Audrey had become firm friends and spent most days together baking or gardening.

Harriet sighed with happiness. To top it all, Jo had sent them an invitation to her wedding. She and Hans were having a ceremony in Wengen. Harriet had already booked the flights. Elspeth and Toby were coming with them. It would be fun to see the old crowd again.

She had been informed that Becky would be at the wedding with her new husband, Tom. Apparently she had surprised them all by settling into the valley as if she had lived there all her life. She had opened up a little boutique where she advised the local teenagers and young women on everything from fashion to deportment to hair and make-up. Her business was becoming quite a success, so much so she had even been able to persuade Tom to hire a cleaner. She was by far the most glamorous lady for miles around and therefore, for once in her life, she was well and truly Queen Bee. And she thrived on it.

Greg spent 90% of his time abroad. Toby went to stay with him for the odd weekend, but his home was largely with Harriet and Philippe. Harriet sold her house and Philippe and Harriet moved around the corner into a house with four bedrooms, which gave Toby a bigger bedroom and left two spare rooms for guests, well for the time being anyway. Jo had already reserved a slot for when she and Hans returned from honeymoon.

Philippe was halfway through his next book. It was, unsurprisingly, set in Berkshire and involved tennis coaching and step children. As usual, he was up against the deadline to submit his first draft.

As for Harriet, she still worked flexible hours for Ed. She loved being back at Hardacres now she'd had time to settle in. Although a few faces were new, she had known many of her colleagues for years. They all noticed how much she had changed: she was more relaxed, laughed a lot and didn't take life or work as seriously as she had before. 'Iron balls' was a nick-name of the past, much to Harriet's relief.

Sophie had somehow managed to take over Philippe's flat in London. She was working for a Treatment Centre at the same time as studying to be a counsellor. Toby went to stay with her from time to time and was taken on whirlwind tours of London, which left him overtired and overfull of sugar and fizzy drinks.

That evening when Toby was asleep upstairs, Philippe and Harriet sat entwined on the sofa, drinking coffee.

'I, um, have something to tell you.' Harriet took Philippe's hand in hers.

Philippe smiled down at his wife. 'You're not getting a dog, are you? As much as I love them, their hair makes me sneeze all the time.'

'No silly, I'm not getting a pet, but we are getting another addition to our family . . .'

Philippe raised an eyebrow. 'Go on, spit it out.'

'We're having twins!'

'How? Why? When? Twins!'

The look of astonishment on Philippe's face made her burst out laughing. 'Dr McKenzie asked me back for another scan. He was concerned about the size of my bump; I was getting huge.'

'But, surely your first scan would've picked up twins?'

'You'd have thought so, but apparently they are so small that one twin can hide behind the other.'

'Ah, so we've got at least one escape artist even before they leave your womb!'

Harriet smiled.

There was silence while Philippe digested the news. 'Why didn't you tell me about the second scan? I would've come with you, you know that.'

'I know you would. But, you see, Dr McKenzie hinted that it might be a multiple pregnancy and, well, I wanted to surprise you.'

Philippe brought Harriet's hand to his lips before grinning. 'Double the trouble, heh?'

'What cupcake d'you reckon your mother will bake to celebrate that phenomenon?'

'Normally I would say double chocolate chip, but knowing mum it will be something eccentric like double aniseed or double beetroot.'

'I honestly don't care what she bakes. She's an amazing granny.'

They cuddled closer together on the sofa. Harriet looked up at Philippe with an intensity that took his breath away. 'I love you, Mr Myers. You've made me the happiest woman alive.'

'Ditto.' Philippe wrapped his arms around Harriet. 'And I will never, ever let you go, Harriet. Never again.'

THE END

ABOUT THE AUTHOR

Writing has always been a passion for Nicky Clifford and as a student she penned poems, short stories and articles, many of which were successfully published. But a lack of confidence in her novel writing led her to follow a different career path and for many years she worked in the corporate world of HR & Training.

Now with her sons having reached their teens and with her husband's encouragement, Nicky has decided to focus on her writing once again and, glued to her writer's chair, has completed three novels. Her debut novel, *Never Again,* is the first to be published. *Never Again* is set in her home county of Berkshire and also in the Swiss Alps where Nicky has many happy memories, having worked there in her student days.

In addition to writing, Nicky also works part-time for a local charity. Once a keen ice-skater, managing to perfect backwards crossovers, mohawks and one foot turns, she has recently hung up her boots. Instead, Nicky cycles by the canal with her husband (the same route that Philippe and Harriet walked), devours book after book and bakes (not quite to Audrey's standard!). She also enjoys relaxing with her friends and family.

Author's Note

Dear Readers

If you enjoyed *Never Again*, it would be wonderful if you could take a few minutes to write a review on Amazon.co.uk and/or Amazon.com; reviews are so important to authors.

With very many thanks and best wishes

Nicky

Nicky Clifford
Author, Writer, Poet

ACKNOWLEDGEMENTS

Never Again has truly been a team effort. I would like to thank the following people for all their help and support over the past two years. This list, however, is not definitive, as I owe a big "thank you" to countless people who advised, helped, supported, suggested and pointed me in the right direction – I am sorry I couldn't name you all in person.

Writing *Never Again* has certainly been a marathon, not a sprint. It has tipped me into unfamiliar territory, such as website and book cover design and other areas I didn't expect to venture into.

A big thank you to all those who read through my manuscript and gave me honest feedback: Beth Huff-Guelbert, who not only completed this twice, but is also my biggest fan, so far(!); Sam Sale, who has been with me through thick and thin for years; Sam, my eldest son; Ann Hope, my muse; Jennifer Forsyth (the journey we've been on together . . .); and Moira Smith (less "howlers" recently!), who also dreamed up the title, *Never Again*. Their observations and encouragement have been invaluable.

My writing group, who have provided endless advice and support over the years. I don't think I would have reached "The End" without them. A particular mention has to go to: Chrissie Cuthbertson, who not only highlighted some key changes, but also edited a large proportion of my manuscript – no mean feat; Bernard Tomlin, who gave me very detailed feedback on the whole novel – I learned a lot from his suggestions and humour...; and Jo Davies who, amongst other things, dreamed up my nifty Twitter handle: "@NickyNovelist".

Emma Barr (in Austria) for her advice and guidance on many topics, including book covers, book blurb and how to decipher Twitter; she also set me on the bumpy path to building up my followers (without buying them...).

Sam Sheppard and Ron Green, who competed with each other for months to try to be the first to 'like' every single post on my NickyCliffordWriter Facebook page. I will keep the winner a secret!

Nibsy's café (www.nibsys.com), my gluten-free haven (heaven), where I have written and edited and sampled their delicious range of cakes . . . home from home.

EmmabBooks (http://emmabbooks.com/) for her wonderful review of *Never Again*.

Caroline James (http://www.carolinejamesauthor.co.uk/), who has so kindly taken me under her wing and mentored me through this rigorous process of transitioning my many, many written words into a published book.

All of my very special friends who get me through life, one day at a time, in a *vaguely* sane frame of mind.

And I have to mention my two teenage sons, Sam and Thomas, who have helped me no end with a great variety of technical glitches, my front cover font (very important!), the 'dos' and 'don'ts' of posting on social media and websites and Thomas for lending me his photo-editing skills. And mum, who always thinks I am fantastic, whatever I do, and champions me tirelessly.

Last, but of course not least, Mark, my hubby, who loses me for hours at a time as I in turn lose myself in my "World of Words". Oh yes, and for proof-reading my novel before publication (so you know who to blame if there are any typos!). Given Mark does not read romances (up until now), I truly appreciate his dedication!

I am indebted to all of you.

I will be making donations from the royalties of *Never Again* to a number of charities that have advised and guided me over the years, but particularly:

Childhood Tumour Trust (http://childhoodtumourtrust.org.uk/) - supports children and young people with the genetic condition Neurofibromatosis 1 (tumours of the nervous system); and

Auticulate (http://Auticulate.org.uk) – runs a club for children and young people with high-functioning Autism and Asperger Syndrome helping them to develop their communication, social and independence skills.

Now that *Never Again* is finally out there, I can begin the same journey with my second book . . . so watch this space!

With very best wishes

Nicky

Author, Writer, Poet
October 2016

Printed in Poland
by Amazon Fulfillment
Poland Sp. z o.o., Wrocław